Genius Summer

PAMELA WOODS-JACKSON

Pamela Woods-Jackson
Christmas 2014

Vinspire Publishing
www.vinspirepublishing.com

ISBN: 978-1976324857

PUBLISHED BY VINSPIRE PUBLISHING, LLC

To my Hall/Yeager family. And to the Conner Prairie interpreters who helped me with historical research. And finally, to Robert, Faith, Caroline and Tom.

Chapter One
Conundrum

"Millie, did you hear me?"

Millie Olson looked up, startled. She'd been in her own world, eating her grilled cheese sandwich while reading her favorite Jane Austen novel, her earplugs firmly in place as she listened to Mozart. Now as she glanced at the clock in Kendrick Hall Preparatory School's cafeteria, she realized the lunch period was almost over.

"Don't sneak up on me like that, Carlye!" Millie removed her ear buds, methodically wrapped the cords around the iPod, and neatly repacked the novel and music player into her book bag. "What did you say?"

Carlye let out an exaggerated sigh. "I said, why are you always sitting by yourself with your nose stuck in a book?"

Millie found most of her classmates intimidating, since they were all so much older than she was and most of them thought of her as an interloper, so she just preferred to drown out the lunchroom social scene with music and reading. Millie had been thrilled when popular Carlye Henderson had befriended her on her first day at Kendrick Prep three years ago, and then introduced her to longtime friend Michael Simmons, who was totally unconcerned about the academic threat she posed.

"Well, you were all the way over there," Millie said, pointing to the opposite end of the cafeteria, "sitting with Emily, and…" No need to finish that sentence.

Carlye scowled, pushed her huge horn-rimmed eyeglasses back up her nose and ran a few fingers through her frizzy red hair. "You could have joined us." When Millie didn't respond, Carlye rolled her eyes and said, "So I came to ask you about study group this afternoon."

"We're meeting tomorrow, Carlye, not today. I checked my online calendar last night."

Carlye shrugged. "Well, yeah, but some of us," she said with a head jerk toward Emily Safire on the other side of the room, "are a little behind, so we should meet every day until we get the history project done."

Millie shook her head. "If Emily can't get her part done then tell her I'll do it, but I can't just change my schedule like that. I have to drive Kaz and Charlie to baseball slash softball after school."

Carlye plopped down in the empty chair next to Millie and propped her feet on the rungs. "Why do you have to drive those kids all the time?"

"Carlye, you already know why. Because Mom's at her office downtown, Dad's away on business in Los Angeles, and Martha doesn't drive. Since we don't have a nanny — or a manny like you Henderson's — I'm elected. Get it?" Millie carefully stacked her dirty lunch dishes onto the tray, preparing it for return to the conveyor belt.

"Geez, Millie," Carlye said in a huff, "I get it. I may not be as smart as you, but I'm not stupid."

Millie saw the hurt expression on Carlye's face and felt guilty. She certainly didn't want to alienate the only real friend she had. "I'm sorry, that was rude," she said as she threw the strap of her school bag over one shoulder.

"It's okay," Carlye said, standing up and shoving the chair back under the table. "Besides, I wanna get home right after school and check the mail. My dorm room confirmation from Indiana University should be arriving soon and I seriously hope I got into that new dorm complex." She cast a sideways glance at Millie. "Assuming you're still planning to be my roommate, because I've gotta have a designated roomie to hold the spot."

Millie squirmed and, to avoid eye contact with Carlye, pretended to be absorbed in a PSA mural about texting and driving. Really, what was she supposed to say? Despite her reluctance, she'd dutifully applied to a number of top schools because that's what was expected of her as valedictorian. But thinking about leaving home at age sixteen…it was all too overwhelming. Even Bloomington, Indiana, one hundred miles south of Indianapolis, seemed like a formidable distance.

"Well?" Carlye asked.

Millie ducked her head so Carlye couldn't see the anxiety on her face. "Um, good luck. Come on. We can't be late for class."

Millie glanced at her phone to read the text from her mom as she walked in the front door of their house. *Call me after school*, it said. She was pretty sure she knew what that was about. She tossed her keys on the entry hall table and felt her stomach lurch as she looked at the stack of mail waiting there. Their part-time housekeeper Martha always sorted it into piles according to type: bills, flyers, fan letters forwarded to her mother from her publisher, and business letters for her father.

Among all the other mundane pieces of mail, a fat oversized envelope addressed to Millie had arrived last week. She'd surreptitiously buried it at the bottom of the stack and hoped no one would notice, but some-one—probably Mom—always did because it kept re-appearing on top every day. She sighed in defeat, grabbed the envelope and stomped up the stairs to her bedroom, tossed her school bag on the floor, kicked off her loafers and sat down cross-legged on her bed. "Thick means yes," she moaned. She took a deep breath before tearing it open and reading the letter.

"Dear Miss Olson:

We would like to welcome you to Huntleigh College for the Humanities in New York City. Enclosed you will find the necessary forms…"

Millie returned the letter to the admissions packet and tossed it all on her nightstand, remembering with a shudder her parents' excitement when they finally convinced her to apply. Millie had hoped to be re-jected—as unlikely as that was—but figured she'd just pretend to be disappointed when the time came. Well, she'd been accepted to this school just like all the others she'd applied to, so now she had to figure out how to finesse her way out of it.

"Millie!" Kaz was leaning against the doorjamb, his arms crossed, that bored pre-teen look on his face. "Hey, genius! Let's go!"

Millie snapped to attention, remembering she had to drive her brother and sister to their respective athletics. However, after the bad news masquerading as good news from Huntleigh, she wasn't in the mood for his adolescent moodiness. She grabbed a throw pillow off her bed and tossed it at him.

Kaz ducked, just as the pillow whizzed by his head and hit the banister in the hallway. "Nice toss. Maybe you should be playing softball."

Millie glared at her twelve-year-old brother. She always loved looking at the pictures of her dad as a kid at her grandmother's house in Oklahoma, and if she hadn't known better she could have mistaken those old photos for Kaz. Millie opened her mouth to answer him, but gasped when she realized he was now standing on her white carpet in his dirty baseball cleats. "Karl Azford Olson—get those shoes off my rug!"

Kaz backed out of the doorway until his toes were just barely touching the edge of her carpet. "Okay, I'm off. See? Come on, we gotta go or I'll be late."

Millie glanced at the bedside clock and winced when she saw it was nearly 4:00 p.m. She took advantage of the fact that Kaz and Charlie rode home with the Henderson's many and stayed too long at the library after school again, and even had to stop typing her English paper mid-paragraph to hurry home and pick up Kaz and Charlie. It was a beautiful day and the librarian had scolded her about spending too much time indoors, about not taking advantage of the lovely spring weather.

"I'm outside at the museum every Saturday," she told him, but he didn't buy it. "Okay, I'll take a walk later," she promised him, but she didn't know when that could happen, because her school final projects were coming due, Advanced Placement exams were just around the corner, and teachers were cranky and hard to please this time of year. That called for more studying, not less.

"Do I at least have time to change clothes?" Millie asked her brother.

"No! Let's go or I'll be at the bottom of the batting order." Kaz turned and went down the stairs, his cleats clunk-clunking on the hardwood steps all the way.

Her school uniform would have to do. She sighed and slipped back into her shoes, grabbed her handbag, and ran down the stairs. She spotted her car keys where she'd dropped them next to the mail and grabbed them on her way to the kitchen.

"Martha? Where's Char—oh."

Charlie was sitting at the kitchen counter eating a peanut butter sandwich with a half-drunk glass of milk next to her. She was dressed in white softball pants, athletic shoes, and her maroon and white uniform shirt with Young Lady Panthers emblazoned on the back. Her curly blond hair was tucked into a ponytail like the kind her older sister always wore, and people said that Millie and Charlie looked enough alike to be twins despite their eight year age difference.

"Charlotte, finish up," Martha said. "Millie and Kaz are waiting." Martha handed Charlie a napkin and waited, hands on hips, while Charlie wiped the milk mustache off her mouth.

Millie smiled at Martha, grateful for all she managed to accomplish in their household with only three days a week, the same three days her semi-retired husband worked at a nearby hardware store. "Thanks for getting her ready."

Martha was dressed in her usual baggy grey sweatpants and oversized blue denim shirt with the rolled-up sleeves, what she called her 'housecleaning wardrobe.' "Between the two of us, we keep things humming around here," she said as she brushed a stray lock of her graying brown hair out of her face.

Millie took Charlie's hand and helped her off the center-island barstool as Charlie made an unsuccessful grab for one last gulp of milk. Millie gave Martha a pleading look.

"I'm on it. You go," Martha said, as she got a rag to wipe up the spill.

"Where's your equipment bag?" Millie asked her sister.

Charlie shrugged.

"Front door," Martha answered. "Oh, and Howard's picking me up soon, so make sure you have your house keys."

Millie led Charlie into the hallway where Kaz was waiting impatiently, his athletic bag on his shoulder, the bat handle protruding out of the end. She paused by the door to hoist Charlie's softball bag onto her own shoulder and pointed to her brother's baseball cleats with a raised eyebrow.

In defiance, Kaz impatiently tap-tapped the hardwood floor with his metal cleats. "I'm laaaate," he said.

"Millie, I have to go potty!" Millie groaned as Charlie scurried off to the downstairs half bath.

By the time Charlie came back, Millie knew they

were very late and she felt guilty for not being more responsible. After all, her parents depended on her. She hurried Charlie out to her Hyundai—the car her parents had bought for her sixteenth birthday and expected her to take to college in the fall—where Kaz had already settled into the front seat, his mud-caked cleats propped up on the dashboard while he tapped a plastic CD case against his knee. She sighed as she slid into the driver's seat, checked the rearview mirror and started the engine. Kaz immediately shoved his heavy metal CD into the player, but Millie lowered the volume to almost zero from the steering column.

"Geez, Millie, killjoy." He folded his arms in frustration. "It's bad enough I'm gonna be late. At least I could listen to some decent music."

"Come on, Kaz. Maybe something a little less—raucous?"

"Whatever that means," Kaz mumbled as he fastened his seatbelt.

Millie drove the ten minute route back to Kendrick and made her way to the athletic fields at the back of the multi-building complex, observing the ten mile-per-hour speed limit despite her brother's impatient pounding on the dashboard. She pulled up to the parking lot just behind the boys' baseball field, but before she could put the car in park, Kaz jumped out and ran to the dugout.

Millie lowered the car window with the automatic button on the door. She started to yell at him about how dangerous that was, but bit her tongue and decided not to embarrass her brother in front of his coach and teammates. Kaz was a popular middle-schooler, unlike her status as top-of-the-class loner. "What time will your game be over?" she called instead.

"I'll text you!" he shouted over his shoulder.

Millie ejected Kaz's CD and pushed in a Mozart violin sonata, and as she upped the volume, made eye-contact with her sister in the rearview mirror. "Ready?" She steered the car around the corner to the softball practice fields.

The parking lot was nearly full, but she was able to wedge her compact Hyundai in between two soccer-mom SUVs. Charlie jumped out of the car and ran off to join her team, who were huddled around the coach near the pitcher's mound.

"Charlie," Millie called, "you forgot your bag!" But Charlie was already out of earshot.

"Sorry she's late," Millie said, handing the equipment bag to the coach.

"No problem," Coach Anderson said. "We'll be done about 6:00." She blew her whistle. "Okay, girls, batting practice!"

Millie got back in the car and turned over the engine, easing backwards out of the parking space. She stopped at the red light at the school's entrance, her left turn signal blinking, and glanced at the dashboard clock. 4:37.

I was supposed to call Mom, she remembered. But the mantra her parents had pounded into her head, not to mention the oversized poster in the school cafeteria, stopped her from reaching for her phone. "Driving and cell phones do not mix!" she told herself, and put her hands back on the steering wheel at ten and two. Instead she'd just drive downtown and take a chance on seeing her mom without calling first. The light changed to green and she turned right instead of left.

Millie pulled into a parking slot in front of the

Wellington Towers Office Complex in downtown Indianapolis, fed the meter, and made her way to the elevator bay in the well-appointed lobby. She pushed
the UP button and tapped her foot while she waited.

On the ride up, she had plenty of time to think
about her current predicament: soon to graduate at the
top of her high school class from a ridiculously expensive private school that her parents had sacrificed for
her to attend; accepted to all the in-state colleges she
didn't want to go to; and just today opened her acceptance to Huntleigh College, her parents' particular
Ivy League favorite.

"It's an excellent choice," her dad had insisted.
"You can major in history, literature, or humanities, all
your favorite subjects. And you'd be in New York City
with access to culture and museums, everything a his-
tory-loving genius could want."

But Millie had remained firmly unconvinced, and
after a virtual tour of the small campus, situated right
in the middle of Manhattan, Millie had decided that
she wasn't going anywhere near New York City. *You
need me at home,* was going to be her argument. *How can
I think about college when I know how busy you both are
and how much you depend on me to help run the household
and look after the kids?*

Well, it sounded good in her head. The real truth
was that she was terrified of going off on her own like
that. Finding her way around an unfamiliar college
campus in a huge city, interacting with complete
strangers, and trying to please grumpy professors in
order to live up to her self-imposed high academic
standards was just too much. She'd have to convince
her parents that the timing was all wrong. Maybe in a
few years….

The elevator opened and Millie stepped out. Down the hall on the right were the law offices of Merritt, Hall and Olson, the small intellectual property firm her dad had helped found with two of his fellow Harvard graduates. That was how her parents had met, when Karl Olson hired Elizabeth McCaffrey as his administrative assistant, and of course it didn't take long for a romance to start. Once they were engaged, Mom quit the firm and put her journalism degree to work, freelancing for various publications in the Indianapolis area.

Millie wished her dad and his partners could hurry up and finish that copyright infringement case they were working on with another firm in Los Angeles, so he could come home. She shrugged her shoulders and walked down the hall in the opposite direction to Trending in Indianapolis, a small bimonthly magazine where her mother wrote a column about parenting gifted children.

"Hi, Sarah," Millie said to the receptionist as she walked into the magazine's front office.

The magazine staff consisted of Editor Larry Solsworth, two part-time staff writers, a business manager, and her mom. Sarah's desk was situated where she could oversee a small waiting area with three comfortable lounge chairs, a coffee table filled with past issues of their magazine, and the most recent edition of their publication containing an interview with the up-and-coming children's book author, Elizabeth Marie Olson.

Sarah looked up from her computer. "Hi, Millie. Did your mom know you were coming?"

Millie shook her head. "Is she busy?"

Sarah glanced at her desk phone. "Well, she was on a call with her agent, but it looks like she's finished now." She pushed a button on her headset. "Elizabeth? Millie's here."

Immediately a door to an office down the short hallway opened and Elizabeth Olson appeared. Millie sometimes wondered why she didn't resemble either her red-haired father or her mom, who was tall and slender with shoulder-length light brown hair, but Millie assumed it was a recessive gene that gave her and her sister the blond hair and blue eyes.

Elizabeth's reading glasses were shoved on top of her head and she was wearing form-fitting skinny black jeans and a crisp white shirt with a black patent belt fastened at the waist. On her left hand was her white-gold wedding band, but otherwise she wore no jewelry. Elizabeth was barefoot as usual, since she swore she couldn't write with her feet pinched into designer shoes.

"This is a surprise, hon," Elizabeth said, giving her daughter a hug. "I thought you were going to call." She held Millie back and looked her over. "And still in your school uniform, I see."

"Well, I didn't have time to change because I got distracted reading a letter…."

"Ah, the letter." Elizabeth grinned and squeezed Millie's shoulders. "So you finally opened it?"

Millie furrowed her brow as her mother piloted her into the tiny office. The huge mahogany desk nearly filled the entire space, and it was piled high with papers which threatened to bury the laptop and printer. Behind the desk was a large picture window that overlooked downtown Indianapolis and offered an excellent view of Monument Circle. From this altitude the famous Indianapolis Motor Speedway could be seen off to the left.

Elizabeth followed Millie's gaze out the window. "I was working on an article, trying to give parents suggestions on how to use the Indy 500 as a teaching tool for their gifted children." She shot her daughter a look of apology as she brushed aside a pile of legal pads containing notes for future articles, and patted the sofa so Millie could sit.

"Tell them to have their children collect data from websites to determine the average speed per lap," Millie said as she settled onto the worn, brown leather sofa. "They need to know the formula d=rt."

"Huh." Elizabeth scribbled all that down on a pad next to the phone before plopping down in the swivel chair behind her desk, and propping her feet up as she reached for a half-empty mug. The herbal tea bag was dangling out of the scratched white and gold embossed Writer's Guild mug, but when Elizabeth took a sip her feet hit the floor as she made a face and put the mug down. "Cold," she choked. "Want some tea? I can get Sarah to make us some fresh."

Millie shook her head. "I wanted to talk about...."

Elizabeth's eyes twinkled. "Yes, the acceptance letter to Huntleigh, right?" Millie shrugged as Elizabeth tapped her cheek with her index finger. "So when do they want an answer?"

"The answer is no."

Elizabeth lifted an eyebrow. "But I thought you were looking forward to college."

Millie sighed and gazed out the window. "I just don't think...." She broke off, unsure how to proceed with this touchy subject.

Elizabeth peered closely at her. "What is it you 'don't think'?"

Millie took a deep breath. "I just don't think I'm

ready for college."

"Not ready for college!" Elizabeth echoed. "Not ready for college? After all your hard work? I know you've never really been on your own like that, but this is a golden opportunity! Being accepted to an Ivy League school is such an honor."

"Mom, Huntleigh's your choice, yours and Dad's, not mine." Millie hated the look of disappointment on her mother's face.

"But if you turn down this once-in-a-lifetime chance, then what?" Elizabeth shook her head and frowned. "You obviously haven't thought this through."

"Yes, I have. Exhaustively."

Elizabeth contemplated her daughter as she pushed a stray lock of hair off her forehead. "There's still time, Millie. You might change your mind about Huntleigh."

Millie shook her head. "I'm not changing my mind."

Elizabeth let out a puff of air in exasperation. "Well, then, what about your second choice—Notre Dame? It's also a prestigious school and it's right here in Indiana."

"Your second choice. South Bend's all the way up there by Chicago. And I don't want to go to Chicago any more than I want to go to New York. I'd take Indiana University over that."

Her mom threw up her hands. "Well, then, go there, I guess. You could always transfer later."

Millie could see she wasn't getting her point across. "Don't you and Dad need me here to help Martha and to watch the kids?"

Elizabeth sat up straight and leveled a stern gaze

at her daughter. "That's not your responsibility. Your job is to use those brains of yours and get the best possible education you can." When Millie didn't answer, she sighed. "What if I speak to your father and we come up with a plan?"

"Oh, good, a plan." Millie said. "One that doesn't include shipping me off to some far corner of the country, I hope."

"Is that what you think?" Elizabeth frowned. "You act like we're trying to get rid of you instead of trying to provide you with the best possible future." Elizabeth stood up and started rummaging through papers on her desk. "In the meantime, did I tell you my agent has a film producer interested in the movie rights to the Millicent books? Now where did I put that email he sent?"

Millie slumped down into the sofa cushions. "Sometimes I think you spend more time thinking about Millicent than you do thinking about your real kids."

Elizabeth lifted an eyebrow. "You know that's not true, and I thought you were flattered that I based my twelve-year-old scientific genius sleuth on you."

Millie reached over to the coffee table and picked up the first book in the series, Millicent the Magnificent and the Case of the Ransacked Laboratory. She studied the illustrated picture of Millicent on the cover of the book, remembering when she was little, when her mom used to tuck her into bed at night and then make up stories about the fictional Millicent. Even at that tender age, Millie was perceptive enough to know that her mom hoped Millicent's adventurous nature would encourage her daughter to be more outgoing as well. At some point Elizabeth started writing the stories down, found an illustrator, then a publisher, and was quite pleased when her children's books began to sell.

"Hopefully I'm prettier than she is," Millie said, a grin creeping onto her face, "since I don't wear thick glasses and clunky shoes and masquerade as a nerd." She set the book back on the table. "She's definitely got more moxie than me, though, and I guess her IQ's higher; 180 versus my measly 150."

Elizabeth laughed. "An IQ of 150 is not measly, Millie." The smile evaporated from her face as she got serious again. "Which is why you can't let those brains of yours go to waste. Besides, Millicent's just a character in a book. Books." She reached down and kissed her daughter on the forehead. "You're the real deal and you need to own your intelligence."

Millie glanced at the clock on the wall. "I gotta go, Mom. I need to get home and change clothes before I pick up Kaz and Charlie, and northbound traffic on Meridian's going to be bumper-to-bumper this time of day."

They both looked up as Sarah popped her head in the door and handed Elizabeth a stack of messages. She nodded as Sarah waved goodbye and told her, "Have a nice evening." Thumbing through the messages, she turned back to Millie. "Looks like I'm going to be here awhile. Can you pick up a pizza on the way home?"

"See? You do need me here." Millie grabbed her handbag and headed to the elevator. She pressed the DOWN button as the elevator door closed behind her, and leaned back against the rail for the ride to the lobby.

Kids in the shower, pizza for everyone, that Eng-lish paper to finish, the school history project looming. It was going to be a long night.

Millie tossed her bulging school bag on the floor next to the booth in the twenty-four hour coffee shop and slid in next to Carlye. "Everybody ready? We've got lots of work left to do on this history project. And I have AP exams to study for."

"You're late," Michael Sommers told her as he blew on his steaming cup of coffee. Even though he looked like a stereotypical private school student—tall, blond hair, chiseled—he differed from his class-mates in that he spent his free time jamming with his garage band instead of playing sports. Unfortunately he didn't budget his time well, so to compensate, he'd acquired a caffeine addiction and a lot of nervous en-ergy to go along with it.

"Sorry, I didn't mean to hold everyone up," she said, "but I was getting the visuals we need for the pro-ject from the museum."

Millie's love of history had caught fire at the age of ten when she and her mom first visited the living history museum in Hamilton County, just north of In-dianapolis, and spent hours conversing with the "res-idents" of the fictional, historic towns. Fast forward six years, and dressing in reproduction clothing and play-ing the part of an early Indiana settler never got old.

In fact, when Millie assumed a role, she became so immersed in it that she often forgot—or maybe just tuned out—her real life in the twenty-first century. She loved dreaming up whole scenarios about her make-believe family, scenes where playing board games, cooking on a wood-burning stove, or helping her 'mother' hostess a tea party was more fun than being a sixteen-year-old genius fending off society's expectations. Nineteenth century life was so much simpler. Millie loved the 'living' part of living history re-enactment. Every Saturday was a new adventure, and she always arrived in a good mood.

"Hi, Allison," she said to the costume shop proprietor. "Who am I today?"

Millie surveyed the tiny costume room, every square inch of which was being used to store, sew or mend the costumes used by the historic interpreters at the museum. On one side of the room were men's frock coats, trousers, top hats, and linen shirts, but the majority of the shop was used to house women's dresses, petticoats, day caps, bonnets, pelerines, and assorted knitted accessories such as muffatees, tippets, and garters. In short, anything that a well-dressed nineteenth century man, woman, or child would need could be found there.

The clothing—in all shapes and sizes and spanning several nineteenth-century decades—took up most of the space, but there was a small area set off to the side for sewing machines, ironing boards, bolts of cloth, and of course a computer to house the inventory data base.

Allison looked up and smiled. "I think they want you in the Civil War area today," she replied as she sorted through a rack of corded petticoats.

Millie groaned inwardly. She much preferred the areas of the museum devoted to earlier nineteenth century. It was much more fun to play fictional Lydia in 1826, whose 'father' was a doctor and whose 'mother' was a former slave-owner. She got to wear empire-style dresses, romantic bonnets with flowing ribbons, and discuss Jane Austen with museum visitors to her heart's content. "Really? Civil War? Those dresses are huge, and it's really hot out today," Millie whined. "Besides, I don't know as much about that time period."

"Think of it as stretching yourself, historically-speaking," Allison told her.

"Okay," Millie said with a shrug. "Where's my dress?"

Allison pointed to a hanger on a rack, from which dangled the hoop skirt, round petticoat, corset, and sunbonnet.

"How did women get anything done in all these clothes? Didn't they have work dresses?"

"Of course they did, but your character wouldn't have been doing housework. Today you're playing the daughter of an army colonel who's gone to fight the war, and you and your mother are at home helping with the war effort. Sewing shirts, rolling bandages, that sort of thing. Oh, and for back story, your character's grandparents arrived in this part of the state via wagon train fifty years earlier."

"Ugh," Millie replied. "I'm pretty sure I wouldn't have survived traveling by wagon train."

"Just remember it's not actually you living in 1863."

So Millie gathered her costume and accessories. "I'll be back at the end of the day to get those dresses for the school project," she called over her shoulder as she headed to the women's locker room.

"You kept us waiting," Emily sniffed, snapping her fingers in Millie's face to get her attention. "It's a volunteer job for heaven's sake, so why couldn't you just leave early? It's Saturday night, and some of us eighteen-year-olds have a life."

Millie blushed and squirmed in her seat at the coffee shop. She always felt uncomfortable when someone pointed out how much younger she was than her classmates, especially when that someone was Emily Safire, the most popular girl in the senior class.

"Don't be so dramatic, Emily." Carlye opened her bulging three-sided notebook and took a pen out of its side pocket. "It's only six o'clock. You still have plenty of time to get your party on tonight. And we need the stuff Millie brought from the museum for the project."

Millie mouthed a 'thank you' to Carlye, but she reminded herself that this was a group project, and she also needed them to maintain her 4.0 GPA.

Michael began playing drums on the edge of the table, beating out a melody using his hands as drumsticks to accompany a tune he was hearing in his head. "Well, I've done my part. The PowerPoint's all ready to go."

Emily shot Michael a look and reached over to still his hands. "Getting the visuals was your job, Millie. Carlye did research and I'm typing the handouts."

Millie frowned. "I did plenty of research and you know it, and anyway the whole idea was mine." The three of them watched in dismay as Michael poured more sugar into his half-drunk coffee, clanked the metal spoon against the mug repeatedly, and then gulped down the last drops.

"How much coffee have you had, anyway?" Millie asked him.

Michael shrugged. "So where are the dresses?"

"In my car."

Michael grabbed his book bag from the floor between his legs, shoved the coffee mug aside and opened his laptop. He punched a few keys and said, "Okay, I'm ready to tweak the PowerPoint. Let's get on with this girly project."

Emily picked up her iPad from the seat next to her and flipped several pages over to where she'd left off. But instead of reading her notes, she peered over the top of the iPad and winked at Michael, who was grinning back at her instead of focusing on his computer.

"Honestly, you two," Carlye muttered, pulling her note cards out of her purse. "At least Ireland and I don't flirt with each other in public." Carlye claimed to be in a 'relationship' with Ireland Hancock, the school's star football player, but to Millie it never seemed to be much more than a convenient friendship. They hung out together on the weekends, either watching movies at Carlye's house or going out with friends, but Carlye frequently told Millie that college campuses were a wide-open dating field and she planned to take full advantage next fall. The idea of college and dating made Millie shudder.

Millie booted up her laptop and rolled her fingers along the mouse pad until she found what she was looking for. "Okay, I'm set," she said, opening the file. "The rise and fall of the sleeve: How nineteenth century women's fashions reflected the economic times."

"Like I said, girly," Michael grumbled.

Carlye glared at him. "Stop complaining, Sommers. You could've worked with the jocks on their he-man project, but you opted for the guaranteed 'A' with Millie."

He shrugged. "I kinda liked *A Complete History of Football – From Pig Bladders to Gridiron.*"

"Seriously?" Carlye said. "At least ours is original."

"Hello? Dr. Reed put us second on the presentation list this week," Millie reminded them. "On task?"

"Okay, okay," Michael said. He grabbed his empty coffee mug and held it up to signal the waitress.

"May I help you, sir?" The scowling waitress was tapping her foot, a full pot of coffee in her hand.

"More swill," Michael said, slamming the mug down a little too hard.

The waitress slopped coffee on the table as she refilled his cup. "And you ladies?"

"Oh, sorry," Millie said, looking up from her computer. "Um, one coffee with cream for me, two iced teas for them," she said, pointing to Emily and Carlye, "and pie," she added. "Four pieces of apple pie with vanilla ice cream."

The waitress finally cracked a smile and said, "Coming right up," before hurrying off.

"I'm on a diet," Emily harrumphed, folding her arms in defiance.

Millie rolled her eyes, since Emily was one of the thinnest girls she knew. "You don't have to eat the pie. But since we're going to be here tying up her booth, the least we can do is order food." She narrowed her eyes at Michael, who'd been there the longest, and who didn't look at all concerned, as he blew on his fresh, hot coffee. "And we're leaving her a big tip."

"Whatever," Emily said. "Michael and I have plans tonight so let's get started."

"And I have tests to study for," Millie shot back.

"Who studies for AP exams anyway?" Michael asked her. "You either know the material or you don't after you sat in the class all these months."

Millie stared at him like he was speaking a foreign language. Well, okay, not a Romance language, because she was fairly conversant in all of those. Maybe more like Chinese. "What are you talking about, not study? That's insane."

"I'm just saying you should get out more, socialize instead of staying holed up in the library all the time," Michael said. "You could join us tonight," he suggested, and then cringed as Emily tossed him a look.

Millie glanced at the time on her laptop and realized that if she was going to get any study time in at all tonight, they needed to wrap this up. But just then the waitress returned with the pie and drinks, forcing everyone to push aside their work.

She sighed. No way could she go out with friends, even if she thought Emily would agree. Instead, it was going to be another long Saturday night of study, study, study.

Chapter Two
Top of the Class

Millie was strict about her school-morning routine: Shower, dress, kitchen for juice, a protein bar needed for energy after late-night studying, and then check her email to be sure her teachers had received her homework. But this morning there was an email from her grandmother that piqued her curiosity, so with a quick glance at the clock, she opened it.

Hello, dear! Thought I'd start making plans for your summer visit. I know there are still a few weeks of school left, but June will be here before you know it. Not sure if you heard, but my dear friend Mac had a heart attack. The doctor says he has to take it easy for a while, and since I use Mac's landscape company exclusively, he's arranged for Zach to come by after school and on weekends to help out. Mac's grandson is a fine boy. I'm sure you'll want to renew your friendship with him while you're here. ☺

Millie was sorry to hear about Mac and promised

herself to reply to her concerned grandmother later, but Mac's grandson? She thought about the last time she'd seen Zach MacMillan two years ago in Rolling Plains, Oklahoma. He wasn't much taller than she was at five feet two inches, and had nothing to talk about except sports, a subject she had no interest in. She and Zach had nothing in common then and even less now, since she was about to graduate high school and he was only a junior. What sort of friendship did Gran expect her to renew? She shook her head, but the rest of the email was a lot more interesting:

Went antiquing on Main Street and acquired some items for the church bazaar that I'm temporarily storing in the attic. See you when I arrive in Indianapolis for your graduation! — Love, Gran

Millie was thrilled at the idea of sorting through antiques in her grandmother's turn-of-the-twentieth century attic and wondered exactly what types of vintage items Gran had been able to purchase. Old toys? Glassware? Perhaps a lamp or Victrola? There were lots of history-laden pieces already stored in that attic, but Millie never tired of going up there and constructing stories in her mind about their origins. Her grandmother's email was both tantalizing and infuriating in its brevity.

"Millie!" Kaz yelled up the stairs. "Come on!"

Millie snapped back, realizing the three of them would be late for school unless they left — she glanced at the clock — five minutes ago. She groaned and thought about all she had to do before the end of the term: the history project presentation, then AP exams, then finals, and every minute counted. She swallowed the lump of anxiety in her throat, closed up her laptop and hurried out to the garage where her impatient siblings were waiting to be driven to school.

* * * * *

Millie loved attending Kendrick Prep. She was hooked as soon as she saw the stately half-century-old red brick buildings on the sprawling campus with the perfectly manicured green lawn that surrounded the fragrant flower garden. Guilford Public Academy, the neighborhood K-through-eight school Millie and Kaz had been attending, left her unchallenged, bored and frustrated. Thanks to her volunteer time at the museum and the extra hours she spent in the local library, Millie was already way ahead of her public school classmates and frequently confounded her teachers as well.

While in sixth grade, she'd jumped mid-year to eighth grade, aced all of those classes, and then tested out of most of the freshman classes the public high school had to offer as well, leaving her in limbo. Her middle school classmates distanced themselves from the weird genius-kid, so Millie compensated for her lack of a social life by spending more and more time in the library or history museum. Her concerned parents put their heads together and talked to the guidance counselor at Guilford, who referred them to the guidance counselor at the nearby private, college-prep school.

Kendrick was so eager to acquire a student of Millie's caliber that they worked out an arrangement with her parents, offering a full ride scholarship for Millie and discounted tuition for their younger two children. Charlie was bubbly and could fit in anywhere once she started kindergarten, but Kaz was perfectly happy at

Guilford and balked at the transfer. In time, Kaz survived the culture shock and soon made a niche for himself at his new school where he felt most comfortable — sports.

Millie arrived from Guilford as a thirteen-year-old sophomore, and then started her senior year last fall at age fifteen. She would be the youngest valedictorian Kendrick had ever had. She'd already passed three Advanced Placement exams with top scores her junior year, but that didn't win her any popularity contests with her age-appropriate classmates. Her presence on campus had pushed Esther Weinstein down to salutatorian, who never got over the humiliation and kept her distance from Millie, and by extension, Carlye.

Millie quietly walked into the first-floor corner classroom just as the fifth period bell sounded — a pleasant ding-dong — and set her school bag on the long, oval mahogany table in front of her wooden chair. "Hi, Dr. Reed."

The teacher, who was sitting at his desk working at his laptop, looked up and smiled at her over his glasses. "Good afternoon, Mildred. Ready for the big day?"

Millie could feel the butterflies in her stomach like she always did before an important school presentation. It didn't matter that she prepared endlessly and every project was perfect, she still got the nervous twitters. "I hope so." She glanced up at the clock with a puzzled expression. "Am I early?"

Dr. Reed chuckled. "Right on time, as usual, but this time of year, well, let's just say the other eleven students must be experiencing senioritis."

Millie sat down at the table, placed her book bag on the floor next to her chair and dug out her laptop as the classroom door opened. Students began filing into the room and talking quietly among themselves as they took their seats around the table.

"All right, ladies and gentlemen, let's begin," Dr. Reed said, loosening his tie and rolling up the sleeves of his blue dress shirt. "We've got to finish these presentations by the end of the week. We were subjected to Group One yesterday," he said with a frown at Ireland and the football players, "so today is group two: Miss Olson, Mr. Sommers…." He glanced around the room. "Where are Miss Safire and Miss Henderson?"

"Um…." Millie craned her neck in the direction of the classroom door, panic gripping her. Why weren't they here?

"Come on, Olson," Ireland said, "just own it. Your group's not ready."

Millie blushed a deep red. "We are ready," she insisted, her eyes silently pleading with Michael for backup.

Michael shrugged. "Yeah, I've got the PowerPoint set to go. But Emily's got the handouts and Carlye…" Michael turned the spotlight back on Millie. "Well, anyway, Millie's got the visuals, right?"

"Dr. Reed, I apologize. I know Emily and Carlye are at school, or at least they were this morning, but…."

Just then the door opened and the two of them strolled in as if their entrance had just been announced. "Sorry, Dr. Reed," Emily cooed, handing him her late pass. "I had to go to the nurse. Girl thing. And Carlye…." The two of them giggled conspiratorially.

Esther Weinstein snickered. In the back of the room the three football players—Craig Albertson,

Marshall Spellman, and Ireland Hancock—rocked back in their chairs until they were all leaning against the back wall, watching the fun.

Dr. Reed cleared his throat. "Well, then, if all the drama's done," he said, "let's see this project."

Michael got up, plugged his laptop into the LCD projector, and scrolled around until his slideshow was on the large screen at the front of the classroom. Emily extracted the handout papers from her overstuffed book bag and passed them around the table, while Carlye produced the hard copy of the research assignment and the Works Cited pages, all neatly bound in an assignment folder, and handed them to Dr. Reed.

Breathe, it'll be fine, Millie assured herself. She stepped into the hallway, gave the rolling clothes rack that she'd borrowed from the theatre department a tug over the bump in the carpet, and brought in the nineteenth century dresses to supplement their Power-Point presentation and her written research paper.

Millie lifted a dress off the rack and held it out. "Our thesis statement is: 'Nineteenth century women's fashions mirrored their economic times.'" She had to wait out the loud coughing fit from the football players before continuing. "In a robust economy, dresses had voluminous amounts of fabric creating large, flowing sleeves, but after the economic depression of 1837, the sleeve became noticeably smaller. As you can see from this first dress…" She cringed at the groaning from Ireland and his football cronies, ignored Esther's exaggerated yawn, and looked straight ahead to focus on her discussion.

Once Millie was sure the reproduction historic

dresses were arranged neatly and wouldn't be damaged, she gently closed the trunk of her car, unlocked
the driver's side door and tossed her school bag on the
passenger seat. It had been a long day, she was tired,
and it was unusually hot for mid-May. She sank into
the driver's seat, resting momentarily before turning
the ignition key to the on position, just long enough to
roll down all the windows and release the heat before
turning it off again.

She leaned her head back and took a deep calming
breath as a hot breeze blew through the car. Millie had
deliberately stayed late in the library after school so
she didn't have to endure any more ribbing from her
classmates, and now the student parking lot was
empty, to her great relief. She closed her eyes and
could easily have drifted off to sleep.

"Unlock the door, okay?" Kaz was standing by the
passenger door, jiggling the handle. "Millie?"

Startled, Millie opened her eyes, taking a minute
to get her bearings. She knew she was sleep-deprived,
but that was the price she had to pay to stay at the top
of her class. "Oh, sorry, Kaz. I was mentally reviewing
the project presentation." She told herself it was just a
small fib.

Kaz rolled his eyes. "Why? It's Miss Perfect Millie.
I'll bet everyone got an A."

Millie punched the door-unlock button and sat
up. "It would've been perfect if it weren't for that mo-
ronic Emily Safire," she said.

"Moro—what? In English, super-genius." Kaz
dragged his sister's school bag off the passenger seat,
heaved it into the back seat, and then tossed his own
lighter bag on the floor by his feet.

"Never mind." Millie fastened her seat belt and

started the engine.

"So what happened with the project?"

Millie glanced over at him as she lowered the volume. "You really want to know?" Kaz just shrugged. "Okay, well, Emily and Carlye were late to class and I just knew Dr. Reed was going to flunk us for sure. Turns out Emily had forgotten the handouts, so she stalled in the nurse's office while Carlye drove over to Emily's house and picked them up. After all that, we were a stellar success!"

Kaz scrunched his brow. "Cellar success? Sounds more like you tanked."

Millie cringed at her brother's poor grasp of vocabulary as she adjusted her rearview mirror. "We got an A+. Despite the inauspicious beginning, Dr. Reed was duly impressed." She turned on her signal and eased the car out of the parking space and around the curved drive toward the elementary building to pick up Charlie.

"Whatever all that means." Kaz reached for the volume control on the radio, but Millie gently moved his hand away.

"See you tomorrow, Charlotte," the carpool monitor said as she shut the car door and waved goodbye. Millie quickly pulled out so that the SUV mom behind them could load her carpool.

Just as she made the curve back toward the school entrance, a late model sports car driven by Ireland Hancock, with Craig Albertson sitting shotgun, swerved in front of Millie on their way out of the student parking lot. Millie hit the brakes and the car skidded to a stop.

"Jerk!" Kaz shouted out the open window.

"Ohmigod the dresses!" Millie put the car in Park,

pulled the trunk latch and jumped out to make sure the borrowed costumes were okay.

"You nearly have a wreck and all you care about is stupid dresses?" Kaz exclaimed. "No wonder none of the seniors wanna hang out with you."

"Well, I don't have time to 'hang out,'" Millie shot back as she got in the car and refastened her seat belt. "I have too much school work to do."

"That's your problem," Kaz snorted.

"Dad!" Millie flew down the staircase from her bedroom to the family entry hall. She tossed her cap and gown over the stair railing and leaped into her father's open arms. "I was so afraid you wouldn't get here on time!"

"Now, come on. You knew I wouldn't miss the big day." Her father chucked her under the chin. "The plane was delayed in Dallas because of weather, so we were late landing in Indianapolis."

"I'm so glad you're here," Millie said, giving him another big hug.

Karl Olson held her at arm's length for a good look. "Have you grown?" he teased. "Or maybe being valedictorian just makes you seem more grown up."

"Oh, Dad," Millie whispered as she wobbled on her new high heels. "I'm really nervous."

"What about?" Karl asked, catching her before she stumbled. "You're surrounded by your loving family, so what could go wrong?"

"Plenty," Millie said with a frown.

"Pay no attention to that girl, Karl. She's just being modest."

Karl looked over Millie's head and grinned. "Mom! It's good to see you." He gave Millie a quick shoulder squeeze and released her, holding out his arms to enfold his mother.

Mildred Olson was an attractive woman, tall, slender, stylishly dressed in white linen pants and button-down pink silk blouse, and she had a streak of silver which ran across her reddish-brown hair. The same reddish-brown hair as her son Karl, and the same as his son Kaz. "It's good to see you, son. It's been awhile."

"How are things at home, Mom? Mac improving?"

Mildred nodded. "Slow going, but he'll be good as new before long, I just know it. Little heart attack can't keep that man down."

"Dad, do you know who Gran hired to help out this summer?" Karl shrugged so Millie drove home her point. "Zach, that's who, and that kid…"

"That 'kid,'" Gran scolded her with a wave of her hand, "is a year older than you, my dear."

"What's going on here?" Karl asked, looking from his mother to his daughter and back again.

"Oh, just a difference in perspective, that's all," Gran told him.

"But Gran, Zach's not…"

Gran clucked her tongue. "Never mind now, Millie. This is your graduation, so let's focus on that."

Karl nodded in agreement and called out, "Elizabeth? Kaz! Charlie! I'm home so let's get this graduation party started!"

Elizabeth came down the stairs wearing a navy blue business suit and beige pumps. With a smile on her face she embraced her husband warmly and added an affectionate peck on the lips. "Welcome home, darling."

"Daddy!" Charlie bounded in from the kitchen and tackled her father around the waist.

"Hey, peanut," Karl said, tousling her curly blond hair with his free hand. "Where's your brother?"

Charlie made a face. "In the kitchen being a gross jerk."

"Hmmm," Karl said. "How so?"

Before she could answer, Kaz sauntered in with an ice cream sandwich in his hand. Naturally it was dripping down his dress shirt and onto the floor.

"Kaz! You shouldn't be eating that now!" Millie exclaimed.

"You're not the boss of me," Kaz retorted. "Hi, Dad!"

Karl leaned on the banister, a bemused look on his face. "Good to see you, son, but now you've got to run upstairs and change that shirt. Hurry!" he clapped his hands together as Kaz stuffed the last of the ice cream in his mouth and raced up to his room.

Millie was already nervous enough without her brother delaying them. At least Gran was here for this momentous occasion, and Dad had gotten back in time. Maybe it would all be okay.

At precisely seven p.m. guests and spectators were in their seats, all the dignitaries had taken the stage, and the school orchestra began playing Pomp and Circumstance, as the sixty graduating seniors in purple and gold caps and gowns walked solemnly into the school auditorium. Millie was at the head of the class with her special white sash denoting her status as valedictorian, followed by disgruntled salutatorian, Esther Weinstein.

The two of them walked onto the stage and took

their seats next to Headmaster O'Reilly and adjacent to the four school board members, the chairwoman of the Kendrick Alumnae Association, and the mayor of Indianapolis. The rest of the graduating class were seated in a roped-off section at the front of the auditorium, and behind them sat their proud families and friends.

Headmaster O'Reilly stood and addressed the graduates, congratulated them on their hard work throughout their high school years, and began calling students onstage to accept scholarships, awards, and accolades. Millie accepted her awards graciously — full ride scholarships to three state universities plus private universities in Indiana, Oklahoma, and the dreaded Huntleigh College in New York City — all the while hoping she didn't have to actually attend any of them.

"And now," said the Headmaster, "I'd like to introduce our valedictorian. This young lady — and I do mean young; she's only sixteen years old — has distinguished herself by not only having the highest grade point average in her class, but by being our first student ever to sit for seven Advanced Placement exams and earn top scores on each. Please welcome Miss Mildred Olson." He began the applause and the audience politely joined in.

Millie blushed as she shook his hand and took her place at the podium. She was so tiny and the microphone was set so high that Mr. O'Reilly had to readjust it for her, much to her chagrin. All eyes were on her while the audience waited for her to begin speaking, and she had a moment of panic as her throat went dry. *You've practiced and practiced. Pretend it's a class presen-*

tation. She took several cleansing breaths while everyone in the audience seemed to be staring a hole through her.

"Headmaster, Board of Directors, parents, friends, honored guests, and my fellow graduates," Millie began in a thin, high-pitched voice. She paused, swallowed hard, and anxiously looked out into the sea of faces. She heard mumbling among the graduates, followed by some quiet giggling, but then she made eye contact with her grandmother who gave her a wink and a head-nod. Millie straightened her shoulders, cleared her throat, and began again.

"This graduating class of Kendrick Hall Preparatory School has accomplished great things during these past four years. You've all listened as individual students were honored with well-deserved awards and scholarships. And truthfully, we've got a great group of young people here tonight, thanks to the help and encouragement of all the dedicated faculty, administrators, and parents." Millie awkwardly waved at her fellow graduates and then waited as the audience applauded.

"Commencement means beginning, and we're all beginning a new phase of our lives. But even when you think you know where life is taking you, sometimes life is just plain surprising.

"I've learned three life lessons in high school that I want to share with you. First of all, I learned that I could always count on my family for support. Like with this speech—my mom, whom you may know does a little writing…"

Millie had to wait for the laughter to subside. "…Mom offered to help me write this speech, but I told her I had to do it on my own. Secondly, although

I personally struggle with this one, I've been told that life isn't all schoolwork, homework, and academic competitions. Sometimes you just have to stop and smell the roses, which I know is a cliché, but it's springtime, and the flowers in the garden smell really great!" She stopped again to wait for the tittering to die down. "And lastly, I learned that it's okay if you disagree with someone as long you respect their right to have an opinion.

"So how do these three things translate into life lessons? First, no matter how great your family is or how many friends you have for support, ultimately you can only count on yourself. Second, the joy in life can be found anywhere, so seek it out. Finally, listening to other viewpoints is how we learn tolerance and diversity. Pick your battles and save your energy for the important struggles you'll face. Thank you and congratulations to this year's senior class!"

Applause erupted as Millie returned to her seat. She looked out at the audience to see her mother applauding loudly, her dad with a huge grin on his face, and Gran beaming with pride. Even Kaz was grudgingly clapping. Somehow she'd made it through the speech without stumbling or sounding awkward, and for once she was actually proud of herself.

All the graduates and their families were milling around Kendrick's meticulously manicured Oval Garden after the ceremony. Millie hugged both of her parents and even smiled when Kaz high-fived her. She was in the middle of accepting congratulations from several of her now-former teachers, when Dr. Reed approached her.

"We expect to hear good things from you in the future, Millie," he told her. "I always knew you'd study history. Huntleigh College? Congratulations."

"Um, thanks," Millie demurred. "Oh, there's my grandmother," she said as she ducked her head and scurried off.

Off in the distance, Millie spotted Elizabeth being mobbed by middle school kids, eager young fans hoping for an autograph. Kaz groaned and walked off in the direction of their parked car. Millie knew how he felt and started to follow him when she felt a tap on her shoulder.

"Hey, Millie." It was Emily, standing next to her boyfriend, Michael. "Nice speech."

"Thanks," Millie said, surprised at Emily's uncharacteristic graciousness. "And congratulations to both of you, too."

"Millie," Emily said, "don't forget there's that party at the Hendersons' tonight."

Emily was intentionally trying to assure Millie's attendance? "Um…" Millie started, "well, I don't have a date, and my grandmother's in town …"

"Come on, Mill," Michael urged, "it wouldn't be graduation without the valedictorian. You don't need a date."

"Or hey, my brother Peter's not doing anything tonight," Emily said. "You two hit it off Prom night, didn't you?"

Now I get it, Millie thought. Emily's thinly-disguised dig was one final attempt to humiliate her, and Millie's heart sank as she thought about that fix-up date a few weeks ago with sophomore Peter Safire, okay, a junior now. "I appreciate what Peter did, Emily, agreeing to be my Prom date and all, but he and I clearly have nothing in common."

Emily rolled her eyes. "Well, I just thought, since

you two are the same age and all…."

"Right, same age." Boys Millie's age who were two grades behind her were intimidated by her intelligence, and her own classmates thought of her as a kid. So Millie had reluctantly allowed herself to be fixed up with Emily's younger brother so she wouldn't miss her senior Prom. She'd carefully selected a sophisticated pink satin and silk evening gown in an attempt to look like she belonged at the Prom instead of the sophomore spring dance, bought matching heels and handbag, had her hair styled at a pricey salon, and let her mom do her makeup.

When Peter arrived he had the obligatory wrist corsage, which he awkwardly placed on her right wrist, but which Millie surreptitiously moved to her left. She actually thought the photos her dad took of her and Peter turned out pretty well since Peter was a little taller than she was and kind of cute when he smiled. He was wearing a nicely tailored black tuxedo and had slicked his dark brown hair back into a stylish short ponytail. But Millie realized upon a second viewing of the pictures that they did look more like they were off to that tenth grade dance. Nevertheless, she'd been determined to have a nice time at the only Prom she would ever attend, despite having a sophomore for a date.

It didn't go well. On the drive downtown to the Hilton, Michael and Emily sat up front in Michael's car while Millie sat on one side of the backseat hugging the door, and Peter stared out the window on the other side. Once at the Prom, Peter danced the first dance with Millie and then wandered off to talk to some of the guys from the Kendrick varsity football team. *I guess Peter will be quarterback next year, now that Ireland*

Hancock's graduating, she remembered thinking.

Millie had spent most of the evening at a table waiting for Carlye to sit down and rest between dances. She tried to look as if slowly sipping her soda and watching other kids dance was exactly what she wanted to do.

Emily dragged Michael over to her table, tightly linking her arm through his. "Where's my brother, Millie? Did you bore him to death?"

Michael jerked Emily's arm. "I hear there's a coffee bar in this hotel someplace and we're off," he told Millie.

But Emily jerked Michael's arm right back. "It's too early for coffee, Michael."

"Well, then," Michael said with a steely glare at Emily, "I guess we could spare a few minutes to sit with Millie."

Millie didn't want to be the cause of a fight between them, and she sure didn't relish the idea of making small talk with Emily. "It's okay, you two go ahead," Millie told them. "I'm sure Peter will be right back."

Emily shrugged. "Then sit by yourself. That's what you get for being stupid smart anyway."

Millie had to laugh despite her discomfort. "That's an oxymoron, Emily."

Emily had put her hands on her hips and glowered. "What did you call me?"

Thank you, Michael, Millie thought as he dragged Emily away.

"So you coming to the graduation party?" Michael repeated. "Everyone's expecting you."

"I don't know..." Millie replied, her eyes darting around for an escape.

"Just be there, okay?" Michael took Emily's arm and piloted her away.

Millie rolled her eyes and hurried back to her dad, who was introducing Gran to Carlye Henderson and her parents. She tugged his arm and said, "Let's go."

"Millie," Karl scolded, "you're being rude."

"Nice speech, Millie," Dr. Henderson said.

"Oh, yes, dear, quite inspired," Mrs. Henderson agreed. "And congratulations on all your scholarships."

Carlye checked the time on her cell phone. "You'll be over to the house later, right? Party starts at ten."

Millie sighed, sneaked a glance at her father whose expression told her she was going, and realized she was stuck. "Yeah, I'll be there."

"Well, hurry it up, girlfriend," Carlye said with a laugh. She nudged her parents in the direction of the parking lot. "Come on, Mom. I want to make sure the caterers have everything ready."

Mrs. Henderson nodded pleasantly, linked her arm through her husband's, and together they leisurely strolled away.

"Let's go, Dad!" Millie repeated. Shoving her way through the middle-schoolers she said loudly, "Mom, Dad's ready to go."

Elizabeth looked up and over the knot of pre-teens and caught her husband's eye as he shrugged, and then began to politely extricate herself from her fans. Millie hurried ahead to her mom's car, only to find Kaz leaning against it, arms crossed in front of his chest, listening to his iPod. Millie decided that her brother had the right idea about drowning out the crowd noise, and even though she didn't have her iPod, she mirrored his stance and stood staring at the night sky.

Finally Kaz pulled out one of his earbuds. "What's eating you? Your speech didn't suck and you're outta high school, so you should be happy."

"Thanks. I think." Millie slumped deeper against the car door. "I have to go to that graduation party at Carlye's."

"Oh, tough break," Kaz said with a smirk. "Swimming, dancing, food, no curfew…."

"No date," Millie added. "Unless I want to go with Peter Safire."

Kaz stared at her in disbelief. "He's a soph—junior. And why do you need a date anyway? You're the vale-whatever, so shouldn't you be the guest of honor or something?"

Millie looked down at her feet and kicked a rock out of the way. "Sometimes I just feel so superfluous."

"Super what?"

"Like a fifth wheel," Millie explained. "Out of place."

Kaz rolled his eyes. "Geez, Millie, at school you're some kind of super-genius and knock it out of the park, but when it comes to people, you strike out."

Millie smiled at him. "Nice baseball analogy." She sighed with resignation. "I guess I'll just go to the party and make the best of it."

Millie drove her car into the Hendersons' cul-de-sac only to discover that all the available parking spaces were taken. The party invitation was sitting open on the passenger seat all but screaming at her, "Ten p.m. till?" She was late, which explained the lack of parking. *Now what?*

As if in answer to her unspoken question, an older couple—probably friends of the Henderson's—

emerged from the house and beeped open their parallel-parked Lexus. Millie put on her turn signal and zipped into the vacant space once the Lexus maneuvered its way out.

She rang the doorbell and waited, but no one answered. She tried the door and it wasn't locked, and the party seemed to be in full swing, so she cautiously pushed it open and stepped inside.

"Finally!" Carlye shouted from across the room. She hurried over, grabbed Millie's arm and pulled her all the way into the living room, which was crowded with both teenagers and adults. "What took you so long?"

Millie looked chagrined. "Sorry, but I wanted to spend a little time with my grandmother. She's only here for the weekend."

"So? Aren't you going to visit her in a few weeks?"

"Yeah, but…"

"Oh, Millie, we're so glad you finally arrived," Mrs. Henderson called from across the room.

"Sorry, Mill, you're stuck," Carlye whispered as she gave Millie a little shove in her mom's direction.

Millie reluctantly joined Mrs. Henderson, who politely indicated the gentleman next to her. "Millie, have you met Mayor Albertson?"

Millie shook her head. "But I just graduated with his son, Craig."

Mrs. Henderson turned to the mayor and said, "The school expects great things from this young lady."

The mayor offered his hand. "Craig's off to Duke. And where will you be going next fall with all that scholarship money?"

Millie shook his hand and felt her cheeks burn.

"Well, I'm still trying to decide."

"Meaning she's too afraid to leave home," said a voice behind her.

She turned around and saw Emily standing there, her arm linked through Michael's. Millie opened her mouth to defend herself but thought better of it, especially with the mayor of Indianapolis right in front of her, so she merely said, "Nice to meet you, Mr. Mayor. And this is a lovely party, Mrs. Henderson. Excuse me."

Millie hurried over to join Carlye, who was standing next to the open patio door, which led to the pool. She was deep in conversation with some of their other classmates and everyone was chattering away about their college plans. Millie felt overwhelmed by inertia in the midst of all her focused fellow-graduates, feeling like the sixteen-year-old kid she actually was. She envied all those eighteen-year-olds who already knew which schools they'd be attending, what their future career plans were, and who in fact seemed to have their whole lives mapped out. Oh sure, she had options, thanks to all the hard work and study she'd put in over the years, but the thought of leaving home still made her stomach churn.

Michael looked over Emily's head. "Hey, Mill, everyone says you're off to New York this fall."

Millie's eyes widened in surprise. "Well, that's one of my options," she hedged. "What about you?"

Michael rocked back on his heels and thrust his hands in the pockets of his khaki shorts, grinning broadly. "Notre Dame Irish all the way!"

Ireland Hancock sauntered over to join them, a cup of punch in his hand. "So does that mean I'll see you around campus up in South Bend, Mike?"

"You bet," Michael replied. "Say, Millie, didn't you apply to Notre Dame?"

"Ummm…" Millie began to feel overheated and noticed sweat forming on the back of her neck. Surely it was because the patio door was open, letting in all the heat and humidity. "Notre Dame? I…"

"Only if Millie recently grew a backbone," Emily snarked.

A waiter was right behind them with a tray of hors d'oeuvres. Carlye deliberately stepped on Emily's freshly-pedicured toes as she reached across for one. "Mmmm, these are so good. Here, Emily, try one of these bacon quiches," Carlye said as she shoved it near Emily's face.

Emily backed up and winced. "Hey, watch it," she said, rubbing her toes and readjusting her sandal. "These are expensive. And I'm on a diet, so get that away from me."

Carlye winked at Millie as she popped the quiche in her mouth and turned back to Ireland and Michael. "Forget Notre Dame. My best friend and I are gonna be roommates at Indiana University next fall."

Although Millie appreciated Carlye's intervention, she hated to get her friend's hopes up just to ease the tension. "I'm giving it some thought."

"For all your so-called accomplishments, you sure are indecisive," Emily said.

"They aren't 'so-called,'" Carlye corrected her. "Did you see how many times Millie was up on stage tonight accepting awards? And you were up there when?"

"I'm starved." Michael grabbed the last two mini-quiches off the waiter's tray and popped them both into his mouth at once, practically swallowing them whole. "And thirsty. Got any coffee made?"

Carlye jerked her thumb in the direction of the kitchen. "Fresh pot just for you."

Ireland gingerly took a bite of his hors d'oeuvre and then spit it into his napkin. "Yuk! Anyway," he said, taking a big gulp of his punch, "it's late May, Millie, and everyone else has already signed their dorm leases. If you don't hurry up, there won't be any decent rooms left, to say nothing of getting your pick of the best classes. At School X," he added.

"It's complicated," Millie said, knowing how lame that sounded.

Ireland looked puzzled. "I don't get what you're waiting on. Can't be finances. You got all those full rides."

Emily tossed her hair and rolled her eyes as she linked her arm through Michael's. "Don't be dense, Ireland. We'll all be in college this fall and little Millie will still be in Indianapolis chauffeuring her sibs around town."

Michael shot Emily a look and pushed her ahead of him toward the kitchen for his caffeine fix.

Millie put her hands to her flushed face. She turned to Carlye and said quietly, "I gotta go." She glanced at the time on her cell phone as she headed to the front door. She'd lasted at the party a full fifteen minutes.

Chapter Three
Making Plans

Millie had tossed and turned half the night, waking frequently with nightmares about being lost and alone in New York City. Then there was the weird dream where she was stranded in the wilderness with her siblings, and finally one about some skinny boy in overalls and a corn pipe. She chalked that one up to too much museum time.

It was 6:30 a.m. Exhausted but unable to go back to sleep, she got up and went downstairs to the kitchen. She knew her dad would already be up and hard at work, since he claimed to do his best thinking at five a.m. Sure enough, there he sat at the breakfast table, laptop up and running. She yawned and glanced at the screen.

"Morning, Dad," she said. She leaned over his shoulder and pointed to the page he was working on. "Don't you mean 'intangible'? You've got 'intangled' here."

Karl lifted an eyebrow. "What would I do without

my genius valedictorian?" He grinned and turned to face her. "Aren't you supposed to sleep in during summer vacation?"

"I'm sleepwalking."

Karl got up and stretched his arms overhead, and then walked to the coffee pot to refill his cup. "Something keeping you up?"

"Nightmares," was all she would admit to.

"What sort of nightmares?"

Millie sighed, knowing her nightmares were personifying her waking fears. How could she tell her dad about the panic that gripped her whenever she thought about leaving home and living in some distant city surrounded by strangers, all while trying to please exacting professors and making friends among much-older and more sophisticated classmates? "College," she told him.

"That's it? Just qualms about college? This should be the time of your life."

"Well, it's just that, well, I've been struggling…."

"Millie," Karl said with what Millie thought was a maddeningly patronizing tone, "you've been accepted to some fine universities. You know without me telling you that you must choose one soon before it's too late."

Millie went to the cupboard for a juice tumbler and turned her back so her father couldn't read her expression. "What if I postpone college for a while?" she suggested, and then took a quick peek over her shoulder to gauge his reaction.

Karl frowned as he sat down again at the breakfast table, removed his glasses and tossed them aside. "Mildred, I needn't remind you that you're brilliant, graduated top of your class, and your mother and I have every reason to expect you to use your scholarship money at a top university."

Millie rolled her eyes. She went to the refrigerator and pulled out a half-empty bottle of orange juice and poured herself a large glass, sloshing most of it over the side. "Since you're using my formal name, I guess that means you're miffed."

"Disappointed is more like it. You know how hard we worked to send you to Kendrick, all with an eye toward getting you into an Ivy League school. Now you're telling me we did all that for nothing?"

Millie grabbed a towel and wiped the spilled juice off the counter, but she couldn't look her father in the face. Yes, her parents did sacrifice a lot for her education—and her brother's and sister's—and she felt guilty for letting them down. "It wasn't for nothing, Dad, but…" She shook her head and fought back the tears. "I'm just not ready for college yet."

"How can you say that? As hard as you pushed yourself in high school, I'd say you're more ready than most of your classmates. You can't tell me you aced all those AP exams for the sheer sport of it."

Millie processed that for a moment. Her dad was right, she had worked hard in high school, but at the time her only goal was to stay ahead of her peers. "There's just so much more pressure in college, to make good grades and compete for the best post-grad program, career, whatever." Saying it out loud, it sounded even scarier and made her more determined to put off going, knowing she couldn't handle all that right now.

Karl sighed and rubbed his forehead. "Millie, you're your own worst enemy. You could lighten up on yourself and still do fine in college. It wouldn't be the end of the world to earn a B+." She didn't answer. "What about OLAC?"

Millie's eyes widened in surprise. "Oklahoma Liberal Arts College?"

Karl shrugged. "It might be just what you're looking for," he said with a grin. "Small private school in a community you're familiar with, and it's got one of the best humanities departments in the Midwest. You'd fit right in."

Millie slumped into a kitchen chair. "Why can't I just stay home for a while," she pleaded, "help out with Kaz and Charlie?"

"Because you can't hide out here forever," Karl told her, the playful smile fading from his face, "going to the library or playing make-believe at that museum. OLAC's undergrad program got me into Harvard Law School, and it could do the same for you."

Millie swallowed hard. "Boston?"

"Okay, one step at a time, but OLAC could be the perfect solution. And don't forget your grandmother lives nearby if you have problems. You've been accepted there, right? Sent them your SAT and AP scores?"

Millie let out a huge, exaggerated groan. "You know I did. You and Gran nagged me mercilessly."

Karl reached over and squeezed Millie's shoulder. "Another bonus—my old school buddy, Alex, is a tenured professor there. Can't hurt to have a family friend on staff. What do you think?"

"I'll give it some thought, Dad," she fibbed.

Back upstairs in her bedroom, Millie threw herself on her bed in agony, the pressure from family and peers reaching a crescendo. Huntleigh? Notre Dame? Indiana University? OLAC? It didn't matter, because she just knew she lacked the courage to go to any of them. How would she ever navigate all the hurdles involved? Too much pressure. What to do?

She decided to make good on her former promise to Kendrick's librarian to get out in the fresh air and go for a walk, which might help her get some perspective. But instead of getting dressed and putting on her walking shoes, she stretched out on her bed and fell asleep.

Millie rolled over several hours later and glanced at her bedside clock, which read 11:50 a.m. She berated herself for sleeping through the cool morning hours when walking outside would have made sense, forced herself to put on her walking shoes, and stepped out the front door where she was met with a blast of June heat. "Too hot," she mumbled, and retreated back into the comfortable air conditioning.

She pulled a bottle of chilled water from the fridge and slowly sipped it as she headed to her bedroom, checking her phone for messages as she climbed the stairs. There was one from Carlye. *Pool. My house. TODAY!* It was a marvel of brevity.

She punched in her response: *Can I bring Kaz and Charlie?* She hit send.

Carlye's response pinged right back. *Sure. Matt and Krissy will be glad to have them. Be here by 2:00 and come around back to the pool. We MUST talk!*

Well, at least Carlye had bestirred herself enough to write complete sentences, but that didn't clarify the urgency. Millie sighed and headed to the bathroom for a shower.

Promptly at two that afternoon, Millie arrived with Kaz and Charlie at the Henderson's expansive home for a swim. She'd insisted that both kids slather themselves with sunscreen before even leaving their house, since she knew once they arrived there'd be no reasoning with either of them about sunburn precautions. Kaz balked as always, but Charlie was her usual sweet, compliant self.

The car's interior digital thermometer said it was eighty-nine degrees outside. Millie sucked in her breath when she turned off the car's air-conditioning, but she remembered to leave the windows cracked an inch to allow heat to escape. She reached over, patted Charlie on the head, and then flipped open her little sister's seatbelt.

Kaz gave the front passenger seat a shove from behind. "Get out, Charlie. Matt's waiting."

"Give her a minute, okay?" Millie snapped, then immediately regretted her quick temper. She reached into her side door pocket and pulled out the windshield-covering shade and methodically stretched it across the front window.

"Geez, Millie, it's like you're afraid you'll get hot or something," Kaz groused as he rattled the locked door handle. "Let's go!"

Millie ignored him until the covering was perfectly in place. Once she released the door locks, Charlie slid out of the front seat onto the curb and Kaz bounded out of the backseat. With his towel draped around his neck and swim fins flapping on the sidewalk, he made a comical sight as he attempted to run up the winding walkway.

"Hurry up, Millie!" Charlie called out as she tried to catch up with her brother, who was already halfway to the front door. She had on her favorite purple Lil Filly-embossed swimsuit, flip-flop sandals, and water wings, her towel tucked under her arm and goggles on top of her head. With all the gear she was carrying and her sandals that kept slipping off, she wasn't making much progress either.

Millie easily caught up to them and took Charlie's towel from her, stuffing it inside her own bag. "Carlye said to just go around back to the pool and not bother ringing the front doorbell. Kaz? Did you hear me?" But he was already out of earshot.

Millie took Charlie's hand and together they walked more leisurely. "It's really hot today, don't you think?"

Charlie bobbed her head up and down and giggled.

"But that means great pool weather!"

The Henderson's backyard consisted of a perfectly manicured lawn and landscaped flower garden, a tribute to Mrs. Henderson's status as president of the Marion County Garden Club. In the corner off to one side of the immense yard was a tennis court that Millie had never seen anyone use, and she often wondered why they'd even built it. On the other side of the property was the large, oval swimming pool.

The house reflected the Hendersons' wealth, not unlike the stately homes of so many of her former Kendrick classmates whose parents were corporate CEOs, doctors, architects, politicians, and on and on. Oh, sure, her parents were also professionals—her father a partner in a small law firm, her mother a magazine columnist and author of children's books—but their home in a decidedly middle-class neighborhood was no comparison to the mansions in this part of town.

It seemed like a long hot walk from the front of the

house to the backyard, so Millie was more than ready to dive into the pool, but only after she had on enough sunscreen. It wouldn't do to get sunburned. She was wearing her pastel green maillot swimsuit for more protection and modesty than a bikini would afford. She carried a beach bag stuffed full of her pool necessities, which included UV-ray sunglasses, sunscreen with SPF 45, bottled water, and her dog-eared copy of Jane Austen's Emma, should she get a chance to read. But she doubted it, because even from this distance she could hear the loud heavy-metal rock music blaring from the outdoor speakers.

Carlye waved at her from the shallow end of the pool, and then hopped out and hurried over to open the white wrought-iron safety gate for the three of them. She was wearing a skimpy yellow bikini, DKNY sunglasses, and had stuffed her frizzy red hair into a now-wet, bulging ponytail. "It's about time, you guys," she said. Kaz was standing there impatiently, and as soon as Carlye opened the gate he blew past her.

"You said 2:00, right?" Millie fixed Carlye with a quizzical look and then turned to her sister. "Go ahead to the pool, Charlie. I'll be right there."

Kaz had already tossed his towel on the pool deck and jumped into the water with a cannonball splash, right next to Matt, who was floating on a rubber raft. The two of them immediately began splashing, laughing, and playing. Matt and Carlye's five-year-old cousin, Krissy, was already in the shallow end of the pool, kicking her feet and making lots of noise, under the eagle eye of the Henderson's manny, Paul.

"Start in the shallow end by the steps, Charlie," Millie called out, "and you can play with Krissy when you get used to the water."

"I know how to swim and I'm not a baby," Charlie whined. "She is."

"She's five. And you've played with her before, so go on." Millie looked up at the manny/lifeguard, sunning himself in the guard chair. "You're watching, right?" she called up to him.

"That's what they pay me the big bucks to do," he answered.

"They're fine, Millie," Carlye insisted, heading toward the deck chairs. "Come on. We've got to talk."

"Preferably on the other side of the pool," Millie replied with a head-tilt toward the speakers, "if you want me to actually hear you." Millie chose a comfy-looking deck lounge away from the blaring rock music, under a large umbrella attached to a patio table. She carefully spread her towel over the chair, pulled sunscreen out of her bag and began applying it to every inch of exposed skin. Carlye plopped down in the deck chair next to her, took the sunscreen and squirted out a dollop into her hand to rub on her legs.

Millie checked the back of her legs to make sure they were completely coated. "Okay, what's so urgent?"

Carlye looked her square in the eye. "August."

"Kind of a broad subject, don't you think?" Millie settled into the lounger and pulled her sunglasses into place. "Please be more succinct."

"Succinct, huh?" Carlye pulled a face and then took her time as she stretched herself out the length of the lounge chair to sunbathe. "I can't believe you're still procrastinating about college."

To hide her frown, Millie pulled her sun-visor

over her eyes and answered with as much self-assurance as she could muster. "I'm still weighing my options."

Carlye shook her head. "You are not! Why don't you just suck it up and sign those admission papers?"

Millie fidgeted. "What's the rush?"

"Because…" Carlye said, slowly rising to her feet to draw out the suspense, "…I've been accepted into that British Lit study abroad program I applied to! Ta-da! I'll be spending my first semester in London."

Millie slumped down as she let that news wash over her. "So that means if I go to IU—big IF—I'd be all alone with no best friend, and…." Her voice trailed off as she let out a huge groan.

"'Congratulations, Carlye. Way to go. Great program you got into,'" Carlye said as she flopped back down onto the lounger.

Millie forced a smile. "I'm sorry. That is a great program. So what does it matter if I send in the paperwork? You don't need a roommate now."

"I'll just be in London for one semester. You'd have that nice, new room in the brand new dorm all to yourself till I get back."

Even though Carlye obviously thought that was a selling point, Millie blanched. Before she could explain away her hesitancy a big splash of water hit her in the face. "Matt, you jerk! Cut it out!" She jumped up and grabbed her towel to dry off.

"Aw come on, Millie," Kaz called out from the edge of the diving board. "It's summer and you're sitting by a pool. What'd you expect?" He dove in with a big splash.

Millie glared at her brother when he surfaced and made a face at her. "I'm going for a swim," she told

Carlye. As far as she was concerned, the news of Carlye's trip to London was an end to this discussion about Indiana University.

Family dinners were an anomaly in the Olson household, but since everyone was soon to be off in different directions for the summer, Millie had insisted, and Martha had agreed, to go all out preparing the meal. Karl and Elizabeth were seated next to each other at their oval dining room table that was seldom used, with Millie on one side and Kaz and Charlie on the other.

Elizabeth held up her glass of white wine in a toast. "To Millie. And Martha, of course."

Karl held up his half-full glass of wine and clinked it against Elizabeth's.

Kaz craned his neck to eyeball Millie. "Hey, how come she gets ginger ale?" he asked his parents. "And I'm stuck drinking milk?"

"Because you're a growing adolescent in dire need of extra calcium and vitamins," Millie answered.

Kaz rolled his eyes. "Couldn't you just say it's because I'm still a kid?"

"You know your sister's a sesquipedalian," Karl teased with a knowing wink at Millie.

"What?" Kaz demanded, looking from his dad to his sister and back again.

"Dad means I use big words," Millie told him.

Kaz rolled his eyes with a Duh expression, tossed his napkin in his chair and pushed back from the table, rattling the glassware as he did. "You and Millie are so boring! I'm gonna go play video games."

"Make sure you're all packed before you do!" Karl called to him.

Kaz turned back around. "Dad, just how long do we have to stay in Oklahoma anyway? You know I gotta be back for football conditioning the end of July."

Karl's brow furrowed. "Well, son, it depends on this case in LA. But the end of July is several weeks away, so football shouldn't be a problem."

"Good," Kaz said as he turned to go, "because I wanna get back here and spend some time with my friends, since I actually have some."

"That's not fair!" Millie called out, but he was already gone.

"Can I be excused, too?" Charlie asked, and without waiting for an answer, jumped up and raced from the table.

"I'll read you a bedtime story, Charlie!" Elizabeth called after her.

"No thanks!" Charlie answered in sing-song. "I'm tired of Millicent."

Karl smiled warmly at his wife. "Fortunately your other fans disagree, darling," he told her.

Elizabeth poured herself another glass of wine and shifted to a more comfortable position in the high-backed dining chair. "I'm still pinching myself that a Hollywood film company wants to make a movie out of Millicent the Magnificent! I'm meeting with my agent as soon as I get to Los Angeles."

"What about work?" Millie asked her mom.

Elizabeth shrugged. "I've got a two week vacation coming up, and after that I just told Larry I'd be writing 'on the road' for a couple of weeks."

"And you're entitled," Karl told her in response to Millie's dubious look. "The last issue of Trending in Indianapolis sold out as soon as it hit the stands, because of that feature article about you." He took a sip of wine and squeezed her hand. "It'll be good to have you in California with me. This case has been complicated and drawn-out, but if we win, the firm stands to make good money. That should help pay Kaz and Charlie's school tuition."

"And fortunately," Elizabeth added, "Millie's got all that scholarship money for college."

Millie choked on her strawberry shortcake and grabbed her ginger ale, draining the glass.

"You okay, hon?" Karl asked.

Millie nodded and jumped up, using her coughing fit as an excuse to leave the table before the topic of college came up again. She couldn't wait to get on that plane for Oklahoma, a place she always felt safe. *Maybe some distance and sound advice from Gran is exactly what I need right now,* she thought. Getting away from Indianapolis and everyone pressuring her sounded like the perfect respite.

Chapter Four
Discoveries

The plane touched down on the runway at Oklahoma City's Will Rogers Airport. Millie had allowed Charlie to sit next to the window and Kaz was in the aisle seat where he could stretch out his gangly legs, so she'd been cramped between them for hours and was ready to get up.

"Hey, Millie," Charlie said as the plane taxied toward the gate. "Look outside. The air looks wavy!"

"That's from the heat," Millie told her. "It's a mirage, caused by refraction."

"You couldn't just say it's hot," Kaz said.

"This is it, folks," said the pilot over the address system. "Oklahoma City, Oklahoma. Local time is 4:05 p.m. and the outside temperature is 101 degrees."

Millie groaned at the thought of going outside in all that heat, but Kaz jumped up as soon as the Fasten Seatbelt sign was turned off. He hoisted his backpack over his shoulder and took off up the exit ramp. She sighed as she juggled her overstuffed backpack and purse while simultaneously hanging onto Charlie's bag stuffed with toys. The Oklahoma City airport was considerably smaller than the one in Indianapolis, but Millie still had to look around to get her bearings. "Gran's meeting us in baggage claim," she said as she took Charlie's hand, but there was no keeping up with her brother as he bounded down the escalator stairs two at a time.

"Millie, she's here!" Charlie shouted gleefully as she spotted their grandmother waving at them enthusiastically from the bottom of the escalator. She jumped down the last step and ran over to throw herself into Gran's arms.

"Charlotte!" Gran staggered back a bit on impact. "It's so good to have you three here," she said, folding Charlie and Millie into her embrace. She reached over to include Kaz, but he backed away.

"Hey, Gran," he said, "can we go to the pool?"

Gran lifted up Kaz's baseball cap so she could see his face. "Yes, I suppose so. But I know how your sister feels about heat. It might just be you and Charlie."

Millie searched the signage to determine which carousel belonged to Midwestern States Airlines. "Gran, the luggage will be arriving soon, and if you'll drive your car around, Kaz and I will put all of it in your trunk," she said. "But first…" She looked at Charlie, who was dancing up and down. "We need to make a stop."

"Got it," Gran said, winking at Millie.

"Come on, Gran," Kaz said, tugging on her arm. "It's hot and the swimming pool's calling my name."

Millie was pensive on the half-hour drive north to her grandmother's country home, thinking about the problems she hoped she'd left back in Indiana. She watched the city disappear as the scenery turned more rural, and when eventually they turned off onto a two-lane stretch of road appropriately named Olson Road, she felt like she always did when coming to her grandmother's: a comforting sense of home.

Before her father was born, this used to be an unpaved dirt road with a hand-painted sign her grandfather had stuck on a fence which read "Olson's," with an arrow pointing the direction to his house. In the 1970s, when the town extended the pavement out that far, Rolling Plains put up an actual street sign officially naming it after her grandfather.

There it was off in the distance, sitting on two full acres of land: a large two-story, wood frame house in the ornate gingerbread style of the early 1900s. The exterior of the house sported freshly painted brown shutters and yellow trim on the lattice work, which in turn framed the white-columned wraparound front porch. And on that porch was Millie's favorite spot to think and read—the old-fashioned whitewashed wooden swing with the chain link suspension.

By the third week in June, the Oklahoma heat and drought had already produced parched brown fields as far as the eye could see, and someone with good eyes could see quite a distance because of the flat terrain. Millie leaned her head on the passenger side window to let the cool air-conditioning hit her face as they pulled into the lengthy blacktop driveway.

Gran slowly maneuvered the car up the drive and parked adjacent to the house's side entrance and in front of the detached garage. "Here we are!" she announced.

"Goody!" exclaimed Charlie as she opened the

back door and jumped out.

"Can everybody carry their own bags?" Gran asked, specifically peering at Kaz over her prescription sunglasses. "I've hired some temporary help for the summer, but baggage transport is not his job."

"Zach MacMillan," Millie muttered.

Logically Millie knew that Gran couldn't manage two acres by herself, so she depended on MacMillan Landscape. Millie could see that the lawn had been recently mowed and the bushes trimmed, but she still didn't have much confidence in Zach's ability to stay on top of things, based on what she remembered of him from two years ago.

"I'll try to help out as much as I can, Gran." Millie got out of the front seat and stretched her arms overhead, twisting right and left to work the kinks out of her back, and then blew out a big puff of air as she tried in vain to acclimate herself to the Oklahoma heat.

Gran smiled. "I appreciate that, Millie, but I've got Zach for the outside and Esperanza for the inside, so you can just enjoy your vacation." She pulled the vehicle's hatch-door release and walked around to the back of the car.

"Pool!" Kaz shouted as he located his baseball bag from the bottom of the pile of luggage and yanked it out, ignoring his suitcase and everyone else's as he took off for the kitchen door.

Millie put her hands on her hips and called after her brother. "You're not helping! And just how do you think you're going to get to the pool?"

Kaz turned around and rolled his eyes at her. "Gran. Duh."

Millie looked apologetically at her grandmother, as if she were responsible for Kaz's rudeness. "Dad said he'd rent me a car while I'm here so you don't have to be their chauffeur. It should be delivered tomorrow." Loaded down with three heavy bags, packed with all the clothes and gear they would need for an extended visit, she walked the few steps to the side door, working up a sweat with each step.

"That's fine, dear," Gran replied. "But keep in mind that I only have a one-car garage, converted as it was from a barn all those years ago, so the rental will have to sit out in the driveway." Gran peered over her sunglasses at Millie. "In the heat, dear."

Millie nodded stoically as she opened the door into the modern, updated kitchen, a distinct contrast to the exterior of the house. Gran had redone everything a few years ago, adding granite countertops, stainless steel appliances, and new cabinets to complement the original hardwood floors. Off to the side was what had originally been a morning room, but once the wall between the two areas had been knocked down it became one, bright, sunny breakfast area. There was a large picture window that overlooked Gran's flower garden, which Millie noticed was withstanding the heat quite well, meaning somebody must be watering it. Zach? Well, she assumed he could manage a garden hose at least.

Despite the contemporary look of the kitchen, the breakfast table was a round antique oak with a set of six mismatched high-backed chairs, circa 1920, all acquired from antique shops on the town's Main Street. Millie dumped all the heavy suitcases just inside the door, tossed her purse and airplane carry-on bag into one of the breakfast chairs and reached into a cabinet for a green Depression-era drinking glass. She went to the refrigerator door and first filled the glass with ice, then cold water. She sipped slowly to avoid an ice headache, but put the glass to her forehead anyway, enjoying its refreshing coolness.

Upstairs Millie could hear Charlie and Kaz stomping around and laughing. She carefully set her empty drinking glass in the sink, walked through the spacious living room and stared up the staircase where the four bedrooms were located. The master bedroom, Gran's room, was on the left at the top of the stairs, large and with its own bathroom, a later addition to the previously one-bathroom home. Gran kept special rooms for the use of each of her grandchildren during their frequent visits, plus she had added a second master suite downstairs off the side of the laundry room for Karl and Elizabeth's use.

"Kaz!" Millie called up the stairs. "You left your other bag on the ground by the car. You know, the one with your swimsuit in it!"

Kaz blew past Millie on the stairs, taking them two at a time, landed on the hardwood floor with a thud and slammed the kitchen door. Millie sighed and went upstairs to the bedroom she always occupied, the one that doubled as a guest room if anyone besides family should visit. She loved all the antiques in the room, decorations reminiscent of the house's original furnishings, and she liked to envision the first owners living and sleeping in there. She tossed her bag on the vintage trunk at the foot of the double bed and flopped down on the white eyelet coverlet. The reproduction antique ceiling fan whirred silently overhead, generating a cool breeze that was both refreshing and relaxing.

"Knock, knock." Gran peeked in the doorway and stepped into the room.

Millie sat up and smiled as Gran sat down next to her on the edge of the bed and patted her knee. "I couldn't help noticing you've got things on your mind, dear. Karl tells me you've got some college decisions to make, something about an Ivy League school."

"Dad has grandiose ideas."

Gran chuckled, which set her eyes to twinkling. "You know, Millie, of all Karl's children, you're the most like him. Oh, I know, Kaz is named for him and looks just like my son did at his age, but your intelligence and temperament are so like your father."

Millie's shoulders slumped. "At least Dad didn't have to make life-changing decisions at age sixteen."

Gran patted Millie's arm. "You know, dear, your father could have graduated from high school early like you did, but he also wanted to play football, so he languished in unchallenging classes in order to do that. You, on the other hand, have been given a golden opportunity."

Millie flopped down on her back and watched the ceiling fan whir. "It's all so…overwhelming."

Gran winked at Millie. "Wherever you go, you'll be the best student that school has ever seen, just like you were at Kendrick."

Down the hall they could hear Kaz and Charlie taunting each other, racing up and down the stairs and slamming doors. Gran tilted her head in the direction of all the commotion. "I think I have some ideas about entertaining your brother and sister, but I'd like to see you get out and enjoy your visit, meet some young people." Gran lifted Millie's chin and looked her in the eye. "I can introduce you."

Millie looked at her grandmother suspiciously. "I already know Zach MacMillan, if that's what you mean."

"Well, dear, you haven't seen Zach in a couple of years. He was off at that sports camp when you were here last summer. People change."

Millie was trying to respect her grandmother's opinion, but seriously, Zach? "Maybe I'll just take a few days to settle in, go to a museum or the library," she said.

Gran smiled and hugged Millie's shoulder. "A pretty young girl shouldn't spend so much time alone with books and computers. And Zach is such a nice young man."

Millie nodded politely as her grandmother quietly closed the bedroom door. Zach MacMillan indeed.

* * * * *

Millie overslept the next morning. After a quick glance at the clock — eleven a.m.! — she jumped out of bed, showered and dressed in khaki shorts and a yellow cotton blouse, tied her blond hair back in a ponytail, slid into her sandals, and ran downstairs just in time to see Kaz yanking open the front door. "Where are you going? And where's Gran?"

Kaz was dressed in cutoff jeans, a Colts football t-shirt, an Indianapolis Indians baseball cap pulled low over his brow, and had his baseball glove clutched in his left hand with a tight grip on the ball. "Kitchen," he said, tilting his head toward the front door. "And out to play catch if it's any of your business."

Almost immediately after Kaz slammed the front door, Millie could hear his ball banging against the wooden garage door and hoped it wouldn't do any damage. She went into the kitchen, where her grandmother was busy at the stove, cooking something that smelled delicious. "Morning, Gran," she said sheepishly. "You shouldn't have let me sleep so long."

Gran turned around from the stove and smiled. She had an apron tied around her waist to protect her white linen skirt and bright green golf shirt. "You don't have to apologize, dear. You needed your rest."

"What's that you're cooking?" Millie asked, standing on tiptoe to peer over her grandmother's shoulder.

"I'm making Kaz and Charlie some homemade chicken noodle soup, an early lunch because we have an appointment at the Rolling Plains Recreation Center. But I saved you some muffins from breakfast, if you'd prefer."

"Maybe I'll skip breakfast and go right to lunch," Millie said, breathing in the soup's aroma. She pulled four bowls out of the cupboard and went to the fridge for some juice. "What appointment?" she asked.

Gran turned off the burner and slid the boiling pot to the back of the stove, covering it with a lid. "Remember I mentioned an idea for entertaining your brother and sister?"

Millie nodded.

"Well, it seems the community recreation center offers day camps for children in various age groups. Charlie will be in the eight- to nine-year-olds, and Kaz can join the summer baseball camp they're offering this year for the first time. A couple of the Triple-A league ballplayers from Oklahoma City are conducting the camp, with a trip to the Fourth of July ball game and a chance for one of the boys to throw out the first pitch."

"That's great! Now what about Charlie? What will she be doing?"

"Swimming, team sports, crafts, you know, day camp activities. They're taking some field trips to museums and the zoo as well. Charlie's excited."

"Oh, Gran, thank you for doing this!" Millie said. "And I'd be glad to help chaperone Charlie's group to museums or field trips," she added as she got busy setting the table for lunch.

Gran began dishing the soup into the bowls. "I think they have enough chaperones, dear. You spend too much time in a museum as it is."

"I like the museum. It gets my mind off…" She noticed Gran's raised eyebrow and sighed.

Gran pulled a box of crackers from the pantry and set it on the table. "Now you've got some free time, dear, perhaps you could drive over to Oklahoma Liberal Arts College for a campus tour. The rent car arrived this morning."

Millie scowled and sat down in one of the chairs. "I only applied there because you and Dad insisted, but…" She stopped herself when a totally unrelated thought popped into her head. "Gran, how are Kaz and Charlie going to get to camp every day? Do I need to drive them?"

Gran laughed. "My, my, your mind does jump around. But no, no need to trouble yourself. There's a bus that picks them up at eight o'clock every morning and returns them home by five every evening."

THUD thud BAM!

Millie jumped to her feet. "What was that?" she exclaimed as she ran to the kitchen window.

Gran craned her neck, trying to see out the window around Millie. "Can you see anything, dear?"

Millie shook her head before running outside to investigate. There was Kaz, staring up at the roof over the garage in disgust. He pulled his hat off his head as he wiped the sweat from his brow, put one hand on his hip and kicked a rock out of his way.

"Kaz! What did you do?"

"Oh, chill, Millie," he said, pointing to the roof. "The ball bounced up off the garage door, hit the roof and landed in the gutter."

Millie shaded her eyes with her hand as she looked up over the garage and did a few logistical calculations. "It's not going to roll down by itself."

Kaz narrowed his eyes at her. "I'll get the ladder."

"You'll do no such thing!" Millie exclaimed. "I'll get the ladder. Go tell Gran everything's okay, it's just a ricochet ball."

"A what?"

"Just do it, okay?" Millie said. She'd already walked around to the garage's side door entrance and jiggled the handle to see if it was locked, but the door latch was rotting and it opened easily with a shove. "And Kaz," she called out, "tell Gran she needs to get this garage door lock replaced." Millie heard Kaz groan and slam the still-open kitchen door behind him.

Millie surveyed the rusting door lock. Note to self: Call a locksmith. She reached inside and pushed the wall button that opened the automatic garage door, which cranked open with a blast of hot air. She fanned herself with her blouse and began visually searching the garage for the step ladder.

She located it, propped up against the far corner wall and wedged in pretty tightly, so first she had to scoot around her grandmother's Escalade to even reach it. She briefly thought about going inside for the keys to move the car out of the garage, but that meant also backing the rental Toyota down the drive, so she decided if she was careful she'd be able to inch the six foot wooden ladder out without leaving a ding on the car's finish.

It must be 100 degrees out here, Millie thought as sweat ran down her face and dampened her shirt. She carefully maneuvered the ladder out of the garage and set it on the driveway, opened it up and tested it for strength. It was pretty rickety, but she was determined to get that baseball out of the gutter, not so much for Kaz but for her grandmother's peace of mind. She tightly gripped the rungs above her and tried the first step, got her footing, stepped up one more, felt the ladder wiggle beneath her and stopped in mid-climb. She squinted in the sunlight as she looked up, realizing the precariousness of her situation. Salty sweat was stinging her eyes as she tried to figure out what to do next.

"Need some help with that?"

Startled, Millie tried to turn around to see who was there, but caught herself as the ladder teetered. The adrenaline rush caused her heart to beat wildly and forced her to grip the rails even tighter. "No. No thanks," she said.

"Suit yourself."

Millie ever-so-slowly backed down the ladder, sighing with relief when her feet touched ground again, and then turned around to see who was speaking to her. Staring back at her was a tall, muscular, teenage boy, covered in sweat, black grease stains all over the front of his sleeveless white t-shirt. His jeans were also smudged with grease and his formerly white athletic shoes were untied and caked with mud.

Millie looked up into his vivid green eyes. She wiped off the sweat as it rolled down her cheeks and suddenly felt quite self-conscious. "I'll figure some-thing else out," she told him.

He shrugged. "Whatever. Like I said, I can get the baseball down for you."

"How do you know there's a baseball up there?"

"I was over there," he said, jerking his thumb over his shoulder, "in your grandmother's yard, changing the oil in the lawnmower. So you want that ball or not?"

Well, that explained the grease stains. "I'm not helpless!" Millie said, stomping her foot, hands on her hips. But she had to admit that the thought of going back up that unstable ladder unnerved her. She re-laxed her arms, tap-tap-tapped her foot and finally said, "Fine."

The boy centered the ladder on the driveway and locked the side hinges into place, something Millie had neglected to do, tested it for firmness, gave her a wink and quickly scampered up. He retrieved the ball from the gutter, held it up like a prize, and jumped down the last three steps.

"Tell Kaz to be more careful next time," he said, putting the ball in her hand.

He knew her brother? She shaded her eyes with her hand and took a step back to get a good look at him. In the glare of the sunlight, she hadn't recognized him. "Zach? Zach Macmillan?"

"In the flesh." He looked her up and down. "You haven't grown much in the last couple of years."

Millie couldn't help staring. "You sure have." Suddenly she couldn't catch her breath. This was Zach Macmillan? She was blushing and embarrassed, but she hoped Zach thought she was flushed from the heat and exertion. "Appreciably."

Zach smirked. "You never did sound like a regular kid."

Millie squirmed under his intense gaze. "Sorry, habit. I tend to use big words and sometimes people don't understand."

Zach grinned at her. "I'll bet."

Millie hoped to appear nonchalant in front of this guy she'd known practically all her life but had never given a second thought to. It wasn't working. "So how's Mac doing?" She felt like a hypocrite after all the disparaging remarks she'd made about Zach, but now she understood why Gran hired him.

Zach's faced clouded over with concern for his grandfather. "He kinda gave us all a scare. Doctor called it a 'cardiac event,' which I guess is fancy for heart attack."

"Tachycardia, I assume," Millie mused, tapping her cheek thoughtfully.

Zach burst out laughing, dropping his hands to his knees to catch his breath. "So is that how kids talk up north in Indiana?"

"Nice to see you again," Millie said in a huff. Clenching the baseball in her fist, she turned on her heel and started back to the house.

"Hey, Millie!" Zach called after her. "What about the ladder?"

She called over her shoulder before storming back in through the kitchen door. "Put it back in the garage. Through the side door that doesn't lock!"

Millie nearly slammed the door but stopped herself and closed it gently instead. She leaned against the inside door to catch her breath and looked up to see Gran standing in front of her, a twinkle in her eye.

"Yeah, okay, he's taller, but he's still a jerk."

"Millie? Millie!"

Millie's eyes popped wide open to find Charlie hovering over her bed, inches from her face, and at a very early hour judging from a quick glance at the bedside clock. She shook her head to get the dream out—that one where she'd forgotten to study for a major exam—and rubbed her eyes to focus. "What's wrong, Charlie?"

"I can't find my doll," Charlie said, shaking Millie's bed.

Millie rolled over onto her elbow and peered through half-opened eyes at her little sister, dressed in hot pink shorts with a flowered tank top, and noticed that she was growing out of them already. Millie covered a yawn and said, "Your doll was in your bed where we put her last night. Did you look on the floor?"

"Not that doll. Lucinda!"

"Oh," Millie said, "Lucinda." That was the rag doll Gran had found in an antique shop sixteen years ago, shortly after Millie's birth.

The shop owner told Gran that the doll had been handmade from scrap muslin and yarn around the time of Oklahoma statehood—1907. With her new baby granddaughter in mind, Gran had bought the doll and set out to restore her to beauty. Lucinda's eyes had to be re-stitched and she needed a new button nose, but her mouth still had its original embroidered smile. Her hands had what appeared to be two fingers—a thumb and the other four fingers sewn together, and instead of feet she wore shoes permanently sewn on.

The poor doll had been wearing a shabby, stained

pinafore dress, but Gran handily sewed a new blue and white gingham dress which Lucinda wore over a white doll's shirt bought at a discount store. Gran proudly gave the newly refurbished doll to Millie as a Christmas present that first year, but all it did for a while was lie in the crib next to her.

Two years later, even though the doll was nearly as big as she was, Millie loved Lucinda and dragged her around her grandmother's house at every visit, conducting tea parties and carrying on imaginary conversations with her. Even at that tender age, Millie was showing signs of precociousness, and one day she announced to her surprised parents and grandparents that the doll's name was Lucinda.

"Where did you hear that name, Millie?" Gran asked her.

"In a story," two-year-old Millie replied matter-of-factly.

Elizabeth recalled reading her a story with pictures from a bygone era, at the time thinking it was probably too advanced for her. "I guess Millie was paying more attention than I thought," Elizabeth mused.

Millie's parents were convinced that they had a very bright child on their hands. Elizabeth encouraged Millie's interest in history by first taking her to museums and then eventually signing her up as a museum youth volunteer in Indiana.

The doll always stayed at Gran's house so that Millie knew she had a special toy when she came to visit, and even though Lucinda occasionally showed signs of wear through the years, Gran lovingly restitched whatever was necessary. Millie had outgrown the doll a long time ago so she'd willingly passed her on to Charlie, who was again shaking Millie's bed in earnest.

"Where is she, Millie?"

"Don't worry, Charlie, I know she's around here somewhere. I'll find her."

Millie had the house all to herself that afternoon. With Gran gone to a church committee meeting and Kaz and Charlie in day camp, Millie had some time on her hands and decided to make good on her promise to Charlie to locate Lucinda. Approaching the problem with logic, Millie began a systematic search of the upstairs, starting with Charlie's room. She looked under the bed, on the top shelf of the closet, and in the vintage wardrobe closet in the corner. No Lucinda.

Next she went into her grandmother's bedroom and gave it a visual search, but realized it would never end up in there. So she went to Kaz's room and searched under his bed, choking at the smell of dirty socks and athletic shoes, before going through the dresser drawers and digging under the sweaty clothes he'd tossed on the closet floor. She coughed, covered her mouth with her hand and went back into the hallway. Where would Gran have put Lucinda?

Or maybe it was Esperanza, the disorganized housekeeper who came once a week and often left the house in more disarray than she found it. Millie had told Gran many times that she needed a new housekeeper.

Gran was having none of it. "She's not young anymore, dear, and jobs are hard to find. Essie means well, even if she's forever putting things in the wrong places. A search of the attic usually turns up whatever is missing."

The attic! Of course! Millie walked to the end of the hall and reached up to grab the rope attached to the folding stairway, and made sure this ladder was steady before climbing up. Years ago when Millie was a toddler, the attic was unusable space because it was either stifling hot or freezing cold, depending on the season. Grandpa Karl decided to make good on his promise to Gran to refurbish it, so he had contractors install new drywall, a solid hardwood floor, adequate insulation, new air ducts and a ceiling fan.

Millie flipped on the electrical switch at the top of the stairs which operated both the ceiling fan and its light fixture, and then did a visual search of the attic. Everything was neat and orderly, exactly as Gran always kept it, but Esperanza hadn't dusted up here in ages, causing Millie to sneeze three times in a row. *Bring a broom and feather duster next time*, she told herself.

Millie thought about the many happy times she'd spent playing up here. The attic, with Grandpa Karl's improvements but still with its original architecture, was a great place for Millie to get lost in her fantasies about her grandparents' house at the turn-of-the-twentieth century. She loved picturing the home's first owners, whoever they were, going about their daily lives, and mentally transported herself back to a simpler time, one in which girls—even smart ones—weren't forced to leave their homes and go away to college.

She sighed and sat down in the antique rocker, in the corner next to the window that overlooked the front lawn, near the doll house her grandfather had built her. Millie still missed him, even though he'd died over ten years ago. She knew Gran missed him, too, and Millie always loved hearing stories about him.

"Tell me again about when you met Grandpa." Millie always settled in to hear the story she'd heard so many times before about her grandparents' romance.

Gran began telling the story in the exact same way she always did, like she'd never told it before. "That was 1964, I think. He was thirty years old at the time, smart, handsome, all the girls wanted to date him. But," she assured Millie, "he didn't date the college girls." She shook her head. "As a college professor, that wouldn't have been professional."

Millie winked at her grandmother. "I've seen those pictures of Grandpa when he was younger."

Gran continued, "I was just twenty years old, a good deal younger than Karl, Karl Senior, that is. There was a dance at the college — they had those back then, mixers they called them. I was friends with some of the students and those college girls insisted on dragging me along. But don't worry, dear," Gran told Millie with a playful pinch of her cheek, "there were lots of chaperones there that night, keeping a watchful eye on all us single ladies."

Millie couldn't help but giggle at the old-fashioned idea of chaperones looking out for the virtue of the young women. "And then what?"

"Seems like Karl danced with every other girl there and I didn't think he even knew I was in the room."

"But he did," Millie said, "because you were the prettiest."

Gran blushed. "Well, he finally asked me to dance — 'At Last' was playing — and he whispered in my ear that he'd had his eye on me all evening." She paused, lost in her memories, and began to hum the tune and sing quietly, "At last, my love has come along…"

"And then?" Millie would prompt.

Gran opened her eyes and continued. "Well, dear, after that we dated steadily until we got married a year later, and I moved into this house with him after our honeymoon." She clucked her tongue. "Up till then the house was what you young folks today call a 'man cave', so I had my work cut out for me."

"And Dad was born two years later. Right?"

"That's right!" Gran exclaimed. "Strong, healthy boy, nine pounds ten ounces. Karl Jr. was smart, athletic as you know, loved sports, good at most of them. Your grandpa coached him in football, which helped him get that scholarship to OLAC, and then he was off to Harvard." She sighed. "Your grandpa was always so proud of our boy." She shook her head. "He died too young."

Millie came out of her memories, sat up in the rocker and looked around the attic. Next to the doll house was a large, painted, wooden toy chest. She got down on her knees and carefully opened it. Inside were stored some of her dad's old toys that Kaz had played with as a little kid — worn stuffed animals, faded Tinker toys, a baseball bat and an old mitt. She carefully dug down to the bottom of the chest, hoping she'd find Lucinda. No such luck. Millie rocked back on her heels as she wracked her brain. Where would Esperanza put the doll?

Across the room in a nearly-hidden recess under the eaves she spotted several old quilts that she didn't remember ever seeing before and went over to have a closer look. "Where did these come from?" she asked herself. They'd been tossed rather haphazardly on top of an old trunk, another item Millie had never seen before. Puzzled, she gathered up each handmade quilt and carefully laid all six of them on the floor. They'd obviously been lovingly made decades ago and were still in remarkably good condition. Millie recognized the flying geese design on one quilt, dating it to the nineteenth century, and the Sunbonnet Sue design on another, placing it mid-twentieth century.

She ran her fingers along the top of the wooden trunk and flicked the dust off. "And what's your history?" she asked it.

It was definitely an antique, made of cedar, which was used back in the day to protect textiles, and it sported decorative wrought iron clasps and hinges. Millie gingerly touched the latch, found it unlocked, and gently lifted the lid, allowing the smell of cedar and mothballs to waft out. It was filled to the brim with what appeared to be old bedding—embroidered sheets, pillowcases, and dust ruffles—and lying on top of all that was Lucinda!

Millie lifted the doll out and planned to firmly tell Esperanza to leave Lucinda on Charlie's bed from now on. Lucinda didn't seem any worse for wear, so Millie gently set her on top of the folded quilts on the floor and went back to the trunk, its contents too good to resist.

She was extra careful as she lifted each linen piece out and examined it. At least the cedar had done its job, protecting all the linens from moths. These, she realized with some excitement, must be the items from the antique shop that Gran mentioned in that email back in May. She assumed Gran intended to donate them to the annual church bazaar where they would command top dollar, but Millie almost hated to see them sold.

To be sure everything was out of the trunk, Millie ran her hand around the interior, in case she'd overlooked anything in this poorly-lit corner of the attic. She'd just about satisfied herself that that was all the treasure the chest would yield when her hand struck something on the bottom, something wedged into a corner of the trunk and wrapped in a faded brown muslin dish towel. Gently she removed what felt like a book wrapped tightly inside a tiny, faded baby quilt, which was in turn covered by the towel. She unwrapped the book, blew the dust off the leather-bound cover and read the blocked lettering penned in bold ink, "Property of Synthia Elizabeth Whitfield."

Puzzled, Millie cautiously opened the cover and looked inside. Some of the top page was smudged, but what she could read said, "…on this day in 1865."

1865? Millie's jaw dropped. Who was Synthia Elizabeth Whitfield and how did her book get in this trunk in Gran's attic? This was someone's journal, someone she'd never heard of! Eagerly she opened it and began reading.

> May 18, 1865. Today is the fifteenth anniversary of my birth! Mama presented me with this journal, as she said I am now a young woman and would hereafter want to record my private musings.
>
> Mama has promised me a birthday cake, but otherwise it is a typically busy day on the farm. I have chickens to feed, a new dress to sew for my sister Mary Ann (at age seven, she is growing so quickly!), and the washing and

mending to do. My brother TJ is a rowdy ten-year-old boy, so of course he soils and tears his clothing regularly, making extra work for Mama and me.

TJ and Mary Ann are at school and I must go and fetch them before supper. At fifteen, Mama says I am too old for formal schooling, so I must content myself with being taught at home. To be assured that I am not neglecting my education in favor of housework, though, Mama instructed me to read one of Mr. Jefferson's essays, explain to her its meaning, and then be able to recite three Bible verses to her satisfaction. All this before I can celebrate my birthday tonight.

Good news! There is hope that the end of the Great War has come! Papa says word has come all the way from St. Louis up to our little town of Sedalia, Missouri, concerning General Lee's surrender to General Grant, but little else is forthcoming. We all pray that it is indeed finished and that our young men will soon be coming home. I again thank God that TJ was too young to serve, and that Papa could not be induced to leave his family.

It has been a wet spring. The planting is done and buds are poking through the soil, which Papa says is a sign of an abundant crop in the fall. We are all praying it is so.

So ends my first journal entry as a woman!

Millie's curiosity grew as she read and reread the entry. She quickly but gently replaced the textile items in the trunk, closed it, grabbed Lucinda and the journal, and hurried to her bedroom with her newly discovered treasure.

Chapter Five
Research

By late afternoon, Millie had moved from her bedroom to the kitchen, her laptop open, and she was lost in her research on the origins of the diary she'd just found. The back door opened and she looked up long enough to see Gran, Kaz, and Charlie walking in loaded with grocery bags, before returning her attention to the screen.

"Millie! Guess what we did at camp!" Charlie exclaimed as she raced around the table and tugged on her sister's arm, pulling it right off the keyboard. The bag of paper products Charlie was holding fell to the floor and its contents spilled out.

Millie sighed, closed her laptop, and began to retrieve the paper towels and boxes of tissue. "I can't guess, Charlie. Tell me."

"Rode horses!" Charlie said, covering her mouth with both hands to stifle her giggles and jumping up and down.

Millie thought about that for a moment as she

opened the cabinet where the paper products were stored and wedged them in on the top shelf. When she was Charlie's age, she'd been briefly enrolled in a summer day camp near Indianapolis, but her mother had withdrawn her because Millie was afraid of bugs, snakes, and the horses the counselors insisted they ride. "That doesn't sound safe," she muttered to herself. "Gran, is that safe?" she asked aloud.

Gran winked at her. "I'm sure the camp counselors know what they're doing, dear."

"Silly, Millie. It was fun! My horse's name is Apple!"

Millie forced a half-smile. "I'm glad you're enjoying camp, and I hope you'll obey all the safety rules." Millie took Charlie's hand and led her to the kitchen table facing the garden's bay window. Once she was seated and not wiggly, Millie handed her a juice box from the fridge. "Be careful not to spill," she cautioned. "Kaz…"

"Don't start," he told her as he dropped the grocery bags on the kitchen counter with a thud. "Where do these go?"

"I'll put them away, Kaz," Gran said. "Didn't you say you wanted to call your father?"

"Yeah," he said, cocking his head toward Millie, "but I was trying to help out before genius got on my case."

Millie narrowed her eyes at him and then immediately felt guilty, telling herself she shouldn't be so hard on her brother, even when his attitude got on her nerves. A normal summer for Kaz would have included swimming, Little League, and Indianapolis Indians baseball games with Dad, so in his mind, Millie reasoned, this extended Oklahoma visit must be more like exile. *I need to try to be a better sister*, she thought, so she impulsively reached out to give him a hug. "Do you like baseball camp?"

Kaz backed away from her and crossed his arms in front of his chest like a barrier. "It's okay. I just need to talk to Dad about some new equipment," he said as he eyed her warily, "and then I'm gonna go out and see if Zach wants to toss a ball around."

"What? Zach…what?" Millie stammered, but Kaz bounded up the stairs and was out of earshot. She took a deep, calming breath, and even though she was secretly glad to be rid of her pre-pubescent brother, the thought that Zach was nearby made her feel prickly all over. She stepped out the kitchen door and took a quick look around. Sure enough, there he was, moving the sprinkler from the front flower bed around to the side of the house. Millie had been so engrossed in her new research project she hadn't realized anyone else was around—let alone Zach—but Kaz must have seen him when Gran pulled in the driveway. Zach turned on the water spigot and looked up, saw her watching him, folded his arms and smirked.

ARGH! "I wish Zach didn't have to be here. He's so arrogant," Millie said, closing the door a little more forcefully than she intended.

"Not so arrogant that you failed to notice him," Gran replied.

"I didn't notice him, Kaz did," Millie retorted.

"It's only for the summer, dear, till Mac's back on his feet. And Zach will be graduating high school next spring, so you won't get too many more chances to see him."

"Good."

"Why, Mildred!" Gran exclaimed with a raised

eyebrow. She shook her head. "Zach's a fine boy, smart and a good athlete, too. Football quarterback. That is," Gran said, turning her back to empty the contents of a grocery bag, "if he can pass that history test."

Millie's radar went off. Brow furrowed, she got in front of Gran and looked her in the face. "What test?"

Gran reached around Millie and began methodically putting away groceries. "Some history course he needs to make up."

"History course," Millie repeated, suddenly understanding. "That's why you're so eager to get us together?"

"Well, dear, according to Mac, if Zach can't pass that test, no football, no athletic scholarship. I sort of promised Mac I'd mention it to you." Gran turned and winked at Millie.

"Why me? His dad's a college professor."

"Oh, pooh," Gran said, dismissing that idea with the wave of a hand. "You're always looking for ways to stick your nose in a book anyway. I was hoping to get you out of the house some this summer, that's all."

Millie groaned. Besides being peeved at her grandmother for blindsiding her, it had been her experience that kids her age only spent time with her if she could help with an important test or a school project. "Kids only want to be friends with me if they can make use of my intelligence, Gran."

"Nonsense."

Millie sighed and sank listlessly into the breakfast table chair next to her sister. "No, Gran, it's true. Except for Carlye and Michael, kids at school treated me like a walking search engine."

"Hey, you're crowding me!" Charlie said as she slurped the last of the juice from the bottom of the box.

"Sorry." Millie scooted her chair over and gave her sister some space.

"So can I tell Mac you'll help out his grandson while you're here?" Gran cajoled.

"I'll think about it."

Gran studied the downhearted look on Millie's face. "I didn't mean to impose, dear," she said gently. "I genuinely thought you'd enjoy spending time with someone your own age."

"He isn't my age. He's one year older and two academic grades behind me." She sighed and turned to her sister. "Hey, kiddo, guess what I found!"

Charlie shrugged. "I don't know."

"Lucinda!"

Charlie jumped up from the chair and began clapping her hands together. "Yippee! Where is she?"

Millie peered over Charlie's head, making eye contact with her grandmother. "I found her in the attic." Leaning down to Charlie's eye level she said, "I put her on your bed. She's a little dusty, so you may want to change her dress." Charlie darted out of the kitchen and up the stairs.

"So you spent your summer afternoon in a dusty old attic, did you?"

It almost sounded like an accusation instead of a question. "I promised Charlie," she said with a shrug. "Gran, did you know there's an old trunk up there? I found Lucinda inside it."

"When Essie's here, things do tend to end up in the attic," Gran admitted with a bob of her head.

"Never mind the doll. What about the quilts?"

Gran looked up in surprise. "Quilts? Oh, yes, quilts. Well, my friend, Abigail—you know, she owns that antique shop on Main Street—she got them at an estate sale down in Oklahoma City, along with that old trunk, and thought I'd like to have them for this summer's church bazaar."

"Do you know anything about that trunk? Its history?"

"Just that it's a cedar hope chest, something a bride would have taken to her new home, and Abigail said it probably dates mid-to-late nineteenth century."

"I know about brides' hope chests," Millie answered. She stood up and started pacing the floor. "Did Abigail tell you which estate sale—who owned the property?"

Gran tapped her chin with a forefinger and thought hard to remember. "Hmmm. Yeoman?" She shook her head. "No, that's not quite right. Oh, yes. Yeager! An elderly gentleman, a Mr. Yeager, now deceased, of course."

"Was he or his family from Missouri?"

"Oh, Lord, child," Gran said as she tossed up her hands, "I have no idea. What makes you ask that?"

"Because of what I found inside that old trunk!"

"Nothing alive I hope!" Gran scrunched up her nose before opening the refrigerator door, rummaging around and pulling out several large white deli containers. She began to set out plates and silverware for a cold supper.

Millie laughed. "No! It was a journal, or diary, or something. It belonged to a girl named Synthia Elizabeth Whitfield from Missouri. Synthia with an S."

Gran was puzzled. "Wonder who she is."

"Was," Millie corrected. "She was fifteen years old in 1865."

"1865? Are you sure about that, dear?"

Millie nodded. "I read the first entry. The journal's

been remarkably well-preserved, assuming it's real, so it seems to me we should return it to the lady's family. Whoever they are."

"Synthia Whitfield? Don't know any Whitfields around here."

"Of course I got right to my online research," Millie said with a head tilt toward her computer, "to see if I could track down her descendants. No luck so far, but I'll keep looking."

Gran sighed and shook her head. "Dear, you're talking about spending your vacation on a computer, researching some dead woman's journal. It's summertime and you should get out of the house, be with other young people."

"If you mean Zach, no thanks. I prefer the company of Google." Millie grabbed her laptop, took a quick peek out the bay window, caught Zach looking back in at her, blushed, and darted for the stairs.

Gran laughed out loud and called after her, "Isn't there some old saying about a girl protesting too much?"

"'Methinks the lady doth protest too much,'" Millie called back. "Hamlet, Act three Scene two. And it doesn't apply to me!"

"Hi, Dad." It was after eleven p.m. in Oklahoma but two hours earlier in California. Millie was sitting on her bed, trying to catch the breeze from the ceiling fan so it would blow on her face.

"And how's my favorite valedictorian?" Karl asked.

Millie rolled her eyes and quickly changed the subject. "How's the case going?"

"Looks like things are going in our favor so far,"

Karl replied, taking the bait. "The jury's pretty easy to read."

"That's good," Millie said as she lifted the hair off the back of her neck to allow the flowing air to circulate. "How's Mom?"

"Doing well. Very excited. Signed the contract her agent worked out and the TV movie will start filming in Toronto later this summer. She's working with the screenwriter now."

"Great," Millie said, trying to sound enthusiastic. She was happy that her mother's books were successful, but she didn't relish the thought of any notoriety that might come her way as the real-life prototype of Millicent the Magnificent. She'd already ducked a few reporters, both from the Indianapolis Star and The Kendrick Prep Herald, because she didn't want anyone thinking she was a science nerd like her mom's title character. "Tell her we miss her."

Karl shuffled some papers on his end and sounded distracted. "Are you enjoying your time with your grandmother? I've already talked to Kaz and he likes baseball camp. Says he needs a new bat. Charlie has a newfound love of horses. So what are you doing with your time?"

Millie sighed and kicked off her sandals. "I went poking around in Gran's attic," Millie said.

"Is that code for 'avoiding all human contact'?"

"Ha ha. No, but I wanted to tell you what I found." She reached into the nightstand drawer, gently pulled out Synthia's journal and carefully turned the pages. "Gran has an old trunk up there that she got from an antique shop. Inside it I found this really old diary that belonged to a girl named Synthia Elizabeth Whitfield."

"Interesting." Karl paused and Millie could hear him tap-tapping a pencil as he usually did while he was thinking. "You've Googled her, of course?"

"Tried. Can't find anything. The first entry is dated May 18, 1865, her fifteenth birthday. Between smudges and torn pages, the next one I can read is June 5, 1865."

Karl whistled softly. "1865? That old?" He was silent a moment. "Say, my old friend Alex is still over at the history department at OLAC. I'm sure he could help you figure this out."

Millie pondered that idea. Even though she liked her dad's oldest friend, Mac's son, she was pretty sure she wanted to avoid any entanglement with Alex's son Zach. "I'll think about it. But listen to this." She started reading aloud to her father.

"June 5, 1865. The summer is already hot, and so begins the sickly season. Cases of cholera are increasing in town and many of our rural neighbors are sick as well. Mama and Papa must go in to town for supplies and they insist Mary Ann, TJ and I stay home to avoid infection. I assured them I could look after my brother and sister while they are away, but I worry for their health with the sickness so rampant."

Millie paused. "Hey, Dad, Synthia and I have something in common—younger sibs." Millie put the phone on speaker and tossed it on her bed so she could roll over onto her back and hold the journal over her head. "Anyway, then she writes…

"Now that the Great War is over, Papa says food and farming supplies are sure to become more readily available.

"Dad? Are you still there? What do you think?"

"Well, Millie, I don't know what to make of it, but it sounds like you've got quite a mystery on your hands," Karl said. "Go over to the college and speak to Alex." She heard him cover the phone and say something to someone. "Room service is here, hon. Gotta go."

"Goodnight, Dad," Millie said, disconnecting the line. She had to admit her dad was right that she needed help with this journal, but all these suggestions about going over to OLAC from both her grandmother and her dad were starting to feel like a conspiracy. But it couldn't be, right? Neither of them knew anything about that diary stashed in the attic. Her palms got sweaty and she felt her pulse race just thinking about walking around a college campus, even a small one. And would a visit to Zach's dad at OLAC include dealing with Zach? She shook off that thought and rolled over onto her stomach to continue reading.

June 10, 1865. Mama and Papa returned from Sedalia with a month's worth of supplies, exclaiming it was a miracle such an abundance of items were on hand. Mama was happy to find several bolts of material for new clothing, since my brother and sister are quickly outgrowing their clothes. My gingham dress is quite worn and faded, too, and Papa needs new breeches. She also bought yarn for knitting winter caps, mittens and scarves for all of us, and intends to begin work right away in order to have them ready by fall when the weather turns cold.

Papa reports that he too was able to purchase much-needed items. He bought a new hammer and nails, bags of cornmeal and flour, some new rope, and then went to visit Mr. Anson, the blacksmith, to discuss repairs to the wagon and plow. Papa says that after spending $120 last year to purchase a new wagon, it is imperative that it be properly maintained. He pointed out to Mr. Anson where the iron strengthening the axles and wheels is already showing wear, and some of the iron bolts and pins need to be replaced, as well. It is a wonder how much use it has seen in so short a time!

My brother TJ asked Papa when he could learn to drive the wagon, but Papa says TJ is too young and (if you will believe it) my father has been secretly teaching me to drive! I am not to breathe a word of this to Mama until I am a proficient driver. So far Papa says I have been a good pupil.

Upon their return from town, I pressed Mama for details. "Town was crowded with folks all clamoring for newly-available goods," she told me. "We ate our noon meal at the café, and I must say the coffee tasted a bit off. Papa agreed, but downed his anyway. Despite my efforts to avoid the filth all about us, as we left the cafe the hem of my skirt became soiled when refuse was thrown into the street from the inn. Then I stepped in horse dung, which very nearly ruined my leather shoes! I was so embarrassed! Papa just waded through the filth, claiming his boots would protect him."

June 15, 1865. Mama has been feeling poorly now for several days since their return from town and I am worried. "What has caused you to become sick?" I asked her.

"Oh, I suppose it is nothing of consequence," she reassured me. "The food at the café was poorly prepared. And the coffee tasted bad. Perhaps the water was tainted." She patted my cheek and added with a smile, "I shall rest for a day or two and feel right as rain in no time."

June 18, 1865. Mama is no better, and in fact somewhat worse. I have been seeing to the children and the house, as well as cooking her favorite foods to try to tempt her, in hopes that she will recover her appetite. But instead, she suffers with the headache, is consumed with a terrible pain in her belly, excessive thirst, and is greatly afflicted with loose bowels. I've pleaded with Papa to send for the doctor, but Papa insists Mama will recover soon enough, and anyway the doctor is too busy with his cholera patients.

"Cholera!" Millie exclaimed out loud. She reached for her laptop and pulled up a search engine. C-H-O-L-E-R-A she typed in. Skimming down to the symptoms, she read with dismay. 'Patient is infected by drinking unsanitary water or by poor hygienic habits. Fever, chronic diarrhea causing dehydration, often leading to death.'

Millie's hand flew to her mouth as she clamped the lid closed on her computer. Did Synthia's mother die? Millie shook her head and tossed the journal aside, almost as if it had become too hot to handle. She put her laptop on the floor, turned off the bedside light, and fell asleep on top of the covers.

Chapter Six
Distractions

BBBRRRRAAAACCCCKKKK!

Millie covered her ears with the pillow and rolled over in bed, trying to block out the hideous noise from just outside her bedroom window.

BBBRRRRAAAACCCCKKKK!

She curled up on her side, buried her head under the blanket to avoid both the noise and the sunlight, and closed her eyes in an attempt to fall back asleep. Still no luck drowning out the grating sound. She opened one eye and squinted at the bedside clock. 9:15 a.m.

With a groan, Millie sat up and realized that after reading Synthia's diary and doing research into the wee morning hours, she'd fallen asleep in her clothes. It just so happened that it was one of her favorite lounging outfits—her pink athletic shorts and match-ing t-shirt with the Indianapolis Colts horseshoe on the front—and now they were all wrinkled. Grumbling to herself, she stepped into her flip-flops and tried to peer through the white lace bedroom curtains to see what was going on outside, but from her vantage point she couldn't see a thing.

BBBRRRRAAAACCCCKKKK!

"What is that?" she cried.

And then the noise stopped. Millie sighed. "Short night," she said to herself as she yawned and headed downstairs.

On the kitchen table was a note from Gran, propped up next to a plate piled high with freshly-baked blueberry muffins, and covered with a red and white checkered linen napkin. She smiled as she reached for a muffin and read the note.

Millie: Fresh fruit in bowl in the fridge — also orange juice, milk or coffee. Kaz and Charlie are at day camp. Off to a church committee meeting, then to our monthly luncheon, and on to errands. Call or text if you need me!

Millie set the note back on the kitchen table and pulled open the refrigerator door, decided on the juice instead of fruit, and retrieved the carton.

BBBRRRRAAAACCCCKKKK!

Startled, she juggled, and nearly dropped, the carton of orange juice before finally getting control of it and setting it down safely on the counter. "Enough already!" She stormed out the back door.

Once outside, though, she sucked in her breath as she was hit with a blast of mid-morning heat. She fanned herself with the palm of her hand, which did no good at all, and was about to go right back in the house when she spotted Zach next to the garage, scrunched down on one knee, a power drill on the ground next to him. She watched as he tested the side door by repeatedly pulling it open and closed, making sure it fastened properly each time.

Millie had to admit that he looked better today than he had a few days ago. He was wearing jeans again, but this time they were clean and paired with a navy t-shirt which was neatly tucked into his pants. He wasn't wearing a hat, which Millie thought was fool-hardy in this heat, but his light brown hair was freshly washed, combed, and parted on the side, making him look quite handsome.

She walked up behind him, crossed her arms and patted her foot. "What are you doing?"

"Fixed it!" he said with a wide grin, pointing to the side entry door.

"At this hour?"

Zach stood up straight and rolled his eyes. "You're welcome."

Millie shaded her eyes as she glared up at him, re-alizing yet again that Zach was no longer that short, skinny kid who'd constantly annoyed her two years ago. "Well, it's just that…" She crossed her arms when the words wouldn't come out, took a deep breath and tried again. "So did you have to make all that noise this early in the morning?"

Zach threw his head back and laughed. "Early? It's mid-morning and if I put it off, it'd be too hot by noon." He then deliberately folded his arms in front of his chest and mirrored her stance.

Millie wanted to slap the smirk off his face, but suddenly she remembered her just-out-of-bed appear-ance. Besides her slept-in clothes, her hair hadn't been combed, and since she'd never bothered to wash yes-terday's makeup off, there were probably black circles under her eyes. She swiped at her hair self-consciously and tried smoothing her shorts and shirt. "So what ex-actly did you do?"

Zach turned to the door and pointed out his repairs. "You said the door wouldn't lock, so I used the
electric sander on the rotted wood and then the drill to
install a new deadbolt." He reached into his front jeans
pocket, fished out two keys on a flimsy metal ring
fresh from the hardware store and placed them in her
hand. "Your grandma can lock up now."

Millie watched Zach gather his equipment and
turn to walk to his truck. She felt a pang of guilt because she was the one who asked him to fix the door,
and his repair job had made Gran's garage safer, and
because she knew her petulance was immature. "Zach,
wait!" she called.

He stopped and turned around, a scowl on his
face. "Your grandma need something else done?"

"Um, well, I…" Again Millie couldn't form a coherent sentence and didn't know why. Zach was just a
friend of the family helping Gran for the summer,
nothing more. "Well, thanks," was all she could manage. "Are you leaving now?"

"I borrowed my granddad's tools to fix the deadbolt and I gotta take 'em back. Why?"

Millie craned her neck to see what sort of trans-
portation Zach had. She spotted a large, late-model
Ford F-150 parked in the driveway, sparkling in the
sunlight, its polished black exterior and chrome attach-
ments showing obvious care. "Oh, never mind."

Zach shrugged. "Whatever," and he turned to
walk away.

"Wait!" she called again, waving her hand over
her head.

Zach turned back around with a puzzled look on
his face. "Now what?"

"Well, I was wondering…" She cleared her throat

in an uncomfortable silence while Zach stood impatiently, shifting his weight from one foot to the other. "I, uh…I talked to my dad last night."

"Okaaayyy…" Zach said. "He want something done?"

"He told me…" She stopped, embarrassed at her inexplicable lack of vocabulary.

Zach put the equipment down on the ground and walked closer and stopped right in front of her. "For a girl as smart as you are, you sure have trouble speaking your mind."

Millie looked down at the ground and kicked at an ant pile on the sidewalk, jumping back in time to avoid them crawling on her bare toes. "How's Mac?" was all she could come up with.

Zach looked confused. "Mac? Better, I guess."

Millie felt flustered and decided it must be dehydration or even impending heat stroke causing her brain to go fuzzy, because it certainly couldn't be Zach staring at her like that. "Good," she said.

"What's my grandpa's health got to do with what your dad wants done on his mom's property?"

"Oh, well, uh, Dad said I should ask him, ask you, I mean ask your dad…."

Zach shook his head in exasperation. "Look, if you wanna ask my dad something, he'll probably be at Mac's this afternoon. One of us is always there, in case he needs something."

Millie couldn't concentrate with Zach glaring at her like that, so she simply said, "Okay, tell Alex I'll stop by today." With that she turned and all but ran back into the kitchen. She shut the door behind her, took a few deep breaths as she leaned against it, and then discreetly parted the curtains to peek out. Zach was still standing where she'd left him, a quizzical expression on his face. Finally he shrugged, picked up the power tools, got into his truck, and roared off down the driveway.

Millie showered and washed the day-old cosmetics off her face, berating herself the whole time for letting Zach see her like that. She applied fresh makeup, combed her hair out straight to dry around her shoulders, and put on a flowered sundress with spaghetti straps. Barefoot, she went to the bedroom closet and rummaged around among the array of footwear on the floor, searching for just the right pair of sandals to complement the dress. Nothing suited her and she wished she had new shoes. She sighed, settled for an old pair of slip-ons, and then surveyed her appearance in the mirror.

She shook her head and kicked the shoes off again. "I definitely have to go shopping," she muttered.

"What did you say, dear?"

Millie spun around in surprise. "Gran, what are you doing home? Don't you have a luncheon or committee meeting or something?"

"Yes, I'm on my way, but I stopped by home to print out the minutes from last month's meeting, only to find my granddaughter in the throes of a wardrobe crisis." Gran surveyed Millie's attractive attire with a nod of approval. "Where are you off to?"

Millie's hands flew to her reddening cheeks and butterflies kicked up in her stomach. "Well, this morning I saw Zach…"

"Oh!" Gran said with a knowing smile. "You're all dressed up for Zach MacMillan."

"No!" Millie replied. "I…well, that is I asked

him…" She stopped, flustered, and stepped back into the shoes she'd just kicked off, stalling for time. "What's on today's committee agenda?"

"Actually, it has to do with the bazaar and the money the church needs to earn from it to break even this year." Gran narrowed her eyes at Millie. "And changing the subject won't distract me, dear. You mentioned speaking to Zach?"

"He fixed your broken garage door lock."

"That's nice." Gran put her hands on her hips and waited for Millie to finish.

Millie frowned and sat down on the edge of her bed. "I talked to Dad last night. He says his old friend Alex who's a professor at OLAC—you know, Zach's father…"

"Yes, dear, I know who Alex is."

"…that Alex might help me authenticate that girl's journal I found, but it's summer so I don't know if he's even at the school right now, but Zach says Alex spends time with Mac, who's home recuperating, so I thought if I went to visit Mac and talked to Alex…." Millie stopped to catch her breath and shook her head in dismay at her inability to form a coherent sentence.

Gran cocked an eyebrow. "And naturally you put on a pretty dress to go see a sick old man and a middle-aged father."

"No, of course not, but…" Millie stopped, flustered. "Is it hot in here, Gran?" She stood up and started for the hallway. "Maybe I need to check the AC."

Gran put out a hand to stop Millie and gave her a look. "The temperature's fine, dear, but I'd say you've got more on your mind today than an old diary." She checked her watch. "I'd love to stay and chat, but I'm running awfully late now. Do you remember how to get to the MacMillan house?"

Millie rolled her eyes. "I've been there a million times, Gran."

Gran winked at her before leaving. "Give my regards to Mac and Alex. And Zach, too, of course."

"Graaaannn!" But she was gone. Millie stood up and looked in the mirror once more. Nope, the shoes were all wrong and a trip to the mall was definitely in order, today if possible. She closed the closet door, gathered her bag with Synthia's journal carefully tucked inside, and had just pulled out her car keys when her cell phone rang.

"Hey, Millie!"

"Michael?"

"Yup. We're all at Carlye's and got to talking about you…."

As his voice drifted, Millie could hear water splashing in the background. "Michael? Are you there?"

"Yeah, just got splashed and was trying to keep the phone from getting wet. HHHEEYYYY!" Michael yelled at someone.

Millie didn't have time to waste listening to her friends play Marco Polo in the Hendersons' pool. She was on an important mission. "What's up?" she asked. Silence from the other end. "Helloooo…?" Still no answer. "Michael…?"

"Oh, sorry. Carlye wants to talk to you." She could hear Michael calling across the pool to Carlye, who finally got on the line.

"How's the desert?"

Millie scrunched up her face, glad Carlye couldn't see her. "Oklahoma's not a desert." More silence and water play. "Carlye, are you there? You called me, I'm on my way out, so…?"

"Did you mail in the forms to IU yet? Clock's ticking!"

Millie winced. Not this again. "Well, soon, I promise, but…" She gently patted her bag where Synthia's journal was safely stored, giddy with excitement and eager to solve the mystery of its origin. "Carlye, you won't believe what I found in Gran's attic. It's this really old journal, and Dad suggested I ask his friend Alex who teaches at OLAC…"

"OLA…what?" Carlye asked.

"Oklahoma Liberal Arts College," Millie explained. "You know, Dad's alma mater? Anyway, Dad's old friend Alex is a history professor there…."

Carlye gasped. "So you're going to school in Oklahoma instead of IU?"

"Focus, Carlye. It's only about this old diary I found…"

Carlye groaned. "Millie…."

Millie ignored her friend's tone, "…and I'm on my way now to ask Alex for his help verifying its authenticity."

There was a lot more laughter and yelling from a distance, and what sounded like the grandfather of all cannon-ball jumps from the diving board, followed by a huge splash in the pool. "I gotta go, Millie," Carlye said. "Ireland just wiped out. Mail those forms pronto!"

Millie disconnected the phone, tossed it back in her bag and sat immobile on the edge of her bed. Even though her friends in Indianapolis were enjoying their summer, the part of her that wasn't envious was glad she was hundreds of miles away from Carlye's pressure tactics. She carefully opened Synthia's journal. Her new project was just too exciting and she didn't want to think about anything else right now.

June 19, 1865. Papa has taken sick. I have been tending to both parents as best I can, but it has become urgent that I send for the doctor. Money is scarce, but I shall offer to do sewing or other domestic chores for him in trade for his services, whatever is necessary to get him here.

"TJ," I said to my brother, "there is no choice but that you must go as quickly as possible to the Cleary farm. Tell them Mama and Papa are both sick, but that I hesitate to send a ten-year-old boy five miles by horseback to fetch a doctor in town. Mr. Cleary must go instead."

"I can drive the wagon!" TJ exclaimed.

"No indeed you cannot!" I told him. "You do not know how! Papa has only just begun to teach me."

"Then you go to town," he said with a pout.

I stood firm with my recalcitrant brother. "You could cover the two miles to the Cleary homestead on foot before I could even have the wagon hitched up. Mama and Papa are too sick to be left alone, and then there's Mary Ann."

Millie looked up from her reading. *I guess whiny little brothers are universal*, she thought with some amusement, except Synthia's situation was worse than anything she'd ever dealt with from Kaz.

"But, Synthia," my brother complained, "can I not at least take one of the horses?"

I considered a moment. "Yes, I suppose that would be best. But then you must also take Mary Ann with you, and the two of you must stay with the Cleary family until the doctor has been here and I send word that Mama and Papa are recovered. Is that understood?"

TJ nodded despite his reluctance to obey. Still, there is no other solution.

"Ugh!" Millie said out loud. She felt bad for Synthia, even from this distance in time, and definitely wanted to talk to Alex about this journal, to ask for his opinion and possibly his help. She carefully placed the diary back in her handbag, grabbed the keys to the rental car and left the house.

Mac lived right in the heart of downtown Rolling Plains. Since it was the middle of a weekday, Millie had to circle the block several times looking for a parking space near his house. She finally located one but cringed when she realized she'd have to parallel park the rental Toyota, something she'd barely mastered in order to pass her driving test last winter, and that was in a car she was more familiar with.

"Stupid truck hogging the spot," she mumbled, as she inched in and out of the space behind the black pickup and in front of a silver Chevy SUV, trying a second and a third time before she was finally able to maneuver the car in and put it in park. She cracked all four windows and stepped out of the car into the mid-day heat.

She hadn't been here for a couple of years, but the MacMillan house across the street looked attractive. It had a fresh coat of black paint on the trim and shutters, the red brick appeared newly power-washed, and the climbing vines had been cut down to eye level. This neighborhood had been built in the late 1950s for young families seeking affordable housing.

What had once been a quiet suburb was now sur-rounded by a bustling and refurbished downtown area, complete with office buildings, quaint shops, a modern big box discount store, restaurants and coffee shops. The whole trendy area was within walking dis-tance of Oklahoma Liberal Arts College, which pro-vided not only consumers but a part time work force as well.

Mac still lived in the same house he'd bought all those years ago when he got out of the army. Gran told Millie that the house had originally contained less than one thousand square feet, but Mac soon became a suc-cessful landscape architect and was able to hire con-tractors to add on to his home. Now it was nearly twice its original size and in Millie's opinion, completely overbuilt for the neighborhood.

"Mac will never get his money out of that house now," she once told her grandmother.

Gran had clucked her tongue. "He doesn't need to, dear. It's paid for and holds memories of his life there with Dorothy, may she rest in peace."

Millie rang the doorbell and fidgeted as she stood on the front porch. She smoothed out her skirt and put on some fresh lip gloss while she waited for an answer. Finally a figure appeared behind the beveled glass door.

"Uh, hi," Zach said as he opened the door.

Millie's eyes widened in surprise and she fought back the urge to make her excuses and run. Swallowing hard she said, "I didn't know you were here. I didn't see your truck."

"You didn't look very close, then," Zach said, pointing behind her.

Millie turned around and sure enough, the truck she'd almost nicked while parallel parking was Zach's F-150. She felt her face flush. "Oh. Well, I wanted to say hi to Mac, and ask your dad...."

Zach shrugged and held the door open. "Come on in."

Millie followed him into the house, a house she'd visited many times with her grandmother, and let Zach lead her through the entry hall and into the cozy family room. She looked at the familiar surroundings and smiled to herself, realizing nothing had changed except for the addition of a flat screen TV over the fireplace. It was now the focal point of the room, across from the white sofa with a crocheted afghan tossed across the back, a 1960s-era upholstered rocker in the corner, and a brown leather recliner.

The fireplace was an actual wood-burning, not the now-popular gas kind, and there was a pile of wood left over from winter still sitting in the rick on the edge of the brick skirt. On the coffee table in front of the sofa was a half-drunk cup of coffee, a newspaper turned to the sports page, and the remnants of a sandwich on a plate.

"Hey, Mac, we got company," Zach said.

Mac was reclining comfortably in his leather chair, his feet propped up and the remote control in his hand. He glanced up from the baseball game and muted the sound on the television. "Millie!" he beamed. "What a pleasant surprise. And pretty as ever, just like your grandma." She leaned down to kiss him on the forehead as she clasped his hand.

"I don't suppose I'm dressed for company, though," Mac said with a chuckle. He tugged at his bathrobe and pulled it tight around his pajamas and, lowering the recliner's foot rest to the floor, slid into his house slippers. "So what brings you here?" Mac motioned for Millie to have a seat on the sofa. Zach sat down on the fireplace skirt, all the way across the room from where Millie seated herself in the middle of the couch.

"Well, first of all I wanted to check on you, reassure Gran that you're on the mend."

Mac's eyes twinkled. "That's mighty kind of you, but your grandmother knows I'm doing fine because she was just here this morning," he said.

What? Why hadn't Gran mentioned earlier that she'd already seen Mac today? Millie promised herself to pursue that later. "I also wanted to talk to Alex. Is he here?" she asked, scouting out the rooms she could see from her vantage point, hoping to locate him.

"Nope, stuck on campus," Zach told her.

At that, Millie decided to make a hasty retreat and stood up. "Well, since Gran's already been by and Alex isn't here...."

"Don't rush off," Mac insisted. "Why Mildred and I were just talking about you when she was here earlier." Mac relaxed back into his recliner. "She's awfully proud of her young valedictorian."

"Really?" Zach asked, turning to Millie with surprise.

"Yes," Millie replied, nervously eyeing the exit. She hesitated and finally sat back down on the sofa. "I just wanted to ask Alex's opinion about something." She pulled the diary out of her bag, "I found this in Gran's attic a few days ago, and it belonged to a girl named Synthia Whitfield, dated 1865. So my dad said maybe Alex…."

"Zach, boy we're forgetting our manners. Run to the kitchen and get a soda for our guest. And I'll take some of that bottled water."

Millie was a little disconcerted by Mac's sudden change of subject. "No, really, I'm fine," she said. But it was too late because Zach was already up and in the kitchen. She could hear the refrigerator door opening, bottles jangling, and then he reappeared with two cans of soda and the bottled water his grandfather re-quested. Zach sat down again on the edge of the fire-place, pulled the tab on his can which made a loud swoosh, and took a long swallow of his cola. "So what is it you wanna talk to Dad about?"

Millie politely took a sip from the soda can and set it on the coffee table. "Well, because he's a history pro-fessor, I hoped…well, Dad thought, well I…" Millie stammered and then wanted to kick herself for stutter-ing. She took another swallow of soda and started over. "I want to get his opinion on the actual age of this journal." Ignoring Zach as he stared a hole through her, she opened the page to where she'd left off earlier. "Here, listen to this.

"June 20, 1865. Mr. Cleary arrived with the doctor two days ago, but it was too late. Papa was beyond medicinal help and soon passed away, and Mama followed him to

Heaven the next day."

Millie gasped. "What?" She looked back at the writing, convinced she'd misread it.

Zach, with little interest asked, "Who died?"

Millie sighed. "This teenage girl's parents in Missouri. That's so sad!

> "Mr. Cleary insists my brother, sister, and I stay with his wife at their farm while he and the doctor make arrangements to bury Mama and Papa on the hill above our farm. I am too distraught to do otherwise, but alas, I must remain strong in order to comfort my brother and sister.
>
> "Oh, why did this have to happen? Life was good, we were a happy family, and now TJ, Mary Ann, and I are orphans. What will become of us?"

"That kinda sucks," Zach said with a shrug, "but it was a long time ago."

Millie agreed, but because of her immersion in nineteenth century history, she understood the predicament Synthia must have been in. Millie counted herself lucky that her parents weren't dead, just busy with their careers. She and Kaz and Charlie missed them, but at least they'd eventually be home. Synthia hadn't been so lucky.

Mac scratched his head. "I never heard of any Whitfield family around these parts."

"Gran didn't know of them either. My dad said Alex is the perfect person to ask for help," Millie said as she stood up to leave. "I should have called first," she said, "but this morning Zach told me his dad would be here."

"Sorry," Zach said with a shrug of his shoulders.

Mac stretched his arms, turned off the TV with the remote and got up from his recliner. "I'm ready for my nap, Zach. Walk the young lady to her car."

"Yes, sir." Zach held the front door open to let Millie out ahead of him, and then dutifully walked alongside her to her car.

"Thanks," Millie said, expecting Zach to turn and head back to the house.

He didn't. "Seems like you're really into that old diary."

"I'd like to know its origin, who the girl was."

"History's not my thing," Zach said with a grin.

Millie dug into her bag for the car keys. "So I hear. Gran said something about a history test you need to make up."

"Yeah, I gotta make up my U.S. History final exam. Coach worked out a deal with my teacher since I missed the test in May when Mac had his heart attack, but if I don't pass it I don't play football." Zach winked at her. "Any chance a history buff like you could give me some pointers?"

Millie was almost taken in by his smile, but caught herself and eyed him suspiciously. She could almost predict what would happen if she helped him, the same thing that always happened with her peers: he'd pick her brain and then afterwards go back to ignoring her. "Why don't you just ask Alex?"

"Yeah, right," Zach said.

Millie looked down at her all-wrong sandals as she fumbled with the keys in her hand. "You know, it's the height of irony that your dad's a history professor and you hate history."

"Yeah, 'height of irony.'" Zach shook his head. "I like math a lot better."

Millie lifted an eyebrow. "Seriously?"

"Yes, seriously. How d'ya think football plays are laid out? It's all math coordinates and statistics."

"Oh," she said, "I guess it is."

"Say, I'll make you a deal. I can take you over to OLAC to talk to my dad about that old diary if you'll help me study."

Millie blushed at the idea of Zach showing her around a college campus. Still, she definitely needed professional help figuring out this journal. She was unfamiliar with the campus layout and got qualms just thinking about being on a college campus anyway, so how bad could it be just to let an old family friend direct her to Alexander MacMillan's office? "Would tomorrow be convenient?"

"Dad's teaching a summer school class. But I'll ask him, since it's almost the holiday and he won't be in his office again for about a week."

"Holiday?"

"Fourth of July. Independence Day. Fireworks, picnics, outdoor concerts. Don't folks in Indiana celebrate July 4th?"

Millie narrowed her eyes. "What time tomorrow?"

"Noon. Meet me on the Quad, in the middle of campus."

"It's a date," Millie said.

It's a date? Embarrassed at her unfortunate choice of words, she quickly got into her car without making eye contact with Zach, turned over the engine and cranked the air conditioning blower up to max. She carefully readjusted her rearview mirror and after a few back and forth tries, eased the Toyota out of the tight parking space.

Some retail therapy was now imperative and those new shoes were a must. She just had to look — what? Attractive for Zach? No, she had to look like she belonged on a college campus. Right?

Chapter Seven
Date with Destiny

As if Millie wasn't having enough trouble juggling all the shopping bags, Charlie chose that moment to bound into the kitchen from the living room and tackle her. Kaz was at the kitchen table playing a hand-held video game and Millie shot him a please help me with these bags look, but he ignored her.

"Millie! What did you buy?" Charlie asked, jumping up and down and trying to peek into the bags. In her excitement she pulled too hard on one of them and the handle broke, spilling its contents on the floor.

Millie sighed and began picking up skirts, dresses and shoe boxes, and stuffing them back into the bag. She set all the bags in the nearest kitchen chair, with the exception of a large sack, which she handed to her sister. "Here, this one's for you."

Charlie snatched the bag, peered inside, and was poised to empty it onto the kitchen table right next to a plate of freshly baked, gooey chocolate chip cookies. Millie adroitly grabbed the plate and set it on the back of the stove, out of harm's way.

Charlie ooohhed and aaahhhed, admiring all her new outfits: a sundress, white sandals, two pair of shorts with matching tops, a new bathing suit, and then gave a whoop as she pulled out a plush teddy bear that Millie had tossed in at the last minute. "He can sit on my bed next to Lucinda!" Charlie exclaimed, and hugged Millie around the waist again. "Thank you, thank you!"

Millie patted the top of her little sister's head. "I could tell your swimsuit was a little faded and you seemed to be growing out of your other clothes. I'm glad you like them."

"I'm gonna go try them on!" Charlie stuffed the clothes and shoes back into the bag, tucked the bear under her arm, and dashed out of the kitchen with her treasures.

Kaz snorted and folded his arms in front of his chest. "I don't need any clothes, so I hope you got me something useful."

Millie pulled a face and bit back the impulse to tell her brother she didn't have to buy him anything at all. "Yes, Kaz, I got you that video game you've been wanting." She sorted through the bags until she found what she was looking for. "Oh, and this came from the sporting goods store," she said, offering him a second plastic sack.

Kaz opened it, pulled out a new metal bat, and carefully looked it over.

"It's just like the one you have, but Dad said you needed a new one, so…"

Kaz shrugged. "Yeah, thanks." He reached down to the bottom of the bag and pulled out an Oklahoma City RedHawks t-shirt and baseball cap. He put the cap on and adjusted it so that it fit snugly on his head. He almost seemed pleased, but all he said was, "Cool." He held the shirt up for a closer look. "Coach is taking all of us in baseball camp to the RedHawks game on July Fourth. And I didn't have a thing to wear," he added in a mocking voice.

Millie ignored her brother's sarcasm. "So now you do."

"You two quit sniping at each other." Gran stood in the kitchen doorway, her hands on her hips as she surveyed the numerous packages covering the floor, chair and table. "I thought you were going to visit Mac, Millie. You went shopping instead?" Gran lifted up the bags and looked at the store logos. "Dinehart & Co.? Taggart's Sporting Goods? You've been busy down there in Oklahoma City."

Millie averted her eyes. "Dad gave me a credit card and Charlie was outgrowing her clothes and I haven't bought anything since I've been here, so I splurged. They were having an end-of-summer sale," she added, hoping to convince Gran as well as assuage her own guilt over her vanity-driven shopping spree.

Gran poked through the skirts, dresses, and sandals as she checked the mark-down on the price tags. "And I suppose that bag I saw Charlie lugging up the stairs came from Dinehart's as well?"

"All stuff on sale, I promise. I bought you something, too," Millie teased. She pawed through the bags on the floor until she pulled out a large, round box. "Hope you like it."

"Carson's Millinery. Hmmm." Gran seemed pleased in spite of herself as she held the box away from her to have a good look at it. She carefully pried the box open and brushed aside the tissue paper.

"Why, Millie Olson! How did you know that's just the hat I've been admiring?"

"A little bird told me, as you like to say." Millie could see that Gran was waiting for a real answer. "Okay, you mentioned a hat you saw there and the saleslady remembered you."

"Well, thank you, dear, that was very thoughtful. But what happened to your visit to Mac?"

Millie reached over to the plate of cookies on the stove and slowly nibbled on one. "I did go to see Mac, Gran, don't worry. But then circumstances conspired to send me off for some serious shopping."

Kaz's head popped up from his video game. "Circumstances did what?"

"Never mind, Kaz," Millie said. "Why don't you go to the living room and boot up your game station, give that new Indy 500 Racing game a try."

Kaz rolled his eyes as he started for the living room. "I'm not stupid, Millie. I know when I'm being sent away for…" He paused as his hands formed air quotations, "…grownup talk." He turned to head into the living room.

Gran faced Millie in concern. "Did something happen at Mac's?"

"Excuuuuse me," Kaz interrupted, reaching between them for his t-shirt. "Forgot this."

"Go!" Millie snapped.

As soon as Kaz disappeared into the living room, Gran frowned at Millie. "It's not like you to be so short with your brother, dear. Is everything all right? And how's Mac?"

"You've asked me that a million times already, excuse the hyperbole. As you know, he's getting better, just tires easily."

"It's just that I hate thinking of him all alone," Gran hurried to explain.

"Oh, he wasn't alone."

Gran looked visibly relieved. "Good. Was Alex there? Or Jane? It's nice to have a nurse in the family who can check on him every day."

"I didn't see Alex or Jane today, Gran."

"Oh, so if neither Alex nor his wife were there, and assuming Zoe was off at some athletic something-or-other, it must have been Zach keeping company with his grandpa." Gran nodded and smiled till Millie wanted to scream. "Is that what prompted this shopping spree, dear?"

Millie really didn't want to admit it, but all her good sense had flown out the window right about the time Zach had offered to meet her on campus. "You heard me say I needed new shoes. Besides, I'm visiting Alex at OLAC tomorrow and I want to look nice." She turned her back and busied herself rummaging through several kitchen drawers until she found a pair of scissors and began methodically cutting off price tags.

"Uh, huh." Gran watched Millie make a big show of cutting off store tags. "Something doesn't add up here, young lady. You visit Mac, his handsome grandson's there, and suddenly there aren't enough nice clothes in your closet?" Gran lifted Millie's chin and looked her in the eye. "You aren't going to the campus alone, I take it?"

Millie blushed. "Well, Zach did offer to show me around and stuff."

"And stuff." Gran helped Millie scoop up and throw away all the tags, re-fold her new clothes and carefully place them back in their bags. "I'm sure Zach will find you quite fetching in whichever new dress you decide to wear."

Millie groaned, grabbed the bags and ran up the stairs to her bedroom.

Millie carefully sorted and put away her new purchases; dresses hung with the dresses; skirts with skirts interspersed with their matching blouses; shoes lined up side-by-side; and beauty products neatly arranged on the bathroom counter. She was actually allowing herself to be proud of her new inventory of summer clothing despite the expense, when she realized she'd carelessly tossed her handbag on the bed. "Synthia's journal!" she gasped aloud. Gingerly taking it out of her bag and turning it over in her hands to ensure its safety, Millie started to set it on her nightstand, but then couldn't resist opening it.

July 4th, 1865. I refuse to let grief overtake me. As our newly reunited country celebrates its birthday, I must look for a different kind of independence for myself and my brother and sister. Of course I am sad, but there is nothing to be done except stand tall and accept the responsibility that has been thrust upon me.

Mr. Cleary asked me about other family who could take us in, but TJ, Mary Ann and I have no relations in Missouri. Our nearest relatives live in northern Texas, near a town called Nevada, which my mother told me is pronounced NevAda.

"You must write to your mother's brother," Mr. Cleary advised me. "Inform him of the tragedy and appeal to him for guidance as to your future."

Mrs. Cleary offered to pen the letter for me, but I refused her help as I knew this sad news must come from me. Subsequently I sat down and wrote the following to my Uncle Miles Graves, Mama's brother:

Dear Uncle,

It is with a heavy heart that I write these lines. Mama and Papa passed away within days of one another, stricken by the cholera. TJ, Mary Ann and I are staying with neighbors, Mr. and Mrs. Martin Cleary, but we cannot stay with them for long as they have their own family to look after.

As to your most natural question, I thought to inquire of Mr. Cleary, "What is to be done about Papa's farm? His animals, our possessions?"

"I will act as proxy for Mr. Whitfield's property," Mr. Cleary promised, "but folks are not eager to part with their money just now, the Great War so recently ended. I have no way of knowing when Mr. Whitfield's farm might sell, my dear. And of course, I must be paid a commission for the time I take away from my own farm."

Uncle Miles, I am only fifteen years old and have no experience with financial concerns. I am confused and frightened. I beg you to write to me immediately, sending instructions as to what we are to do next. I sincerely hope you will want my brother, sister, and myself to join you and Aunt Catherine in Texas, but I do not know how to accomplish that. Please, please, let me hear from you

within the week.
> Your loving niece,
> Synthia Elizabeth Whitfield

Millie set the journal on the bedside table. *That poor girl. I don't know what I'd do if anything happened to Mom and Dad. I'd be saddled with Kaz and Charlie, and if I'm too afraid to go away to college, how would I handle that?* Millie shook her head. At least she had Gran. Synthia didn't seem to have anybody.

Travel to Texas? From Missouri? How would that have even been possible for three kids? She searched her memory for her knowledge of post-Civil War travel. "Train or wagon train," she said as she booted up her computer. Millie sat up on the bed, her legs curled beneath her, and Googled "Wagon Trains 1865." Not much came up, except for The Chisholm Trail. Millie knew that couldn't be it, since it went from Abilene, Kansas, straight down to San Antonio. How would Synthia have gotten from Missouri to Kansas in the first place?

"Millie? Kaz? Charlie? Supper!" she heard her grandmother call.

The aroma from the kitchen suggested her grandmother's mouth-watering fried chicken was ready. She reluctantly closed the laptop. "I guess that's why I'm meeting Alex MacMillan tomorrow," she said to her mirror reflection, "to get his take on this." She gulped. "On a college campus. With Zach." Suddenly Millie didn't know if what she felt in her stomach was hunger pangs or butterflies.

Millie parked her car in the visitor's parking lot on the small campus, easily locating a space in the nearly empty lot. She slid out of the car and nervously smoothed her new skirt and layered t-shirts while she glanced into the car's side rearview mirror to make sure her makeup hadn't run in this unbearable heat. Her hair was pulled back into a sleek ponytail, partly for the look of sophistication she was hoping to achieve, but also to keep her hair from sticking to the back of her neck. She checked the time on her phone. Noon. Right on time. She made sure that the journal was tucked safely in her bag, took a deep breath, and followed the signs to the Quad where she was to meet Zach.

There was not a single cloud in the sky to block the glaring sun, so Millie reached into her bag and pulled out her sunglasses. She'd been here on this campus before, of course, with Dad, so she paused a moment to get her bearings. The century-old buildings were arranged around a grassy common area which in turn surrounded a small pond with a billowing fountain. Last summer she and Dad attended a performance of A Midsummer Night's Dream here, one of her favorite Shakespeare plays.

The temperature was broiling. Millie impatiently wiped the sweat off the back of her neck and began to scout out a shady place to sit and wait for Zach. Even the sidewalk was hot and Millie could feel the heat through her sandals, forcing her onto the cooler grass and under a shade tree. She hadn't really expected much midday activity on a college campus during summer session, but this campus seemed exceptionally deserted. She located a concrete bench near the pond and put her hand over it, but even that was too hot to sit on, so she set her satchel on it as she checked the time on her phone again. Ten after. Great. Maybe

Zach forgot, and here she was sweating through her new clothes and totally wasting her time. Just then a rare gentle breeze blew through her hair and she closed her eyes to savor it.

"Hi."

Millie's eyes popped open. "Hi," she replied as she looked up at Zach towering over her. "I didn't hear you walk up," she told him, shading her eyes, "which is surprising since there's not a soul around."

"Coming up on the holiday weekend, everybody's probably gone. You ready?"

"I'm beyond ready. It's sweltering out here." She silently chided herself for her tone of voice. Just because she was hot was no reason to get cranky and take it out on Zach, who was doing her a favor, even if he was almost fifteen minutes late.

"Dad's office is this way," he said, pointing to a building on the northeast side of campus.

At the classroom building's main entrance, Zach paused and held the glass door open, allowing Millie to go ahead of him. She breathed a sigh of relief once they were inside the air conditioning, and then looked around in confusion when she saw only classrooms on that floor. "Where's your dad's office?"

"Third floor, but there's no elevators so we'll have to take the stairs."

Millie sighed, thinking about how sweaty she could get climbing up three flights. Zach took the steps two at a time while Millie held the rail and took each flight slowly. By the time she caught up to him on the third floor landing, he was waiting with a sly grin on his face while she was forced to gasp for air. Okay, Millie had to admit that Zach was pretty athletic and that her high IQ hadn't helped her climb stairs at all. But he didn't have to look so smug!

They passed a cluster of offices with names on the doors—'Professor Theodore Southmore', 'Dr. Mary Alice Wheeler'—before arriving at the end of the hall at an open doorway marked 'Dr. Alexander MacMillan.' Zach tapped lightly and peered in. "Dad?"

Alex MacMillan was working at his computer with his back to the door, but he stood up and smiled as Zach and Millie walked in. Millie had never seen Alex anywhere but family gatherings, and for some reason she had the clichéd idea that all college professors wore tweed jackets with leather patches at the elbows. She quickly tossed out that stereotype when she saw Alex casually dressed in jeans and a green golf shirt with the OLAC logo embossed on the front.

Alex took off his reading glasses and tossed them next to his computer. "Hey, you two." He gave Zach's shoulders an affectionate squeeze and turned to Millie, looking her up and down. "My, how you've grown. The last time I saw you…."

"Daaadddd…." Zach moaned.

Alex craned his neck over Millie's head and winked at Zach. "Got it." To Millie he said, "Well, you look more like your grandmother every day."

Millie smiled. "So I've been told."

"But I also see a resemblance to your father. How is Karl, by the way? It seems like just yesterday we were playing on the football team, sharing a dorm room, eating late-night pizza. I imagine he's up to his eyeballs in legal briefs these days, while I'm up to my elbows in term papers."

"Dad's fine," she replied.

"And your mother?" Alex gazed out the window.

"She's quite the busy lady, I hear. Karl was pretty smitten with her from the start, as I recall. I didn't meet her until their wedding day actually, but I liked her immediately. Who knew she'd be a writer one day?"

"Well, she does have a degree in journalism," Millie said with growing impatience, wondering when the walk down memory lane would be over so she could get to the reason for her visit.

Alex took the hint. "So what's this Zach tells me about a journal you found?"

Finally! "I'm really hoping you can help me." Millie dug into her satchel and gently pulled out Synthia's diary. "It was buried in the bottom of a cedar chest in Gran's attic, and before that the cedar chest was in an estate sale in Oklahoma City. The date on the journal is 1865 and I'd like to find out if it's real or a reproduction."

Alex took the journal from her and gently turned it over in his hands, examining the leather binding. He opened the first page, but then had to reach over to the computer for his glasses to decipher the handwriting.

Millie literally held her breath. "So…what do you think? Is it real?"

Alex removed his glasses and rubbed his forehead. "Hard to tell. This sort of verification isn't really my area of expertise. Have you read any of this?"

Millie nodded. "Some of the pages are smudged, and sometimes her handwriting's hard to read, but Synthia lost her parents when she was fifteen and she and her sibs had no family up in Missouri where they lived."

"What happened to the parents?" Alex asked, perusing the page.

"Cholera. And now I'm completely hooked on her

story, probably because I can relate to Synthia, about siblings at least. Our lives do seem to have a certain synchronicity."

Zach coughed into his hand while simultaneously repeating, "Synchronicity!"

Millie sighed. "What I meant is that I also have a younger brother and sister like she did."

Zach shrugged and plopped down in a chair. A slow grin and what Millie hoped was a hint of admiration crept onto his face. "You sure get excited reading stories about dead people." Zach gave her an infectious smile.

Millie's knees went weak. In spite of herself, she smiled back at him. "I am excited." Turning to Alex she said, "She mentions writing to an uncle in Texas. Here, let me show you. I've marked the place with ribbon so I don't damage the paper." She took the journal from Alex and carefully opened the journal to where she'd left off the previous day. "Listen to this:

"July 12, 1865. At his wife's request, Mr. Cleary stopped by the post office on his trip to town and returned with a letter addressed to me, a reply from my Uncle Miles. It is so good to hear from family, even under these sad circumstances. Unfortunately I am quite disappointed at Uncle's response. I read his letter aloud to TJ, Mary Ann, and Mr. and Mrs. Cleary."

Millie laid the ribbon to mark her place and explained to Alex, "She wrote a letter to her uncle in Texas on July 4th. I guess getting an answer in eight days was pretty good back then."

"I would imagine so, considering the recent end to The Civil War and the damaged railroad lines," Alex said.

Millie was intrigued. "Civil War era isn't really my thing. I'm more into early nineteenth century."

"I still can't believe you actually like history," Zach said.

Alex frowned at him. "Don't disparage history lovers, son. That's how your old dad makes his living, you know. And," he added, "since you won't let me help you study for that exam, maybe you should take advantage of this bright young history enthusiast while she's here for the summer." Alex turned to Millie. "That's if you're willing, of course."

"Maybe," Millie hedged. "But I won't be here much longer."

"Off to college, I presume," Alex said with a nod. "I hear you were valedictorian. Karl's quite proud of you, telling me all about the offers you've had. Which school have you chosen, Millie?"

Millie ignored his question, which didn't have an answer anyway, and redirected Alex's attention. "So do you think it's possible all this really happened? The diary, I mean."

Alex took the journal from her, put his glasses back on, and began reading aloud.

> "Written this day July 8, 1865, from our farm in Nevada, Texas.
> 'My dear niece Synthia,
> Tears flooded my eyes as I read your letter. I am broken-hearted to hear of the loss of my sister Mary Elizabeth and—"

"Mary Elizabeth?" Millie interrupted in surprise. "There's another coincidence! My mom is Elizabeth Marie." She looked over and saw Alex waiting patiently. "Oh, sorry."

Alex adjusted his glasses and continued reading.

"...I am broken-hearted to hear of the loss of my sister Mary Elizabeth and brother-in-law John, but my heart most certainly reaches out to you, their children, during this time of grief. Be assured that our prayers are with all of you.

I have given a great deal of thought to your request to join us here in Texas, and of course that is the only solution. Unfortunately, it is impossible for me to come to Missouri to fetch the three of you until spring, and there will be no discussion of a girl your age attempting such a journey alone with two children. There are no North-South railroad lines at this time, the tracks having been nearly destroyed during our recent Civil War. Assuming the expense could be accounted for, the only solution would be to join a wagon train and that, too, is out of the question without an adult male escort.

We are newly-settled here in this part of Texas and are eager for our crops to take hold. The planting is long done, but northern Texas enjoys little rain this time of year, so it is necessary to be vigilant about irrigation until the fall harvest. I have the help of my sons—your young cousins William and Bartholomew—but I cannot leave the farm alone with them and their mother, nor can I afford to spend the money on travel just now, and of course it would be foolish to even think of undertaking such a journey in winter. You made mention of your parents' particular friends, Mr. and Mrs. Martin Cleary, and how kind they have been to you. I have enclosed a separate letter for Mr. Cleary requesting that you stay on with them, working at whatever occupations you are able, to pay for room and board until I can come for you next April or May, June at the latest.

Your loving uncle,
Miles Graves'

"There ends my uncle's letter, and a discouraging one it is. Mr. and Mrs. Cleary are not eager to take on three more mouths to feed for the next several months. TJ is willing to help Mr. Cleary with farm chores, but Mary Ann is still young and unable to be of much use to Mrs. Cleary, at least not without a great deal of assistance from me.

"I shall go to town to see if I might find employment. Mama taught me domestic skills, and I am now a very good cook and seamstress. If I can find work, perhaps I can pay our room and board until spring brings my uncle to fetch us south.

"July 20, 1865

"My hopes for gainful employment in Sedalia have been dashed. All the shopkeepers, restaurant owners and millinery or dressmaking establishments expressed sympathy for my plight, but were unable to take on extra help due to a shortage of money after the War.

"However, there is exciting news in town: a gentleman is organizing a wagon train headed south, in order to recoup his losses on a cattle drive north from Texas. He and his hired cowboys lost many of their longhorns to disease, which ate into his profits. He seeks to sign on families to travel down the Sedalia Trail, intersect with the Shawnee Trail, and then continue south through Indian Territory toward the Red River Station. There he hopes to find healthier longhorns and drive them north for the profit that slipped through his grasp before.

"I heard all this from Mrs. Anson, the blacksmith's wife, who has an ear for all the local gossip, and then I came upon a bill posted on the door of the hotel inviting interested parties to sign on for this wagon train. It leaves Sedalia, Missouri, on September 1st, with an expected arrival in Texas of mid-October. I snatched the bill off the door and brought it back to the Cleary farm with me.

"Upon my arrival I was at first greeted with eager anticipation by my sister and brother, but then they were sorely disappointed to learn I had returned without employment. We are poverty-stricken orphans depending on the kindness of our neighbors, and the situation is untenable.

"'What are we going to do until April, or later?' TJ fretted. 'We have no money and we are a burden here, yet if we return to Pa's farm we will starve, or freeze, or both.'

He is right; we are indeed desperate. He

has been to the farm daily to see to the animals, but every day he returns more downhearted. 'Thieves have broken in again, Synthia. What is not stolen is damaged.'

"'You must hide whatever equipment is left under bales of hay in the barn. Mr. Cleary offered to sell Papa's farm,' I told him. 'If a buyer cannot be found, he can at least sell the animals and remaining equipment, but not if it is stolen or in disrepair.' I sighed with the uncertainty of it all.

"So I have determined to speak once again to Mr. Cleary about brokering the sale of my father's property as quickly as possible. I have an idea brewing in my head, and it is the only possible solution."

Alex shook his head and set the diary on his desk. "They were in a tight spot, that's for sure. Assuming the journal's authentic."

"So how you can find out if it is?"

"I'd like to take it over to the forensic science department and have a colleague of mine analyze a section of the paper and the ink. That should tell us something. But he won't be able get to it till after the July 4th holiday weekend."

Millie pulled her phone from her bag and turned over several pages in the diary as she took pictures of them.

Zach came and peered over her shoulder. "Why are you doing that?"

Millie snapped a few more photos and tucked the phone back in her bag. "In case I want to read some more or do some more research." She turned back to

Alex. "Can you contact me when you find out anything? I really appreciate your help."

Alex nodded. "My pleasure. Give my best to Karl."

"I will," Millie said as she pulled her sunglasses out of her bag and reached for the door.

Alex cleared his throat loudly as he turned to his son, who was once again sprawled in a chair. "Zach…"

"Oh, sorry." Zach immediately jumped up and opened the office door to let Millie walk out ahead of him. "Let me walk you to your car," he said loudly over his shoulder for his dad's benefit.

Millie put her sunglasses back on and sucked in her breath as she and Zach stepped out into the heat. "I'm parked in the visitor's lot," she said, visually scouring the campus, "which now I can't find."

"Yeah, I saw your car. I'm parked on the other side of the same lot."

They walked together in silence for a few minutes as Millie wracked her brain for polite conversation. She didn't have much experience with small talk, especially with a boy who wasn't a classmate, but she told herself that with her intelligence she should be able to come up with something. Nothing came to mind, though, and the silence between them was getting uncomfortable. "It was nice of you to…" she began.

…just as Zach said, "What got you into all this history stuff?"

They both laughed nervously before Zach said, "You first."

Millie squinted up at him. "Mom got me involved volunteering at a museum years ago, since I'd already been through most of the books in the public library anyway."

Zach shook his head. "It must be crazy inside that brain of yours."

Millie smiled. "Sometimes. It's just who I am, but then my parents start obsessing about my…" She raised two fingers in each hand for air quotes, "…academic future."

"What about your…" Zach held up his hands in imitation, "'academic future'?"

Millie kicked a rock out of her way as she looked down at the pavement in embarrassment. "It's a little uncertain at the moment."

Zach stopped walking and turned to face her. "So is that why you dodged Dad's question?" Millie opened her mouth to respond but nothing came out. "Yeah, I noticed. You haven't decided yet which Ivy League school to attend, right?"

Millie looked up into his face. It occurred to her that he was quite handsome, in that rugged Oklahoma cowboy kind of way. Definitely not like the sophisticated boys she was used to back in Indianapolis at Kendrick—the ones who always ignored her—but he wasn't hard to look at, and he did have an endearing smile. "It's complicated."

"Well, maybe we could get together and you could tell me just how complicated it is."

Millie's pulse began to race. "Um, well, I guess that would be okay." She was excited for a brief moment, but then sighed when she figured out what he must really be asking. "Study for that test?"

"That's not what I meant."

Millie's heart skipped a beat. They walked on toward their cars in silence until Zach impulsively took Millie's hand. The air temperature had to be hovering near one hundred degrees by now, and Millie wondered if the sweat she felt in her palms and trickling down the back of her neck was from heat or nervousness. Zach was walking along the pavement, his leather sandals slapping on the concrete, apparently oblivious to the fact that Millie was staring up at him through the dark UV lenses of her sunglasses.

"Well, here we are," he said as they arrived in the visitor's parking lot.

Millie jiggled the car keys in her hand and punched the remote to unlock the door, stepping back to let the interior heat pour out. "Ugh," she said, "I'm never going to get used to the climate down here."

Zach folded his arms in front of his chest and looked down at her. "So what do you do in the winter up there in Indiana?"

Millie opened her eyes wide. "Winter? Isn't that kind of a non sequitur?"

"No, I'm making a point. And yes, I do know what 'non sequitur' means."

Millie was a little embarrassed that Zach thought she was talking down to him. "We stay indoors and wait for the snowplows," she replied.

Zach grinned. "See? Trade-offs. You know how hot it is in Oklahoma in the summer, but the winters here are pretty mild. Dad's been known to play golf in January in sixty degree weather."

Millie pushed her sunglasses back up her now glistening nose and gave that some thought. "Hmmm. Interesting concept—reversal of climates." She tossed her bag onto the passenger seat and started to get in, but the car's interior was still too hot so she backed out again, right into Zach, who was still standing by the open car door. For once Millie was glad it was so hot outside, because her cheeks felt bright red and she fervently hoped Zach attributed their color to the summer heat.

"Say, Millie," Zach said, putting his hands on her shoulders to help her regain her balance, "if you were serious about getting together to talk and stuff, there's this Fourth of July picnic that my Mom's bosses host every year for the hospital employees. It's a huge event, held at a picnic pavilion near Lake Hefner. Wanna come?"

Millie could feel her pulse racing. "Huh?" *Did I just say 'huh'?* She blushed all over again.

Zach's whole face lit up with a grin, setting his green eyes to sparkling. "Millie Olson speechless. That's gotta be a first. I'm asking you out, Millie. Ever been on a date?"

Millie looked down at her now dusty new sandals and mumbled, "Not really. Except the Prom, and it was a fix-up." She drew a figure eight in the dust with her shoe.

"Then it's about time. I'll pick you up at 4:00. Bring a towel and swimsuit. And sunscreen, but I figure you won't forget that."

Zach winked at her as he sauntered off toward his truck. He casually got in, started up the engine, rolled down all the windows and waved at her as he pulled out of the parking lot.

Millie watched as he drove off, completely forgetting she was standing out in the open in the blazing sun. After a moment the sweat began to pour off her brow, snapping her back to reality. Zach MacMillan was a senior, the star quarterback of his high school football team, and could go out with any girl he wanted, yet he'd just asked her on a date. Millie told herself he must be used to asking girls out, and she shouldn't read too much into an invitation to spend the July 4th holiday with family friends. But still….

She climbed into the car and turned on the engine, cranking up the air conditioning to full blower. "I just accepted a date with Zach MacMillan," she said to her reflection in the rearview mirror. Millie's stomach quickly tied itself in knots.

Chapter Eight
Antiques & Angst

Gran stood at the bottom of the stairs, tapping her foot and checking her wristwatch. "Millie, dear, hurry up or we'll be late," she called.

Millie did a final wardrobe check in the bedroom mirror, assured herself she looked fine for an event attended mostly by elderly church members, and bounded down the stairs. "We're not going to be late," she said. "We don't have anything to load up this year since Zach already took everything to the church yesterday."

Gran had decided that Zach could transport the rummage sale items in his truck—of course she'd reimburse him gas money—but Millie was just as convinced that they shouldn't inconvenience him and surely someone from church could come and pick it all up. Gran insisted it had to be Zach. Millie didn't understand that reasoning, but she dutifully took him up to the attic yesterday morning.

He looked around and took mental inventory of

everything he'd have to carry down the stairs. "That thing going?" Zach asked her as he pointed to the cedar hope chest.

"Absolutely not," Millie told him. "It's an antique bride's hope chest."

"Well good. Looks heavy."

"Gran's keeping it until I can figure out its origin," Millie explained as she ran her hand lovingly over the lid. "It's where I found Synthia's journal." Zach leaned down for a closer inspection, although he seemed to be doing it for her benefit and not to satisfy any particular curiosity of his own. Still, she thought it was a nice gesture. "But those quilts on the floor next to it need to go."

There were several more rummage items in the attic beside the quilts, such as an old Monopoly game, some framed still-life drawings, a table lamp circa 1970, and Charlie's old high chair. Zach inched his way down the pull-down stairs with each individual item, placed them in the back of his truck and set off to the church, with Gran calling after him to drive slowly.

Despite her initial reticence, Millie now had a completely different perspective on Zach MacMillan, especially after their visit to OLAC. She had to admit she was eagerly looking forward to their Fourth of July date tomorrow.

But today was about the church's fundraiser. "Will there be any interesting pieces to look at this year, Gran?" Millie asked as she checked her bag for sunglasses and sunscreen.

"I should think so, dear, enough to keep even you busy. Oh, some of the donations should've been tossed in the trash bin long ago, but there might be some hidden treasures there." She clucked her tongue. "Now we're on a tight schedule, dear. We only have a few hours while Kaz and Charlie are at day camp, and we want to get to the bazaar early to have first pick of the goods." Gran glanced once more at her watch. "Let's see, it's 9:30 right now, so a fifteen minute drive across town to the church, time to look for parking…Well, let's hope we're there at 10:00 when the sale begins."

Millie laughed. "Gran," she said, as they walked out the back door, "Rolling Plains is a small town and it won't take us that long to drive over there." She opened the garage's side entry door, the one that Zach had so recently repaired, and let Gran go in ahead of her.

"Maybe so," Gran said as she pushed the inside wall button and waited for the garage door to crank open, "but it never hurts to be early."

Millie climbed in the passenger side of her grandmother's car and fastened her seatbelt as Gran pushed in a Frank Sinatra CD, turned on the car's air conditioning, and backed slowly out of the garage. Millie leaned back against the leather headrest as she listened to Sinatra crooning "Everybody Loves Somebody," then got her phone out of her bag.

"Calling someone?" Gran asked as she turned onto Olson Road.

Millie shook her head. "Before I left Synthia's journal with Alex, I took pictures of some pages. I just got so caught up in the story…" Her voice trailed off as she flipped through the menu until she brought up the photos. "This girl's got a world of problems, yet she's tough as nails."

"Maybe you should follow her lead and power through your fears," Gran advised, checking her rearview mirror before turning onto Main Street. "Why don't you read it to me?"

Millie reached over to the CD player and lowered the volume.

"August 18, 1865

"'We are leaving Missouri,' I told my brother.

"TJ fixed me with an emotionless stare. 'Yes, I know. Uncle Miles will come for us next spring.'

"I shook my head. 'No, TJ, we cannot wait. Mr. Cleary has just this week brokered the sale of Papa's farm to Dr. Olmstead from town. The doctor is willing to pay $600 for the farm, equipment, and any remaining animals. Of course Mr. Cleary will take $100 in commission for his trouble.'

"My brother sighed and hung his head. 'I suppose that means we are now homeless as well as orphans.'

"My heart ached for my brother. I knew he was trying to be the man of the family that Papa would expect him to be. Nonetheless he is only ten years old, and the tears forming in his eyes were those of a child.

"'We have nothing left,' he said, clenching his fists.

"I took my brother by the shoulders and looked him in the eye. 'Oh, yes we have! We are not defeated. We have Papa's wagon, small though it is, and I will spirit away two of the horses from the farm before Dr. Olmstead takes possession. We must pack what we can and make for Texas!'

"TJ was all amazement. 'Synthia, no!

How are we three children to make it all the way to Texas by wagon? What about traveling through Indian Territory? That alone is dangerous!'

"'As you know,' I replied with the courage I hoped I exuded, 'Papa taught me to drive the wagon, and with your help I shall hitch it and make all preparations for this journey. Papa very recently had repairs made, so the wagon is fit for travel.'

"'But…Papa isn't here, and we are but orphaned children…' My brother's words stuck in his throat and he began to sob.

"'See here, TJ, I am not a child, but I must have your help. I have decided to take our portion of the money from the sale of the farm, and the three of us shall join a wagon train. We leave in three weeks.'

"TJ shook his head. 'We are forbidden, Synthia. You read Uncle Miles' letter. He will come for us in the spring.'

"I understand my brother's concern, but my mind is set. By joining a wagon train rather than striking out alone, we can achieve a measure of safety, so that should allay some of TJ's fears. My hopes and prayers will be answered when we arrive safely in Texas. I strengthened my resolve and said, 'There will be no need. We shall save him the trip by six months!'

"Now she's joining a wagon train?" Millie asked, incredulous. "But how…" She marveled at the moxie this unknown woman was displaying. Dead unknown woman.

"What did you say, dear?"

"It's just that this girl, Synthia Whitfield, she's got—had—more guts than I ever did. I'd be scared to death to take a long-distance trip like that with Kaz and Charlie—in a car. And here she's talking about driving a covered wagon!"

"Don't sell yourself short, dear. You've traveled with your brother and sister numerous times."

"In an airplane that only takes a few hours," Millie replied. "She's planning a journey that could take weeks."

Gran clicked on her turn signal to change into the left lane, preparing to turn into the church parking lot. "Why not take a train?" she asked.

"Even before the war there were very few railroads operating between Missouri and Texas, and even fewer by 1865." In response to Gran's surprised reaction, Millie laughed and said, "Okay, I just Googled it."

Millie loved Ogden Church's annual silent auction and rummage sale. She knew several of the church members, mostly friends of her grandmother's, but she wasn't here to socialize. The chance to wander among all the vintage items and create stories about them in her mind was why she came, why she always came.

Gran easily found a parking place in the church lot. She and Millie got out of the car, and while Gran punched the remote door lock, Millie adjusted her sunglasses and smoothed the wrinkles from the back of her shorts.

The rummage sale was being held on the church lawn this year, much to Millie's chagrin. "Gran, what were you and your committee thinking, planning an outdoor event in July?" It was only mid-morning and already it was hot and sticky as the sun beamed down from a cloudless sky.

"We were too crowded last year in the church hall, dear," Gran explained, "and we can't afford to turn folks away. Besides, most Oklahomans don't notice the heat the way you Hoosiers do."

Millie moaned and reached into her bag for a ponytail holder to pull her hair up off her neck. She was glad she'd dressed comfortably in khaki walking shorts, golf shirt, and white sandals.

"We had to make some costly repairs to the building this past winter, so we have to do better than just break even this year, Millie. Luckily church members stepped up with lots of donations, put up flyers in local businesses and then publicized the event on social media," Gran told her. "Hopefully we'll have a good turnout." She shaded her eyes with her hand and did a visual search of the yard. "Hmmm, let's start over here with the kitchen items." Gran strolled toward the display tables set up with clipboards and pens for writing silent bids, and began perusing the already-placed bids ahead of hers.

Aside from the costlier items reserved for silent auction, there were a dozen or more tables set up around the yard with a variety of items priced individually for immediate purchase. Each table was piled from end to end with merchandise, and all were organized into specific categories as stated by posted signs. There were kitchen gadgets and pots and pans; antique dishes and glassware; floor lamps and table lamps; baby clothes and layette items; children's toys from bygone eras; modern tools and tool chests; gardening implements; old books; vinyl records in both 45 and 33 rpm; men's and women's jewelry; and one table simply labeled 'Miscellaneous' with a mishmash of goods.

Millie browsed for what she thought was only a couple of minutes, getting lost in her daydreams about the items' histories, but a glance at her phone told her it had been closer to a half hour. She turned around to discover she'd lost sight of her grandmother, so she had to stand on tiptoes to see over the heads of the thickening crowd of bargain-hunters. She finally spotted Gran at the opposite end of a long table and waved both arms over her head as a signal. Gran waved her over.

"Dear, I'd like you to meet my friend, Abigail Collins. She owns that antique shop on Main Street I told you about."

Millie was thrilled to finally meet the woman who had originally acquired the cedar chest with Synthia's journal inside, and a million questions raced through her mind.

"This must be the brilliant granddaughter I've heard so much about, Mildred," Abigail cooed, and then turning to Millie she asked, "Will you be attending Oklahoma Liberal Arts College this fall like your father did?"

Millie pretended she hadn't heard that. "Nice to meet you," she said. "I wanted to ask you about that cedar hope chest Gran bought in your shop last spring."

"Yes, fine piece from an estate sale."

"Well, what do you know about its history?"

Abigail thought for a moment, tapping her cheek

with a long, red fingernail. "It's a bride's hope chest…."

Millie wanted to groan because she already knew that, but she bit her tongue and tuned out the rest of Abigail's long-winded discussion of wedding hope chests. When Abigail finally came up for air, Millie jumped in. "Did you know there was an old journal buried in the bottom of it?"

"Why, no. I wonder I never saw it."

"It was pretty well hidden," Millie explained, "but it belonged to a woman named Synthia Elizabeth Whitfield, written in 1865. Do you know anything about her?"

Abigail shook her head. "I'm afraid not. You'll have to Google her."

Disappointed, Millie mumbled, "Thanks anyway." Why did people think Google was the answer to everything? Sure, there were plenty of unanswered questions that could be resolved with an online search, but sometimes people at estate sales had inside information about their artifacts, and could tell a compelling story without benefit of the Internet. Synthia's journal certainly had an amazing story to tell.

"Why don't we go over to the furniture section, dear," Gran suggested, "which is conveniently located in the shade."

Millie appreciated that, so she squinted and looked in the direction Gran was pointing. Not only did she enjoy the knick-knacks and household items she'd already seen, she loved to look at the antique furnishings and imagine the people who had owned them, how the pieces got particular dents or scratches, and what their owners' lives might have been like.

She paused to admire a handmade afghan tossed

over the back of an old Bentwood rocker sitting all alone near a shade tree, and began an imaginary narrative in her head about its origin as she stroked the afghan's soft texture with her fingertips.

Her grandmother walked on ahead at a brisk pace. Millie couldn't imagine how anyone, let alone her grandmother, could walk that fast in this heat, but she was forced to quicken her step to catch up.

"Well, well, my dear Mrs. Olson," said a short, rotund, middle-aged man as he stepped toward them.

Gran stopped, smiled, and extended her hand to the proprietor of Keller's Antiques & Auctions, the company that donated their time to conduct the church's silent auction. "It's nice to see you again, Mr. Keller. Could you point us toward some interesting pieces?" Gran asked. "Millie here is quite fascinated with antiques."

"Why, Mrs. Olson, I'm surprised you have to ask!" Mr. Keller reached over and patted Millie on the head as if she were Charlie. "My, my, how your little granddaughter has grown."

Millie was mortified, but fortunately Gran came to her rescue. "Mr. Keller, our girl here just graduated at the top of her high school class up in Indianapolis, with numerous scholarship offers."

"Is that so?" Mr. Keller winked at Gran before turning back to Millie. "Valedictorian, interested in antiques, and off to college. Does that mean a history major in your future?"

"Well…." Millie looked around for an avenue of escape. None came into view.

"You know," Mr. Keller continued, "the twins just graduated from Rolling Plains High School. Both Kendall and Arthur are off to The University of Oklahoma soon."

"Well, that's exciting news for all of you, Mr. Keller," Gran said, "and I know Millie has met them at some point, haven't you, dear? So perhaps while you're in town…."

"Gran," Millie interrupted through gritted teeth, "Mr. Keller's grandchildren are nearly nineteen. We don't have anything in common."

"I don't suppose you're off to OU as well, Millie?" Mr. Keller persisted. "You could always look them up down in Norman."

Millie nearly rolled her eyes at that remark, but stopped herself and managed to say politely, "No, I'm not going to school in Norman, Oklahoma."

"Our Millie is considering offers from Ivy League schools and of course our own OLAC. Isn't that right, dear?"

Millie cleared her throat. "Did you see that Bentwood rocker over there? I'd like to get a closer look." She knew how rude that was, but she couldn't take it anymore. She walked away, even though she'd had a good look at the rocking chair the first time.

This day was not going as planned as far as Millie was concerned. All she'd wanted to do was look at the merchandise, maybe buy a few things, and enjoy being surrounded by all the history that was here. Instead she'd been cornered repeatedly with questions about her nonexistent college plans. Millie decided to move that antique rocker directly under the shade tree and read some more of Synthia's journal. Maybe there was some inspiration in there.

August 28, 1865. TJ persists in his reluctance to set out on this journey to Texas, but despite his misgivings he has been of some help to me. I make my excuses to Mrs. Cleary every day after breakfast by telling her I must pack our personal belongings before Dr. Olmstead moves into our former home. I am not lying exactly, since I am indeed packing, but I am guilty of a lie of omission and hope she does not see the truth in my face.

The wagon is still on my father's property and has not as yet fallen victim to the vandals. I am filling it with all the items I know we must have for our trip, and then hiding the boxes and chests under old horse blankets to disguise them from thieves. I wrapped Mama's china in her beautifully sewn quilts, and I also made use of blankets, clothing, and old towels for packing breakables. I then carefully and lovingly packed the dishes into her cedar hope chest, alongside the family Bible which notes marriages and births, documentation I am sure to need in Texas.

"Cedar chest!" Millie exclaimed. "I wonder if it's the same one where I found the journal." She shook her head. It couldn't be just a coincidence!

I found an old wooden box in Papa's now-abandoned barn and set about filling it with such items as we would need on our journey. I located some stout canvas sacks that Mama had stored in the house under the dry sink, and salvaged food from the kitchen that I deemed necessary for such a long journey. On Mama and Papa's final trip to town,

she stocked up on smoked bacon, dried apples, beans, rice, coffee, and flour, so I carefully stored all those foodstuffs in individual
bags. During the day when the wagon train
travels and I cannot cook, I must plan ahead
so that my brother and sister are properly
nourished. To that end I shall prepare extra
bacon and biscuits every morning and wrap
them in muslin towels to eat midday.

Cooking utensils will be necessary, so I
packed two cast-iron skillets, carving knives
and wooden spoons, tin plates, tin cups, and
eating utensils. I packed all the bars of
Mama's lye soap that I could find, as I fully
intend to wash bedding, clothing, dishes, and
children while on our journey. Cleanliness is
next to Godliness Mama always said, and I
share her aversion to filth. I must also set
aside sewing notions for repairing the few
outfits we will wear, as I have packed all our
extra clothing and personal items in the hope
chest along with the china. There they will
stay, and since children will naturally snag
their clothing or perhaps grow, I have sewing
notions for mending, so that we may make do
with what we are wearing until we arrive in
Texas.

Although I am used to cooking on a
stove, I am skilled at starting a fire for cooking, but as we cannot transport firewood in
the wagon, I took Papa's ax from the barn in
the hopes that TJ is able to chop wood as we
travel. Failing that, I shall have to use dead
brush or tree limbs.

Our journey begins in three days, but it

is a few hours' ride to Sedalia. The wagon is packed and ready to leave, and all that remains is to hitch the horses. I have written a letter to Mr. and Mrs. Cleary explaining our sudden departure and thanking them for their kindness, but I will post it from Sedalia, ensuring that they will not receive it until we are well on our way south. God Himself knows how frightened I am at the prospect of striking out alone with two children, so I do not wish to be discouraged (or prevented!) from making this journey.

Wow! She's so brave, Millie thought. *I'd never be able to plan and execute a trip like that. Would I?*

Millie lapsed into silence on the drive to Kaz and Charlie's day camp. "Gran, what am I supposed to do about college?" she suddenly asked.

"Why go, dear," Gran answered.

Millie twisted in her seatbelt so she could face her grandmother. "But it's not that simple."

"Of course it is," Gran said. "You've been blessed with a brilliant mind and plenty of opportunity to make use of your intelligence. Go to college. Have some fun. Create a wonderful life for yourself."

Millie felt her body tense up at the thought. She lowered her eyes and fidgeted with a loose thread on the hem of her shorts. "I'm scared."

"Why are you so frightened, dear? This should be the best time of your life."

Millie stared out the window. "I'm afraid I'll choose the wrong college, or I won't make any friends, or my professors will think I'm just a kid who doesn't belong there, or…" She sighed and then shook her head. "It may be too late to register anyway."

"You have procrastinated a bit, dear," Gran agreed. "But there are still options. You've been accepted to Indiana University and Oklahoma Liberal Arts College. Are they closed to admissions?"

Millie swallowed hard. "Well, no," she said. "But I'm really just considering community college in Indianapolis. I could take a few classes, live at home, help out with Kaz and Charlie…"

"Don't squander your potential," Gran advised her. "Young people with your mental aptitude are the future of this country." She silently concentrated on her driving before asking, "What do you suppose Synthia Whitfield would do in a situation like this?"

"From what I've read so far, she doesn't back down from a challenge. Pretty inspiring, whoever she was. Maybe I'll spend some time tomorrow reading and doing research." Millie noticed her grandmother's scowl. "What?"

"Don't you have plans with Zach tomorrow for the Fourth?"

Millie blushed. "I'm still going!" she answered with a bit more enthusiasm than she intended. "He's not picking me up till 4:00."

Gran put on her turn signal to pull onto a side road which led to the recreation center. They rode on in silence for a while before Millie reached into her bag and pulled out her phone, scrolling down to where she left off reading Synthia's journal.

Gran glanced over at the phone in Millie's hand and then back to the road as she clucked her tongue. "Mildred Olson, if that fifteen-year-old girl could make life-altering decisions, the least you can do is nail down a college."

"But things were so different in her era…."

"People in every age face all kinds of adversities," Gran replied. "Could you read me some more?"

Millie smiled. "You're right. Okay, well, as you know, she's decided to travel by wagon train between Missouri and Texas, which means she's got to cross through…"

"Oklahoma, aka Indian Territory," Gran finished.

"September 1, 1865.

"I awoke my brother and sister hours before dawn, and the three of us stole away to our farm. TJ and I were able to hitch the horses to the wagon by moonlight, and then I drove us safely to Sedalia, where we arrived at sunrise. TJ was impressed with my driving skills, and appeared rather less fearful of this whole enterprise than before. Mary Ann is all amazement, as no word of any of this was spoken to her for fear she could not keep the secret.

"I posted my letter to Mr. and Mrs. Cleary, and then I paid our fare to the wagon train's captain. He frowned at me and growled, "Girly, do yore folks know what you young'uns are up to?"

"I held my head high and replied, "Sir, my mama and papa would approve, may they rest in peace, and my uncle awaits our arrival in Texas!"

"The captain grunted and warned me repeatedly of the perils ahead. I turned a deaf ear to his concerns, and will do the same to anyone else who might complain that a girl of fifteen is incapable of making this journey. He shook his head but willingly took my money, and now we have the remaining $200 from the sale of Papa's farm to start our new life in Texas. Should Uncle Miles and Aunt Catherine not welcome us into their home, we will have money enough to live until I can find gainful employment and see to the children's education, as Mama would want.

"TJ made the acquaintance of a boy his age by the name of Samuel Carrington, whose family is also traveling in the wagon train, and Mr. Carrington suggested that I place my wagon behind his. It is a very kind gesture, meant to offer us protection of sorts. However, although TJ is of help hitching the horses, I alone am responsible for driving the wagon and seeing to the children while we travel.

"Oh, this is a heavy burden! I am still grieving the loss of Mama and Papa, and yet being their oldest child, I must accept the torch that has been passed to me. I have been praying every night that the journey is uneventful, and that Uncle Miles will welcome us when we arrive."

Gran shook her head as she parked the car in the recreation center parking lot. "The girl is brave, I'll give you that, but I'll be interested in what Alex has to say about the diary's authenticity." She turned off the engine, and she and Millie got out of the car and headed into the recreation center to collect Kaz and Charlie.

Inside, the building was stuffy and humid, as if

the door had been opened one too many times and the air conditioning was working overtime trying unsuccessfully to keep up. Children were running everywhere, some wearing stained t-shirts and smudged jeans, while others were still in their swim suits with towels wrapped around their waists. Stressed-out teenage camp counselors were trying to get control of various groups divided up by age, making dismissal time very chaotic.

Millie did a visual search of the area and finally spotted Kaz at the far end of the building, dressed in baseball pants with his athletic bag tossed over one shoulder, the new bat protruding from the partially-opened end. He casually sauntered over, a wide grin on his face.

Gran gave him a hug and then recoiled. "Kaz, boy, you're soaking wet, and I'd bet it's not swimming pool water."

Kaz was exhilarated. "Gran, you knew our coach set it up for us to go to the RedHawks game tomorrow night, right? Well, now one of us gets to throw out the first pitch! And since I'm the best pitcher it's gonna be me! I've been practicing all afternoon. And after the game they're shooting off fireworks! I just need a ride to the ballpark to join Coach and the guys. And guess what! The Oklahoma City RedHawks are playing the Indianapolis Indians!" He let out a whoop with a fist pump to the air.

"Oh, my, that's a surprise," Gran said, and her expression didn't look like it was an agreeable one.

"Well?" Kaz said.

Gran and Millie exchanged glances. Kaz was obviously excited about this, but Millie was supposed to be at the picnic with Zach, and Gran was planning to attend a pitch-in supper at church.

Kaz crossed his arms in front of his chest and tapped his foot impatiently. "Well?" he repeated.

Millie took a deep breath. "We have kind of a conundrum, Kaz. Gran and I both have plans, and Charlie's spending the day with one of her friends from camp, so…"

Kaz did a slow burn. "What's a con…drum… whatever you said?"

"Scheduling conflict," Millie explained.

He glared at his sister. "So as usual, it's all about you! Forget what's important to me, Genius Millie always comes first!" He pushed his way through a knot of kids and out the door before Millie or Gran could stop him.

Millie was stunned. "Is he right, Gran? Am I that selfish?"

Gran shook her head. "I'd say you're pretty selfless, dear. But we've got to figure this out, because this is clearly important to your brother."

Disappointed, Millie nodded. "I'll just tell Zach I can't go."

"No, ma'am, that's not the right answer! Let me go have a word with Coach Long." Gran headed in the direction of the main offices and was soon out of sight.

"Hi, Millie!" Charlie was tugging at her arm. "Mandy's mom's here, and we're stopping for pizza on the way to their house."

Millie smiled as she hugged her sister. "You got everything? Toothbrush? Jammies? The new teddy bear?"

Charlie giggled and bobbed her head up and down. "Freddy, his name's Freddy. Gran packed my backpack this morning." She turned completely around as she searched for her friend. "Hey, there's Mandy! Bye!"

Gran reappeared from the office area and gave Millie a thumbs-up as she approached. "Problem solved. Coach Long will drive Kaz to the ballpark, but he can't pick him up until after 4:00."

Millie was relieved. "That'll work, I hope." She headed out the front door, sucked in her breath as she got hit with the late-afternoon heat, and spotted her brother sulking as he leaned against Gran's car.

"Gran fixed the problem, Kaz," Millie said, breathing hard from the exertion in the sultry humidity.

Kaz rolled his eyes. "Yeah, right. Fixed it so you can go on your stupid date."

Millie rolled her eyes right back at him. "You're welcome."

"Like I said, always about you."

It was approaching supper time and Millie knew she should be hungry, but between the heat, the constant reminders about her nonexistent college plans, and the argument with her brother, she'd lost her appetite. Kaz was scowling in the backseat of Gran's car, and Millie was fanning herself with a pizza flyer they found under the windshield.

"Do we have something for supper, Gran, or should I go and pick up a pizza?" she asked, examining the brochure in her hand.

"Whichever you prefer, dear," Gran said as she pulled up alongside her mailbox at the end of the long driveway. "Kaz, can you hop out and get the mail for me?"

Kaz grunted, but opened the car door and walked

the few steps to the mailbox. Millie watched as he stood staring down the driveway toward the house before finally opening the box and pulling the mail out. He made a circular motion with his arm for Millie to roll down her window.

"Whose car's that in your driveway, Gran?" Kaz asked, pointing ahead.

Millie craned her neck but couldn't see anything. "Is it a truck?" she asked a little too eagerly.

"I said car!" Kaz got back in and pulled the door shut.

Gran drove slowly up the drive and parked behind the metallic blue, late-model sedan which was blocking her garage entrance and Millie's rent car. She furrowed her brow and said, "Now I wonder…" Before she could speculate further, the back door opened and out walked Karl, grinning broadly, his arms outstretched.

"Dad!" Millie exclaimed. She jumped out of the front seat and lunged into his open arms. "Dad, I can't believe it!"

"Hey, guys, thought you'd never get here!" Karl said with a twinkle in his eye. "I'm starved and all I can think about is that Mexican restaurant in town." He tousled Kaz's hair and hugged his shoulders. "FYI, Mom, my partners and I settled the case out of court and I took the first available flight out of LA. Wouldn't you know there'd be a long layover in Denver!"

"You settled?" Millie asked.

Karl nodded. "Yes, indeed, and the unfortunate gamers who hijacked our clients' video game will be paying hefty damages."

Gran was beaming. "What a pleasant surprise, son." She walked over to Karl as Millie and Kaz stepped aside to let her hug him. "But where's your wife?"

"Off to Toronto." Karl looked around and over the tops of their heads. "And where's Charlie?"

"She's sleeping over at a friend's house tonight," Millie told him. "We've all got plans for the Fourth tomorrow and…" Suddenly she stopped when the obvious dawned on her. "Well, naturally, I'm sure you're welcome to join us—Alex's family—Jane's company picnic."

Karl put a hand on Kaz's shoulder. "Actually, I did some online research while I was stuck in Denver, and I see the Indianapolis Indians are in town for a game with the RedHawks." He got down to eye level with his son. "You interested?"

"You bet, Dad! Wait till I tell you what Coach has planned!" Kaz talked animatedly to his father as they headed for the back door.

Millie smiled, glad that her Dad was here and relieved of some of the guilt she was feeling about her July 4th plans.

"Millie? You coming inside? I've never known you to want to stand outside in the Oklahoma heat," Karl said as he held the kitchen door for her.

Millie's cell phone buzzed in her pocket. "Be right there, Dad," she said as she checked the text message. Zach? Zach!

Looking forward to some fireworks tomorrow! was all it said. She was both excited and nervous about her first real date. She replied to his text, *See you at 4pm!* Sudden optimism caused her appetite to return and she couldn't wait to join her family for dinner and order lots of her favorite Mexican foods.

Chapter Nine
Fireworks

Fresh from her morning shower, Millie practically danced back to her bedroom, her bathrobe tied around her waist and a towel wrapped around her head. The anticipation of spending the holiday with Zach was making her giddy and nervous all at once.

POP POP POP! WHOOSH! BOOM!

A quick glance through the white lace bedroom curtains told her that the popping and whizzing sounds outside were courtesy of Kaz shooting off firecrackers in Gran's front yard. She tossed aside the wet towel, threw on shorts and a t-shirt, and ran downstairs barefoot.

"Kaz!" she shouted, pounding on the kitchen window. "That's dangerous — and illegal!"

"Shut up, Millie!" he shouted back.

"Problems?"

Millie turned around to see her dad with a bemused grin. "Where did Kaz get fireworks?" she asked him.

"I'm afraid that's my fault," Karl told her. "As long as I can remember, there's always been this fireworks stand just outside the city limits, so I drove over there last night."

Millie clenched her fists in frustration and opened the back door, positioning herself so that she stood with one foot in and the other foot out, ready to run outside if Kaz set anything on fire. And with no supervision, Millie thought that was likely. "What if he gets caught?" she fretted. "This isn't Indianapolis where private fireworks are legal."

"Don't worry, kiddo, I'm keeping a close eye on your brother. We're so far out in the country that he won't disturb the neighbors, and I won't get a ticket from the local police."

Millie didn't understand his cavalier attitude. "We're in a drought, you know," she said. "Let's hope we're not so far out in the country that the fire trucks can't get here."

Millie continued to watch her brother's activities, since she was pretty sure her dad wasn't really paying attention, but when the coffee pot announced the end of its brew cycle with a burst of steam and a loud grinding sputter, Millie reluctantly closed the kitchen door. She took two mugs from the cabinet, put milk and sweetener into hers and handed the cup of black coffee to her father.

"Good morning, Gran," Millie said, peeking over her mug. Her grandmother waltzed into the room, a certain glow about her that Millie couldn't ferret out. "You look nice," Millie observed. Gran was dressed for the holiday in a white linen skirt, red, white and blue striped button-down shirt with an American flag pin on the lapel, and bright red canvas sneakers with blue and white laces.

"I agree, Mom," Karl said with a quick glance out the bay window.

"All dressed up for a bunch of women at a church picnic?" Millie asked, eyebrow raised.

"You needn't sound so surprised, dear." Gran went to the refrigerator and pulled out cartons of strawberries and blueberries and began busily arranging the fruit in a serving bowl. "Why, you act as if I never take care with my appearance. Rest assured, dear, there will be all sorts of people at that picnic and it never hurts to look nice." She surveyed Millie's thrown-together look. "I would imagine you'd want to look your best for a certain young man today, too."

Millie blushed and decided to let the topic go before it completely turned back on her. Instead, she got busy setting the table for breakfast. She pulled five plates out of the cabinet, remembered Charlie was at a sleepover and put one back, but then put them all away when she remembered the holiday plates her grandmother stored in the pantry. She set out placemats, silverware, and checkered napkins that complemented the American flag-embossed plates, and then stood back to admire the results. Maybe Gran was on to something with all the holiday dishware, corny as it was, because the table did look festive.

"I wish Mom could have come with you, Dad," Millie said.

"Mom misses you, too. All you kids." Karl gave Millie a bear hug. "We had a great time in LA and she's in Toronto with the production crew, scouting locations for Millicent's TV adventures. Which reminds me, Millie, I promised your mother we'd talk." Karl turned to face Millie with the 'serious discussion' look that ignited her fight or flight response.

"After the holiday weekend I'm flying back to Indianapolis to get caught up at the office. Your mom suggested I get an extra ticket and take you with me. You could drive down to Bloomington, maybe take Carlye along, and finally get registered for fall classes, since you've squandered your better offers."

Gulp. Millie didn't know how to respond. She definitely resented his dig about Huntleigh, but how could he expect her to just up and enroll at IU without ever having been there? Her hands flew to her throat as it tightened, and she wasn't sure she was going to be able to speak at all. "I can't..." she squeaked out. She swallowed hard and tried again. "I can't just dump Charlie on Gran, Dad, but..." Suddenly the perfect solution came to her. "Didn't Kaz want to be back for football? Take him instead."

"Kaz may have to be a little late for middle school football conditioning," Karl replied, his arms crossed and a frown on his face. "On the other hand," he said, unfolding his arms as he addressed his mother, "my daughter's procrastinated long enough, and I'm sure you wouldn't mind keeping Charlie for a few days."

"You know, Karl," Gran said thoughtfully, "we have a perfectly good liberal arts college right here that our girl's already been accepted to. She even visited the other day."

Millie put her hands on her hips and stomped her foot. "Stop talking about me in the third person!"

"Well, dear," Gran said as she obligingly faced Millie, "assuming a big university is too intimidating, our small local college might be just the solution."

"A good suggestion, Mom, but she's not enrolled

there either."

Millie rolled her eyes and sat down at the breakfast table next to her father.

Gran took a seat at the kitchen table and began passing the fruit and muffins. "Didn't you just drop off that girl's diary with Alex?" Millie nodded warily. "Well, then you'll have to go back for it, I assume. Since you didn't stop in at the admissions office before like I suggested, why not make the most of your second opportunity?"

Instead of answering, Millie popped a too-large strawberry in her mouth and began vigorously chewing.

Karl reached for a muffin. "I've been hearing a lot about this mysterious journal."

Finally something she wanted to talk about! Millie spit out the strawberry stem, swallowed the rest of the berry and said, "Hang on a minute, Dad." She dashed upstairs and grabbed her cell phone. She focused on the screen as she walked back into the kitchen and touched open the file. "Here. Listen to this.

"September 20, 1865.

"We are slowly making progress, but I had no idea of the difficulty of this journey. We travel for days on end and see nothing but tumbleweeds and barren plains. There was a rain storm early one morning, and as the lightning flashed through the sky, the thunder seemed to crackle forever across the prairie, with nothing to rein it in.

"Driving this wagon is responsibility enough, but the care of two children from morning till night weighs heavily upon me. I constantly remind myself that this is what

Mama would expect me to do.

"Our day begins before dawn. Every morning I must light a fire to prepare a breakfast of pancakes, biscuits, bacon and coffee, set aside extra food for midday, and then see to the dirty dishes and repack them by the time the 7 a.m. bugle sounds to roll the wagons. Mary Ann generally rides in the wagon next to me, but TJ often complains of the discomfort and sometimes chooses to walk alongside, chatting or playing with his friend Samuel. Since we cover as much as twenty miles per day, TJ is constantly jumping in and out of the wagon. Mama always said boys will be rambunctious, so I just keep needle and thread at the ready for mending. Before sunset we stop travel for the day, and supper usually consists of dried beef, beans, biscuits, and cooked apples. If TJ has been able to find fresh water and catch some fish, of course we substitute fresh fried fish for the beef.

"All told there are twenty families in this train, and folks are saying that the reason the captain is pushing us this hard is so that he can get in one last trail drive back north before winter sets in. I heard Mr. Carrington say that Texas was mainly settled because of the cattle industry, and cattle trails are an important source of revenue, so our speed makes sense in that regard.

"I have the family Bible with me, and often take pleasure in instructing Mary Ann, listening to her hesitant reading whilst I drive the wagon. In the evening Mary Ann goes to sleep shortly after supper, TJ sees to the horses and then plays with Samuel, and I have many chores such as washing and mending to keep me busy. I try to write in this journal by firelight if time permits. Hardly anyone brought candles, so unless there is a full moon, everyone retires early.

"Tonight as I lie in the wagon attempting sleep, I pray yet again for guidance, hoping I have made the right decision.

"September 29, 1865.

We awoke this morning to find a large number of the Natives of this area blocking our path, about a mile distant from our camp. Now that we have crossed into Indian Territory, we have frequently seen members of the Choctaw and Chickasaw tribes, (it is rumored that these tribes are the most financially well-off in this uncivilized land), as well as other indigenous peoples whose heritage we are unable to determine. Up till now, although we have seen the Indians off in the distance, they have generally ignored us. So there was a great murmuring amongst the travelers this morning, considerable fear from some of the wives and their children, and consternation among the men as to the meaning of this en-counter.

"At length the captain and some of the men—heads of households—rode out to greet our visitors. TJ begged to be allowed to join them, claiming he is the 'man' of our family, but Mr. Carrington told him the captain would not allow it due to his tender age. He was angry and crestfallen but did as he was told.

"There was suspense as we waited and watched for over an hour. Eventually the men returned to our camp and began going from wagon to wagon, collecting what money or trinkets they could, and offering little explanation. When they came to me, I at first balked.

"'Girly,' the captain growled, 'you signed on for this journey and knew the risks, so if you and those young'uns expect to continue with this train, you'll do as everyone else does.'

"I knew we would be in grave danger if I tried to continue on alone, so I was forced to dig into the bottom of Mama's hope chest and give them $10 from our savings, an expense I hadn't counted on. Now my brother, sister and I are left with less than $200 for our new life in Texas, and I hope it will be enough.

"The men went back to our Native visitors with the money collected to pay the toll for our safe passage. Everyone waited breathlessly as the transaction was completed and our way cleared. Finally the captain returned and gave the order that we should set out for the day.

"The indigenous peoples did not again impede our travels, and thereafter were frequently seen in our midst, seeking trade while we continued our travel near their homes. When they occasionally approached, families were eager to trade such small items as they had on hand (jewelry being a favorite)

in exchange for woolen blankets, freshly har-
vested corn, or firewood, all of which are in
short supply amongst us.

"I must quickly end this in order to make
my preparations for the day's travel."

"That's fascinating," Millie said, pushing some
buttons on her phone to return to the main menu.

Karl drummed his knuckles on the tabletop. "I
must say, it's an interesting story if it's true. What did
Alex say?"

Before Millie could answer, KAPOW! POP POP
POP! WHOOOOSH!

"Dad!" Millie exclaimed as she jumped up and
started for the door. "That was too close to the garage!"

Karl motioned for her to stay put as he bolted out
the kitchen door and shouted, "Karl Azford Olson!
You're about to set the roof on fire!"

Millie stood staring at the carefully selected outfits
lying on her bed. The idea that she might not look her
best for this 'official' date with Zach was giving her
qualms. What to wear? The spaghetti-strap polished
cotton sundress with the colorful flowers on a white
background with her new sandals? The navy blue
walking shorts with the white eyelet blouse, a red
headband and red deck shoes? Or the plain old jean
shorts, Old Navy t-shirt with an emblazoned American flag, and white athletic shoes?

She glanced at the clock: 3:45 p.m. Zach would be
here in fifteen minutes and she still hadn't made a decision. How embarrassing would it be if he got here
and she wasn't ready? What to wear, what to wear….

Okay, logic, Millie. We're going to an outdoor picnic

by a lake which means Oklahoma red clay and dust; it's over 100 degrees outside; you want to be able to change in and out of a swimsuit quickly. "And I don't want to seem pretentious," she scolded herself, as she ran her fingers across all the wardrobe choices laid out.

She got dressed, checked her canvas beach-bag one last time to make sure she had towel, swim suit, sunglasses, and sunscreen, and then went downstairs to wait for Zach.

Gran was already gone to the church pitch-in supper, her homemade apple pie carefully packed in the carry-all, and she'd been very insistent about being on time. Millie wondered again why it mattered if she was a few minutes late to an event with a bunch of old ladies and a few widowers, but at the moment there was no answer for that. As for Dad and Kaz, they'd spent the morning shooting off illegal fireworks from Gran's driveway, and by now they should be arriving at the ballpark in Oklahoma City, all set for Kaz to throw out the honorary first pitch of the holiday baseball game.

Millie decided to wait on the front porch for Zach. She eased herself onto the porch swing and envisioned herself casually swinging when Zach drove up, but the swing was mostly made of metal and when Millie tried to sit, she jumped back because it was radiating heat. So instead of looking picture-perfect like a proper Southern lady on an old-fashioned swing, she had to sit down on the front step and lean her elbows on her knees to keep from getting her hands dirty. *Cut it out, Millie,* she groused at herself. *Zach's the son of longtime family friends and we're just going to a picnic.* That little pep talk didn't settle her nerves any, though. Since

she'd become reacquainted with Zach, for some unknown and illogical reason she wanted him to like her.

Zach's truck ambled up the drive at 4:02 p.m., according to Millie's cell phone. He left the engine running and hopped out the driver's side. Millie knew
that wasn't too fuel-efficient in his gas-guzzler, but she
was secretly glad he'd left the AC turned on so she
wouldn't have to get into a hot vehicle.

"Hi," Millie said. She stood up and adjusted her
bag on her shoulder.

Zach was wearing what looked to be freshly-
washed denim cutoffs which showed off his muscular
quads, an untucked OLAC logo-emblazoned golf shirt
like the one Alex had worn the other day, a backwards
baseball cap, and the same well-worn sandals as before, again with the clasps unfastened. A guy thing,
she assumed, but then again she didn't really have
much experience with guys. He looked her up and
down and nodded in approval. "You dressed down
for a change."

Millie smoothed her already-rumpled jean shorts
and Old Navy t-shirt with the flag waving across the
front, and shifted the bag yet again. "I can go
change…."

"What for? You look great."

Millie hesitated before stepping off the porch. *AM
I underdressed?* Before she could puzzle it out, Zach
smiled at her, took her hand and helped her down the
porch steps, making her feel like Cinderella about to
go to the ball—without the dress.

"Come on, hop in." He held open the passenger
side door for her and she climbed into the truck's cab,
grateful for the cool air inside.

"How far is this picnic area?" Millie asked, fastening her seatbelt.

"You mean you didn't Google it?" Zach asked as he snapped his seatbelt closed.

Millie smiled with a blush. "Okay, yes, I did. It's about a half hour away, right?"

"Right. Ya like music?"

"Of course I do," she said and stopped herself before adding a juvenile-sounding Duh, "but not that country stuff everyone around here listens to, and I doubt you have The 1812 Overture, so whatever you've got is fine."

Zach lifted an eyebrow at her as he flipped through his iPod selections on the console and turned up the volume. Tchaikovsky's famous overture began blaring through the speakers and he grinned mischievously when Millie's jaw dropped. He pulled onto the freeway ramp and stepped on the accelerator.

Zach found an empty space in the paved parking area adjacent to the public park, and eased the truck in backwards. He turned off the engine and reached behind his seat and pulled out a rolled up beach towel. Millie went for the door handle and started to get out on her side when he held up his hand. "Hang on. Both my dad and my grandpa got on me about my manners." He walked around to her side of the truck, opened the door and handed her out, again making her feel like the belle of the ball.

Zach tucked his towel under his arm and punched the remote door lock before stuffing the keys in his front pocket. "Ready?" he asked her.

She nodded. Millie had to adjust her jeans and shirt, both sticking to her with sweat despite the truck's AC on full blower, but that gave her time to survey their surroundings. She estimated there were over a hundred people here for this picnic, all doctors, nurses, or administrative staff from St. Agnes Memorial Hospital in Oklahoma City. Some of them were still dressed in scrubs, obviously having come straight from work, but others were wearing shorts or swimsuits, and most had their families with them. In the background she heard some illegal firecrackers popping and marveled again at the scofflaws here in Oklahoma.

"Where do people get those bootleg fireworks?" she asked Zach. "Kaz had some this morning that Dad bought him."

Zach grinned at her. "Bootlegging's an Oklahoma tradition."

Millie laughed. "Right." She stood on tiptoe and tried to see over the crowd.

"What are you looking for?" Zach asked, following her gaze.

The sun was blazing overhead, not a cloud in the sky, but even with her sunglasses on Millie still had to shade her eyes with her hand. From where they stood, she could see sailboats out on the lake, so many in fact that it looked like a regatta. Off to the left of the picnic area was a roped-off section of water creating a beach, complete with diving-board and water slide, and the beach was filled with swimmers. Overseeing the swim area was a lifeguard tower with a handsome, tanned, muscular twenty-something man sitting in the chair, keeping an eye out for everyone's safety.

"Your parents," she replied to his question. "Are they here yet?" She scouted out the many picnic tables with families swarming around them, wondering which one the MacMillan family had claimed.

"Yeah, they're here," Zach said. "Mom sent me a text. Come on."

He led her on a short walk down a dirt path to a wooden picnic table that was blissfully sitting under a large oak tree, and festively covered with a plastic red and white checkered cloth. Millie said a silent thank-you for the shade.

"Hi, Mom," Zach said, kissing her on the cheek.

Jane MacMillan was a short, amply-padded woman in her early forties, dressed in khaki shorts, an oversized blue scrubs shirt, and white athletic shoes. Her hair was pulled back into a tight bun, from which a few stray hairs had escaped, and when she smiled her face lit up and her green eyes sparkled. Millie could see where Zach got his smile and gorgeous eyes.

Jane beamed with pleasure as she hugged Millie. "So glad you could join us. Alex told me how much you've changed since the last time we saw you."

"Mom...."

"Oh, I know, I know. Kids hate it when grownups say stuff like that."

"Where's Dad? And Zoe?"

Jane plopped down on the picnic bench and wiped her brow with a paper towel. "They went for a swim. I'd join them, but I came directly from work and don't have my suit, not that I'd like my coworkers to see me in a swimsuit anyway, but I told the two of them to go ahead while I get set up here."

"Do you need any help?" Millie asked. Truthfully she hoped she didn't have to exert herself in this heat, but she didn't want to be rude.

Zach shot his mother a look but Jane didn't need the warning. "No, Millie, thanks for offering. Since the hospital's providing drinks and the burgers and hot dogs, I brought all the side dishes. Including," she said with two thumbs-up to Zach, "my famous homemade potato salad. The master chefs — aka the on-call ER resident and the head of neurosurgery — said we'd eat promptly at 6:00." Jane laughed out loud at that idea, a deep guttural laugh that had a few other picnickers turning their heads in her direction. "That means it'll be ready about 7:00 at the earliest, depending on who gets stuck in the OR." Jane nodded a greeting toward those same hospital coworkers before turning back to Zach and Millie. "You two have plenty of time for swimming, volleyball, softball, whatever."

Zach looked at Millie, who was fanning herself with her bag. "Millie's not used to this heat, Mom, so I think we'll hit the beach."

Jane smiled at Millie. "I understand, and truthfully I doubt I'd survive one of your Indiana winters."

Zach again took Millie's hand, a turn of events she never would have believed she'd allow much less enjoy, and together they walked back up to the parking lot and followed the same path in the opposite direction to the roped-off swimming area. Adjacent to the beach was a wooden structure — a shack really — divided into men's and women's sections.

"Meet you back here!" Zach called as he squeezed and then released her hand.

Millie paused in the doorway to let her eyes adjust to the darkness, and hesitated before entering the women's side. Inside there were some outhouse-type bathroom stalls and a few extra booths with wooden benches for changing. The whole area smelled of urine and sweat; flies were swarming everywhere; wet toilet paper trailed along the mud-covered cement floor; and spiders had attached their webs to the corners of the only window, left open and letting in even more heat. Millie clapped a hand over her nose and mouth to ward off the stench, wondering if she was actually willing to change clothes in this place. But there was no alternative if she wanted to go for a swim with Zach. And she certainly did. Steeling herself, she looked inside each dressing stall for one that was even marginally clean, shaking her head at each one.

"You 'bout ready?" Zach called from outside.

Millie briefly removed her hand from her face. "Yeah, in a minute." She reluctantly chose a changing booth and hung her bag on a hook inside so that it wouldn't touch the floor. She managed to change out of her shorts without removing her shoes, her t-shirt draped around her neck, and into her swimsuit without touching the walls or seating bench. She shoved her arms back into the t-shirt, wrapped the towel around her waist, grabbed her bag and hurried out, shuddering. Suddenly a phrase from Synthia's journal popped into her head. *Cleanliness is next to Godliness Mama always said, and I share her aversion to filth.* Millie agreed and was beginning to feel a real affinity for this girl she'd begun to think of as her nineteenth century counterpart.

"That place is disgusting," Millie told Zach. She pulled a bottle of hand-sanitizer out of her bag and squirted a large blob into her palm, smearing it liberally onto her hands, neck and arms.

"Yeah, this ain't the Ritz," he chuckled. "Come on, it's hot out here."

"If you think it's hot…." Millie didn't finish her sentence but allowed Zach to put his hand on her back and pilot her to the beach area.

They had a good time in the water, splashing, playing Marco Polo with some younger kids, and just basking in the sand with the water splashing over their toes. Zach caught sight of his dad and sister swimming laps out in the deep water, but they didn't see him when he waved. It was early evening when they left the swimming area, the sun still broiling hot, and Millie assumed her swimsuit would dry just fine if she kept on wearing it underneath her shorts and t-shirt. No way was she going back into that filthy changing room.

"Millie! It's so cool you're here!" Zoe gave Millie a bear hug that nearly knocked her over as she and Zach approached the picnic table. Zach's fifteen-year-old sister was built like her father and brother—tall and chiseled—and Zoe had to reach down in order to enfold petite Millie in her arms.

"Thanks," Millie said, politely extricating herself before she was smothered. "You've—" she stepped back, holding Zoe at arm's length—"grown." She knew how that sounded, like she was so much older, but it was true. The last time she'd seen Zoe two years ago they were roughly the same height, and now Zoe towered over her.

Zoe giggled. "The women's basketball coach hopes I grow a few more inches."

"Yeah, that's all you need," Zach said with a playful punch to her shoulder.

Millie looked at brother and sister standing side by side and realized Zach was in danger of becoming the shorter of the two. "I hear you're quite good," Millie told her. "At basketball, I mean. Any chance for a scholarship?"

"Nothing like what you've got, I guess. Wow, Millie," Zoe gushed, "what's it like to be out of high school already? Top of your class at that cool private school up there in Indianapolis? Bet you've got your pick of colleges!"

Millie smiled at the unexpected hero worship. Truth be known, Millie envied Zoe her athletic ability and charismatic personality, with her tons of friends and active social life. "Well, um, well…" Millie stammered and then tried again. "I really don't have any definite college plans. My mom's really busy right now and might need my help."

"Hey, I was wondering if your mom would autograph one of her books for me." Zoe snickered behind her hand.

"Sure," Millie told her. "I'll text Mom to send you the latest one."

"Wow, thanks!" Zoe craned her neck and scouted out the crowd. "I'm starved. Where's Mom?" she asked Zach.

Millie had refrained from checking the time on her cell phone, not wanting to appear rude, but she was sure it was nearly eight o'clock by now and her stomach was growling fiercely.

"So it turns out our esteemed head of neurology is also a decent chef," Jane said from behind them as she set a plate of steaming food on the table. "Fast, too, since he got held up in surgery and still managed to grill up a storm! Burgers and hot dogs are served. Help yourself, kids. Where's your dad?"

Alex sauntered over with an armload of sodas, water, and lemonade. "Right here! A little help?" Zach grabbed the gallon jug of lemonade as his dad set the cans and plastic bottles down on their table alongside the cooked meats and side dishes.

Jane began passing around her filled plastic containers and Millie loaded her plate with more food than she would ever be able to eat: one hamburger, two hot dogs, coleslaw, watermelon squares, and a large scoop of Jane's homemade potato salad. Eyes bigger than your stomach she knew Gran would say. Still, since it was way past supper time and she was famished, she ignored her inner voice and forked up a big bite of the potato salad.

"Yum!" Millie exclaimed.

Jane blushed. "Old recipe of the family — Alex's mother's in fact."

Millie nodded, swallowed, and turned to Alex. "Dad's here," she said before catching herself. "Oh, sorry. Non sequitur."

"Non what?" Zoe asked.

"It means it doesn't follow," Alex explained to his daughter. "Literally that Millie changed the subject without notice." Zoe shrugged and went back to her burger, chasing it down with a long swig of canned soda. Alex turned to Millie and said, "So Karl's in town?"

"He got in last night and sends his regards to you and Jane."

Zach stopped in mid-hot dog bite, furrowed his brow, and then threw one leg over the picnic bench to turn sideways and face Millie. "If your dad's here, does that mean you," he blushed and then amended his statement, "I mean you and Kaz and Charlie — you're heading back to Indiana?"

Millie watched the expression on his face and thought she saw more than mild interest in their travel plans. At least she hoped she did. Zach was waiting for

an answer so she shook her head. "This is just a stopo-
ver before Dad heads to Toronto to join Mom."

Zach looked visibly relieved. "Good," he said as
he quickly squeezed her hand and just as quickly released it before anyone noticed.

Millie felt a chill run up her spine and wondered
if there had been a change in the wind. She looked up
at the nearby tree but not a leaf was stirring. Weird.

With a sideways glance at Zach, Alex said to Millie, "Apparently I'm not the only one who's glad
you're sticking around for a while." When Jane shot
her husband a warning look, he added, "So we can
delve into this journal mystery a little deeper, I mean."

"I don't get what you guys find so interesting in
that old book," Zach said as he turned back around
and addressed his burger.

"Synthia was in a tough spot and I really admire
how she handled it. Wish I had some of her courage,"
Millie admitted.

"What did she do that was so courageous anyway?" Zach asked.

Millie shrugged. "I'm pretty sure I wouldn't have
wanted to drive a covered wagon through Indian Territory in 1865."

Zach took off his hat, ran a finger through his hair,
and then put the baseball cap on backwards again.
"Boorrinngg. Pass the coleslaw."

Alex frowned his displeasure. "It's history, son, a
subject it wouldn't hurt you to put a little more effort
into."

Zoe jumped up from the table and waved at some
kids at the other end of the picnic area. "Gotta go,
Mom. Volleyball game!" She tossed her napkin on top
of her empty paper plate and grabbed the swim towel

she'd been sitting on, rewrapping it tightly around her waist. "See y'all at the fireworks!"

"Ten o'clock, missy! Meet us there and be on time!" her mother called after her.

Jane started clearing off the table and Millie took that as a signal to get up to assist. Jane wouldn't hear of it. "I got this. You and Zach should go hang out with kids your age. We'll all meet up at the fireworks later."

Millie hesitated. "Are you sure?" Jane nodded and continued stuffing trash into the large plastic garbage bag.

"See ya, Mom," Zach said before Jane could change her mind.

He took Millie's hand and led her in the direction of the playground, which was accessed from a downward-sloping dirt path not too far from the picnic area. With the lack of rain this summer, dust flew everywhere and made the path difficult to navigate. Loose pebbles scattered easily when stepped on, making the gravel slippery and causing Millie to lose her footing. Zach grabbed her arm to steady her just as she skidded on the rocks and nearly fell. She smiled up at him gratefully, and his response was to put his arm around her waist and hold on tight, making her feel completely safe as they walked the path.

When they reached the bottom of the hill, Zach looked around for a likely group to join and Millie fretted about which of the ongoing games she might get forced into. In the early-evening heat, no less. She thought it prudent not to mention her distinct lack of athletic ability and silently began dreading the inevitable.

Over on the swing set were some younger children and their parents. There was that volleyball game

off to the left, with Zoe serving up one zinger after another, and there was a basketball game of shirts versus
skins going on in the distance, but the court was filled
with grown men, so at least that was out. And then
there were the teenagers on the baseball diamond engaged in a raucous game of softball, a game Millie was
particularly bad at, unlike her siblings. Zach waved at
some of the outfielders and Millie sighed. "I could sit
and watch the game if you want to go play."

"Watch? Geez, Millie, don't you ever get any exercise? Weren't you on any teams at school?" She
shook her head. "Aw, come on. I know they have actual sports teams at that private school of yours, 'cause
Kaz plays on 'em."

Millie's heart sank. Would Zach lose interest in
her if he knew the truth? She busied herself dusting off
her sandals so she wouldn't have to look him in the
eye. "Debate team," she muttered.

"Debate?"

Millie finished dusting her shoes and stood up.
"Well, sort of. Robby Grayson was State Champion
and my junior year he wanted me to join his team, but
I was way too self-conscious to get up and speak ex-
temporaneously in front of strangers, so I did all of
Robby's research for him and went to tournaments to
help him organize his speeches."

Zach whistled softly. "Debate. No sports, just a lot
of talk. And you didn't even do the talking."

Millie tried to sit down on a large rock but it was
too hot and she jumped back up. "If it makes a difference, Robby's pre-law at Harvard," she said, "so I'm
proud I could help him." She wiped the sweat off the
back of her neck as they stood in silence. "Are those
your friends down there? Don't you want to go join

them?"

"Thought about it."

"Go ahead. I'll just sit under that shade tree and wait." Millie set off toward a large tree where there was some shaded grass, away from the red dirt that seemed to be everywhere in Oklahoma and would no doubt stain her jeans. She sat down cross-legged and began picking through the grass, hoping for a four-leaf clover, all while keeping an eye on Zach out of the corner of her eye.

Zach stood watching her from a distance, cast a wistful glance at the softball game, but instead walked over and sat down on the ground next to her. "It's kinda funny, I guess."

Millie looked up from her search. "What's funny?"

"How we met, or should I say 're-met?' A girl who doesn't like exercise climbing a ladder at her grandmother's house. Sort of a, a…" He fumbled for the right word.

"…an aberration," Millie finished for him.

Zach laughed and picked at the grass awhile himself. "People would think we're total opposites. You use all those big words and get all excited about an old diary, and I'm struggling just to pass a history test so I can graduate and get an athletic scholarship," he said. "Say, here's a four-leaf!" He pulled up his prize and placed it in Millie's hand.

Millie was flabbergasted. Without even trying, Zach had found a lucky clover, making it seem so easy, when to her the whole search was such a struggle. "We are different," she sighed, "and you even found that four-leaf when I completely overlooked it."

"I gave it to you, didn't I? What does that tell

you?" Zach leaned back on his elbows, his long legs outstretched and his ankles crossed. "What I meant was, we're different, but so what? That's what I like about you — how smart you are."

"Smart, right," Millie nodded, getting his point. "I guess that's why you want to spend time with me, so I can help you pass that test."

Zach sat up straight and looked at her in dismay. "Is that what you think?" He shook his head. "Millie, I like you, I've always liked you, and I wouldn't use you like that. When we were little kids I was always trying to impress you, but I'd end up rambling on too much about sports and then you'd get mad and rattle off some big words I didn't understand and..."

Millie smiled at him. "And then I'd get incensed because I thought you were annoying me on purpose."

"'Incensed' huh?" Zach said with a smirk. They sat in silence awhile, watching the softball game in the distance. "Good hit, Thompson!" he shouted to a muscular teenage boy running bases toward a homerun. After a few minutes he turned back to Millie. "So what'll you be studying your freshman year in college?"

Millie forced down the lump in her throat. "I'd be a sophomore."

"Huh?"

"Advanced Placement tests," Millie explained. "I got fives on AP Lit; AP Lang/Comp; AP Chem; AP French; AP Gov; AP History; and a stupid four on my AP Calculus exam, 'cause that's my hardest subject."

"Wow. Cool. So what college are you gonna be a sophomore?"

Millie squirmed. "I still have a few decisions to make."

Zach's jaw dropped. "It's the Fourth of July and you don't know where you're going to college yet?"

Millie stood up and dusted off her shorts. "My parents want me to go to New York, my best friend's pushing Indiana University, Gran's insisting on Oklahoma Liberal Arts, and…" Her voice trailed off, "…and I'm tired of being pressured." She started walking briskly, retracing her steps along the path. She took a quick glance over her shoulder and saw Zach standing there looking stunned.

It was getting dark now, stars were appearing in the sky, and off in the distance someone was shooting off more firecrackers. It would be time for the fireworks display soon so Millie quickened her step, walking pretty fast for someone who disliked heat and exercise. She hoped to put some distance between her and this latest bout of peer pressure.

"Hey, wait up!" Zach called as he sprinted to catch up to her. He took her hand and slowed down his pace, forcing her to slow down, too, and together they walked on in silence, side-by-side.

People were beginning to gather in the baseball bleachers for the fireworks display that was set to start at 10:00 p.m., courtesy of the hospital administrators who got a special permit for the show. Zach helped her climb up over the metal benches, where she steered clear of the spilled soda and half-eaten hot dog someone had discarded on the steps. They found a seat at the very top and settled in. He stood up to search the crowd, spotted his parents and waved, and sat back down again. Someone had a portable radio and it was tuned to a local station playing patriotic music, a perfect complement to the fireworks.

BOOM BOOM BOOM

The opening white flashes introduced the program, and Millie watched in awe as the colorful display filled the sky. Zach took her hand in his and wouldn't let her pull away.

"I agree with your grandma," he whispered in her ear. "You should go to OLAC. I'd like it if you were nearby."

Millie wondered if the tingle down her spine was just a reaction to the pyrotechnic electricity in the air, or if it was these new feelings for Zach. The light display in the sky on this warm evening created a romantic mood, and couples all around were cuddling as they oohed and ahhed and pointed skyward. Zach pulled her close and kissed her, her first kiss ever, and she got so caught up in the moment that it felt completely natural to kiss him back.

As the grand finale splayed across the night sky, Millie chided herself for having a crush on a boy in Oklahoma, a popular high school boy who could date any girl he wanted, and wondered why he would pick someone like her with all her neuroses. Zach didn't seem to notice her introspection, though, so Millie sighed, leaned her head on his shoulder and told herself that, like Scarlet O'Hara, she'd deal with that tomorrow.

Chapter Ten
A Different Perspective

October 5, 1865

During our journey over the last few days, Mary Ann has been listless and shown little interest in our usual games, such as I spy with my own little eye… or ABC Bible characters.

"Synthia," she whimpered yesterday, "my head hurts."

When I put my hand to her forehead I noticed she was warm to the touch. She has not been eating well, which I attributed to the strain of travel, but now I am quite worried because we are so far from civilization, not to mention a doctor. I am hoping that she will rally her spirits soon. I have tried some of Mama's home remedies, those at hand in this uncivilized territory: beef broth, a cold compress, lemon drops, but Mary Ann still does not improve. We must needs continue our journey, so my sister has taken to riding with her head in my lap or lying on a pallet in the back of the wagon, undoubtedly an uncomfortable place for a sick child. I am quite concerned and can do nothing except pray for her recovery.

October 9, 1865.

Another day and Mary Ann is still feverish and listless, and now I am getting frantic. I refuse to lose another family member, and certainly not here in the wilds of Indian Territory! I spoke with Mrs. Carrington, who was busy lighting her fire to cook the evening meal, as she has more experience in these matters than I.

Mrs. Carrington was of necessity distracted. "Miss Whitfield," she replied as she carefully placed her prepared biscuit dough into the spider pan and placed the lid on tightly, "children can suddenly take sick and just as quickly recover. Let her be."

"Too many days have passed with no improvement," I insisted. I knew my next question was borne of desperation, but I inquired anyway. "Is there perhaps someone among us with medical knowledge?"

Mrs. Carrington stood up from her now-lit fire and shook her head. "You could ask the captain, but I expect that will come to naught." She thought for a moment. "If this were Samuel, I might be tempted to approach some of the Natives who are frequently among us. I have heard their medicine men are quite skilled. But mind you, that would be my last resort."

I certainly gave that serious consideration, but approach an Indian? Did I dare?
Speaking to Indians was a frightening propo-
sition, but I was running out of options and
must do what I could to keep my family safe.
I thanked her and turned to leave, but then
thought of one more question. "Do they
speak English?"

At camp time I prepared supper for the
three of us as usual, and again Mary Ann refused food, so I told my brother, "Stay with
our sister until I return." And off I went to
seek help from any of the imposing Natives
who might offer assistance.

I was forced to walk the entire length of
the camp until I spied two Indians negotiat-
ing a trade with a family I did not know. Unlike depictions of half-naked men in feather
headdress that I have seen in newspapers or
books, these men were fully clothed in quite
colorful attire—red trousers, work shirts fes-
tooned with ribbons, and boots that were not
unlike what all the other men in camp wore.
Their hats were adorned with feathers and sat
atop their long, dark braided hair. I felt my
heart beat wildly as I approached one of
them, a man who seemed about the age of my
late father. "I beg your pardon, sir," I began.

He said nothing but turned to me with a
bemused expression.

"My sister is taken with a fever. I wonder
if there is any remedy you might suggest…"

He did not respond, nor did I know if he
even understood me. He turned and walked

away, leaving me bereft.

October 10, 1865.

"Synthia! Synthia, wake up!" I opened my eyes to note that it was not even dawn, yet my brother was shaking me vigorously.

"What is it, TJ?" I asked with a yawn. "It's not yet time to arise."

"Synthia, we got company!" he practically shouted. At this news I sat straight up in the wagon and peered out through the canvas. TJ was correct. Outside stood the same Native I had spoken to earlier about a remedy for Mary Ann. I quickly grabbed my shawl and scrambled out, tentatively approaching him.

I knew no way to begin the conversation, but I was quite certain I must remember my manners. "Good morning, sir," I said.

He pressed into my hand what looked like a wad of leaves. I looked up at him, confused.

"Common sumac. Make tea. The child will recover." And as quickly as he'd come, he was gone.

October 12, 1865.

I did what the Indian told me. I sent TJ to the nearby fresh-water spring where he had caught fish for our supper the night before, and instructed him to bring back plenty of clean water in a jug. I heated some of the water in a tin mug near the fire and Mary Ann drank the tea (with a bit of sugar added, as she complained of its bitterness) until the tea was gone. I repeated this process with the remaining leaves at supper and as predicted, she was well in two days' time. I am so relieved!

Millie sat cross-legged on her bed, staring at her phone, reading and rereading the last entries she'd photographed in Synthia's journal. Approach a Native American in the middle of Indian Territory? What that girl did to find a cure for her little sister was beyond brave. Millie leaned her head back against the pillow and marveled at the girl's bravery and determination. *Would I have had the courage to do something like that for my sister? If Charlie or Kaz got sick, what would I do?*

At home in Indianapolis, her mom kept a list of important phone numbers on a bulletin board in the laundry room, but Millie seldom looked at it since she had a near-photographic memory. Now she closed her eyes and visualized the list. It contained the usual police and fire emergency numbers, but it also listed the pediatrician and the nearest pharmacy. Millie was confident that if either sibling got sick she would call the doctor, describe the symptoms, call Mom or Dad, and then drive the sick child to the pediatrician's office.

But wait, would it be that easy? What if it was winter? Snow, sleet or ice are frequent occurrences in Indianapolis and sometimes the sand trucks or snowplows can't keep up. Roads can quickly become impassable, and a simple trip to the pediatrician might take hours or even be impossible. What would she do then?

Millie wracked her brain for a logical solution to her hypothetical problem. Synthia was bold and approached a total stranger out of necessity, but in the twenty-first century Millie would need a more practical plan. *Well, there's always Dr. Henderson,* she thought. Even though Carlye's father is a busy surgeon, he's always available for his children, so she was sure Carlye would be willing to call her dad for her and ask for advice.

Millie's spirits rallied a little. Reading Synthia's diary reminded her that she wasn't helpless when it came to making important decisions and maybe, just maybe, she could even overcome her inertia about her education. "So now I just need to figure out how," she told herself.

"What did you need to figure out, dear?" Gran was standing in the open doorway, a pile of freshly-laundered clothes in her hand.

"Oh, nothing," Millie said. She toggled to a different screen on her phone and pretended to be absorbed in the information. "I was just figuring out if Dad's plane would arrive in Toronto on time, and hoping Mom was at the airport to greet him." Millie took the laundry from her grandmother and began putting things away in the proper dresser drawers.

"What are your plans for the day, dear?" Gran gave her a knowing wink. "Meeting up with Zach?"

Millie shook her head. "I haven't seen too much of Zach this past week." Oh sure, he'd been here to mow and water Gran's lawn and prune the bushes, and Millie had even taken him a glass of Gran's lemonade, but otherwise she hadn't really seen him. That July 4th kiss confused her, and she didn't know what to do about all her mixed up emotions and fears.

Gran sat down on the edge of Millie's bed. "You two seemed to be getting along so well. Did something happen?"

Millie slumped down on the bed and leaned her head on her grandmother's shoulder. "No. We had fun, but then at the fireworks…." Her voice trailed off.

"Fireworks can be romantic," Gran said with a twinkle in her eye.

Millie first blushed and then smiled. "Okay, it was nice. But Zach and I are just too different. He even said so. I mean, he's got to finish high school, and I'm…." She shrugged. "I don't know what I am."

Gran lifted Millie's chin. "I know you pretty well, dear, and I can tell you have a crush on that boy."

"Maybe, but…."

Gran gave Millie's shoulder a hug. "I'm sure Zach likes you, too. Mac said as much."

"Mac?" Millie's eyes widened with surprise, but then she shook her head. "It doesn't matter anyway. I'm going home soon, and Zach…."

"You're giving up too easily," Gran told her with a tsk-tsk.

"What are your plans today?" Millie asked, deliberately changing the subject.

Gran took the bait, stood up and smoothed the wrinkles from her skirt. "Well, I'm off to church for a meeting post-auction, which was financially successful this year, by the way. Then I'm joining Ma…a friend, for lunch."

Millie was barely listening, her mind turning over all the seemingly insurmountable problems she had to deal with, so she didn't even notice Gran quietly shut the bedroom door behind her.

So what am I going to do? Millie wondered. Suddenly she remembered Synthia's journal that was at OLAC with Alex's colleague and knew that, if nothing else, she had to get it back and learn the results of his analysis.

Millie had survived her first trip to the campus with Zach's help, but going back solo required a lot more courage, and definitely the right wardrobe. She began rummaging in her closet for the perfect outfit to make her feel like she actually belonged on a college campus, but before she could decide what to wear, her cell phone rang and she had to search around in the bedcovers to unearth it. "Hello?" Silence. "Hellooo?" She pulled the phone back for a look at the origination but the caller ID had gone blank. Frustrated, she disconnected the phone and tossed it back on her bed. It rang right back.

"Geez, Millie, I was trying to swallow my coffee and you hung up on me. Give a guy a chance!"

"Michael?"

"Who else? Didn't you check your caller ID?" He took a large slurp of coffee. "Bad news. Notre Dame closed fall admissions, so you're probably on a wait list now."

Thank goodness! "Oh, too bad," Millie said.

"Call Carlye," he suggested. "Maybe she'll take you down to IU if it's not too late. Isn't that your safety school?"

"Well, no, well, yes, it's just that, um, Indiana University, it's so...so huge," she sputtered, "and Carlye's not even going to be there first semester. I don't know...."

"Ugh, Millie. All that whining sounds like your kid brother. Use those valedictorian brains of yours and figure something out!"

"I'm working on it!" Millie exclaimed as she disconnected her phone.

Millie gave up on the wardrobe search and instead went out into the hall, pulled down the ladder to her grandmother's attic, walked up and flipped on the light switch at the top of the stairs which set the ceiling fan to whirring. She started to sit down in the rocking chair but realized Charlie's doll Lucinda was sitting there. She picked the doll up, hugged her and sat down to rock.

"Well," she said to Lucinda, "I guess Charlie's going to wonder where you ended up this time."

Millie rocked back and forth. For a fleeting moment she wished she hadn't graduated from high school so young. She'd spent all her years at Kendrick studying hard to get ahead and stay ahead of her classmates, oblivious to the social isolation she was creating for herself. If she were a year or two older, maybe she'd have enjoyed high school more and acquired the maturity and self-confidence to be happily making plans to attend college in a few weeks. Instead, that idea still sent chills down her spine.

She sighed as her gaze drifted around the attic, finally settling on the trunk where she'd found Synthia Whitfield's journal. She got up from the rocker and walked over, carefully lifting the wooden lid with the wrought iron handle. The smell of cedar wafted out again, just like the last time, but this time Millie just stared inside. *What do you think you're going to find in there this time? A magic wand?* She laughed softly and shook her head.

"What now?" she asked herself as she gently closed the lid. "What would Synthia do?" Not sit around feeling sorry for herself, that's for sure.

Suddenly it came to her, almost like Synthia had whispered the answer in her ear. The library! The only places Millie had ever felt comfortable were academic settings—schools, museums, libraries—so that's where she knew she had to go. She would do a genealogy search on the Whitfield family and maybe get that question resolved. Then she would force herself to get onto Indiana University's website and see what courses were still available for fall semester, which might help her decide if she could actually enroll there without the comforting presence of her best friend.

Millie waltzed into her bedroom and changed out of her cutoffs and into a sundress. She quickly ran a comb through her hair and put on a headband, grabbed her purse and raced out the back door.

Millie easily found a public parking space in front of OLAC's library. She put the Toyota in park and as usual, cracked all four windows down an inch. Late July in Oklahoma had brought on an unprecedented heat wave and drought, and Millie felt a little homesick for the relatively mild Indiana summers. She locked the car door with the remote and hurried into the air-conditioned university library.

The building was old, probably dating to the turn of the twentieth century like most of the buildings on campus, but she felt an instant affinity with its history and architecture. As she stepped in the door and admired the stately dignity, she felt completely at home. She thrilled to the sound of her heels clicking and echoing on the original tile flooring as she made her way across the entry.

There was a hub adjacent to the entrance that had originally been the check-out desk, but now it housed a computer bay with access to the online card catalog, and was staffed by an elderly librarian standing in front of an INFORMATION sign. The gray-haired lady peered over her glasses which had slid down her nose. "May I help you, Miss?"

Millie had to stifle a giggle. If there ever was a stereotypical librarian, she was it: gray hair in a topknot, old-fashioned white blouse with a knee-length navy-blue skirt, and an antique watch dangling from a chain on her blouse. Her nametag read Harriet Sullivan.

"Um, yes, Ms. Sullivan, I'm interested in doing some research on a family named Whitfield, who possibly lived in Oklahoma City in the early twentieth century."

Very unstereotypically, Ms. Sullivan went to a nearby computer and began rapidly keying in information. She hit enter and then smiled over the glasses on her nose. "I don't see anything here, but I can certainly help you locate what information we may have in the stacks. I just need to see your student ID."

Millie's spirits flagged. "I'm not a student here," she admitted. "Does that mean I can't even look?"

Harriet eyed Millie closely. "Potential student?"

"Well, I was accepted for the fall term, but…" She stopped, not willing to tell an outright lie just to get access to the genealogy records, so she decided to try another approach. "Do you know my grandmother, Mildred Olson? She lives here in Rolling Plains."

Harriet's face suddenly lit up as she smiled at Millie. "I do indeed know your grandmother. We're on several committees together at Ogden Church."

Millie relaxed. "Then you probably know Alexander MacMillan. He's a history professor here and he's been helping me…"

"Well, of course I know Alex!" Harriet exclaimed. "In fact, he was just in here. I'll tell you what…" She paused and lowered her voice. "What is your name again?"

"It's also Mildred Olson. But everyone calls me Millie."

Harriet cocked her head to one side and scrutinized her. "So you're Karl Olson's daughter. What a football star he was back in the day!"

Millie smiled and nodded politely.

"Well, that settles it! Let me show you where to begin your search. You know," Harriet added as she walked Millie to the back of the library, "I'm a huge football fan and I went to every game your dad played in. We all expected he'd go pro, but instead he went to law school."

Millie was completely taken aback by this woman who looked so much like an old-fashioned Marion-the-librarian-type, but who turned out to be not only computer savvy but a football enthusiast as well. She happily followed Harriet Sullivan through the stacks and up a flight of metal steps to an area in the back of the library where very old books and public records were housed. Harriet placed her fingers to her lips to indicate silence, pointed to a row of books, and winked at Millie before turning to leave.

Millie ran her fingers across the leather-bound edges lined up chronologically, looking for a year or reference to point her in the right direction. "Aha!" she said, but then clapped a hand over her mouth and scolded herself. *You're in a library.* She pulled several books off the shelf and dropped them with a loud thud on a nearby table.

"Hey, people are trying to study around here!" someone behind her admonished.

Startled, Millie wheeled around and came face-to-face with Zach! Her mouth dropped open. Zach had been sitting at a study table in a far corner, books and papers spread everywhere, his laptop computer open in front of him.

"Um, sorry. I didn't mean…I didn't know…" Millie was flabbergasted and had no idea what she meant to say, so she took a deep breath and tried again. "What are you doing here?"

Zach rolled his eyes. "Dad brought me up here. And you don't have to look so surprised. I've been in libraries before."

Millie walked over to the table where Zach was sitting, turned some of his notes around to get a good look at them, and then thumbed through the scattered papers. "What are you studying?"

Zach leaned back in the wooden chair, clasped his fingers behind his head and grinned. "I guess you wouldn't believe me if I said I was just trying to get ahead for fall." Millie pulled a face. "Busted." He shrugged. "This is where I've been hanging out lately."

Millie realized that she'd been worried about not seeing Zach and he'd been in the library studying, not ignoring her. She turned aside since she didn't want to meet his gaze and instead pretended to be re-examining his papers. "History," she said, looking up from his notes. "Nineteenth century?"

Zach nodded and set the chair back down on all fours. "Government, history, politics, pre-Civil War stuff." He looked overwhelmed. "Dad said if I'm going to pass that history test before school starts, I'd better get studying." He sighed and tossed his pencil on top of his notes.

"Why isn't your dad helping you?"

"Did you ever let your dad help you with school-work?"

Of course not, there was no need! was what Millie started to say, but stopped herself. She understood his meaning, that asking a parent for homework help was a last resort. She flipped through the pages of the high school history textbook and then looked again at the notes he'd been taking. This was simple stuff really, material she'd covered at least three years ago.

Zach rubbed the back of his neck, and then leveled his gaze at her. "What are you doing here?"

Millie dragged a chair across the floor and sat down across from Zach. "Trying to figure out where Synthia Whitfield's journal came from, or who it came from. Found some reference material," she said, pointing to the books she'd dropped so loudly on the table. Then an idea came to her. "Hey, what if I help you with your history and then you can help me!"

"Help you what?"

"Get the results of the paper analysis on Synthia's diary from your dad's colleague. Maybe you could walk me over there."

Zach gave her a crooked half-smile. "Well, yeah, I guess I can take you there. If you're sure you've got time to help me. Since I haven't heard from you lately I figured you were packing for Indianapolis."

Millie could feel the color rising in her cheeks and she looked away. "I guess we've both been preoccupied."

Zach leaned across the table and reached for Millie's hand. "I thought we had a good time at the picnic, that we were good together."

"We did. We were, but…"

Zach released her hand in frustration. "But a high

school boyfriend doesn't fit into your plans. Right?"

"No, that's not it, I…"

"Then what?"

"I've got some decisions to make, and I'm still fending off everyone's expectations about college," she said with a frown, remembering Michael's earlier phone call.

"Hey, would you look at that?" Zach made a big show of standing up, turning completely around and waving his arms at their surroundings. "We're in a college right now."

Millie thought his gestures were pretty funny and she had to bite her lip to keep from laughing. Finally, when she had the giggles under control, she said, "I know we're in a college library, but…"

Zach shook his head. "Oklahoma Liberal Arts is a pretty decent school, Millie. You've been accepted here. Your dad went here. So what's the problem?"

"I don't know…"

"What's not to know? Just get online and sign up for classes." He reached out and gave her hand a squeeze.

Millie shook her head, but with Zach this close she couldn't focus, because her heart was beating so fast it felt like it was going to jump right out of her chest. She took a deep, calming breath and said, "Right now I just want that journal back, so I'll help you study but that's all I'm willing to commit to for the moment."

Zach grinned at her and his smile made her quiver all over. Millie turned his book around. "Political theory. That's so…" She started to say 'easy,' but stopped herself and said, "Okay, let's start with the Lincoln-Douglas debates."

Zach plopped back down in the chair and looked

at the section of the page Millie was pointing to. "Okay, fine, but then we're going to dad's office, and then we're going for frozen yogurt."

This time Millie couldn't stop the smile that was creeping over her face as she tried to be serious about his history lesson. "Yogurt sounds good," she said without looking up.

"Hey, Dad!"

Millie and Zach had both been so engrossed in nineteenth century politics that they hadn't noticed when Alex walked up.

"Millie, what a pleasant surprise," Alex said. "What brings you in here?"

Millie began gathering up the reference books she hadn't even touched to place them on the re-shelving cart. "Well, I was planning to do some research on the Whitfield family, but I sort of got side-tracked." Zach winked at her and she blushed all over again.

Zach jerked his thumb at her. "She's as smart as everyone says." He stood up and started packing up his book bag. "I was going to bring her over to your office in a while anyway, because of that journal...."

Alex slapped his forehead and nodded. "I forgot all about that. And good timing, too. Steven's on campus today, so we could walk over to the chemistry department right now if you're free."

"That's great!" Millie exclaimed.

"And then," Zach added, "I promised to 'pay' Millie for her tutoring with a scoop of Mrs. Swenson's homemade frozen yogurt."

Alex helped his son shove the chairs back under the table. "Thanks for your help, Millie. I know Zach struggles with history," he said, "in spite of my best efforts."

Millie stopped at the INFORMATION desk on her way out with Zach and Alex. "Thanks again for your help, Ms. Sullivan."

"You come back any time," Harriet said. "Karl Olson's daughter is always welcome in this library."

Millie felt a comforting sense of welcome and familiarity from both Ms. Sullivan and the people on this small college campus. It was true what Gran always said about Oklahomans: they're very friendly and helpful.

Alex, Zach, and Millie stepped out into the midday heat and Millie instinctively sucked in her breath. She pulled her sunglasses out of her bag and adjusted them on her face as Alex led the way to the forensics department across campus. All the way over there? Millie groaned inwardly. She could already feel the sweat glistening on her forehead as they circled around the pond in the Quad and walked between some very old stone buildings on their way to the more modern structure across from the men's dormitories. Alex swiped his campus ID badge in the access panel, and when the door buzzed, he held it open to let Millie and Zach through.

"This way," he said, pointing to a long corridor at the end of the hall.

They walked through the 1960s era building and down the narrow hallway to a door near the opposite exit. Millie looked at the nameplate which read Dr. Steven Riley, Forensic Science Department Chair—Students Admitted by Appointment Only.

"Do you think it's okay to just pop in on him like this?" Millie asked as she read the notice.

Alex knocked on the door and then tried the knob,

which turned easily in his hand. "I guess we'll find out." He pushed the door open and led the way in.

Chapter Eleven
The Reveal

Alex extended his hand to Professor Riley as they all walked into the office. "Sorry to barge in, Steven, but this young lady," he said with a nod toward Millie, "was eager to hear your findings about that old journal."

Millie could barely control her excitement, despite her efforts to appear calm and patient. Was Synthia's diary real? Millie always prided herself on her intellectual logic, so if the diary was a hoax, she didn't think she could bear the disappointment or the embarrassment of being duped. And never mind how much she'd begun to admire the courage of a fifteen-year-old girl from nearly two centuries ago.

I just know it's real, she told herself. Still, the suspense was killing her. It was all she could do to keep from jumping up and down in anticipation, like Charlie sometimes did when she was excited. She reminded herself to behave in a mature fashion while in the presence of these college professors, because valedictorians didn't giggle and jump around like eight-year-olds. "Did you get a chance to look at it, Professor?"

Professor Riley rummaged through a pile of scattered books on his cluttered, old-fashioned wooden desk. For a moment Millie panicked, wondering how he could treat such an artifact so carelessly, assuming it was an artifact. But instead of the journal, he yanked a printed report out from underneath some used exam blue books and nodded as he looked it over. "It's real, all right. It dates to late nineteenth century for the most part, although some of it appears to have been written earlier than that."

Millie instinctively exhaled and didn't even realize she'd been holding her breath. "Oh, that's good. I was so afraid I'd been wrong, that it was a reproduction."

Millie did a visual search of the room, but in all the clutter she couldn't lock in on the actual journal. On the back wall of the office was a set of built-in cabinets with sliding glass doors. Inside the cabinets Millie could see every kind of book imaginable, some of them vintage leather-bound volumes, and others more modern. She stared at the collection in awe, but then she blanched at the thought of Synthia's diary being shoved in there with all that mess.

Professor Riley followed her gaze. "Don't worry, Millie, I've taken good care of it." He reached into his pocket and pulled out a set of keys, fumbled for the correct one, and opened a metal drawer underneath one of the cabinets. He pulled out a white muslin bag with a drawstring and, holding it flat, carefully handed it to her. "I'd recommend you keep it in this bag from now on. The journal's old, but it's obviously stood the test of time, so just treat it with care and it should be fine."

"So, Steven," Alex said as Millie gingerly lifted the diary out of the bag, "tell us exactly how you determined its authenticity."

"Elementary, my dear Alexander," the professor said in a feigned English accent with a flourish of his arms. Alex laughed, Zach winced, and Millie looked on in amusement at their easy camaraderie. Professor Riley continued, "It's written on a wood-based paper, which by about 1850 had become cheap and readily available, frequently used in letter writing and personal diaries of the late nineteenth century. You've also probably noticed that most of it is written in pencil, and pencils were being mass-produced from about the 1830s on."

"But some of it's written in ink," Millie pointed out, gently thumbing through the pages.

"Fountain pen, also mass-produced, although I'd say Miss Whitfield had more pencils at her disposal than pens."

Millie nodded as she carefully turned the pages. "Here's where I left off when I snapped those photos," she told Zach, pointing to the spot. "Synthia was actually driving a covered wagon!"

"What happens next?" Alex asked.

Millie was also eager to read more of the story, so she was happy to oblige and began reading aloud.

"October 15, 1865.

"Our wagon train crossed the rest of the way through Indian Territory with few other encounters with the Natives. Eventually we came to The Red River that divides Indian

Territory from Texas, aptly named for its reddish color due to a type of mud called red clay. We stopped and all of us stood in awe of its immenseness. The captain said we were fortunate that there had been a drought during the summer, and therefore the waters are quite low enough to safely drive the wagons across. Otherwise we would have had to hire a ferry and that was one more expense I had not planned on. Crossing the river caused a delay of two days, as it was very slow going with twenty wagons attempting to cross, one at a time.

"I guess that so-called Civil War drought was good for something, huh?" Millie said. "And now she's encountered the infamous Oklahoma red clay!

"Once on the other side, though, I knew that TJ, Mary Ann and I must part company with the wagon train and strike out on our own, as they are headed to Dallas. I consulted with Mr. Carrington, who assured me that Nevada, Texas, is but two or three days' journey to the west of our current location. I gave the captain our notice and now we must go it alone."

Millie stopped reading, her eyes wide. "She's leaving the wagon train?" She turned to Alex. "Wouldn't that be dangerous? She's only fifteen."

"She made it that far," Zach pointed out.

"Texas was considerably more civilized than Indian Territory in 1865, so once they'd crossed the border she was probably much safer," Alex replied.

"Where's she headed?"

"To her uncle's farm in north Texas, but I don't want to bore anyone." By that Millie meant Zach, but she was surprised to see him actually listening.

Zach plopped himself into a chair, stretched out and crossed his ankles. "It doesn't suck. Go on."

Millie eyed him suspiciously, but her curiosity about the journal won out. "Well, okay, just a little more.

"October 20, 1865.

"The weather here is quite warm for late October. In Missouri an autumnal chill would have been in the air by now, but here the sun shines directly down upon us, the vegetation is still green albeit sun scorched, and my brother, sister and I are free to go about during the day without a wrap. The land appears to be rather flat, mostly prairie, and farmland is all there is to see for miles around. I would assume some of the farmers have been late bringing in their crops due to the dry weather. There are worn dirt roads which are easily navigated, indicating a population of some sort nearby, but as of yet we have met not a soul. We are all of us very tired, running out of food, and ready to be at the end of this journey.

"Arriving at my uncle's farm outside the little town of Nevada took longer than anticipated, five days instead of the promised three. We had seen no one on the road from dawn till dusk and I had begun to despair for fear of being lost, when finally we encountered folks traveling. I asked for directions, but one (I suppose) well-meaning gentleman unfortunately pointed me nearly a mile out of our way. Then I approached another solitary traveler on foot who corrected our mistake, and we were at last set on the right path.

"At last we spotted our destination, the culmination of weeks and months of worry and travail. From a distance I estimated Uncle Miles' farm to be over forty acres, his house a sprawling wooden structure. I held the wagon and horses back a safe distance and sent TJ ahead to announce our arrival. He walked to the barn door and hollered "Hallooo!" A farmer who greatly resembled my late mother emerged, brushing the straw from his clothes as he walked over to offer his hand to TJ. Even from afar, I could see the perplexed look on Uncle Miles' face as TJ introduced himself. As I lifted Mary Ann down from the wagon and we walked across the field to greet him, I hoped I would not incur his wrath for disobedience. That would be an inauspicious beginning for forging a new relationship with the only family we have.

"'Synthia Elizabeth Whitfield!' he exclaimed, embracing me warmly. 'I have never been so surprised in all my born days. Did I not instruct you to await my arrival in the spring?' He pulled back and held me at arms' length, shaking his head. 'Howsoever did you manage?'

"'Uncle, we could not continue in Missouri,' I told him emphatically. 'We were unwanted orphans and dared not depend on the kindness of our neighbors till spring. Papa taught me to drive the wagon, so here we are.'

"Uncle Miles gasped. 'You drove it by yourself?'

"I smiled triumphantly. 'Yes, sir!'

"The farmhouse door opened and out came a woman who most assuredly was my aunt, with two young boys at her heels, both approximately my brother's age.

"'Miles? Is this…?' she asked, scrutinizing me. 'Well, of course it is. You look just like that miniature of your ma that your uncle keeps on the mantle.'

"I found myself smothered in hugs and kisses by Aunt Catherine, and heard peals of laughter ring out from my cousins William and Bartholomew. I drew Mary Ann and TJ to me and said a silent prayer of thanksgiving. Tears of pure joy and relief came to my eyes as I realized we were home at last."

Millie gently closed the journal and sighed. "A happy ending."

"That's not the end," Professor Riley said. "There's a lot of that journal left. I've examined every inch of it."

Millie thumbed through it. "You're right."

"You know, Alex," Steven said, "Oklahoma Liberal Arts could sure use a bright young student like Millie. We don't get many with such an avid interest in history and artifacts."

"I agree," Alex said. "Millie, have you given our school any more consideration?"

Millie opened her mouth to answer, but Zach interrupted as he pointed at the institutional clock hanging above Professor Riley's desk. "Going on four," he said to Millie. "If we're getting that yogurt, we'd better get on it."

Millie was eager to read the rest of the journal but it would have to wait until she was back at Gran's and had leisure time to look through it. She carefully laid the ribbon bookmark in the page, replaced the diary inside the muslin bag, tied the drawstring, and smiled at Zach. "You said something about Mrs. Swenson's homemade?"

Alex laughed. "Ah, the good stuff. Would it do any good to remind you not to spoil your dinner, son?"

"Nope!" Zach took Millie by the hand and led her out.

* * * * *

Mrs. Swenson's Homemade Frozen Yogurt and Custard Shop was located near the historic downtown area in another one of those renovated turn-of-the-twentieth century buildings just off Main Street. It was situated between a bed and bath boutique and a vintage bookstore that also housed a popular coffee shop frequented by college kids. Zach held the door open for Millie and stepped aside as she entered ahead of him. She breathed in the smell of sweets that wafted about the large room as she walked across the creaking wooden floor. A ceiling fan churned lazily overhead, but Millie noticed that aside from the air it stirred up, it wasn't particularly cool inside.

"It's kind of warm in here," she told Zach. "Do you suppose their AC went out?"

Zach grinned as he took her hand and pointed to the counter. "Don't worry. The ice cream will cool us down."

She giggled to hide the nervous tingle she felt

whenever Zach held her hand. "What do you recommend?" she asked, gazing through the glass at the various colorful concoctions.

"You'd probably like the frozen yogurt, but I usually go with the custard."

"Then I think I'll step out of my comfort zone and try some." She pointed to the mint chocolate chip. "One dip of that in a cup, please," Millie told the girl behind the counter. She smiled up at Zach as the young woman scooped out her selection, set the cup on the counter, and plopped a plastic spoon in it. Zach opted for a double-dip of chocolate fudge with whipped cream.

"Thanks Kristen," Zach said to the girl as he handed her the money.

"You know her?"

Zach nodded and took a bite of cold ice cream. "We had trig class together last year."

Millie remembered Zach saying he liked math, but trigonometry? That meant he was heading for calculus his senior year. Sometimes the guy just surprised her. He struggled with history but breezed through sophisticated mathematics. Of course most teenagers weren't as good at all subjects as she was, but it was increasingly apparent that Zach wasn't just a dumb jock either.

"Come on, let's eat outside," Zach said, pointing to some iron-mesh tables with matching chairs on the covered porch next to the store's picture window, "and maybe catch a breeze." He held the door open for her, but Millie hesitated as she peered out the door. Despite the broiling sun earlier in the day, dark clouds were starting to roll in.

"Wow! It's really cooled down out here!" Millie

said as they stepped outside. She knew from experience that Oklahoma weather could change dramatically—and quickly.

"Yeah," Zach agreed, surveying the sky. "Probably dropped twenty degrees in the last half hour."

She pointed in the direction of the incoming storm as she removed her sunglasses and laid them on the table next to her. "Squall line," she said, spooning up a bite of frozen custard. "We'd better not stay out here too long. These storms can be dangerous."

Zach scooped up a huge bite of his custard and popped it all into his mouth. "You're a scaredy-cat, Millie Olson."

Millie dropped her spoon in surprise. "Seriously? Did you just say that or did I misunderstand you with your mouth full?" Zach nodded. "'Scaredy-cat?' Are we kindergartners?"

"Yeah, okay," he said once he'd swallowed, "but what I meant is, you're afraid to take chances. Afraid of a little rainstorm…"

"Squall line," Millie corrected him, "big storm…"

"…afraid to commit to college," he continued right over her, "and afraid to admit how you feel about me."

Millie's eyes opened wide at that last remark, and her stomach started to churn so loud she was sure he could hear it. To avoid having to answer him, she took her own big bite of ice cream.

Zach shoved his custard aside and lowered his face to her level. "Go out with me."

Millie turned her palms up in a 'duh' gesture. "We're out."

"No, I mean on a date. Not like the Fourth with my family, not for a quick scoop of fro-yo, just the two of us. Tonight. I'll pick you up at eight."

Millie could hardly believe her ears. A real date with Zach? Now that was a scary thought. "Okay." *Did I just say that?*

Just then a loud clap of thunder broke the silence and big raindrops began splashing on the table and the ground around them. Zach grabbed her hand. "Come on, let's run!"

"But we'll get drenched!"

"Good!" He urged her onto her feet and together they ran across the parking lot to his truck, arriving just as the downpour began in earnest. He opened the door for her and she scrambled inside as he ran around to the driver's side. He wiped the water off his face with the sleeve of his now-soaked football jersey and turned to Millie with a grin. "See? You didn't melt!"

Millie sat there for a moment in awe, realizing she wasn't all that upset about getting rained on, and in fact, admitted to herself that it felt pretty good after the afternoon heat. Maybe she could take a risk or two. What would it hurt to go out with Zach, for just one evening?

* * * * *

What do I wear? What do I wear? Zach hadn't told her what they'd be doing, so she rummaged through her closet in yet another obsessive attempt to be per-fectly dressed, to look like going on summer dates were commonplace for her. She ruled out a sundress, since Zach had already seen most of her dresses any-way. The denim cutoffs were fine for a lakeside picnic but not for a special date like tonight. That left shorts. What about those khaki-green linen shorts, the white peasant top blouse with the three-quarter length sleeves and drawstring neckline, and her closed-heel sandals? Perfect! Millie glanced at the clock and saw it was nearly eight o'clock. She had to hurry if she wanted to be ready on time.

Sure enough, the doorbell rang precisely at eight and she heard Kaz call out, "Mill…your boyfriend's here!"

UGH. She needed to have a serious talk with that smart-aleck brother of hers. Millie stepped into her sandals and checked her look in the mirror one last time. She grabbed her canvas bag off the hook in the closet, the one with the multi-colored yarn stitching that conveniently matched everything, picked up the purse she'd been carrying earlier and without thinking started to dump its contents into the canvas bag.

"Ohmigod!" she gasped in horror and dove for the bag containing Synthia's journal, right before it landed on the floor. In her rush to get ready for this date she'd forgotten all about it being in there. How could I forget something as important as a nineteenth century diary? She sighed and carefully set the muslin bag and its contents on her nightstand.

Millie shut the bedroom door quietly, hoping not to disturb Gran, who was watching TV in her bedroom with the door closed. Unfortunately, Gran had ears like a fox. The door opened wide to reveal Gran with a huge grin on her face. "Have a lovely time, dear!"

Millie was excited, no doubt, but she hoped neither she nor her grandmother had unrealistic expectations. "I won't be late, Gran," Millie called back.

"Ready?" Zach asked from the bottom of the stairs.

Millie hurried down the stairs. "Where are we going?" she asked, surveying Zach's clothing. He was wearing khaki walking shorts, a clean Rolling Plains

number seventeen football jersey, and those ubiqui-
tous unfastened leather sandals. "I didn't know what
to dress for," she said.

Zach looked her up and down and nodded approval. "Perfect for miniature golf."

"Golf? You know I don't have an athletic bone in
my body!"

Zach held the front door open. "It's mini-golf, not
the real thing. Come on, it'll be fun."

Millie was about to check her bag for bug spray
when Zach took her hand and pulled her out the door.

As soon as they arrived at the miniature golf
course and got their clubs and balls — red for her, blue
for him — she didn't give the possibility of bug bites another thought. Normally it took a lot to distract her
from her physical comfort, but Zach managed to keep
her happily occupied.

And they had fun. A lot of fun, in fact. Millie hit
the ball at all sorts of cockeyed angles and ended up
with a huge score, yet Zach didn't tease her about it.
For his part, he proved to be the well-rounded athlete
her grandmother said he was, and a perfect gentleman
as well.

Is this what it's like to date a boy? Just going out
to do goofy things and enjoying the time together?
Millie didn't know, and admitted to herself that she
probably wouldn't have a chance to find out because
if she decided to go to college, she certainly wouldn't
have time to go on dates. Pretty soon she'd start having that recurring nightmare of being unprepared for
class and being looked down upon by both peers and
professors, which would cause her panic reflex to kick
in and force her into social isolation for more study

time. *Don't think about that now,* she told herself. *Just have fun.*

Millie was mildly surprised that she didn't have any mosquito bites after a two-hour round of miniature golf in the evening humidity with no bug spray. Probably those mosquito-zapper machines were responsible, or maybe the recent drought had kept the mosquito population at bay. Whichever was the case, she was itch-free and, okay she admitted it, carefree.

"Thirsty?" Zach asked as they turned in their putters, balls and scorecards.

"Um, do you mean that concessions stand?" Millie shied away as she pointed to the little shack next to the admissions gate which was surrounded by parents with small children eating snow cones. She spent enough time with her younger brother and sister as it was, so a conversation interrupted by squealing kids didn't hold much appeal.

Zach followed her gaze. "No. Come on, I want to introduce you to some of my friends."

Millie gasped in horror. "What? Where?" Zach didn't answer but quietly escorted her to his truck. They rode for a few minutes in silence, and then Zach put on his signal to make a left-hand turn into the parking lot of a drive-in restaurant with a huge neon sign blazing its name into the night sky, Canby's Old-Fashioned Root Beer. Once in the parking lot, Zach slowed to a crawl and began looking for an empty space, finally locating one at the far edge of the lot. He turned off the truck's ignition and came around to help Millie down from the truck.

"Here we are," he said as he handed her out.

She stepped down and looked around in wonder. "Ohmigod I'm in an episode of Happy Days!"

"What?" Zach asked.

Millie looked down at her feet so Zach couldn't see her smile to herself. "Never mind. Something we studied in Pop Culture class." But one look around told her the Happy Days analogy was dead-on.

It was pretty loud in the outdoor patio seating area. Zach took her hand and led her toward some tables where a crowd of teenagers was mostly just standing around, since there weren't enough chairs for all of them. Some were drinking root beer, some eating hot dogs, and some just drinking bottles of water as they laughed and chatted, moving around from one group to another, and occasionally sitting down if someone vacated a seat. The outside speakers were blasting music, but the kids just talked right over it.

"Is that Beethoven's Ninth?" Millie asked in astonishment.

Zach squeezed her hand and shrugged. "Yeah, ol' man Canby thought if he played classical music outdoors during summer instead of rap or heavy metal, he'd scare off the teenagers and draw in more families. Didn't work. The families mostly eat inside, and the high schoolers still hang around out here. I guess us Rolling Plains kids are more highbrow than he gave us credit for!"

"Hey, MacMillan!" A large, blond-haired boy with a sleeveless white muscle shirt and cutoff jeans slapped Zach on the back. "It's about time you came around. Who ya got here?"

"Millie Olson, meet Brad Thompson. Remember him? He's the guy who made that homerun at the July 4th softball game."

"I only saw him from a distance," she told Zach. "I'm from Indianapolis," she said to Brad, offering her hand to shake.

Brad sized her up. "Pretty clear you ain't from around here, what with that Yankee accent."

Millie lifted an eyebrow. "Yankee?" She had no accent she was aware of, and this coming from someone with poor grammar and a distinct Oklahoma twang.

He turned and shouted into the crowd, "Hey, Zoe! Look who's here!"

Zach's sister pushed her way through the throng. She was wearing her softball uniform and cleats, and from the sweat and grime on her clothes, she appeared to have come straight from a game. Zoe reached down and gave Millie her usual bear hug which caused Millie to momentarily gasp for breath.

"Millie!" Zoe squealed. "Zach, I didn't know you'd be here! Come on, I'm with the softball team." She got between them, hooked her arms in theirs and led them to where her teammates were scarfing down hot dogs, fries, and root beer by the gallons.

"Y'all, this is an old family friend, Millie Olson from Indianapolis. Her mom writes those Millicent the Magnificent books." There was lots of giggling from the girls when they heard that.

"Zoe, we didn't come here to hang out with sophomores," Zach said, rolling his eyes.

By then Brad had caught up to them. "Rude, Zoe," he growled.

"Hey, Zach," cooed a very attractive girl standing behind Brad.

She shoved aside a couple of loiterers in her path and joined them. Millie recognized her as the girl from the custard shop that afternoon and her stomach started to churn, just like it did at the ice cream store earlier.

"Zach," Kristen purred, "who's your little friend?"

Little friend? Millie opened her mouth to speak but nothing came out.

"Kristen Baker, Millie Olson," Zach replied.

Standing next to this attractive friend of Zach's, Millie began to experience a completely foreign emotion: jealousy. Kristen was tall, slender, and wearing a stunning spaghetti-strap sundress made of expensive polished cotton. She had long-brown hair pushed back on her forehead with DKNY sunglasses, which Millie thought looked silly at ten o'clock at night, but she had a level of sophistication and aloofness Millie hadn't seen since Emily Safire. Zach was looking at Kristen with approval and Millie's heart sank. This girl must be nearly eighteen, and Millie felt as immature next to her as she always did around Emily, making her want to sink into the ground or dive under one of the wrought-iron tables.

"Zach says you go to school together," Millie said in her best imitation of polite conversation.

"Millie was valedictorian of…" Zach turned to her and asked, "what's it called?"

"Kendrick Prep," Millie said, putting a firm emphasis on the 'Prep' part.

"Private school?" Kristen asked.

"Valedictorian? Hey, how old are you anyway?" Brad asked.

"Sixteen," Millie replied.

"And a genius!" Zach exclaimed.

Brad and Kristen exchanged glances. "Cool!" Brad exclaimed as he wrapped his arms around Kristen, pulled her close and planted a passionate kiss on her lips. She responded by kissing him back.

Wow! I didn't see that coming, Millie admitted to herself as she looked away.

"They've been together since ninth grade," Zach whispered in her ear. "Come on, I want you to meet some of the other guys on the football team." He took Millie's hand and steered her away from that embarrassing make-out session.

Millie was a little ashamed of herself, thinking that Zach had a crush on Kristen. But really, how would she know? She didn't live in Rolling Plains, knew nothing of the teenage social structure here, and in fact had little idea how to behave around kids her own age at all.

Zach led her to a group of boys and girls huddled around a table with their heads together in a serious conversation. He dragged two more chairs to the already-crowded table and shoved his way in, motioning for her to have a seat once he'd created enough space for them.

"...but I still say he wasn't the third murderer."

Millie's ears perked up. Murder? What in the world were these kids talking about?

"Callie," insisted one of the girls, "it was him. He followed his two hired guns to make sure the job got done right—that Banquo and Fleance both died."

Millie's jaw dropped. "Are you talking about 'The Scottish Play'?" Then she slapped her hand over her mouth when she realized she'd jumped uninvited into their conversation.

The girl named Callie and the other one turned, eyeing her suspiciously. "Zach!" Callie said with surprise. "What are you doing here? Slumming?"

"Oh, sorry, guys," Zach said. "We just sort of

barged in. This is my friend Millie from Indianapolis, staying with her grandmother for the summer. How was Shakespeare in the Park?"

"You were supposed to be there, Zach," Callie said. "Thanks for blowing us off."

Zach shrugged and put his arm around Millie's shoulders. "Something came up. Fill me in."

One of the guys with a scruffy almost-beard, ponytail and several ear piercings shook his head and said, "Sorry, dude. You're on your own."

Millie looked around the table at the six kids, the diverse kind she assumed you could find in any public high school, crowded together and discussing Macbeth. Shakespeare. Shakespeare? These kids were definitely the intellectual type despite their outward appearance, and she immediately felt like she fit right in.

"You must be familiar with Shakespeare if you call it 'The Scottish Play,'" said the boy. "Anyone with half a brain and a thorough knowledge of theatre history knows you only say the 'M' word on stage."

The other boy with the ponytail stood up, gave a courtly Shakespearean bow to Millie, and extended his hand. "Since your date here's so rude, I'm Keith," he said pointing around the table, "and this is Callie, Izzie, Terri, Blaine, and Lisa. We're rising AP Lit seniors, and seeing Macb…'The Scottish Play'…is a summer assignment."

Millie eagerly shook his hand and turned to Zach. "I thought you said they were football players."

"Blaine and I are," Keith answered her. "What d'ya think? Ya can't have brains and brawn?"

Chagrined, Millie said, "Of course you can. There were plenty of smart jocks at Kendrick Prep." She turned to Zach. "And you didn't tell me you were taking AP Lit."

Zach shrugged. "It'll be my first AP class."

"Prep school, huh," Keith said to Millie. "Gonna be a junior? Senior?"

Millie shook her head. "I already graduated, valedictorian."

Keith whistled softly and punched Zach in the arm. "Got yourself a smart one there, boy!" He turned to Millie and asked, "Where ya headed to school?"

"I…" She suddenly developed a coughing fit and couldn't finish her sentence.

"She hasn't decided yet," Zach finished for her. "Want a root beer, Millie? The floats here are amazing."

"Sure," she said, relieved at how easily he diverted the conversation.

Zach got up to place their order at the walk-up window and Millie happily settled into a long discussion of the literary and theatrical merits of *Macbeth* with these kids she'd just met. It was amazing how at ease she felt, and how easily they included her in their group. If only she'd had friends like this at Kendrick. Well, she had Carlye and Michael, but mostly she'd just spent all her time studying alone while her classmates were out socializing. She was starting to see the benefits of a social life as well as an academic one.

Millie had a lot to think about as she sank into the pillows on her bed at Gran's. Tonight had been eye-opening. She had fun with Zach, fun with his friends, and actually felt like she fit in with a group of kids her own age for the first time since…well, she couldn't remember when. She glanced at the clock and noticed it was already past midnight, and she was not at all sleepy. She closed her eyes to try to fall asleep, but all she could think about was the incredible date she'd just been on with a boy she'd always thought of as a crashing bore.

Her brain wouldn't shut off. She went to the bathroom for a drink of water, came back to bed and fluffed her pillow, kicked the covers on and off, tried lying on her stomach and then on her back, and peeked open an eye at the clock again. 1:30 a.m. She groaned, rolled over to her handbag and pulled out her cell phone to check for messages. There was a text from Zach and she couldn't help but smile. *Thnx for fun time. See ya tomorrow?*

Her quick reply, *I had fun, too* was keyed in and sent. She stretched and was about to give up and go downstairs for some herbal tea when she spied Synthia's journal sitting on the nightstand in its muslin bag where she'd left it, and now more than ever she wanted to draw in some of Synthia's wisdom. Carefully Millie opened the diary.

October 31, 1865

We are settling into our new life here in Texas. Mary Ann and I share a bed in a small bedroom in the back of the house, a room intended for a hired man but currently unoccupied. TJ is bunking in with his cousins Will and Bart, but I am sensing a growing resentment on the part of William. He is thirteen, older than TJ, and up till now has fancied himself a man, one who does not relish the thought of a tagalong cousin. Bart is nine years old and eager for a playmate, but my brother pouts and refuses to play.

Perhaps TJ's sulkiness is the result of our changed circumstances, or perhaps he just does not like his cousins. I am unable to ascertain which, but I do know that William and TJ have been arguing of late. Uncle Miles says he will not have such discord in his home, that everyone is to remember we are family and are to be welcomed here.

Tomorrow I will accompany my cousins to their school in town in order to enroll TJ and Mary Ann, but at above age fifteen I am much too old to attend grammar school. This past year their education has been sorely neglected and I intend to see that remedied. Uncle Miles vouches for the schoolteacher, a Mr. Yeager, who is a veteran of the Great War, albeit on the Confederate side. I look forward to meeting such a distinguished gentleman.

November 1, 1865

Mr. Thomas Perry Yeager keeps school in town, but his keen interest in education has helped him gather support among School Board Members for establishing a larger academy in the near future. Uncle Miles says his current school is considered quite progressive with its advanced curriculum, largely due to Mr. Yeager's forward-thinking approach to teaching children. He insists they learn more than rote memorization; that they actively engage themselves in their studies with research and writing, and that has caused a stir among some of the parents. They have been silenced for the most part, though, as the results they see in their children's education are most satisfying. Uncle Miles is pleased with the progress of his own sons.

Mr. Yeager is not at all what I expected. I assumed he was middle-aged with a family, being a war veteran and school board member, but in fact he is a mere twenty years old and a bachelor.

"Good morning, Mr. Yeager," I said with a curtsy upon our introduction. "We are newly arrived in town and residing with my Uncle Miles Graves. I hope to enroll my sister and brother in your school."

Mr. Yeager looked stern, rendering me embarrassed and confused. "Miss Whitfield, I presume," he growled. "Your uncle notified me of your coming. However, I am not at all convinced that your brother and sister are academically prepared to matriculate here. Where have they been in school most lately?"

Nervously, I tied and untied the ribbon on my bonnet. "Well, sir," I hedged, "they attended a country school near Sedalia, but when both my parents passed away last summer…" A lump formed in my throat and I could say no more, but I had no need to finish anyway as the look on Mr. Yeager's face registered his displeasure.

"Please, sir, give them a chance," I pleaded. "My brother TJ does quite well in mathematics and often helped my father with the bookkeeping on our farm, and Mary Ann can read, write, and recite her Bible verses."

Finally Mr. Yeager agreed to take them on as pupils, as a favor to Uncle Miles, but only upon the condition of their proving themselves worthy. I left in a huff.

I do not think I like Mr. Thomas Perry Yeager.

Millie could easily sympathize with Synthia's plight because she understood what it was like to have exacting teachers. She was about to turn the page and read on when her cell phone rang. "Carlye? It's two o'clock in the morning!"

"You didn't mail in those admissions papers, did you?"

Millie was trapped. "Um…well…no. Actually they're in Indianapolis."

"Seriously? Ohmigod, seriously?"

"That's redundant."

Carlye groaned. "Then you've got to hop a plane to Indianapolis so we can hurry down to Bloomington and get you enrolled at IU."

"What?" Millie sat straight up in the bed.

"You heard me!"

"Carlye, are you nuts? I can't do that."

There was anger and impatience in Carlye's voice, tinged with a hint of desperation. "You know I'm leaving in a week for my study abroad semester in England, right?"

"Well, I didn't mark it on my calendar, but okay."

"So you've got to get home pronto."

This time Millie groaned in exasperation. "What does you leaving for England in a week have to do with me enrolling at Indiana University 'pronto'?"

"Because—you've procrastinated so long we're going to lose our dorm spot! You know, the one in that just-opened building with its own gym and all the amenities, right in the heart of campus."

Millie yawned. "It's not 'our' dorm space. Just designate someone else to be your roommate. Whoever she is will have the place all to herself first semester anyway. I hear Esther Weinstein's available."

"Millie, I want to room with you, not Esther."

Millie had been deliberately avoiding this very conversation for weeks. She ticked off all her logical objections on her fingers. "First of all, Carlye, you're assuming I've made the decision to enroll at Indiana University and I've done no such thing. Secondly, there's Kaz and Charlie. I can't just dump them on my grandmother. And if I could settle that problem, there's no guarantee I could get a flight out."

Carlye fired right back. "First of all, Millie, you've just got to go to college and not waste those brains and all that scholarship money, and IU's a great school. Secondly, I'm sure your grandmother could watch your sibs for a couple of days. And flights can be booked any time. Got a credit card?"

Millie sighed. "Yes, Dad gave me one. But he certainly never said anything about last-minute plane tickets, which will cost a fortune, by the way."

"Millie, please," Carlye begged. "I really, really want to spend the rest of my college years rooming with my bestie, and I want to do it in that fantastic new dorm complex. Do us both a favor and hop a flight. Tomorrow."

Millie thought about it for a very long time, so long in fact that Carlye said "hello?" a couple of times to make sure she was still on the line. Millie hadn't made up her mind about college at all yet, and she was still leaning toward community college in Indianapolis. True, she'd just recently given some serious thought to Oklahoma Liberal Arts, but that wasn't settled either. No, this crazy scheme of Carlye's was out of the question. Right? She thought about the ramifications of suddenly flying to Indianapolis, enrolling at IU against her better judgment, and leaving Zach.

"Come on, Millie, quit stalling. Once you've seen the dorm and figured out what classes you can take, you'll be glad you did it."

Millie was torn. "This really means that much to you?"

"Yes!"

"Well, let me talk to my grandmother...."

"No, Millie, it's too late, for a lot of things. Get online and book a flight and text me the details. I'm sure your grandmother will be okay with it if you tell her it's because you're enrolling at a university. No. More. Stalling. Hear me?"

Millie ended the call and felt turmoil bubbling up inside her. She replayed the events of her just-ended date with Zach and the interesting conversation she'd had with his friends, turning over in her mind how much fun she'd had. But did it mean anything about a future with Zach?

She heaved a huge sigh and booted up her laptop to search for last-minute flights, pulled her Visa card out of her purse and began keying in information.

Chapter Twelve
Missing

Sunlight streamed through the bedroom window early the next morning, which would have awakened Millie had she ever been asleep. She'd gone ahead and booked a flight to Indianapolis, but her conscience was gnawing at her because the cost was exorbitant and she hoped Dad wouldn't be too mad at her. Maybe it would lessen the blow if she told him it was for a good cause — she was planning to enroll at IU for the fall semester. Not her parents' first choice of a school, but at this point they'd probably see it as positive step. She also felt guilty about making all these impromptu plans without consulting her grandmother. And then there was Zach. Would he be mad, or hurt? Who could sleep with all that in her head?

She checked the time: 7:15 a.m. Millie decided she might as well get up and start packing, even though she had several hours before she had to leave for the Oklahoma City airport. She slowly climbed out of bed, stretched, and from habit parted the window curtains to see if anyone, okay Zach, was outside. After all, Gran's front yard needed mowing... But it was very early so of course he wasn't out there. She let the curtain drop.

In the back of her closet was the carry-on bag she always used, so she pulled it out, took out way more dresses and sandals than she needed for three days and tossed them on the bed. *Don't forget, it's not as hot in Indiana as it is in Oklahoma,* she reminded herself, so she went back to her closet for jeans, a blouse, and flats to wear on the plane. She sighed in frustration at the pile of clothing on her bed, knowing it wouldn't all fit in the carry-on. And there was no way she was paying the extra money for baggage check.

Just then Millie caught a glimpse of her bedraggled reflection in the mirror, frowned, ran her fingers through her tangled blond hair and pulled out the ponytail holder from the night before. "Go take a shower and figure it out when you get back," she advised her reflection.

"Don't even think about it, Millie!"

Startled, Millie flipped around to find her brother standing in her doorway. "Think about what?"

Kaz stood there in his pajama pants, his arms crossed in front of his bare chest, a bath towel flung over his shoulder. Millie wondered when he'd gotten so tall and why she hadn't noticed before. They used to be about the same height, and yet in the course of one summer he was now nearly a head taller than she was. She also asked herself when the start of a beard had appeared on his face and when his arms had become so muscular. Millie had to admit that she really hadn't been paying much attention to Kaz for most of the summer, or Charlie either, for that matter, and another wave of guilt swept over her. After all, orphaned Synthia had almost single-handedly raised her siblings, while Millie had more or less dumped Kaz and Charlie on Gran and was now about to abandon them further. She promised herself she'd try harder.

"I'm sorry, Kaz. What did you say?"

"I said — Don't even think about hogging the bathroom. I need to get ready for camp."

Millie, with her new determination to be a better sister, said cheerfully, "Okay, let me know when you're done." She watched with amusement as Kaz screwed up his face in surprise when he didn't get an argument, and then shrugged and headed for the hall bath.

Millie had turned her attention back to her packing when Synthia's journal caught her eye, waiting like an open invitation on the bedside table. She lifted the journal off the nightstand and found her place, glanced at the date, flipped a few pages back, and realized a large chunk of time had gone by since Synthia had written in her diary. Wonder why?

> December 6, 1865
> I must admit to being remiss in my journal-writing. I have been so busy helping Aunt Catherine with her increased domestic duties, seeing to TJ and Mary Ann's homework, and attempting to keep abreast of my own reading and sewing, that the time has slipped away since last I wrote.

Millie nodded. Makes sense.

Uncle Miles says we will have a big feast tomorrow. President Johnson declared an official Day of Thanksgiving the first Thursday of December, saying, "Reconstruction is over. America is once again whole."

I will go to Mr. Yeager's school earlier than usual today to collect my brother, sister, and cousins, as their help is needed in the preparations for the special celebration. My aunt says I must invite Mr. Yeager to join us, as he is a bachelor and unlikely to get a proper meal otherwise. I do not like that idea, but I shall do as I am told.

Mr. Yeager had dismissed the pupils earlier than normal when I arrived, as their excitement over the holiday spoiled their concentration. Mary Ann, William and Bartholomew emerged from school with the other children, but TJ was nowhere to be found.

"Mr. Yeager," I said upon entering the schoolroom and finding him busily erasing the chalkboard, "where is my brother, Thomas Jefferson Whitfield?"

Mr. Yeager turned about in surprise. "Why, Miss Whitfield, I assumed you knew your brother did not come to school today."

My mouth fell open. "No, sir, I did not know. He left home with his sister and cousins this morning. Where can he be?"

TJ is unfamiliar with the area around our new home and knows few people here in Texas — only family and a few classmates. He is but ten years old and ill-equipped to be wandering about in strange surroundings on his own, amongst people he is unacquainted with. And he had already been missing for hours! Mr. Yeager immediately took charge of this frightening situation and went outside to question my sister and cousins. I followed close on his heels, eager to hear their answers and determined not to be left uninformed.

"Miss Whitfield," he said when finished questioning them, "you are most likely aware of the discord between TJ and Bart and Will."

"I am aware, Mr. Yeager, but I hoped they would settle their differences on their own." I shook my head. "It doesn't appear that they have."

"Apparently not," Mr. Yeager agreed. "As you heard, there was an altercation between TJ and his cousin William this morning on the way to school. TJ left their company and has not been seen since."

"Mary Ann!" I exclaimed, getting down to my sister's eye level and speaking sternly to her, "Why did you say nothing to Mr. Yeager about this?"

Mary Ann hung her head at my scolding, so I hugged her to my breast and attempted to both comfort my young sister and ease my own guilt at not doing more to put a stop to this rancor.

"We must notify my aunt and uncle immediately!" I told Mr. Yeager.

Mr. Yeager directed Bartholomew and William to escort Mary Ann home and fetch Uncle Miles. "Fear not, Miss Whitfield," he said. "TJ cannot have gotten far. I shall find him. You must wait here for your uncle."

"Indeed I shall not!" I told him. "I have little enough family left and TJ is my responsibility. I shall accompany you in your search."

Mr. Yeager frowned his disapproval, but as I was not to be dissuaded, we set forth.

Missing? That poor kid, Millie thought. Poor Synthia, really. That girl had to deal with more than any fifteen-year-old should have to, even in the nineteenth century when kids were expected to take on more responsibility.

Kaz emerged from the bathroom and stuck his head into Millie's bedroom. "All yours!" But instead of heading back to his own room, he pointed to all the clothes strewn around her bed. "Hey, what gives?"

Millie started straightening up the mess and avoided eye contact with Kaz. "I'm going to Indianapolis." She looked sideways at her brother to gauge his reaction, but she already knew what it would be.

"WHAT?" he shouted. "Why do you get to go and I don't?"

Millie lowered her voice before speaking, hoping he would lower his as well. "It's only for a few days, Kaz. I have to get registered for fall classes."

"When are you going?" Kaz demanded.

Turning her back on him, she began carefully folding clothes and placing them in the open carry-on bag. "Today."

"What?" he shouted again. "And what're me and Charlie supposed to do while you're gone?"

Millie bit her tongue to keep from correcting his grammar, remembering her moments-earlier resolve.

"You'll stay here with Gran until I get back." She saw the angry and confused look on his face. "I promise I'll be back."

Kaz threw up his hands and yelled, "No way! If you're going, I'm going!"

Millie rolled her eyes. Okay, her bratty pre-teen brother was back and she didn't have as much patience as she'd hoped. "You can't go, Kaz, because there's no one to take care of you there."

"Then I'll stay with the Hendersons!"

"My, my, my, what is all the yelling about?" Gran asked, stepping into the room and inching between the two of them.

"Sorry, Gran," Millie said, narrowing her eyes at Kaz. "Just a little sibling difference of opinion."

"Gran," Kaz said as he pointed a finger at her, "did you know Millie's going to Indianapolis?"

"No, indeed I did not!" Gran lifted an eyebrow and folded her arms, waiting for Millie to explain.

Millie sighed and pushed a stray lock of hair behind her ear. "It all happened so fast last night. I wanted to tell you but it was way late. Carlye insists I've got to enroll at IU like yesterday, mostly so she doesn't lose her dorm room for lack of a roommate."

Gran tapped her foot. "So what I'm hearing is that this is Carlye's plan. I'm wondering if you've given this enough thought, dear."

"I was wondering that myself." In her mind, Millie reran all the pros and cons of this whole idea, asking herself if this was the right thing to do.

"Do your parents know?"

Millie snapped out of her head, picked up her phone, rapidly pushed buttons and tossed it back on her bed. "They do now."

"And you couldn't text them about me?" Kaz asked as his face reddened and his fists clenched. "Gran, I wanna go, too!"

Gran took a backward step, both to get perspective and to avoid Kaz's shouting and temper. "But what on earth for, Kaz? I thought you were enjoying baseball day camp."

"I need to be at football conditioning," Kaz said to Gran before getting up in Millie's face. "You already knew I was gonna play football. Way selfish, Mill."

"Football?" Gran asked.

"Dad played football, her boyfriend plays football, so yeah, football!"

Millie blushed at the mention of Zach being her boyfriend, but shook her head and said, "Calm down, Kaz. I know Dad said you could play, but it's too early for Kendrick football practice to start."

"Two-a-days start the end of the month, but conditioning is ongoing, and I'm not there!"

"I'm sorry, Kaz," Gran said as she gave his shoulder a squeeze, "but since I have no instructions from your father about this, you'll have to wait until your folks come fetch you, like we planned all along. Now go get dressed and eat your breakfast."

Kaz stomped out, grumbling about his 'privileged' sister all the way to his room.

"Thanks for understanding, Gran," Millie said, reaching out for a hug.

Gran held Millie at arm's length. "I'm not too happy with you either, young lady."

Millie flopped down on the bed. "I know. I'm starting to regret letting Carlye goad me into this." Millie sighed. "I could use some advice, Gran."

"Millie dear, is this really what you want to do—

attend a huge state university? I was under the impression you and Zach…Did things go wrong last night?"

Millie winced at the mention of Zach's name. "Just the opposite."

"Then why this rushed trip to Indianapolis? Why not stay here for a bit and see how it goes?"

Millie took a deep breath. "I wish I hadn't rushed into it, but I promised Carlye, and I've already bought the ticket and it's nonrefundable. So will you be okay taking care of the kids for a few days while I'm gone?"

Gran cocked her head at Millie and placed her hands on her hips. "Of course, but that isn't the issue, Mildred. It's a question of what you want. Think hard about this, dear." She sighed. "I suppose you can text me from Indianapolis."

Millie nodded. "Where will you be today?"

Gran walked over to the bedroom window and pulled the curtains back as she gazed with appreciation at the clear blue sky. "It's a lovely day for a garden picnic, don't you think? A bit cooler than it's been lately."

"Oh," Millie said, her mind elsewhere, "your garden club. Have fun."

She went back to her packing but she couldn't concentrate. Too many things were rattling around in her head: her fight with Kaz, leaving Zach when their friendship was just beginning to blossom, the question of whether or not she really did want to attend IU, and dumping the care of her hormonal pre-teen brother and trusting little sister onto her grandmother. Millie's head ached from all the mental exertion and lack of sleep and then her stomach growled, reminding her she hadn't eaten breakfast. She went downstairs to the kitchen, hoping she'd feel better after some food and strong coffee.

Kaz glared at her when she reached into the fridge for juice, swallowed the last of his cereal, and made a big show of scraping the chair on the floor as he got up and stomped out of the room.

Charlie was sitting at the table, nibbling on her toast and jelly, but when she saw Millie she jumped up and tackled her around the waist. "Kaz says you're leaving. Is that true, Millie?"

Now Millie really felt guilty. She hugged Charlie's shoulders and led her back to the breakfast table. "It's only for a few days, Charlie. I have to enroll for college, kind of like you have to enroll for third grade next month." Millie tousled Charlie's hair and got her sister to giggle. "You'll be okay here with Gran until I get back, won't you?"

"I guess," Charlie said with a sigh, but then brightened up. "We're going to the Butterfly Exhibit at the zoo today."

"See? You'll be so busy at camp you won't even notice I'm gone."

Charlie shrugged, drained her juice glass, and ran from the table as the camp bus honked outside. "Bye, Millie!"

Millie waved to her sister and then peeked around the corner in time to see Kaz heading out the front door behind Charlie, carrying what looked like an extra bag over his shoulder.

Millie smiled, her conscience eased a bit, at least as far as Charlie was concerned. As for Kaz…

Millie was all packed and ready to leave for the airport and decided to call an airport shuttle, the one located in nearby Rolling Plains that her dad always used. Gran had picnic plans that Millie didn't want to disrupt, and the idea of navigating the freeways in Oklahoma City in her rental car and then finding a parking space completely unnerved her. It was now close to noon, and even though her flight wasn't until later this afternoon, she still thought it would be better to go ahead and order the car to pick her up.

Outside, the lawn mower roared into action and Millie tingled with delight. It wouldn't hurt to go out and say goodbye to Zach. Goodbye? Millie felt paralyzed at the thought of actually telling Zach that, after their great date the night before, she was hopping a plane to Indianapolis to enroll in college. Not OLAC like he'd hoped, but Indiana University. She dreaded that conversation.

But first things first. She checked to make sure her carry-on bag was securely zipped and set it down near the back door, and then reached into her purse for her cell phone and the slip of paper where she'd scribbled the phone number of the shuttle service.

"Hello, my name is Mildred Olson, and I'd like to request pickup at two o'clock for a 4:57 p.m. flight to Indianapolis." She sat down in the kitchen window seat and looked out in hopes of catching a glimpse of Zach mowing the lawn while she was on hold. Her patience was rewarded when he pushed the mower within feet of the front flower bed and waved at her. Blushing, Millie waved back. "Yes, I'm still here," she said into the phone. "Oh, of course. I'll be using Visa." Millie fished into her wallet to pull out the credit card. It wasn't there.

"What did I do with that card?" she muttered. She searched through every compartment in her wallet, and then dug to the bottom of her bag but couldn't find it. She unzipped all the interior pockets and ran her fingers around the edges of each, but everything was in order. Finally she dumped everything out of her purse onto the kitchen table and pawed through its contents, but still no Visa card. "Hello?" she said to the customer service agent. "I must've misplaced my card. Can I call you back?" Annoyed with herself for being so careless, she hung up and went back upstairs to her room.

Where is that credit card? She stood in her bedroom doorway, hands on her hips, trying to mentally retrace her steps after she used the Visa card to make the plane reservations at two a.m. Millie did a visual search of the room, wondering why she hadn't just put it back in her wallet like she always did. Exhaustion must be the culprit. She got down on her hands and knees and looked under the bed, pulled the covers back exposing the sheets, and then stripped all the bedding off the bed, but no card. She went through the pockets of the pajamas she'd been wearing, dug through the dresser drawers, opened the nightstand, and even checked the bathroom just in case, but still no Visa. Millie was getting panicky. How could she have lost that card?

Her cell phone rang. Assuming it was the shuttle service, she pushed the button in irritation. "Hello?"

"I'm trying to reach Millie Olson."

It wasn't the car company. She pulled it back from her ear to check the caller ID but didn't recognize the number, only that it was a local area code. "Yes, speaking. Who is this?"

"This is the Rolling Plains Recreation Center. We have your number on file as an emergency contact for Karl Jr. and Charlotte Olson."

Millie's heart leapt into her throat. Something had

happened at day camp! She tried to calm herself but she was shaking all over, imagining all sorts of horrible accidents. "Yes, I'm their sister. Is there a problem?"

"Charlotte is fine, but Karl Jr.—Kaz, isn't it?—well, he's been missing since shortly after roll call this morning."

Millie opened her mouth to speak but it felt like her throat had closed shut and she couldn't get a word out. Finally she sucked in her breath and said, "Mis—missing? How can that be?"

The woman was apologetic. "Your brother asked to use his camp counselor's cell phone this morning. Afterwards the counselor took roll and sent the kids to their various activities. No one missed Kaz until the line-up for lunch about half an hour ago."

"What?" Millie was horrified. "Didn't his baseball coach notice he wasn't there? How can you lose one of your campers like that?"

Just then her call waiting beeped and she checked to see who it was. "Can you hold a minute? My grandmother's on the other line." She clicked over. "Gran?"

Gran was talking very fast. "Millie, oh thank goodness, Millie, I just got a call from the day camp, and..."

"I know, Gran, they're on my other line. They say Kaz is missing!" Millie's head was spinning with all the possibilities, none of them good.

"I'm leaving here now to go to the rec center and see what they can tell me. I'll call you when I know something." Gran disconnected.

Millie clicked back over to talk to the day camp and repeated the conversation she'd just had with her grandmother. She hung up and felt a kind of fear she'd never known before. Now she understood what Synthia was going through when her brother disappeared from school! She started to send her parents a text, but stopped and thought better of it. After all, what could they do all the way up in Toronto, except worry?

Millie raced down the stairs and out the front door. Zach was taking a break in the midday heat, leaning against the towering shade tree and fanning himself with his baseball cap while slurping down bottled water. Millie realized she must look a fright—out of breath, wild-eyed, heart pounding—but she didn't care. She was desperate.

Zach wiped the sweat off his brow with the corner of his t-shirt. "Say, Millie, I'm doin' all the work out in this heat, and you look…" He stopped mid-sentence and jumped to his feet. "What's wrong?"

"Zach, I'm scared!" Millie exclaimed. "Kaz disappeared from day camp and no one's seen him for hours!"

Zach's eyes opened wide. "Wow. How can I help?"

She began pacing. "I need to figure out where he'd go. He was just so mad at me this morning…"

"Wait. You two had a fight?" Millie nodded. "What about?" Zach asked.

Millie leaned against the tree next to Zach to catch her breath. "I'm going to Indianapolis this afternoon and…"

"You're what!"

Millie was afraid to look him in the face. "My best friend wants me to enroll for college," Millie told him, knowing how inadequate that explanation was. "Kaz wanted to go with me and I told him no."

Zach's face blanched. "Seriously? After last night

meeting my friends? I thought you'd decided on OLAC." He didn't say anything for a while, kicked a rock and then picked it up and threw it all the way across the yard. "That sucks, Millie."

Millie looked up into his face. She didn't blame him for being mad at her. "I'll be back in a few days and we can talk...But Kaz." She took a deep breath. "I'm really worried, Zach."

Zach fanned himself with his baseball cap while he thought through everything she'd just dumped on him. He wiped the sweat off his brow with his forearm, put the hat on backwards and said with measured words, "Any chance your kid brother would try to go to Indianapolis on his own?"

Millie was stunned. That thought hadn't occurred to her, but now she began putting the puzzle pieces together. Kaz had left for camp this morning with not only his usual baseball bag, but a second large backpack as well. "My Visa card is missing," she told Zach. "Do you think..."

"Kaz took off to the airport? If he's got a credit card and he's bull-headed enough, maybe."

"Ohmigod, now what do I do?" Millie looked around the yard as if an answer would come to her from among the foliage, because this was one problem she didn't know how to solve. "I've got to think logically, figure this out."

"This isn't a mathematical equation, Millie, it's your brother," Zach said. "I'll drive you to the airport. Does your grandma know?" Millie nodded. "You can call her from the road." Zach sprinted to his pickup, reached behind the driver's seat and pulled out a clean t-shirt from an athletic bag and changed out of his soiled one.

"Let me get my stuff!" Millie heard the engine turn over as she ran into the house to collect her carry-on bag and purse. She was truly grateful for Zach's calm demeanor and assistance, despite knowing how much she'd just hurt him. Now if only they could catch up to Kaz before he…She didn't want to finish that thought.

Chapter Thirteen
Search

Zach pushed the highway speed limits all the way to the south side of Oklahoma City, making good time to the airport and somehow avoiding a speeding ticket. Millie sat in the front passenger seat, alternately watching Zach's speedometer and her cell phone for news of Kaz. Zach slowed down at the entrance to the short-term parking lot just long enough to push the button and grab the ejected parking ticket before zooming in.

"There!" Millie said, pointing to a vacant spot close to the entrance. She had her hand on the door handle before Zach even turned off the ignition. "Come on!" she exclaimed as she jumped out the passenger side door.

"Right behind you!" Zach hopped out his side, hit the remote door lock over his shoulder, took her hand and together they sprinted for the terminal.

Once inside, Millie scouted out the main ticket lobby, craning her neck to see over or around the crowds. People were everywhere, standing in ticketing queues, blocking pedestrians while reading the overhead Arriving and Departing signs, dragging luggage or urging small children along, and then she had to dodge out of the way of one of those beeping golf carts loaded down with senior citizens and their luggage. "There's no way I'll be able to spot him!" she cried in frustration.

Zach tapped his foot nervously and thought for a moment. "If he was here, where would he go first? He's got a decent head start on us, so whatd'ya think, could he be on a plane already?"

"Oh, please, I hope not. I mean I guess it's possible, but...."

"Millie," Zach said, putting a calming hand on her shoulder and looking her in the eye, "use that genius brain of yours and think. You know your brother better than I do."

Millie bobbed her head up and down and choked back tears while she tried to think rationally. "Kaz is only twelve years old. Unaccompanied minors need a form signed by a guardian in order to board the plane," she said. "I've flown with Kaz and Charlie enough to know that."

"Okay," Zach said, "but could he buy the ticket online without an adult? Then bluff his way through?"

"Kaz can be pretty convincing when he wants to be." Millie pulled out her cell phone and fired off a text message.

"Who'd you send it to?" Zach asked, looking over her shoulder.

"My Visa card company, asking if there's been any unusual activity on it today."

Millie's cell phone beeped back with a reply. She

opened the message and flashed the caller ID to Zach before reading the message.

Attempt to use Visa card xxxx xxxx xxxx 3369 issued to Mildred Olson in payment for first class seat on Midwestern States Airlines from Oklahoma City to Indianapolis, unaccompanied minor. Please advise if charge is authorized.

"He's trying to buy a ticket to Indianapolis with my Visa card, first class, no less!" Millie felt dizzy and her knees wobbled, but Zach put his arm around her waist to steady her. She wished she could just collapse into his comforting embrace, but time was of the essence. She did another visual search for a sign directing her to the Midwestern States Airlines ticket desk. "That way!" she exclaimed, pointing down a corridor.

The two of them took off running again, dodging more beeping golf carts and jogging around people leisurely strolling through the airport. They came to a crosswalk, but another sign pointed left, so they jumped over a pile of luggage in the middle of the floor and raced on. Unfortunately, when they finally arrived at the Midwestern States ticketing desk there was a long line of people ahead of them at the counter.

Zach stopped to catch his breath, leaning his hands on his knees and breathing hard. "Now what?"

Millie was breathing even harder than Zach and had to lean over and rub a stitch in her side, so talking was out of the question. But she still knew exactly what to do. She pulled out her cell phone and hit Reply to the text message. Responding to unauthorized Visa charge re: Mildred Olson. Standing at back of line at airport ticket desk. Help!

It worked. A voice came over the public address. "Will Mildred Olson please report to the Midwestern

States Airlines ticket desk?"

"That's me!" Millie shouted, waving her arms in the air to attract attention. She and Zach endured dirty looks from frustrated passengers as they pushed their way to the front of the line.

And there was Kaz! He was not in the line, probably told to stand aside until the Visa charge cleared. He had his baseball cap pulled low over his brow as his eyes darted furtively around the area, and his shoulders drooped because both his overstuffed backpack and his athletic bag were slung over his right shoulder and nearly weighed him down. Millie thought her brother looked like a frightened little boy and her heart went out to him.

She shoved her cell phone into Zach's hands. "Send a text to Gran and tell her we found him." Zach nodded and stepped aside, quickly scrolling through the options on her phone.

Millie tapped her brother on the shoulder. He turned around, startled. "Hey, watch it...Uh-oh!"

Relief swept over Millie as she clamped her hand firmly around the back of his neck. "Karl Azford Olson! You scared us all half to death! What were you thinking?" She pulled her photo ID out of her pocket and turned to the ticketing agent. "You paged me. I'm Mildred Olson and I believe you have my credit card," she said, showing the woman her ID.

The agent raised an eyebrow as she carefully compared the information on the Indiana driver's license to Millie. "Yes, we do indeed. Is there a problem, Miss?"

Millie shot Kaz a dirty look and said, "No, just a family misunderstanding."

The ticket agent gave Millie back her credit card

and craned her neck to see around her. "May I help you, sir?" she asked the man behind Millie.

Millie piloted her brother out of the queue line and turned him around to face her. "Kaz, what got into you?"

Zach handed Millie's phone back to her. "Your grandmother's on her way and she says to meet her at the main entrance." He gently took Kaz's heavy bags from him and easily slung them over his own shoulder. "You okay, Kaz?" Zach asked, getting down to eye level with him. "You had us worried."

Tears flooded into Kaz's eyes and he tried to wipe them away, but the floodgates opened. "I'm homesick, Millie. I wanna be at football, and go swimming with Matt, and, and…" He broke off in sobs. "I miss Mom and Dad," he sniffled.

A lump caught in Millie's throat, too, as she reached out to give her brother a hug, and was surprised when he actually let her. "I know, I miss them, too. Come on, you're probably hungry since you missed lunch, so let's get you something to eat while we wait for Gran." She glanced at the time on her cell phone. Nearly four o'clock. "Doesn't look like I'm going to make my flight to Indianapolis today either," she told Kaz with a sigh.

The three of them walked slowly to a nearby ice cream counter in the food court, and Zach ordered a double scoop of mint-chocolate chip for each of them. They sat down in the lobby near a picture window overlooking the airport entrance and parking garage to eat and wait for Gran.

Millie was now seriously reconsidering this trip to Indianapolis. She felt selfish leaving her distraught brother in the care of their worried grandmother when

Kaz clearly wanted to go home, too, and Zach...

Suddenly an idea popped into Millie's head. *If Synthia Whitfield could take her siblings across two states in a covered wagon, the least I can do is take Kaz to Indianapolis on an airplane!* She immediately started working out the details in her mind.

Fifteen minutes later Gran strolled through the automatic revolving lobby doors, followed by Mac! Millie ran over to give her a hug. "Gran, I'm so glad you're here. And Mac...?"

"Mac!" Zach exclaimed. "How did you...?"

Mac winked at his grandson. "Nice day for a picnic."

Millie looked from Gran to Mac and back again, but was as surprised and confused as Zach. "Kaz's fine, Gran," she said with a stern look at her brother, "but when did you have time to call Mac?"

"Millie, dear, what a day!" Gran said as she exhaled and flopped down into a lobby lounge chair. "Why, I told you this morning I was going on a picnic. I believe you assumed it was with my garden club." She winked at Millie but turned to Kaz and scolded him. "Young man, you gave us all quite a fright. Whatever possessed you?"

Kaz opened his mouth to reply, but Millie jumped in. "He's homesick." She smiled at her brother, who was chagrined, but gave her a thumbs up in response to her unexpected support. To distract him and give Millie time to talk to her grandmother, Zach playfully snatched Kaz's cap off his head and the two of them played a game of keep-away. Kaz actually laughed, and Millie was grateful all over again for Zach's calm assistance.

Millie took her grandmother by the arm and

pulled her aside. "This football thing is really important to Kaz, so I thought maybe I'd take him along with me to Indianapolis."

Gran shook her head. "We haven't spoken to your father about this."

"I know, but he did want Kaz to play, and I haven't missed my flight yet, so if I hurry and buy him a ticket…" When Gran didn't argue, Millie pulled out her cell phone, got on the Internet and began punching in buttons. "Done."

"This is all so disconcerting," Gran said as she nervously pushed back a stray lock of hair.

"I'm still coming back in a few days to help you with Charlie, but I can probably leave Kaz with the Hendersons until Mom and Dad get back from Toronto."

"Won't that be something of an imposition on poor Mrs. Henderson?"

"I doubt it. The Hendersons have a manny and Mrs. Henderson won't be inconvenienced at all. And Martha will be at the house some, too. Come on, Gran, it'll be fine," Millie insisted.

"Well, I suppose…."

"Thanks, Gran. You're the greatest!" Millie gave her grandmother a quick peck on the cheek and beamed at Mac. "Thanks for being here for her."

"My pleasure," he said with a warm smile.

"So what's the verdict?" Zach asked Millie with a glance at Kaz. "Grounded?"

Kaz was crestfallen, but Millie playfully elbowed him and said, "Come on, Kaz, we're going to Indianapolis!"

"Really?" Kaz shouted.

Millie hugged his shoulders. "Really. We've got to

hurry, though. They're boarding our flight soon." Her hands flew to her face as she remembered her packed carry-on bag, hurriedly stashed in the back of Zach's truck. "My stuff…."

"I'm on it," he said as he ran for the exit. "I'll meet you at the screening line."

Millie felt a tingle race down her spine as Zach clasped her hand before releasing her into the passenger screening line. "Millie, I…" he began but didn't finish. "I'll call you later."

"Better hurry, Miss," the screening agent said. "They're about to close the doors."

She and Kaz hurried through the metal detectors, grabbed their shoes and bags and raced down the corridor. Millie handed the gate attendant two boarding passes, waited while the woman ran them through the scanner, and then she and Kaz headed down the ramp to board their flight to Indianapolis. It felt like it was a lifetime ago that she'd even been home, and as eager as she was to be back, she still had some serious doubts. Yes, she'd promised Carlye, and yes, Kaz wanted to go home for football conditioning, but Millie now knew she was going to miss…her grandmother? Her sister? Be honest, Millie. You're going to miss Zach.

Millie shoved thoughts of Zach aside as she walked with her brother down the ramp. One problem at a time, she decided.

She hoped her dad wouldn't be too mad about the expense of the last-minute airline tickets, never mind the taxi ride Kaz took from Rolling Plains Recreation Center to the Oklahoma City airport. But it was a full flight so she'd changed her seat to an aisle at the back of the plane so she could sit next to Kaz. Her gut told her she was doing the right thing.

Once their belongings were stored in the overhead bins, their seatbelts fastened, and items stored underneath the seats as directed by the flight attendants, Millie pulled Synthia's diary out of her satchel and opened it.

Kaz pulled his earbuds out and reached over to touch the diary. "Hey, what's that?"

Millie blocked his hand before he touched the journal and gently removed it to his side of the armrest. "It's that girl's diary I found in Gran's attic," she replied. "And it's really old, so the fewer people that touch it the better."

Kaz shrugged. "I thought you gave that old thing to some teacher at OLAC."

"I didn't give it to him, I just let him examine it to determine its approximate age. I keep trying to do an online genealogy search to find out if any of Synthia Whitfield's descendants are still living in Oklahoma, but so far nothing has surfaced."

Kaz stared at her and then rolled his eyes. "I guess that's genius-speak for 'figure out who it belongs to.'"

Millie smiled at her brother before opening the journal. "That's exactly what it means." Kaz put his earbuds back in and Millie settled in to read as the plane taxied down the runway. *I hope Synthia found her brother as quickly as I found mine.*

December 6, 1865
I am beside myself with worry. Uncle Miles assures me that Nevada, Texas and Collin County are sparsely-populated, having only been settled four years ago, and in this

flat terrain, TJ has few places to hide or get lost. As comforting as that sounds, I will only be satisfied when my brother is home again with his family. My uncle is out this very minute with my cousins, searching for TJ. Mr. Yeager and I have taken the opposite path, hoping to cover more ground that way.

As is usual in December, twilight has come early, and that has added to my fear that TJ will not be found before the light of day.

"Where do you suppose your brother might go, left to his own devices?" Mr. Yeager asked.

I tried to concentrate, and after several moments, I was rewarded when an idea came to me. "He and Papa used to go fishing. Papa always said it helped him collect his thoughts whilst at the same time providing for his family's supper, and Papa frequently took TJ along. Is there a place nearby where folks fish?"

"Bear Creek," he replied, and quickened his step as I hurried to keep up.

We had no lantern, and except for the moonlight it was completely dark when we spotted a figure near the creek's edge, his back to us, a handmade pole and twine in his hand. My heart leapt into my throat when I realized it was my brother! Mr. Yeager and I rushed to greet him, and at that moment I did not know which emotion was stronger: anger at my brother for worrying us all, or relief that he had been found.

"Well, well, here we are," Mr. Yeager

said as he tousled my brother's hair. "Safe and sound, although I daresay young TJ's a bit chilled."

I hugged my brother tightly, threw my shawl about his shoulders, and then pulled him back at arm's length. "Thomas Jefferson Whitfield, you frightened us all half to death. What on earth possessed you?"

That sounds familiar! Millie looked up from her reading as the plane soared to cruising altitude. *Did I already read this part?* No, she was sure she hadn't.

TJ cast his eyes down. "Sorry I scared you, Sis," he said. "It's just that this has all been…"

I nodded as nothing more need be said between us about the ordeal we have endured this year. I hugged him tightly to my breast and offered a quiet prayer of gratitude for my brother's safe return.

After an awkward silence, Mr. Yeager cleared his throat and said, "Miss Whitfield, at recess one day, TJ here inquired after a ball and bat and told me his Pa had been teaching him a bit about the game of Base Ball." He leaned down to my brother's eye level. "We have a team forming here, mostly farmers and such, but there was a suggestion at our last game that we teach some of the young boys to play as well. What do you say, TJ? Would you like to join us?"

TJ brightened up and said, "I would like that very much, sir!"

I am so grateful to this fine gentleman,

not only because he helped locate my missing brother, but also because he has taken such a kindly interest in the welfare of an orphan. Mr. Yeager apparently knows a great deal about children, more than I gave him credit for, and not just what they should learn in a schoolroom. TJ has been adrift since the death of our father, and even though Uncle Miles is kind to us, he is very busy on his farm and with his family, as he should be. However, TJ desperately needs a man to look up to, and I now believe Mr. Thomas Perry Yeager is that man.

"Thank you for your assistance, Mr. Yeager," I said with great sincerity. "My aunt sent me to invite you to join our Thanksgiving dinner tomorrow before..." I frowned at TJ. "Well, the offer of dinner stands. Is there anything else I can do to repay you for your kindness?"

Mr. Yeager tipped his hat to me. "You're welcome, Miss Whitfield," he said with a fetching grin. "And as for repayment, I'd be pleased if you would walk out with me after dinner tomorrow."

I cocked my head to one side and studied him a bit. Although I originally found Mr. Yeager to be quite odious, I can plainly see I was wrong. "Yes, I would like that," I said, returning his smile.

"Hey, Kaz," Millie said, poking him in the arm and pointing to Synthia's journal. "This girl's kid brother also plays baseball."

"Huh?" He pulled his earbuds out. "What year is

that?"

"1865. I guess it was getting pretty popular after the Civil War."

Kaz looked impressed while attempting to maintain his pre-teen nonchalance. "Cool."

Lucky girl, Millie thought. She had a great guy like Thomas to help her find her brother when he ran away. But wait! Zach had been there for her when Kaz ran away. Thanks to Zach's quick thinking and her logic, things had worked out today when they could have gone horribly wrong. *Did I remember to thank him?* She wasn't sure. In fact, she wasn't sure of anything right now.

But one thing was sure. Millie was proud of herself for powering through her fears about Kaz's disappearance and using her intelligence as a resource rather than a safe-haven. Reading Synthia's story was helping her realize she'd been a spectator in her own life, immersing herself in her history books to avoid the here-and-now. It had always been so much easier to role-play a nineteenth century life in a museum than to fully live a twenty-first century one. And now, on her way to Indianapolis, Millie knew she had some hard choices to make.

Home. Millie hadn't realized until now that she was just as homesick as her brother. She missed her parents, her friends, Zach... Wait. Zach's in Rolling Plains, Oklahoma. She shrugged. Well, thinking about him—wherever he was—made her happy.

Millie smiled contentedly, and then closed her eyes for a quick nap before they landed.

Chapter Fourteen
Reservations

It was nearly eleven p.m. when Carlye Henderson pulled her late model compact sedan into the Olson driveway, put the car in park, and popped the trunk latch. "Okay, here you go, Millie." She cast a glance over her shoulder to the backseat. "And Kaz." She rolled her eyes. "Still can't believe the stunt you pulled."

"Thanks, Carlye," Millie said as she slowly climbed out of the shotgun seat and walked around to the open trunk to unearth their belongings. "You're great to come out to the airport so late and pick us up." Millie arched her back to stretch, and then began vigorously tugging at their bags, dislodging Carlye's haphazardly-arranged belongings in the process. "Honestly, Carlye, don't you ever clean out your trunk? What's this?" Millie opened a school folder with a typed report inside and frowned. "Seriously? This paper was due in December!"

Carlye snatched the folder from Millie and shoved

her glasses back up her nose to get a good look at the report. "I wondered where this was. It's a good thing I back up my files." She tossed it back into the disorganized pile of tennis rackets, swim towels, unreturned school books, filled shopping bags and dirty laundry.

"You're going to have to be more organized in college, especially if we're roommates," Millie told her, "and…"

"IF?"

"…and professors don't accept excuses like 'my dog ate my homework.'"

Carlye pulled a face. "We don't have a dog. It's late, Millie. Can you save the lecture?"

The car's back door opened. Kaz stumbled out, yawning and stretching as he headed up the walk to the Olson's front door.

"Hey, Kaz!" Millie called. "You forgot your stuff…again!"

Kaz rolled his eyes as he turned back, yanked his heavy backpack from the trunk, hoisted his athletic bag over his shoulder, and lugged them to the porch. He dropped both on the step with a loud thud and scowled, crossing his arms in front of his chest as he waited to be let into the house.

"Okay, Millie, since you dragged your kid brother along," Carlye said with a sideways glance at Kaz on the porch, "I guess we'll leave him with Matt before going down to Bloomington in the morning. What time are you picking me up?"

Somehow Millie had assumed Carlye would pick her up, not the other way around, but since her car had been parked in the family's garage for weeks now, she really should drive it. "Well, I guess I need to find all the forms Admissions sent me, make sure they're filled out correctly, take my car to be serviced, and…."

"Ohmigod, Millie! You're stalling, aren't you?"

"No," she hedged, "it's just that it's been a long day."

"Uh-huh," Carlye said. "Well, get some rest because tomorrow's a big day."

Millie couldn't understand her motives, either. Maybe it was just exhaustion due to lack of sleep or stress from the day's events, maybe it was that she missed her parents, maybe it was ongoing qualms about the whole going-away-to-college thing. Whatever the reason, a good night's sleep couldn't hurt. "I'll text you in the morning," she said as Carlye stepped back into her car.

Millie dug around in her purse until she found her keys and let herself and Kaz into the house. She flipped on the entry hall table lamp and sighed with contentment as she looked around at the familiar surroundings. Everything was pretty much the same as she'd left it, including the pile of unread mail stacked neatly on the side table. Martha had kept the house in good order during their absence and it felt good to be home. Kaz bounded up the stairs to his room even before Millie had a chance to shut and lock the front door.

In all the chaos of locating Kaz, Millie realized she'd never notified Martha of their imminent arrival. She decided to leave a note for Martha to avoid startling her when she came to work in the morning, so she went into the kitchen to write on the dry erase board they kept on the refrigerator for just that sort of thing. Once in the kitchen, her growling stomach also reminded her she hadn't eaten, so she began rummaging through the fridge to see what might be edible. Not much, she realized, as she stared at the nearly-bare shelves. A few eggs, a loaf of bread, some English muffins, half a box of uneaten pizza she assumed her dad had left behind, several bottles of water, and some yogurt.

She grabbed a carton of yogurt and checked the eat-by date. It hadn't expired yet, so she took a spoon from the drawer and had just stuffed a large bite in her mouth when her cell phone rang. She set the spoon in the yogurt and dug her phone out of her pocket.

"Hello?"

"I guess you made it home okay."

Millie smiled and swallowed her yogurt. "Hi, Zach. Yeah, we're here."

"I just wanted to check on you, say goodnight, tell you I already miss you."

Zach could still make her blush, on the phone and hundreds of miles away. She missed him too, but she had a lot of things to work through in her mind. "Thanks for all your help today," she chirped, as if all he'd done was give her a ride to the airport. "Can I call you when I get back from IU tomorrow?"

Zach waited a beat before answering. "Yeah, call me tomorrow. And for the record, I hate that you're going to IU."

Guilt hit her again full force. If it hadn't been for Zach she wouldn't have been able to get to Kaz as quickly as she did, and to complicate matters, she'd made unspoken promises to him that she was about to renege on by putting her signature on some admissions papers somewhere else.

What were these undefined feelings she had for Zach? Gratitude? Her gut told her it was more than that, but she shook the feeling off. She grabbed the phone to call him back and apologize, but stopped herself and hung up again. Maybe that restful sleep she'd been planning would actually give her some needed perspective.

Well, it didn't help. After two nights in a row with little sleep, a frantic search for her missing brother, plus a long drive from the Indianapolis airport with her chatty best friend, Millie had just assumed she'd collapse into her own bed in her own room and sleep soundly. No such luck. She'd tossed and turned all night, waking up to check the bedside clock nearly every hour and making to-do lists in her head. She needn't have bothered writing that message for Martha the night before. She'd been up for two hours, showered and dressed, and was poring over Indiana University's admissions forms when Martha came through the back door at nine o'clock.

"Millie!" Martha gasped in surprise.

Millie gave Martha a quick hug and set her coffee mug in the sink. "Sorry. I didn't mean to startle you, but this trip came up on short notice and I completely forgot to text." She went back over to the breakfast table and stacked all her papers in a neat pile, making sure all the edges matched and the tops of the pages all faced the same direction, as if organization would solve the problem they represented. "Oh, yeah, and Kaz is here, too."

Martha lifted an eyebrow and put her hands on her hips. "Okay, Millie, your folks aren't due back for a while, so what's going on?"

Millie looked away, convinced Martha could read the sleep-deprived confusion written all over her face. "What's going on is that it's the end of July and Carlye wants me to go down to IU to enroll and be her roomie, so I planned a quick trip from Oklahoma. But then Kaz ran away and I ended up bringing him along, and…."

"Kaz ran away!"

"Oh, sorry," Millie said when she saw Martha's obvious surprise and concern. "It's okay now, we found him, but he scared us yesterday."

"Us?"

"Well, yeah, Gran, Mac, me, Zach…."

"Wait," Martha said, putting up her hand like a traffic cop. "Zach? Mr. MacMillan's grandson, right?" Millie nodded and Martha rolled her eyes. "Uh-huh. Go on."

Millie's hands flew to her face as if she could stop the color rising, but then passed off her embarrassment by readjusting her headband. "Well, see, Kaz was upset because he was going to miss out on football conditioning, so I brought him home with me. Once we found him. Anyway, I was hoping between you and the Hendersons he'd be okay for a few days. Their manny will pick up Kaz this morning and take him and Matt to conditioning, so Kaz won't be underfoot here."

"I'll revisit this business of Kaz later," Martha said, hands on her hips. "Tell me about Zach MacMillan and why you're suddenly blushing whenever his name comes up."

"Is there anything for breakfast?"

Martha lifted an eyebrow at Millie, but pulled out a fry skillet and grabbed some eggs from the fridge. "Toast or English muffin?"

Millie thought she was ready to go. She'd put all her carefully organized IU enrollment papers in a folder, and even had her car keys in her hand, yet she couldn't make her feet move.

Her mind rewound to Zach, his intellectual friends, Synthia Whitfield's journal, and how much she admired the two professors at Oklahoma College of Liberal Arts who'd helped her with it. *Should I enroll there? Live at Gran's? No Way! Why not?* Millie kept going back and forth in her mind, arguing each side of the question and coming up with logical reasons for both and no decision either way. Her cell phone beeped with yet another text from Carlye. She sighed, caught a glimpse of the time and knew she'd kept Carlye waiting long enough, so she sent a reply: *On my way.*

She went out to the garage, almost hoping her Hyundai wouldn't start after sitting idle for several weeks. But it started up immediately and purred like a kitten, so she realized the excuse of taking it for a tune-up was just that, an excuse. The dashboard digital clock read 10:15 — a late start considering the ninety minute drive ahead of them — and she still had to pick up Carlye and get gas.

Ten minutes later she pulled into the Henderson's circular drive and honked. Carlye flew out the front door and hopped into the passenger seat.

"Drive!" Carlye commanded as she fastened her seatbelt. "They close the admissions office at 3:00 during the summer."

Millie took her time readjusting her rear-view mirror, checking her seatbelt, and signaling as she pulled out onto the busy street. "That's over four hours from now, Carlye," she said as she made a slow right-hand turn. "We've got plenty of time. Anyway, I need gas."

Carlye groaned as they drove down Meridian Street headed for the I-465 Loop. "Stop here," she said, pointing to a self-serve gas station with easy access in and out.

Millie shook her head. "Too expensive. I'm sure I can do better down the street."

"What difference does a few cents make?"

Millie drove about a mile south on Meridian, eye-balling gas prices and ignoring Carlye's frustration all the way, made a U-turn at a stoplight, and eventually drove back to the gas station Carlye had suggested in the first place. Carlye drummed her fingers on the dashboard while Millie took her time locating her credit card, popping the gas cap, and pumping the gas. Millie tore off the receipt, shoved it in her pocket and started for the convenience store.

Carlye leaned out the window. "Now what?"

"I'm thirsty!" Millie ignored Carlye's loud groan and went inside, returning several minutes later with a diet soda and a bottle of water.

"Come on, let's go!" Carlye urged. Millie again took way too much time getting back into the car, fastening her seatbelt, checking and re-checking her mirrors, and starting up the engine.

Carlye snatched her soda from Millie, popped open the pull-tab and took a long swallow. "Girlfriend, I don't know where your head is today. Want me to drive?"

Millie also wondered where her head was, but she didn't answer. Instead, she set the water bottle in the cup holder next to the driver's seat and made the left turn onto the interstate loop. "Music?" In fact, that was exactly what she needed: some quiet, soothing, classical music, something to help her collect her thoughts while she drove. She popped in her CD of Vivaldi's Four Seasons and cranked up the volume.

Carlye reached over and turned the volume way down. "What gives, Millie?"

"I haven't been sleeping well, that's all," Millie replied, which was true as far as it went. Could mere insomnia be the problem?

"Well, maybe you can finally relax once all this registration stuff is done."

"But that's what's keeping me up at night!" Millie told her.

Carlye pooh-poohed Millie's doubts with a wave of her hand. "I'm doing all this for your own good, you know, so you can thank me later." She looked around at the cars whizzing by them going at or above the posted speed limit of fifty-five, and then craned her neck to check Millie's speedometer. It read forty. "Unbelievable! You're driving like an eighty-year-old woman!"

Millie realized she had to drive the speed limit on the freeway or she would get run over, or worse yet, ticketed for impeding the flow of traffic, so she increased her speed to fifty-five and set the cruise control. "Better?"

Carlye tossed Millie a look but said nothing. They drove the rest of the way in near silence, only speaking when Millie needed Carlye to check the GPS on her phone.

A flummoxed Carlye crossed her arms in front of her chest as she leaned against Millie's car, scowling as Millie dragged her feet walking across the parking lot to join her. "I can't believe we wasted an entire day just so you could chicken out! Thanks a lot."

Millie fought back tears as she searched for her keys in the bottom of her bag, beeped open the car doors and slumped into the driver's seat, embarrassed and confused all at once. She rubbed her forehead to relieve the throbbing and caught a glimpse of her bloodshot eyes in the mirror. "I'm so sorry, Carlye," she sputtered. "I don't know what's wrong with me. I just couldn't do it—turn in the admissions packet. I just froze."

"Ya think?" Carlye opened the passenger door, slid into her seat and slumped down in a sulk. "You may be a genius, Millie, but your insecurities have bad timing. Seriously, unless you go back inside and turn in that paperwork, we're both screwed."

Millie absent-mindedly played with the keys dangling near the ignition. "IU just seems so..."

"What? Indiana University is one of the most respected schools in the country!"

"I was going to say huge," Millie replied. "Maybe I should wait awhile, go to community college, and sign up for some online courses..."

"Ohmigod, Millie! You can't spend your life hiding behind a computer." When Millie didn't answer, Carlye heaved an exasperated sigh and fastened her seatbelt. "Let's go home," she said in frustration.

Millie dutifully started the engine, turned on the air conditioning, and put the car in reverse. But then an idea came to her, so she pulled the car back into the space so she could get out her cell phone and send a text.

"Who's that to?"

Millie handed her phone to Carlye. "Michael. I can't text and drive, so tell me when he texts back."

"Why do you want to talk to Michael?" Millie

didn't answer, so Carlye took the phone and set it in her lap as they drove in silence. They were well on their way north to Indianapolis when the cell phone pinged with his response. "It says 'meet me in our old study place,'" Carlye told her. "Why?" she asked again.

"He's a guy. Maybe he can give me some perspective," Millie said, and then concentrated on her driving.

An hour later they pulled into the coffee shop parking lot, and this time Millie sprinted toward the entrance with Carlye trailing behind her.

"Millie? What gives?" Carlye asked for what seemed like the hundredth time since they got Michael's text.

Michael was sitting in his favorite booth in the far corner of the twenty-four hour coffee shop, the same booth where their high school study group always met. Millie smiled to herself because Michael was doing what he always did, sipping black coffee and scrolling through apps on his phone, occasionally beating out a rhythm on the table's edge. Just like old times.

Except so much had changed over the summer. "Good, you're here," Millie said as she slid in across from him.

Carlye scooted into the seat next to Michael and almost tossed her handbag on the bench between them before stopping herself. "Or should I save a spot for Emily?"

Michael gingerly took a sip of hot coffee, set the mug down and poured two packets of sugar into it. "Emily's at The Fashion Mall. She leaves for Ball State in three weeks and claims she's crunched for shopping time." He shrugged and stirred his coffee vigorously before taking a second swallow.

No one spoke, just sat there looking at each other, each one waiting for the other to begin. The waitress came over to take orders and cleared her throat to get their attention, and then went to retrieve their drinks from the kitchen.

"Okay," Michael finally said, "why have I been summoned?"

The waitress returned and carelessly slammed an ice tea and diet soda on the table, ignored the sloshing, and let Millie and Carlye each claim their own. "Anything else?" she asked as she tapped her foot impatiently.

Millie wasn't in the mood to placate the waitress. "We're fine." She took a sip of tea through the straw and leaned forward on the table. "I found a journal," she told them both in a conspiratorial whisper.

"Huh?" Michael said.

Millie retold the story of finding Synthia Whitfield's diary in her grandmother's attic earlier this summer.

"So now you're Nancy Drew?" Michael asked her.

"No," Millie said, but was rather amused at the comparison. "Well, it is sort of a mystery, since my grandmother has no idea who this girl was or how the diary ended up in that trunk in her attic. See, my dad's old college friend, Alex, is a history professor at Oklahoma Liberal Arts College, and his son Zach took me over there. Alex's forensics science-professor-friend analyzed the journal and it really is old just like I thought, and then Zach asked me out and..." She paused to catch her breath.

"I sure am hearing the name 'Zach' a lot," Michael said. "Who's he?"

Carlye frowned. "Great. Millie found an old diary and dated a boy. So what's that got to do with what just happened down at IU?"

"Wait," Michael said. "What just happened at IU?"

Carlye pointed to Millie and said, "This one blew her last chance to go to college this fall and cheated me out of my dorm pick, that's what happened!"

"What? No way!" Michael exclaimed. "Miss Valedictorian, Miss all-kinds-of-scholarships, Miss Queen of the AP Exams, not enrolled for fall classes?" He took a sip of his cooling coffee, shaking his head all the while, and then brightened up. "Hey, does that mean you're holding out for Notre Dame?" He gave her two thumbs up. "Don't blame you."

"Doesn't anybody ever listen to me?" Millie cried in frustration. "I'm not interested in any of those mega-universities. All through high school everyone had all these preconceived notions about my future, but no one bothered to ask me what I want."

Carlye was silent for a moment. "Okay, so what is it you want?"

"If I go to college…."

"IF?" both Michael and Carlye exclaimed at once.

"IF I go, I want a life—a social life, with friends and football games and dances…and to not be under constant pressure like I was in high school."

"Pressure in college is a given," Michael told her with a shrug.

But Carlye understood and nodded sympathetically. "You pushed yourself so hard at Kendrick that now you're burned out," she said. "Maybe if you took a semester off it wouldn't be the end of the world."

"See, that's what I thought, but no one thinks it's a good idea," she said. "Not my parents, not my grandmother. I was thinking of just working at the museum and taking a few online courses."

"Well," Carlye mused, "if you take some time off, then you'd be ready to enroll at IU in January when I get back from England. Maybe we can still be room-mates after all."

"Won't you lose your dorm room by then?" Millie asked.

"Probably," Carlye said, sighing, but then a smile slowly spread across her face. "The dorm's not im-portant. You're my best friend and…."

"We'll always be friends, Carlye," Millie assured her. "But after high school when people go to college, things change…."

"Relationships change…" Michael interjected. "Hey, who knows if Emily and I will still be together by Christmas?"

"Or if Zach will still want to be with me by then," Millie mumbled.

"This Zach guy," Carlye said with a swirl of the straw in her soda. "He's in Oklahoma, right?"

"Where there's a perfectly good liberal arts school that your dad went to," Michael added.

Millie blushed and lowered her eyes. "Yeah, Zach's a great guy, but he's only seventeen and still in high school."

Michael threw his head back and laughed loudly, causing people to turn and stare. "Millie," he said be-tween gasps of breath, "most seventeen-year-olds are still in high school!" The laughter stopped, people went back to their food, but the smirk on Michel's face didn't go away.

"There's no future for us unless I go back to Oklahoma," Millie said.

"So that's why you didn't sign up at IU?" Carlye demanded.

"Well, no…well, yes…well, maybe," Millie stammered.

Michael drained the last of his coffee and slammed down the empty mug. "Well, nothing. This Zach guy. He likes you, too?" Millie nodded. "So then if you go to Oklahoma and it doesn't work out with loverboy, you'll still be outta there in three years and off to Boston to follow in your dad's footsteps. Right again?"

Millie thought hard for a moment and then cocked her head to one side. "Well, it's too soon to think about Harvard, but everything else you said is true. Thanks, Michael!" She pulled some money out of her purse and laid it on the table before sliding out of the booth. She was halfway out the door when she remembered Carlye. "You coming?" she called over her shoulder as she pushed open the glass doors.

"Yeah," Carlye called after her. "As soon as I text Esther."

Millie dropped Carlye at her front door as Kaz came running out of the Hendersons' house and hopped in the shotgun seat.

"Home, James!"

"Ha ha," Millie said. "Fasten your seatbelt," she told him as she pulled out of the Hendersons' driveway. "How was conditioning?"

"Fine," he said, but Millie could hear his enthusiasm and read his body language.

She started to push in a Mozart CD, but then changed her mind and instead turned the radio to Kaz's favorite heavy metal station. She winced when the sound came blasting out of the speakers and turned the volume down, but not too much. Kaz didn't seem to mind at all, though. He was playing air guitar and drumming on the seats all the way home.

Millie pulled the Hyundai into their driveway and shut off the engine. "Come on, Kaz, I've got a lot to do before I head back to Oklahoma City. Get your stuff."

Kaz groaned but for once did as he was told, grabbing his athletic bag from his feet and slinging it over his shoulder before heading into the house. He tossed his bag in its usual spot on the entry hall floor, next to the table near the door where the pile of mail had been sitting unsorted last night, but now was gone. "I'm starved, Millie," Kaz called over his shoulder as he started for the kitchen. "Suppose Martha left anything for supper?"

"There's plenty of pizza!" a voice called from the dining room. Millie and Kaz exchanged surprised looks, but before either one of them could say another word, their dad appeared in the foyer, grinning broadly. "Don't I get a hug?" he asked.

"Dad!" Millie and Kaz exclaimed at once, running headlong into his open arms. Karl scooped his children to him in a group hug and danced them around in circles.

"Dad!" Millie repeated. "Why didn't you tell us you were coming?"

"He thought it would be a fun surprise!"

Millie pulled away from her father and her jaw dropped. "Mom!" Sure enough, there stood an amused Elizabeth, her hands on her hips.

The four of them laughed, jumped up and down, hugged, and talked all at once. Millie couldn't believe her eyes. Both of her parents home, so welcome, so unexpected. But then she pulled back and looked at them. "How…" She couldn't even form the question.

"Come on, the pizza's getting cold," Karl said, pointing everyone to the dining room.

"Hi, Millie!" Charlie waved from the table, her fingers sticky with cheese.

Millie felt weak in the knees. She gave her sister a quick hug, shook her head and sank into her usual seat at the table. "Somebody please explain this to me."

"Your grandmother called us after the incident with Kaz," Karl said with a stern look at his son. "You gave Gran quite a scare, young man."

Kaz smirked and reached for a slice of pizza.

"Mildred told us you two had flown up here," Elizabeth explained, "and we knew our family needed us, so we went straight to the Toronto airport and hopped on a commuter flight to Chicago."

Karl picked up the story. "We then flew from Chicago to Oklahoma City last night, collected your sister here," he said with a playful pinch to Charlie's nose, "drove your rental car to the airport this morning, and the three of us grabbed a last-minute flight back to Indianapolis."

"We all arrived here midday, only to have Martha tell us you'd gone to Bloomington and Kaz was at football conditioning." Karl turned to Kaz. "So how did it go?"

Kaz gave the thumbs up sign and washed his mouthful of pizza down with a large gulp of milk.

"So now you're officially enrolled at Indiana University, I suppose?" Karl asked with resignation.

Millie nearly choked on her bite of Mushroom-lovers Delite, but she swallowed some water while everyone around the table waited expectantly for an answer. "Oh, that," she squeaked out, then cleared her throat and took another sip of water. "Well, no, I kinda messed that up."

"You messed what up?" Elizabeth asked in wide-eyed surprise. "Millie the Invincible? Messed up? Impossible!"

Millie wondered why her mom was always comparing her to that fictional character. She wasn't anything like Millicent, who never did or said the wrong thing, and always solved the mystery du jour with the logical use of her considerable brain power. In many respects, Millie was a normal sixteen-year-old girl, filled with insecurities and doubts just like any other teenager, even though her high intellect set her apart from her peers.

Elizabeth had originally invented Millicent to inspire Millie to overcome her fears, but a made-up character was no role model as far as Millie was concerned. And before this summer, real-life role models had been in short supply until she learned about Synthia Elizabeth Whitfield. The girl was real, someone close to the same age, had overcome the worst of obstacles, and she'd done it all with aplomb. Millie wanted to emulate Synthia's real-life courage, and Millicent's fictional heroics paled in comparison.

She took a deep breath. "No, Mom, I'm not Millicent, I'm me, just a confused kid. I let Carlye drag me all the way down to IU today so I could turn in the paperwork and sign up for classes, only to renege on the whole thing."

Kaz scowled as usual when she used a word he

didn't understand. "Re…what?"

"I backed out," Millie explained.

Karl leaned back on the two legs of his dining room chair, causing them to creak, until Elizabeth shot him a look and he set the chair back down. He smiled at his wife across the table before winking at Millie. "Does your reluctance to attend school in Indiana have anything to do with a certain star quarterback in Oklahoma?"

Millie blushed at the mention of Zach. "Umm, well, I…" She sighed. "I could really use some advice."

"We advise you to make use of your intelligence and scholarship money and go to college," Elizabeth informed her.

"The only reason I ever thought about going to IU was to be roommates with Carlye, but she's not even going to be there first semester, and after spending time with Zach and getting help from his dad and Professor Riley…."

"Sounds to me like your decision's been made," Karl said. "It's Oklahoma Liberal Arts College, isn't it?"

"Oklahoma Liberal…?" Elizabeth gasped, looking from her daughter to her husband and back again. "Really? With all your options, that's your choice?"

"Hey, watch it," Karl joked. "But think about it Liz, our girl here can use that scholarship money you're concerned about, feel comfortable in her surroundings, and still get a fine undergrad education. Just like I did."

Elizabeth mulled that over. "Okay fine," she finally conceded, "on one condition. No living with your grandmother. Live on campus, meet people, join activities, have the whole college experience. No more hiding out in the library or holed up in your bedroom with Google."

Millie suddenly felt a sense of peace. She wanted to go back to Oklahoma. She could study history in a well-respected humanities program, spend time with her beloved grandmother, and take part in teenage activities with Zach—and his friends—activities she'd mostly missed out on in her accelerated push to graduation at Kendricks. It was all so simple! She jumped up from the table and tossed her napkin in her chair. "I'll go send the Admissions office an email right now."

Millie fairly danced up the stairs and into her bedroom, opened her laptop and sent the email. She leaned back on her pillow and thought about everything that had happened since May. She'd graduated valedictorian at the age of sixteen; she'd spent an exciting summer in Oklahoma that was completely different from any she'd ever spent there before; and she'd found a journal and gained insight into her own life from reading about a girl from the past. Millie glanced at her bedside table where Synthia's journal lay. She gingerly opened it to read the final entry.

June 15, 1868
I have not had the leisure to write in this journal for a very long time, and may not write again for a while as I will be quite busy in the future.

Today is my wedding day! I am being married to Mr. Thomas Perry Yeager at the Mt. Pleasant Baptist Church just south of Nevada, Texas. My Uncle Miles is giving me away, my brother TJ, at age thirteen and practically a man, will stand up for Thomas, and my sister Mary Ann (now ten years old!) is standing up for me as maid of honor. When I think back to the loss of our parents, the despair and helplessness I felt at being left with two children to raise, the journey from Missouri to Texas, and ultimately meeting Mr. Yeager when I was only fifteen, I am utterly amazed. I found a strength and purpose I did not know I had, and with God's blessing, happiness and contentment are sure to follow. I am a very lucky woman.

Mr. Yeager proposed to me over a year ago, but although Uncle Miles readily gave us permission to marry, he said we must wait until I was eighteen. I celebrated that momentous birthday last month, so now my new life is about to begin. I pray that Mr. Yeager and I are happy and fruitful, and continue to find joy in one another's company for many years to come.

Millie was stunned. She married Thomas Perry Yeager! Synthia Whitfield Yeager? She now knew why she hadn't found any information on Google, because she'd been searching for a Whitfield instead of a Yeager!

I know that Mama and Papa are smiling down on us from Heaven. I pray God grant us the happiness in our marriage that they enjoyed in theirs. And now, I face the future with contentedness and joy I never knew possible.

Millie closed the journal and grabbed her cell phone off the nightstand and hit Zach's number on speed dial. It rang seven times and she was sure it was going to voice mail.

"Hey, Millie," Zach said, sounding a little breathless.

Millie had already begun mentally composing her voice mail message when he picked up and surprised her. The fact that she loved that Oklahoma drawl of his didn't help her concentration either.

"Ya there?" he asked.

"Oh, yeah, I…" Hearing his voice drove all logical thought processes out of her head.

"We just got done with football practice. I'm leaving the locker room now."

Millie heard a beep-beep as he unlocked his truck, then heard the door slam and the engine turn over. She hoped he was listening, really listening. "I just wanted to tell you something…about my college plans." And that he'd care.

"Yeah?" Zach asked with apprehension in his voice. "What?"

Millie told him about the events leading up to her final decision and then held her breath for his reaction.

Zach was silent for a few minutes, leaving Millie's heart to pound with anxiety, but then he let out a huge whoop. "Yes!" he exclaimed, and she felt a warm, happy relief settle all over her.

He turned off his car engine and they talked for a long time. Reluctantly she said goodnight, disconnected the phone, and fell into a deep, sound sleep.

Chapter Fifteen
Denouement

Mid-August! Millie scratched another day off her wall calendar that showed she had only two weeks before she left for college in Oklahoma. Her mind reeled with the dizzying realization that the collegiate experience she'd so steadfastly resisted for the last year was now becoming reality. What to do? Where to start? She took a calming breath and thought it through. Get organized. Treat it like a project.

Of course. The only way to deal with a stressful situation was to make a plan, so she hurriedly booted up her laptop and began typing.

#1. Check dorm room assignment online.

#2. Find out name of roommate; email or Skype to get acquainted.

#3. Update wardrobe: fall/winter clothes, shoes, handbags, etc.

#4. Verify course assignments and check campus map to locate classrooms. Email professors and request advance reading assignments.

#5. Purchase textbooks, school and dorm supplies online.

#6. Complete research for living relative(s) of Synthia Elizabeth Whitfield-Yeager; return journal?

#7. Talk to Zach. ☺

#8. PACK!

"Should I work down chronologically or in random order, and which is most crucial?" she asked herself. She decided that she needed to shop first. Millie wanted her mother's help with that, and fortunately her mom's office was within walking distance of a downtown shopping mall. With Kaz and Charlie already back in school, she had no pressing responsibilities, so she'd drive to Elizabeth's office and convince her to spend her lunch hour at the mall.

Millie stepped off the elevator and briefly thought about going in to say hello to her dad at Merritt, Hall & Olson, but decided against it because he was probably busy and she was in a self-imposed time crunch, so she turned left toward her mother's small office down the hallway. She pushed open the glass doors and walked inside, thinking about the last time she was here, way last spring. She shook her head in amazement at how much had changed since then.

She waved at the receptionist. "Is Mom free?"

Sarah smiled and jerked her head towards Elizabeth's office. "She's on the phone, but you can go on in."

Millie rapped quietly on the office door and peeked in. Sure enough, Elizabeth was on the phone, but waved her in.

"What happened in here?" Millie exclaimed and then clapped her hands over her mouth when her mom indicated silence. The office, in a state of disarray under normal circumstances, today looked like it had been tossed in a burglary. Everywhere she looked, items were strewn around: yellow legal writing pads, research materials, a Colts hoodie sweatshirt from last winter, and a large stack of Millicent books blocking the view of the picture window that overlooked Monument Circle. Open cardboard boxes were filling up every available space, some already half filled with personal and professional items, and even more items were still lying around waiting to be packed. Confused, Millie shoved aside a box and settled herself on the leather sofa to wait till her mom got off the phone.

"Yeah, Larry," Elizabeth was saying, "go ahead and call my cell or my landline at home if you need anything. Thanks for being so understanding." She disconnected the line and smiled. "Millie! To what do I owe the pleasure?"

"What's going on?" Millie asked her. "Did you quit your job?" If her mother had lost her job, the return trip to Oklahoma and all these college plans would have to be shelved and she'd be back where she started.

Elizabeth reached around a box and gave Millie a big hug. "Of course not. I just didn't have time to tell you about all this. And you didn't tell me you were coming downtown today, so I guess we're even!"

"Touché," Millie replied. "So…?"

"Everything's fine," Elizabeth assured her. "Your dad and I had a long talk, and we want you to be able to go off to college worry-free, so some changes had to be made. I told my boss I'd do most of my writing at home from now on, just come into the office on days we have Martha, and that way I can spend more time with Charlie and Kaz."

"And what about Toronto?" Millie pressed her. "How are you going to be there for the Millicent TV show?"

"Skype, email, quick day-trips. Don't worry, I'll manage."

"Mom, are you sure? The kids have lots of after-school activities and need to be driven around. That's going to cut into your work time."

Elizabeth smiled as she shoved her glasses up onto her head to push back a stray lock of hair. "Believe it or not, Millie, I was taking care of my children before I became a writer, and I'm pretty sure it'll all come back to me. And there's always carpooling."

Millie sighed and took one last look around. "Well, if it's okay with your boss, and you're sure..." She grinned. "Got time to hit the mall?"

Zach and Millie had been texting frequently but had also been playing phone tag a lot. Both of them were busy—Zach with two-a-day football practices and Millie helping out with her siblings and checking boxes off her to-do list—until finally they just agreed to have a phone date every night at eleven p.m., ten o'clock his time. Millie planned her entire day around what she would tell him that night and anticipating their phone time as eagerly as she would a date in person. Tonight her phone rang right on time.

"Hi, Zach! How was practice?"

"Hi yourself, and good, I guess. Kinda tired." He paused and Millie could hear the lid pop off a soda can. "Hey, I need your advice."

Millie's ears perked up. He needs MY advice. She was thrilled at the thought of helping him with whatever he needed. "Okay."

Zach loudly guzzled his soda. "You remember that history exam I told you I had to make up?"

"Zach, I don't forget stuff."

"Right. Well, Mr. Teague—he's the history teacher—he's threatening to get me thrown off the team if I don't quit procrastinating. I think he hates me."

"He hates you? Why?"

Zach sighed long and loud. "Dad says Teague was a frustrated athlete back in the day, so now he thinks all football players are 'entitled' and won't help any of us. I'll probably flunk."

"That is so wrong on so many levels!" Millie exclaimed. "Entitled how?"

"He says I'm one of those athletes who goof off during the season and then expect extra time to complete assignments, and yeah, I admit I sorta blew off history last year. The only reason he's giving me a second chance is because Coach and Dad-the-history-professor nagged him into it."

Millie was angry at this unknown teacher who had decided for whatever reason that Zach's athletic future was of no importance. She'd had plenty of experience with instructors who had preconceived ideas about their students, so no, she decided, his future was not going to be derailed by a vindictive teacher and something as insignificant as one U.S. History final exam. Well, okay, maybe a high school test was insignificant to her, but she knew it was important to Zach and she was determined to help him. "What's going to be on the test?"

"Wait, Dad called Teague and then wrote it down," Zach said, loudly riffling through some papers. "Okay, here it is: Be able to analyze how contro- versy over the extension of slavery into western terri- tories contributed to the Civil War during the years 1845-1861." He tossed the paper aside. "I'm toast."

Millie quickly started analyzing all the possible answers. "No, you're not. We went over that last month at the library. Remember?"

"Maybe." Zach didn't sound convinced.

"Okay, write this down. Ready? Here's what you need to cover in your essay." Millie ticked off the main points on her fingers. "1848 Treaty of Guadalupe Hi- dalgo which gave more territory to the Southwest; the Henry Clay Compromise of 1850, making California a free state; tougher fugitive slave laws in the South; 1854 John Brown massacre; 1860 election when Lincoln won the Presidency without a single Southern state." She took a deep breath. "Got all that?" Silence from Zach's end. "I can text it to you if that helps."

"Wow. How do you do that?"

Millie laughed. "It's my Super Power." She smiled to herself. "Break a leg...Oops, I mean good luck."

They hung up the phone and Millie gave herself a big hug, convinced she'd helped Zach save his spot on the football team and nab his college scholarship.

Millie didn't hear from Zach for almost a week. After she'd been his personal crib sheet for that history exam, he'd missed all of their appointed phone dates. Millie tried texting him but got nothing but short re- plies, mostly things like *Busy. Working on a project. Get back to ya later.* But he didn't and now Millie was wor- ried. Did she give him the wrong advice? Did he flunk the test anyway and blame her? Maybe that petulant teacher changed the topic at the last minute and her help was of no use at all.

Or maybe that was all Zach had ever wanted from her in the first place—help passing a tough test—and now he could go back to his friends and his life the way it was before. Without her. Millie's confidence flagged. She'd planned everything around spending time with Zach and his friends in Oklahoma, and now it was too late to change her mind. Zach or no Zach, she and her mom were leaving for Rolling Plains tomorrow morning. No second thoughts, no backpedalling, no stalling.

Despite her qualms, Millie packed her belongings, all her newly-purchased dorm room supplies, her new fall clothes as well as some old favorites, her study pillow and laptop, her collection of classic literature, and then prepared to leave Indianapolis for her new adventure. Even if Zach was breaking up with her (which was devastating, she had to admit), she told herself she could still look forward to attending her college classes, meeting her new roommate (whose name was Isabelle Ramirez) and getting involved in campus activities, things she never thought she'd have the guts to do before. She would make the best of it, but it wouldn't be easy without Zach.

All the boxes had been ticked off her to-do list and the only thing remaining was one last family dinner tonight, until Thanksgiving anyway.

Her dad wanted to take his family to their favorite Mexican restaurant, so they all piled into Elizabeth's newly acquired soccer-mom SUV and drove to The Fiesta del Sol Restaurant. Considering it was late-August and after seven o'clock on a school night, the restaurant was pretty crowded, and they had to wait about fifteen minutes before the hostess finally led them to a table.

Charlie plopped down in the chair next to her older sister and tugged on her arm. "Millie, I'm starving!"

"Okay." Millie automatically started to pass her the bowl of tortilla chips.

Elizabeth held up her hand to Millie. "I've got this." She turned to Charlie and patted her head. "We're all hungry, hon. Here, eat some chips and tell me what you want for supper."

Millie now found herself in unfamiliar territory, considering she'd been sort of a surrogate parent to her siblings the whole last year. Still, she knew she was leaving and had to let her mom handle it from now on, so she took a calming breath and began reading the menu.

"Three chicken enchiladas and refried beans!" Kaz said to the waitress, tossing his menu on the table.

"In other words, your habitual selection," Millie muttered as she continued to study her menu.

"Shut up, Millie," Kaz retorted.

"Now you two cut it out," Karl admonished. "This is Millie's last night and we want to have a pleasant evening before she leaves for school."

"Good rid…" Kaz started, but then for some reason he checked himself and mumbled, "Yeah, okay."

Millie was taken aback. Kaz was being nice to her? Who was that kid across the table from her? She studied him closely and realized that, not only had he grown several inches over the summer, he seemed to be gaining emotional maturity as well. When did her little brother start growing up?

Millie winked at Kaz and handed her menu to the waitress. "I'll have what my brother's having."

Elizabeth poked her head into Millie's bedroom doorway. "Are you ready? We've got a long drive ahead of us, and it's already eight a.m."

Millie did one last visual search of her bedroom, assuring herself she had everything she needed before she and her mother started the thirteen-hour drive from Indianapolis to Oklahoma. "I think so. I hope I didn't forget anything."

"If you did, I'm sure we can find it at a discount store when we get there," Elizabeth assured her. "But we need to get started because your grandmother's going to wait supper on us."

"Don't forget, Mom, it's an hour earlier in Oklahoma." Millie picked up her bulging duffel bag and slung the harness over her shoulder. "I'm so glad you're going with me, though. There's no way I could make that drive alone and I need my car for school." She took one last look around her childhood bedroom and flipped off the light.

Elizabeth smiled and gave Millie a quick hug. "I wouldn't let my firstborn go off to college by herself. Anyway, it's going to take two of us to navigate all those freeway changes in St. Louis."

Millie laughed. "I'll drive through St. Louis. You monitor the GPS."

Elizabeth nodded. "Good plan."

"Oh, and don't forget, we have to stop in Carmel on our way out of town," Millie said as they lugged baggage down the staircase.

"I didn't forget. I do think we can find our way ten miles up Highway 31 without a GPS," Elizabeth teased. "Glad you solved your mystery."

"Hard to believe, huh?" Millie said as she popped

open the car's trunk. "All summer I'm Googling away, looking for Whitfields, only to find Synthia's descendants were named Yeager, and some are still in Oklahoma and Texas. But I was really shocked when I located a great-great-granddaughter living in a suburb just north of Indianapolis. She was pretty surprised when I called her."

Elizabeth tossed her overnight bag on top of everything that was already crammed into the trunk and attempted to shut the lid. "Did she have any idea how Synthia's journal ended up in that cedar chest in Mildred's attic?"

Millie shook her head, studied the overstuffed trunk, and mentally calculated how to get everything rearranged. She moved things around in a more logical order and slammed the lid shut. "Not really. Might have been stored by some relative in that old trunk that may or may not have belonged to Synthia's mom."

"Synthia's story is fascinating. Driving a covered wagon across two states after burying both parents." Elizabeth pulled the ponytail holder out of her hair and retied it, a nervous gesture she often used when creating story, got in the passenger side of the car and kicked off her shoes.

"Mooommm…" Millie warned as she watched the now-familiar ritual.

Elizabeth was pensive. "I'm trying to figure out how to turn this into Millicent the Magnificent's next big adventure."

"Except yours has to be set in the twenty-first century, so it really can't be the same story." Millie turned over the ignition and checked the mirrors.

"True. But I'm working it out in my head."

Millie rolled her eyes and pulled out onto Meridian Street, headed for Carmel. "Dad's gonna be okay with the kids till you get back, right?"

"Millie," Elizabeth said, "relax. We've got it from here. You're officially off-duty."

Millie shrugged. "Well, if you're sure…."

Elizabeth pulled her sunglasses out of her bag and relaxed into the seat. "Of course I'm sure. Now tell me what else you found out about this Carmel woman's great-great grandmother," she said, while Millie steered the car through morning rush hour traffic.

Millie checked her rearview mirror as she changed lanes on Meridian Street, northbound to the booming community of Carmel as they crossed over the county line at 96th Street. "She said her great-great grandmother, Synthia Whitfield Yeager, and her husband Thomas Perry Yeager, had twelve children, and one of the middle daughters was the mother of her grandfather. She also said Mr. Yeager was struck by lightning on their farm in Texas and died at the age of forty-six. Synthia lived until 1925, never remarried, but had lots—lots—of grandchildren and great-grandchildren."

"Yep," Elizabeth said, "there's definitely a story in there somewhere."

Millie couldn't believe she was back in Oklahoma. Had it really been just a few weeks since she and Kaz hurriedly flew to Indianapolis after his runaway attempt? She parked her car in her grandmother's driveway, honked the horn to announce their arrival, popped the trunk lid and opened the door to get out. It was after eight o'clock, barely twilight in the Central

Time zone, and the intense late-summer heat still lingered in the air. "Definitely back in Oklahoma!" she said to herself.

Elizabeth stepped out the passenger side, stretched her arms overhead and twisted right and left to relieve the tight muscles. Millie had already begun pulling items out of the crammed trunk and setting them on the driveway one by one.

The back door opened and Gran hurried out to greet them. "There are my girls!" She enveloped both Millie and Elizabeth in a bear hug, laughing and nearly knocking them off balance in her exuberance.

"Gran!" Millie said as she extricated herself. "I just saw you a few weeks ago."

"Oh, I know, dear, but so much has changed since then."

Millie quickly glanced around at the house and yard for clues. "What's changed?"

Gran opened her mouth to speak but before she could utter a word, Mac stepped out the kitchen door, with his grandson Zach by his side! Millie was totally surprised.

"Hey, Millie, let me help you there," Zach said with his adorable Oklahoma drawl. He grabbed a large, heavy box filled with dorm-room supplies and easily plunked it down near the door.

"Hi, Mac," Elizabeth said, extending her hand. "Good to see you up and about. How are you feeling?"

"Fit as a fiddle," Mac replied as he clasped her hand in both of his.

Millie looked from Mac to her grandmother and back again, wondering why they were both grinning like a couple of Cheshire cats. Since their faces didn't offer any clues, she had no idea what was going on, but then something else distracted her. "Gran, is that your famous turkey chili?"

"I could smell something cooking in that kitchen all the way out here, Mildred," Elizabeth said as she headed toward the open door. "And it smells divine!"

Gran waved them toward the kitchen. "We're all pretty hungry but we waited for you, so help yourselves. Bowls are set up near the stove. Mint tea anyone?" She strolled back in the kitchen door, which had been left standing open the whole time.

Millie groaned, figured the kitchen would be stifling with the cooking and the outdoor heat, and was in no hurry to step inside, despite the grumbling in her belly. Mac was still pulling items out of Millie's trunk and setting them on the driveway alongside the ones she'd already removed. He grabbed the heavy duffel bag and started to close the trunk, but Millie raced over. "Here let me," she said, reaching for the bag. "You shouldn't over-exert yourself in this heat."

"She's right, Mac. I'll get it." Zach appeared at Millie's side and took the bag from his grandfather, hoisting it over his shoulder as if it were a feather pillow instead of the heavy pack it was.

"You two young people quit treating me like I'm a hot-house flower! My doctors pronounced me cured, so I'll not have you coddling me," he clucked. "But I suppose if you insist on doing the heavy lifting, boy, I'll just join the ladies in the house." He winked at Millie before heading back inside.

Millie looked up at Zach and then looked away in embarrassment. She didn't know what had happened to their relationship, if it had ended before it really got started, but there was no easy way to bring up the subject. The only thing she could think to do was look busy organizing all the bags and boxes sitting in disarray on the sidewalk. She picked up a cardboard box labeled 'bath' and then nervously fumbled it, watching helplessly as it landed back on the ground upside down.

"Looks like you brought half of Indiana with you."

"I hope I didn't forget anything I need…" Her voice trailed off.

"Like…?" he prompted.

Millie sighed. "Like maybe some answers, I guess. Why did you blow me off?"

Zach's jaw dropped. "How'd I do that?"

"You quit calling. You didn't respond to my texts."

He winced in embarrassment. "I sent you some texts."

She'd been hoping Zach would explain his cyber-silence, or tell her he was glad she was here, or at least say something polite about moving on with his life. She didn't know what she expected, but this awkwardness between them was excruciating.

There was a long pause during which Millie kicked at a stone under her feet and averted her eyes. "How's football practice?" she finally asked, while at the same time Zach said, "I passed that test."

They both stopped and stared at each other. Zach motioned for her to go first.

"The history test?" Millie hoped her tutoring had helped him or at least contributed in some way. She would let Zach feign gratitude and then he could let her down easy if that's what he planned to do.

"I couldn't call you anymore because I was either at the gym or on the field twice a day, totally crashing into bed at night, and also I was helping Mac with…a special project." Zach stepped closer and gave Millie a hug, tentative at first and then he enveloped her in a warm embrace. "Anyway, I knew you'd be here soon and I could talk to you in person."

"So you're not dumping me?"

He held her at arm's length. "Is that what you thought?"

"Well, when I didn't hear from you, yeah. I mean, normally the only time anyone needs me is for my brains, so…." Millie stared down at her feet.

Zach kissed her forehead. "I already told you I like that you're smart, but I wasn't using you. You're so different from the Millie I knew two years ago, and even two months ago, and now that you're here, I really hope we can spend more time together."

Relieved, Millie smiled up at him. "You've changed, too."

She leaned into him and let the anxiety of the last few days fall away. He released her and took her hand, and together they strolled across the lawn toward the large shady elm tree that he always had so much trouble mowing around. Millie noticed a few telltale tufts of grass growing at the foot of the tree and nearly slipped back into her old critical ways, but stopped herself. This was the Zach she'd hoped to see, and she wasn't about to spoil the moment.

Zach smiled. "I wanted to thank you for all your help."

"I didn't really do that much."

"Yes, you did, and if I hadn't passed that test I wouldn't still be on the team, so to answer your question, football practice is great. It looks like we're gonna have a team this year, which means lots of college scouts around."

Millie leaned into the tree trunk and felt the tickle of the overgrown grass around her ankles. "College scouts? Already?"

Zach nodded and leaned in a little closer. "High schools are back in session, you know, and we've already played two games. I've been scouted by Oklahoma, Oklahoma State, OLAC of course," he said with a wink, "and—wait for it—Boston College!"

"Omigod, Zach, that's amazing!"

She stepped over the long blades of grass, tripped, and accidentally tumbled into his arms. He steadied her, and then impulsively picked her up and swung her around and around. When he set her back down, Millie had to focus to steady herself. Was she dizzy from being twirled around like a rag doll, or was she lightheaded for another reason? For all her high IQ and education, these strange emotions were something she knew nothing about.

"You're light as a feather," Zach said as he chucked her under the chin.

"Since we're doing clichéd similes," Millie replied, "you're strong as an ox." Once again she marveled at how changed he was from that short, skinny fifteen-year-old boy she remembered from two summers ago. His muscles rippled out from under his t-shirt and he looked every inch the six-foot athlete that he was.

Zach laughed, pulled his cap off his head, and wiped his forehead in that way Millie found adorable. "Must be all that weight conditioning. I am the quarterback," he said.

"I know. I mean, intellectually I know. I've studied all the rules of football, all the positions, all the plays, but…" Millie smiled up at Zach as he put his cap on backwards, "…I've never actually seen many games, so I guess I'm the one who needs tutoring."

Zach grinned back at her. "Maybe. Oh, wait. Here," he said, fishing an envelope out of his pocket, "I almost forgot. I brought you something."

Millie examined the nondescript envelope, turning it over and over in her hand. "What's this?" she asked as she carefully opened it.

Zach shook his head. "Geez, Millie, I guess you really didn't go to many high school football games. It's season tickets."

Millie's eyes opened wide in surprise as she carefully put the tickets back in the envelope. "I was always too busy studying. But believe me, I'll make it to every one of yours from now on," she promised as she carefully tucked the envelope in her pocket.

"And I wanted to ask you," Zach said, but then hesitated. "Well, maybe it's a bad idea, you being a college woman and all."

"Ask me what?"

"Homecoming's early this year—mid-September—and I'd like you to be my date. If you don't mind hanging out with a bunch of high school kids that is," he added.

Millie was elated! She shook off the bad memory of last spring's Junior-Senior Prom and instead, replaced it with the happy anticipation of being Zach's date at his Homecoming Dance, alongside his friends that she hoped liked her as much as she'd liked them. "I spent so much time in high school focused on being valedictorian that I completely forgot to have fun. I'd love to go!" Her hands flew to her face as a thought hit her. "Ohmigod, what will I wear? I have to look…"

Zach put his hands to her lips. "You'll look perfect in whatever you wear."

"Millie!" Elizabeth stuck her head out the kitchen door. "You two come in here. We've got your dad and brother and sister online."

As Zach took Millie's hand and walked her to the house, he beamed down at her. "If I should decide to go to Boston College, I'd actually be in Boston before you, if you go to Harvard law school, that is."

Millie squeezed his hand. "If you do, I'll have that to look forward to when I get there! But maybe I could get ahead in my studies…" She saw Zach frowning. "Nope," she corrected herself. "I'm going to ease up and enjoy college—all three years of it!"

They walked into the kitchen and the smell of homemade chili was enticing, alerting Millie to the hollow rumbling in her stomach. But everyone was in the living room on Gran's computer, so she grabbed a cracker on their way to join Gran, Mac, and Elizabeth, who had Skyped Karl, Kaz and Charlie.

"Hi, guys!" Millie said to her dad and siblings over the computer screen. "What's—" Millie started, but Elizabeth shushed her.

Then—to nearly everyone's utter amazement—Mac got down on one knee, pulled a ring box from his pocket, and took Gran's hand. "Mildred Olson, you're my best friend and confidante, and over the years I came to rely on you. And even when I was sick, you were right there the whole time. Lately I realized I've fallen hopelessly in love. Would you do me the great honor of becoming my wife?"

Gran blushed, held out her left hand, and let Mac slip the diamond ring on her finger. "Malcolm Mac-Millan, you already know my answer, but yes, I will marry you!"

Zach whispered in Millie's ear, "See that ring? I helped my granddad pick it out."

So that's what he was helping Mac with, the project that had kept Zach so busy he couldn't call. Millie giggled into her hand, both from excitement over her grandmother's happiness and from the relief she felt knowing Zach had been preoccupied for a very good reason.

There was loud whooping and hollering and applause from everyone in the room—and the rest of the family in Indianapolis—as Mac and Gran began to waltz around the living room, sans music.

Zach took the cue from his grandfather and began to dance Millie around the room, too, when suddenly he stopped and stared at her, looking both confused and excited. "This doesn't mean we're gonna be related, does it?"

Millie laughed out loud and nudged him to continue their dance.

It was very late that night. Actually, glancing at the clock, Millie could see it was very early in the morning. She got up and flipped on the bedside lamp in her room at her grandmother's house, instinctively reaching for the place where she'd kept Synthia's journal all summer, but then she remembered it was gone, delivered to Synthia's great-great granddaughter. She missed it, and missed the inspiration it had afforded.

What if I write my own journal? Good idea? Yes! She booted up her computer and began typing.

> August 24
> I start college in a few days at Oklahoma

Liberal Arts College, where I'll be a sophomore history and political science major. I
have a boyfriend—Zach MacMillan—who's
older than I but still in high school, and yet
we have a great time with his friends and all
his activities. We've got a whole year to really
get to know each other, even though our families have been friends for eons. I read about
orphan Synthia Elizabeth Whitfield Yeager in
her journal from 1865, and it helped me realize how lucky I am to have a healthy family,
my grandmother, Zach, and soon, a new
grandpa.

After a summer of indecision and pro-
crastination I finally realized, just like Dorothy in The Wizard of Oz, that everything I
had been wishing for was right here all along.
Look out world—here comes Millie the Invincible!

About the Author

Pamela Woods-Jackson is a former high school English teacher and author of Confessions of a Teenage Psychic, which was a 2011 Epic Ebook Contest finalist and received Honorable Mention in the 2013 Hollywood Book Festival contest. She is also the author of Certainly Sensible.

Genius Summer received Honorable Mention in the 2013 Pacific Northwest Writers Contest and was a 2013 Finalist in the San Francisco Writers Contest.

Pamela resides in Carmel, Indiana (just north of Indianapolis), but she is originally from Oklahoma City and a graduate of The University of Oklahoma. Contact her at: https://www.facebook.com/pamela.w.jackson.9

Acknowledgements

The author acknowledges and would like to thank the following trademarks:

Google Inc. 1600 Amphitheatre Pkwy. Mountain View CA 94043

Indianapolis Motor Speedway and Indy 500, Brickyard Trademarks, Inc. 4790 West 16th Street Indianapolis IN 46222

Hilton Hotels 720 S. Michigan Ave., Chicago, IL 60605

Toyota Jidosha Kabushiki Kaisha TA Toyota Motor Corporation JAPAN 1,

Oklahoma City RedHawks
OKC Athletic Club, LLC, 2 S. Mickey Mantle Dr., Oklahoma City, OK 73104

Visa International Service Association 900 Metro Center Boulevard, M1-11A Foster City, CA94404

Old Navy (Apparel), LLC 2 Folsom Street San Francisco CA 94105

University of Oklahoma
(660 Parrington Oval, Suite 213 Norman OK 73019

University of Notre Dame du Lac 203 Main Building Notre Dame IN 46556

Duke University 310 Blackwell Street, 4th Floor Office of Counsel Durham NC 27710

Dear Reader,

If you enjoyed reading *Genius Summer*, I would appreciate it if you would help others enjoy this book, too. Here are some of the ways you can help spread the word:

Lend it. This book is lending enabled so please share it with a friend.

Recommend it. Help other readers find this book by recommending it to friends, readers' groups, book clubs, and discussion forums.

Share it. Let other readers know you've read the book by positing a note to your social media account and/or your Goodreads account.

Review it. Please tell others why you liked this book by reviewing it on your favorite ebook site.

Everything you do to help others learn about my book is greatly appreciated!

Pamela Woods-Jackson

btb

Buch

»Auf Sand gebaut« war die erste literarische Reaktion auf die Ereignisse, die als »deutsche Revolution«, als »Wende«, schließlich als »Wiedervereinigung« in die Geschichte eingegangen sind. Jenseits aller nationalen Euphorie richtet Stefan Heym in seinen 1990 erschienenen Geschichten einen illusionslosen Blick auf die jüngsten deutschen Zustände, auf die um sich greifende Korruption des Denkens und Handelns, auf den Opportunismus und die Wendefreudigkeit ehemaliger Apparatschiks, auf die kritiklose Übernahme westlicher Werte.
Mit »Filz. Gedanken über das neueste Deutschland« knüpft Heym zwei Jahre später daran an. Keine Schönrednerei kann darüber hinwegtäuschen: auf den Vereinigungsrausch folgte bald der Katzenjammer. Die Illusionen waren schnell verflogen. Die paradoxe Situation, daß die Kluft zwischen den geeinten Teilen Deutschlands sich zu vergrößern schien, sich die vielberufene nationale Identität nur schwer einstellen wollte, ist Ausgangspunkt der Reflexionen Stefan Heyms.

Autor

Stefan Heym (1913–2001) floh vor der Nazidiktatur nach Amerika, verließ das Land in der McCarthy-Ära und lebte seit 1952 in der DDR. Seine trotzig-kompromißlose Kritik an Selbstherrlichkeit, Unterdrückung und Zensur machte ihn zur herausragenden Figur der deutschen Nachkriegsliteratur, die geliebt und geachtet wurde. Zeitlebens blieb Heym ein streitbarer Schriftsteller, der »seine Kunst an keine Ideologie verriet« (Die Zeit). 1994 eröffnete Heym als Alterspräsident mit einem engagierten Plädoyer für Toleranz den deutschen Bundestag.

Stefan Heym

Auf Sand gebaut
Filz

Roman

btb

FSC

Mixed Sources
Product group from well-managed
forests and other controlled sources

Cert no. GFA-COC-1223
www.fsc.org
© 1996 Forest Stewardship Council

Verlagsgruppe Random House FSC-DEU-0100
Das FSC-zertifizierte Papier *Munken Print* für Taschenbücher aus
dem btb Verlag liefert Arctic Paper Munkedals AB, Schweden.

1. Auflage
Genehmigte Taschenbuchausgabe Oktober 2005
by btb Verlag, München,
in der Verlagsgruppe Random House GmbH
Copyright © für „Auf Sand gebaut" 1990 by Stefan Heym
Zeichnungen © Horst Hussel
Alle Rechte der deutschsprachigen Ausgabe 1990
by C. Bertelsmann Verlag, München
Copyright © für „Filz" 1992 by Stefan Heym
Zeichnungen © Horst Hussel
Alle Rechte der deutschsprachigen Ausgabe 1992
by C. Bertelsmann Verlag, München
Umschlaggestaltung: Design Team München
Umschlagfoto: akg, Berlin
Druck und Einband: Clausen & Bosse, Leck
MM · Herstellung: AW
Made in Germany
ISBN-10: 3-442-73454-1
ISBN-13: 978-3-442-73454-2

www.btb-verlag.de

Auf Sand gebaut

*Sieben Geschichten aus der
unmittelbaren Vergangenheit*

*Und vierzehn Zeichnungen
von Horst Hussel*

FÜR INGE

Inhalt

Darum, wer diese meine Rede hört und tut sie, den vergleiche ich einem klugen Mann, der sein Haus auf einen Felsen baute.

Da nun ein Platzregen fiel und ein Gewässer kam und wehten die Winde und stießen an das Haus, fiel es doch nicht; denn es war auf einen Felsen gegründet.

Darum, wer diese meine Rede hört und tut sie nicht, der ist einem törichten Manne gleich, der sein Haus auf den Sand baute.

Da nun ein Platzregen fiel und kam ein Gewässer und wehten die Winde und stießen an das Haus, da fiel es und tat einen großen Fall.

Matthäus 7, 24–27

Der Zuverlässigsten einer

Wo sie nur alle wieder hin sind?

Vergangene Woche Freitag, jawohl, Freitag Nachmittag, da war auch schon mal diese plötzliche Stille. Sonst sind immer irgendwelche Geräusche, Schritte, oder es hustet einer draußen im Gang, aber wenn so überhaupt nichts ist, legt es sich wie ein Gewicht auf den Schädel und man kriegt so ein Flattern im Bauch, jedenfalls bin ich hinübergegangen zum Genossen Tolkening ins Zimmer, doch dort war auch keine Seele, nur auf dem Tisch lag ein Haufen Papiere, was sonst gar nicht die Art ist vom Genossen Tolkening, selbst wenn der auf fünf Minuten mal weggeht, schließt er alles ein, und beim Genossen Kallweit war auch keiner, so daß ich gedacht hab, was ist denn nur los, wenn es eine Sitzung wäre, der Genosse Kallweit hätte mich doch gerufen, aber in der letzten Zeit ist auch auf nichts mehr Verlaß und auf niemanden, zwar wird verlautbart, jawohl, Genossen, der Betrieb geht weiter, die Firma kriegt einen andern Namen, aber was sind Namen, die Hauptsache ist, wir bleiben auf Posten, und ich klopf an beim Genossen Stösselmaier, der früh als erster kommt und abends als letzter geht, aber sein Dienstzimmer ist auch leer, sie können doch nicht sämtlich beim Kaffeetrinken sein oder dienstlich unterwegs, und dann ist mir eingefallen, was der Genosse Kuhnt gesagt hat bei der Abteilungsbesprechung, der Genosse Alfred Kuhnt ist ja nicht irgendwer, der Genosse Kuhnt also hat mit dem Finger auf meine Person gewiesen, deutlich und unmißverständlich, und gesagt, der Genosse Bobrich ist der Zuverlässigsten einer, unser Arno, jawohl, und wenn es einmal hart auf hart kommen sollte, der Genosse Bobrich hält den Laden, und außerdem hat er auch so ein Wesen, das beruhigend wirkt auf die Menschen, dem wird also kaum einer was tun.

Ich hab das Martha erzählt, was der Genosse Kuhnt über mein Wesen gesagt hat, und Martha hat gesagt, das stimmt, der Genosse Kuhnt ist ein Menschenkenner, aber trotzdem macht man sich seine Gedanken, besonders wenn die Zeiten so unruhig sind wie jetzt und alles drunter- und drübergeht und sogar ein Mann wie der Chef, vor dem das ganze Volk gezittert hat, jawohl, richtiggehend gezittert, hat aufstehen müssen in aller Öffentlichkeit und sich rechtfertigen vor Leuten, die sonst gekrochen wären vor ihm, rechtfertigen für was, möchte ich wissen, der Mann hat seine Pflicht getan wie wir alle und sonst nichts, und dann haben sie ihn noch verhaftet. Und, hat der Genosse Kuhnt weiter zu uns gesagt, wenn es dahin kommen sollte, was er allerdings nicht erwarte, hat er gesagt, daß wir zeitweilig retirieren müßten, retirieren war sein Ausdruck, tatsächlich, dann können wir unsrem Genossen Bobrich vertrauen, daß er das Nötige tut, denn der Genosse Bobrich weiß ja, daß das, was bei uns in der Abteilung liegt, nicht in unberufene Hände gehört.

Das war vergangene Woche. Und jetzt ist wieder diese Stille. Trotzdem, so eilig hätten sie doch nicht zu retirieren brauchen, wenigstens einer hätte den Kopf noch zur Tür hineinstecken und sagen können, Arno, hätte er sagen können, es ist ja nur zeitweilig, aber nicht einmal das hat einer von ihnen gesagt, und dabei wird von mir erwartet, daß ich meine Pflicht tue und den Laden halte, denn was hier in der Abteilung steht, ist höchste Vertrauenssache, und wie ich Martha gesagt hab seinerzeit, daß sie mich hierher gestellt haben, mitten ins Nervenzentrum vom Ganzen, Nervenzentrum, das war mein Ausdruck, da hat sie gesagt, das laß lieber, warum mußt du dich ins Nervenzentrum stellen lassen, war denn das, was du bisher gemacht hast, nicht schwierig genug, Arno, ich hab nie gewußt, wie du das schon in eins bringst mit deiner unsterblichen Seele, aber das jetzt, mitten im Nervenzentrum vom Ganzen, es wird dir kein Glück bringen, Arno. Und wie ich dem Genossen Tolkening erzählt hab, was die Martha gesagt hat zu meiner neuen Stellung mitten im Nervenzentrum, was doch eine große Anerkennung darstellt seitens der Genossen, hat er gelacht und gesagt, mach dir nichts draus, Arno, was wissen die Frauen von Pflicht und von den Notwendigkeiten des Dienstes. Aber was der Junge gesagt hat, wie er dann nach Haus gekommen ist und Martha ihm erzählt hat von meiner neuen Stellung im Nervenzentrum des Ganzen, das hab ich dem Genossen Tolkening nicht gesagt, so etwas kann man einem Genossen gar nicht sagen, der würde denken, eine Schlange hat der Genosse Bobrich großgezogen an seinem Busen, eine richtiggehende Schlange, und wie zuverlässig kann der Genosse Bobrich wohl sein, mit solchem Schlangengezücht im eigenen Hause. Dabei würde ich nie daran denken, auch nur einen von den Ordnern dort im Nervenzentrum des Ganzen anzurühren, die da stehen mit ihren gelben und grünen und purpurfarbenen und orangenen Aufklebern, je nach Kategorie und in sich wieder alphabetisch gruppiert, auch wenn ich schon manchmal hinaufgeblickt hab zu dem zweiten Regal von oben, viertes Fach rechts, *Bat* bis *Bur,* aber da bin ich ja sowieso nicht drin, die Mitarbeiter werden separat geführt, bei den Mitarbeitern hat nur der Genosse Kuhnt Zutritt und keiner sonst.

Dabei ist der Junge ja kein schlechter Mensch und im eigentlichen Sinne auch nicht mißraten, aber er geniert sich, sagt er, wegen seinem Vater. Was hat ein Sohn, frage ich, sich zu genieren wegen einem Vater, der nur seine Pflicht tut, seine Klassenpflicht und seine Dienstpflicht und seine Vaterpflicht. Das sagt dann Martha auch, aber der Junge zuckt nur mit den Schultern, wenn sie ihm das sagt, und zu mir sagt er, wenn ich's bisher noch nicht gewußt hab, für wen ich mein dickes Gesäß wundgescheuert hab all die Jahre, dann müßt ich's jetzt doch wenigstens kapiert haben, wo der Chef hat aufstehen müssen in aller Öffentlichkeit und sich rechtfertigen, und dann lacht er auf diese Art, daß es mir quer durch die Brust schneidet und ich auf ihn losgehen möchte, aber Martha fällt mir jedesmal in den Arm und sagt, wir haben's doch schwer genug auch ohne solche Streitereien!

Wie lange waren sie weggewesen am vergangenen Freitag? Zwanzig Minuten vielleicht oder dreißig, mehr nicht, dann sind sie zurückgeschlichen gekommen und taten irgendwie verlegen, und nur der Genosse Kallweit hat etwas gesagt, falscher Alarm, hat er gesagt, sie sind vorbeigezogen draußen, sie haben Schiß gehabt, sie könnten eins auf den Deckel bekommen. Ich kann den Genossen Kallweit verstehen, der Genosse Kallweit war immer ein Draufgänger, und nun haben sie ihm seine Pistole weggenommen, er hat noch eine zuhause, sagt er, zur Reserve, aber hier hat er jetzt keine mehr, und er fühlt sich wie kastriert, sagt er, Kallweit ist überhaupt sehr menschlich und auch persönlich interessiert, immer hat er sich erkundigt nach Martha und nach dem Jungen. Martha, hab ich dem Genossen Kallweit gesagt, macht mir Sorgen, Martha hat ihre Zweifel, warum gehen die Leute weg, fragt sie, es können doch nicht nur die paar Plünnen sein und die Bananen, es gibt doch noch andere Werte, und warum können wir den Leuten das nicht begreiflich machen, oder glaubt ihr wirklich, der Druck, den ihr macht,

Die SCHWARZ RöCKE.

überzeugt irgend jemanden? Worauf der Genosse Kallweit den Kopf geschüttelt und mir seine Hand um die Schulter gelegt und geseufzt hat, hast's auch nicht leicht, Arno. Hab ich auch nicht, Tatsache.

Aber jetzt sind sie schon länger weg als zwanzig Minuten oder dreißig, viel länger. Sie werden mich doch nicht, so ganz allein hier, und ohne einen zur Hilfe, der eine Pistole hat, mir haben sie ja nie eine gegeben zum immer bei mir Tragen, du zitterst immer so mit den Händen, Arno, hat der Genosse Stösselmaier gesagt, der verantwortlich ist für die Bewaffnung, da kann so ein Ding losgehen zur unrechten Zeit, beim Reinigen zum Beispiel am Küchentisch, und dann hast du deine Martha getroffen, ganz ohne es zu wollen, und wie stehst du dann da. Das hat mir Martha auch gesagt, habe ich dem Genossen Stösselmaier gesagt, Arno, hat sie gesagt, ich bin froh, daß du so was nicht mit dir rumtragen mußt, der Staat ist eines, aber ein Menschenleben ist ein anderes, und kein Staat auf Erden, auch unserer nicht, ist wert, daß man ein Leben dafür opfert. Und der Genosse Stösselmaier hat die Arme hinterm Kopf verschränkt und gegähnt, und dann hat er gesagt, was die Frauen nicht alles sagen, erstaunlich. Und jetzt ist auch der Genosse Stösselmaier nicht da, obwohl ich ganz gern ein Wort gehört hätte sogar von dem, die Stille legt sich wie ein Gewicht auf den Schädel, diese lautlose Stille, und sie macht, daß man so ein Flattern im Bauch kriegt und laut herausschreien möchte, Genossen! – aber die Genossen sind weg und haben den Genossen Bobrich alleingelassen im Nervenzentrum des Ganzen, der Zuverlässigsten einer, wie der Genosse Kuhnt gesagt hat.

Aber wenn dann die Stille auf einmal aufhört und es kommt ein Krach und ein Gepolter, oder ein plötzliches Geschrei, das ist dann fast noch schlimmer als die Stille vorher. Ich geh hinüber zum Zimmer des Genossen Tolkening, und wieder liegt sein Tisch voller Papiere, obwohl er doch sonst alles weg-schließt bevor er auch nur für fünf Minuten weggeht, und dann geh ich bei Kallweit vorbei und bei Stösselmaier, und auch bei denen ist alles ein Durcheinander, nur bei mir nicht, das macht, weil ich ein ruhiges Wesen habe und einen Vor-gang erledige, bevor ich mir den nächsten vornehme, auch in Zeiten, wo alles sonst drunter- und drübergeht und so-gar ein Mann wie der Chef, vor dem alle richtiggehend ge-zittert haben, sich hat rechtfertigen müssen, obwohl er nur seine Pflicht getan hat. Und der Lärm kommt näher, und es ist wie viele hundert Stiefel, die alle gleichzeitig scharren und trappeln auf Treppen und Fluren, und das Geschrei und Ge-ruf, »Hierher!« und »Nein, hier!« und »Nach rechts!« und »Hier hinauf!« und »Da um die Ecke!«, und es ist, als wä-ren da einer oder mehrere, die wissen, wo sie hinwollen und die die andern anführen, nämlich mitten ins Nervenzentrum des Ganzen, und dann, mit einem Knall, birst die Tür zu mei-nem Zimmer auf, wo ich an meinem Tisch sitze, der tadel-los aufgeräumt ist, Lineal und Stifte und Eingangs- und Aus-gangskorb, alles an seinem Ort, und ich erhebe mich und zieh mir die Jacke zurecht und sage, laut, aber nicht überlaut, und deutlich, »Raus, allesamt!« Und zu dem Jungen, »Los, scher dich zu deiner Mutter!«

»Reg dich nicht auf, Alterchen«, sagt doch da eine zu mir, so eine Fahle, Strohige mit blaßblauen Augen und dünnem Munde, »wir sind das Volk«, und geht hinüber zu den Rega-len und fängt an, die Ordner herauszuzerren, die mit den gel-ben Aufklebern zuerst und dann die mit den purpurfarbenen, und von *A* bis *Atz*, und *Aub* bis *Bas*, und so weiter, und all das streut sie über den Fußboden und die Bänke und die Fenster-bretter, und es fällt alles auseinander und löst sich auf, und es ist ein Geflatter da und Gefetz, und die Leute treten dar-auf herum mit ihren schmierigen Sohlen, und ich fang an zu

Fa.
Alberich
& Sohn

brüllen, »Halt! Halt!« und lauf herum wie ein Verrückter und bück mich und versuch aufzuheben und einzusammeln was immer ich greifen kann, und der Junge steht da und lacht und lacht, bis ich nicht mehr an mich halten kann und die Ordner, die ich unterm Arm trag, und die Papiere, die ich aufgesammelt hab, wieder fallen lasse und ihn bei seinem Anorak pack und ihn schüttle, daß sein strähniges Haar nur so hin- und herfliegt, und rufe, »Schlangengezücht! Schlangengezücht!« und dann weiß ich nicht mehr, was passiert ist mit mir, denn wie ich wieder zu mir gekommen bin, hab ich auf dem Fußboden gesessen in meinem Zimmer und die Tür stand sperrangelweit offen und um mich herum die zertretenen Ordner und die zerrissenen Papiere und die Farbflecken von den Aufklebern, gelb und grün und purpurfarben und orange, und draußen eine Stimme, »Keine Gewalt, bitte! Keine Gewalt!« und ich denke, die Stimme kennst du doch, und dann weiß ich, es ist die Stimme von dem Jungen, und ich spüre, wie es mich in der Kehle würgt, und im Innern von meinem Schädel hör ich die Worte des Genossen Kuhnt, *Der Zuverlässigsten einer,* aber wo waren sie alle, wie es hart auf hart gekommen ist und der Junge vor mir gestanden ist und gelacht hat und gelacht.

Und dann seh ich den Ordner mit der Bezeichnung *Bat* bis *Bur* auf orangenem Aufkleber, und der Ordner liegt da mit der offenen Seite nach unten und jemand ist darübergelaufen, und der Ordner tut mir irgendwie leid, weil ja zwischen *Bat* und *Bur Boh* ist, *Boh* wie Bobrich, und obwohl meine Akte nicht in dem Ordner sein kann, denn die Mitarbeiter liegen anderswo, wo nur der Genosse Kuhnt Zutritt hat und nicht ich, greif ich mir den Ordner und öffne *Boh* wie Bobrich, und natürlich ist da kein Bobrich, Arno, aber Bobrich, Martha, und da kriege ich's doch mit dem Schlucken in der Kehle, selbst nach so einem Tage, wo man glauben möchte,

daß man alles schon erlebt hat und über nichts mehr sich auf-
regen kann: die Martha auch, die Martha haben sie observiert,
die eigene Frau von ihrem eigenen Mitarbeiter, und mir kein
Wort gesagt davon, aber sie durften ja auch nicht, Konspiration ist Konspiration, aber wen, möchte ich doch wissen,
haben sie angesetzt auf Martha, und wer hat sie observiert
und über sie berichtet, und wieso hab ich nichts bemerkt davon, der Zuverlässigsten einer, wie der Genosse Kuhnt immer
sagt?

Und da steht es auch aufgeschrieben, alles schön der Reihe
nach, Römisch I, *wie du das in eins bringen kannst mit deiner unsterblichen Seele,* steht da, und *es wird dir kein Glück
bringen, Arno,* und daneben, unter Besondere Vermerke, *Tolkening,* also von Tolkening ist das gekommen. Und dann steht
da, Römisch II, *Subjekt hat Ehemann gegenüber erklärt, sie
hätte ihre Zweifel und wollte wissen, wieso die Leute weggin-
gen, es könnten doch nicht nur die paar Plünnen sein und
die Bananen, und es müßte da doch noch andere Werte geben, und warum können wir es den Leuten nicht begreiflich
machen,* und unter Besondere Vermerke, *Kallweit.* Und unter Römisch III, *Subjekt äußerte sich, sie wäre froh, daß ihr
Mann nicht so was (Dienstwaffe) mit sich herumtragen muß,
und der Staat wäre eines aber ein Menschenleben ein anderes, und kein Staat auf Erden wäre wert, daß man ein Leben dafür opferte, auch unserer nicht.* Besondere Vermerke,
Stösselmaier. Und zum Abschluß, gezeichnet, *Kuhnt, Alfred:
Trotzdem ist meines Erachtens der Genosse Bobrich, Arno,
des Glaubens, daß wir des Glaubens sind, er wäre der Zuverlässigsten einer.*

Und ich sitze da auf dem Fußboden, um mich herum das
ganze Papier mit den gelben und grünen und purpurfarbenen und orangenen Aufklebern, und in der Hand den leeren
Aktendeckel, und ich seh, daß das Papier voller Flecke ist,

Schweißflecke, so sehr hab ich an den Händen geschwitzt, und ich weiß auf einmal, es sind gar nicht die Genossen Tolkening und Kallweit und Stösselmaier, die im Fall *Bobrich, Martha* observiert und berichtet haben, sondern ich, der Genosse Bobrich, Arno, der Zuverlässigsten einer, und dann hör ich jemanden lachen auf diese Art, die mir quer durch die Brust schneidet, und ich merke, der Lacher bin ich ebenfalls selber, denn der Junge, der vor mir steht, lacht nicht, sondern er beugt sich hinab zu mir und legt mir seine Hand auf die Schulter, ganz leicht und so, als wollte er mich schonen, und sagt, »Komm, Vater, wir können jetzt gehen.«

Außenstelle

Der Bunker ist, obwohl sorgfältig eingezäunt mit Maschendraht, kein auffälliges Bauwerk; allerlei Gesträuch umgibt ihn, und welke Äste, totes Laub und Haufen von braunen Kiefernnadeln liegen dicht an dicht in seiner Nähe und bedecken ihn zu etwa zwei Dritteln; die Leute, die in der Gegend wohnen, wissen nichts darüber zu sagen, wann er gebaut wurde und ob er nicht etwa noch aus den Tagen des Krieges stamme, wogegen der erwähnte Zaun mit der schmalen Tür darin spräche, und ob noch überhaupt einer kommt, der den Schlüssel zu dem verrosteten Hängeschloß bei sich hat und vielleicht sogar den schweren, zementverkleideten Deckel der Einsteigeöffnung dicht über der Erde gelegentlich anhebt, um drinnen nach dem Rechten zu sehen. Spuren eines solchen Pförtners oder Wachmanns sind aber nirgends zu finden; das Erdreich im unmittelbaren Umkreis des Bunkers mit allem, was darauf liegt an halb Verfaultem, scheint unberührt.

Man gehe vom Bahnhof aus etwa südsüdwest quer durch den Wald, einen wenig gepflegten Mischwald, der dieser Landschaft eigentümlich, in Richtung Charlottenhof und Seeufer; plötzlich wird zwischen zwei auseinanderstrebenden weiß leuchtenden Birkenstämmen der Bunker auftauchen, nur um sofort wieder zwischen den verschiedenen

Schattierungen von Grün zu verschwinden: wer beachtet so etwas. Mir fiel der graue Klotz erst auf, als ich neulich daherkam und, auf dem Weg zu diesem Bunker, so schien es mir, einen Mann mittleren Wuchses sah, gekleidet in einen lodenartigen Stoff, über der verschwitzten roten Stirn eine Art Förstermütze: dieser zog einen zweirädrigen, gummibereiften Karren hinter sich her, an dessen stählerner Deichsel sich eine Kupplung befand, wie sie etwa zu einem Trabant passen mochte. Er bemerkte mich, blieb stehen, zündete sich eine Pfeife an und wartete, bis ich ihn passiert haben würde. Aber auch ich hielt an, grüßte ihn, »Wohin bei dem schönen Wetter?«, zugleich einen Blick in den offenen Ladeteil des Karrens werfend; der war leer; irgend etwas sollte also abgeholt werden, aus dem Bunker wahrscheinlich.

Da der mutmaßliche Förster mit der Antwort zögerte, sagte ich zu ihm, der Teufel muß mich geritten haben, »Es gibt eine Menge Leute, die sich für das Ding da interessieren.«

»Wieso das?« sagt er mit allen Anzeichen von Bestürzung.

Jetzt konnte ich nun nicht mehr zurück, ohne mich zu blamieren. »Erst vorgestern waren welche da«, lüge ich. »Zwei Männer und eine Frau. Vom Bürgerkomitee, würde ich meinen. Die schnüffeln ja überall herum neuerdings. Das kommt mit der Demokratie.«

Er blickt mich an, zweifelnd zunächst, doch bald auch erleichtert; er wittert wohl einen Sympathisanten in mir. »Ja, ja«, sagt er, »die Verhältnisse haben sich geändert. Aber es gibt noch Menschen, die wissen, was not tut.«

»Da«, sage ich, »denken wir ähnlich.«

Doch sein Vertrauen geht nicht soweit, daß er mir auch nur andeutungsweise mitteilt, was er hier will; er saugt an seiner Pfeife und rückt nicht von der Stelle mit seinem Karren, denn rührte er sich, so würde sein Vorhaben sich ja offenbaren; nur sein sauber getrimmtes Schnurrbärtchen verzieht sich ein wenig, als wollte er mir sagen, Zeit habe er gleich viel wie ich, und nach einer kleinen Weile wird mir das Spiel zu dumm, ich hebe grüßend zwei Finger und entferne mich.

Ein paar Tage später kam ich, purer Zufall, noch einmal desselben Weges, und da war er wieder; aber diesmal steht der Karren vor der Tür in dem Drahtzaun, und diese ist geöffnet, und mein Mann, der anscheinend soeben den Zementblock vor der Einsteigeöffnung beiseite geschoben hat und sich die Stirn wischt, zuckt zusammen, als er mich sieht.

»Da sind Sie ja wieder!« rufe ich erfreut. Ich freute mich wirklich: Meine erste Begegnung mit ihm hatte mich doch betroffen gemacht; nun ließ sich die Sache klären. Und ich frage ihn, betont freundlich: »Was machen Sie eigentlich hier?«

Nun hätte er mich anraunzen können, was mich das anginge. Aber so sicher war er seiner denn doch nicht. »Ich muß da etwas prüfen«, sagt er.

»Was befindet sich denn dort unten?« erkundige ich mich.

Er besinnt sich: wer ist er, und wer bin ich. »Ich bin hier dienstlich«, sagt er endlich, »und ich habe Ihnen schon zuviel gesagt.«

»Welche Dienststelle?« bohre ich weiter.

Er bleibt stumm. Sein Gesicht trägt jetzt einen gehetzten Ausdruck. Dann entscheidet er offenbar, daß Geheimnistuerei seinerseits, oder gar Schweigen, meinen Verdacht nur vergrößern würden, und sagt mürrisch, »Post.«

»Post?«, sage ich, »und seit wann sitzt die Post in Bunkern? Im übrigen sehen Sie gar nicht aus wie einer von der Post.« Und da er immer noch stumm bleibt, mit einem verbockten Zug unter dem Schnurrbärtchen, »Sie haben doch einen Dienstausweis, oder?«

Seine Hand hebt sich, Gewohnheitsbewegung, zur Brusttasche. Aber dann zieht er sie hastig zurück.

»Von welcher Behörde ist der Ausweis nun wirklich?« frage ich. »Von der kürzlich aufgelösten?«

Warum sagt er mir nicht, scheren Sie sich zum Teufel? Folglich hat er Angst: die Behörde, für die er gearbeitet hat, besitzt die Macht nicht mehr, die sie einst hatte; er muß lavieren.

»Ich bin nämlich«, sage ich, und das ist jetzt die Wahrheit, »im örtlichen Bürgerkomitee, und wir interessieren uns.«

»Für was?«

»Für alles«, sage ich.

Dabei ist mir nicht ganz wohl. Wieviel Autorität hat so ein Bürgerkomitee; wer hat die Mitglieder, sämtlich politische Dilettanten, gewählt und ernannt. Und natürlich sitzt in mir noch der alte Instinkt: nur *denen* nicht auffallen, sie können dir die größten Schwierigkeiten machen im Betrieb, und nicht nur im Betrieb, und du willst doch, daß dein Junge studiert. Aber Anfang November des Vorjahrs, auf dem Alexanderplatz zu Berlin, ist, wie der alte Hegel es ausdrückte und wie es uns beigebracht wurde in den alljährlichen Lehrgängen, Quantität umgesprungen in eine neue Qualität, deutlich erkennbar, und der Forstmensch weiß es ebensogut wie ich. Und so blicke ich ihm bedeutungsvoll ins Auge und wiederhole, »Wir interessieren uns für alles.«

Er zuckt die Achseln. Er sieht angeschlagen aus auf einmal.

»Also was ist nun da unten?« frage ich zum zweiten Mal.

»Eine Anlage.«

»Elektronisch?«

»Teils.«

»Kabel?«

»Auch.«

»Die wohin führen?«

»Mehrerenorts.«

»Zum Beispiel?«

»Das darf ich wirklich nicht sagen«, weigert er sich, zieht

aber sofort den Kopf ein, da ich Atem hole, als wollte ich ihn anbrüllen. »Und außerdem«, fügt er hinzu, »ist das alles längst stillgelegt.«

»Und warum sind Sie dann hier?«

Er sucht nach einer plausiblen Antwort. Schließlich zeige ich Zeichen von Ungeduld. »Soll ich«, so frage ich, »mit Ihnen hinunterkriechen?« und bete zu Gott, daß ich's nicht tun muß, ich habe meinen neuen hellen Mantel an und noch dazu fürchte ich mich: ein rascher Messerstich, unter der Erde, und bis mich dann einer findet . . .

»Es führen da Kabel zum Zentrum.«

»Und weiter wohin?«

»Nach Plockau.«

In Plockau, das weiß hier jedermann, haben sie eine große Zweigstelle. »Und?«

»Zu unsrer Außenstelle.«

»An der Uferstraße? Der weißen Villa?«

Das Kinn klappt ihm herunter.

»Von dort aus«, sage ich lächelnd, »bin ich überwacht worden. Ein blauer Lada und ein weißer Wartburg.«

»Dann sind wir ja Freunde«, sagt er.

Die weiße Villa, ein Jugendstilbau mit schön geschwungenen Erkern und Fensterbögen, gehörte bis etwa 1936 einem Herrn Leopold, der im Textilgeschäft tätig war und, wie die älteren Anwohner zu berichten wissen, nach Australien emigrierte. Dann zog ein höherer Parteigenosse dort ein, man munkelte etwas von Geheimdienst; er hatte eine etwas üppige Frau, die in großer Eile zusammen mit ihm entschwand, als die Russen sich der Stadt näherten; sie soll, so erzählen wiederum die älteren Anwohner, ihnen jedoch auf dem Treck nach Westen in die Hände gefallen sein. Die Villa wurde von den Sowjets beschlagnahmt, und mehrere Offiziersfamilien hausten sukzessive darin, bis im Verlauf der Umgruppierungen diese Einheit der Roten Armee anderswohin verlegt wurde und eine Unterabteilung einer Behörde der neugegründeten Deutschen Demokratischen Republik in den immer noch stattlichen, wenn auch ziemlich verschandelten Räumen Obdach fand. Wer oder was diese Behörde war, blieb der örtlichen Bevölkerung nicht verborgen; nicht gerade daß die Leute einen Schritt zulegten, wenn sie an dem prächtigen, leider lange schon angerosteten schmiedeeisernen Gartenzaun vorbeigingen; wer aber genauer hinsah, bemerkte doch, wie die Köpfe sich duckten.

Nach den vom Volke mit einem Schuß Ironie als Wende bezeichneten Ereignissen des Oktober und November erwartete man eigentlich, daß die weiße Villa zur allgemeinen Benutzung freigegeben werden würde; man sprach von der Einrichtung eines Caféhauses mit Sommergarten, da das Grundstück ans Seeufer grenzte, von anderen zivilen Plänen und Projekten; aber die Stadtbezirksoberen, die wie eh und je selbständige Entscheidungen scheuten, stellten sich taub. Da aber nun von Anwohnern festgestellt wurde, daß neuerdings des Nachts sich hinter den Gardinen ein geheimnisvolles Leben entwickelte und in den frühen Morgenstunden dunkle Gestalten ganze Kleinlastwagen, die vorm Hause vorfuhren, mit vernagelten Kisten und mit Geräten verschiedenster Art beluden, wurde Verdacht geschöpft; der revolutionäre Eifer wogte auf und, am Ende einer Sitzung des Bürgerkomitees, als alle bereits müde waren des Debattierens und zum Schluß kommen wollten, schlug eine schon ältere Bürgerin, Frau Schulz-Lattich, den Mitgliedern vor, einen Ausschuß zu bilden, bestehend aus drei oder vier beherzten Personen, die Eintritt in die weiße Villa verlangen sollten und erkunden, was hinter ihren Mauern vorgehe; danach werde das Komitee beschließen, was zu tun sei, um das Besitztum öffentlich einzuklagen.

Mich rechnete man zu den beherzten Personen; und so kam es, daß ich, zusammen mit Frau Schulz-Lattich und einem Herrn Dr. Czesnik, den ich flüchtig kannte, wir drei verstärkt durch einen Hauptwachtmeister von der nahen Polizeiwache, an diesem Spätnachmittag vor dem schmiedeeisernen Tor der Villa standen und lautstark Einlaß begehrten.

»Sind Sie verrückt, so einen Lärm zu machen?«

Der Kerl steht da in ausgelatschten Pantoffeln, die Hängebäckchen aufgeplustert und den Bauch unter der offenen Hausjoppe vorgeschoben wie den Bug eines Schubdampfers drüben auf dem See; der Wind streicht ihm über den weißen Flaum auf der Glatze.

Der Dr. Czesnik macht Anstalten, das Gittertor aufzustoßen, aber die Kette, mit dickem Schloß daran, hindert ihn.

»Aufschließen«, kommandiere ich.

Die Hängebäckchen zittern. »Ist verboten. Zutritt zur Villa nur gegen Berechtigungsschein.«

»Berechtigungsschein von wem?«

Er hüstelt, wischt sich, mit dem Zeigefinger, die Tröpfchen von der Oberlippe. Dann, plötzliche Erleuchtung, »Von der Volksbildung.«

»Die weiße Villa«, frage ich, »gehört der Volksbildung? Seit wann?«

»Seit kurzem.«

Ich winke dem Hauptwachtmeister, der sich nur zögernd in Bewegung setzt: weiß man, ob das Haus nicht doch dem Ministerium für Volksbildung zugesprochen wurde? »Machen Sie«, sagt der Hauptwachtmeister dann doch, »keine Sperenzchen.«

Das genügt. Die Kette klirrt, die Eisenstäbe schurren über das Pflaster. Die Gardine hinter dem Fensterchen neben der Haustür bewegt sich; von dort beobachtet einer die Vorgänge. Frau Schulz-Lattich, den Rücken entschlossen gestrafft, schreitet vor uns her, aber die Tür öffnet sich lautlos, wie auf Knopfdruck, und nach einer gemeinsamen Schrecksekunde betreten wir, wiederum mit Frau Schulz-Lattich vornan, das Haus, das den örtlichen Bürgern so lange vorenthaltene.

Dann ist es wie im Märchen, nur daß die Zwerge, die da beim Werkeln sind, nicht solch hübsch bunte Wämser tragen und auf dem Kopf keine Zipfelmützen; aber sonst blitzt und funkelt es von den Instrumenten her wie von kostbaren Steinen, und piept und fiept und klinkt und klappert, und keiner kümmert sich um uns, so vertieft sind sie samt und sonders in was auch immer sie da treiben; und wir, Frau Schulz-Lattich und der Dr. Czesnik und ich, bewegen uns auf leisen Sohlen von einem zum andern der Zwerge, gelegentlich den Hals reckend, um ihnen über die Schultern zu blicken; nur der Hauptwachtmeister ist am vorderen Ende des Raumes stehengeblieben, die Hände auf dem Rücken gekreuzt, und wippt auf den Fußballen, wie eben Polizisten wippen, wenn sie darauf warten, daß die Aktion beginne.

»Ach!«

Überraschend, der erste menschliche Laut. Und die Stimme kommt mir bekannt vor. Ich wende mich um – das sorgsam getrimmte Schnurrbärtchen: der Forstmensch, jetzt aber nicht mehr in Loden, sondern mit einem weißen Kittel über dem Anzug, wie ein Tierarzt oder ein Laborleiter. Er sieht, warum, bleibt mir unklar, auf seine Uhr, möglicherweise hat er uns längst schon erwartet und ist ein wenig ungehalten.

Dann zieht er uns beiseite, als wolle er vermeiden, daß seine Zwerge unser Gespräch mit anhören, und beginnt, in unterdrückten Tönen, »Früher«, sagt er, »wären Sie nie bis hierher gelangt. Doch in Zeiten wie diesen...« Müde hebt er die Schultern; es sind ermüdende Zeiten, in denen keiner mehr weiß, was morgen auf ihn noch zukommen mag.

Darauf nimmt er meine und Frau Schulz-Lattichs und des Herrn Dr. Czesnik Frage voraus, was denn hier vor sich gehe. »Dies«, sagt er, »ist eine der modernsten Abhöranlagen der Welt. Unser Stolz.«

Frau Schulz-Lattich hat es den Atem verschlagen. Der Dr. Czesnik jedoch nickt fachmännisch und läßt den Blick über die Schalttafeln schweifen. »Dafür«, sagt er, »war Geld da.«

»Aber um Gottes willen«, sage ich zu dem Forstmenschen, »wen hören Sie denn jetzt noch ab?«

Eine Handbewegung. Ob Hunderte von Menschen oder Tausende, und Dutzende von Ämtern und Institutionen, was tut es.

»Und wohin«, frage ich, »gehen die Informationen? Die Gespräche, die Auswertungen, die Millionen Worte?«

Er senkt die Stimme noch weiter: das ganz große Geheimnis. »Nirgendshin.«

»Nirgends?«

»Die Empfänger sind fort, die Kabel durchtrennt.«

»Aber der Rücklauf?« frage ich. »Sie brauchen doch Rücklauf: Bestätigungen, Änderungen, Anweisungen.«

»Schreibe alles ich.« Er schaut mich an, Heiterkeit im Blick, ein Mann im reinen mit sich selber.

»Und Ihre Leute? Hat denn keiner von denen etwas gemerkt bisher?« sage ich.

»Möglich«, sagt er. »Was weiß ich.« Und runzelt die Stirn. »Trotzdem, sie kommen immer wieder. Pünktlich zu jeder Schicht. Drei Schichten am Tag. Tag für Tag.«

Frau Schulz-Lattich hat sich gefaßt. Etwas bewegt sie jedoch, sichtlich. »Aber warum?« fragt sie, in ihrer Stimme, tief von innenher, ein großes Staunen. »Warum das Ganze?«

Der Forstmensch überlegt, streicht sich die Falten aus dem Kittel, überlegt noch einmal. Dann sagt er, »Aber, gute Frau, das Leben muß doch einen Sinn haben!«

Auf Sand gebaut

»Und all das wird sich ändern bei uns«, sagt meine Elisabeth und hat dabei diesen Glanz im Auge: ihr Intershop-Blick, wie ich ihn nenne, der sich stets zeigt bei ihr, sobald sie den Shop betritt und die Auswahl an bunten Westwaren sieht, nur für harte Währung zu erwerben; aber jetzt braucht ja keiner den Shop mehr, jetzt geht man einfach nach drüben; nur mit der Währung ist es immer noch problematisch. »Sehr ändern«, sagt sie, »und bei Immobilien besonders, die werden ungeheuer steigen im Wert.« Ich staune: Immobilien. Woher sie das Wort überhaupt kennt!

»Richtig froh sein können wir«, fährt sie fort, »daß wir das Haus gekauft haben von der Kommunalen Wohnungsverwaltung, als keiner noch an dergleichen dachte, und für 35000 Ost, ein Klacks, nicht lange und das Haus wird eine halbe Million wert sein, wenn nicht eine ganze, und in harter D-Mark, während die lieben Nachbarn immer nur ihre Miete gezahlt haben an die KWV und daher jederzeit rausfliegen können, sobald die deutsche Vereinigung da ist mit den neuen Gesetzen; aber Besitz ist Besitz, den kann keiner antasten, jetzt nicht und später ebensowenig. Und wer hat dir eingetrichtert, daß du kaufen sollst, und immer wieder gebohrt, bis du endlich den Anwalt genommen und den Kauf rechtsgültig gemacht hast?«

»Elisabeth«, sage ich, »du bist die Klügste.«

Das liebt sie zu hören, meine Elisabeth, und das Gespräch hätte gut und gern so weiterlaufen können, alles Freude und Harmonie, wenn der Kies nicht geknirscht hätte vorm Hause: ein Auto, und offenbar ein ziemlich schweres. »Besuch?« sage ich. »Mitten in der Woche?«

Sie tritt ans Fenster. »Das ist doch der –«

»Wer?«

»Der schon mal hier war«, sagt sie, »zweimal sogar.«

»Und wieso«, frage ich, »erfahre ich das erst heute?«

»Ich wollte dich nicht beunruhigen«, sagt sie. Und fügt hinzu, »Er parkte schräg gegenüber, stieg aus, und strich mehrmals ums Haus. Mehrmals blieb er auch stehen und schaute sich um, als hätte er irgend etwas verloren, und ich wollte schon hinausgehen und ihn fragen, ob er vielleicht von der Stasi wäre, doch die war ja aufgelöst, und bevor ich mich entschließen konnte, war er fort.«

»Du bist sicher, daß er es ist«, sage ich, »denn ich sehe ihrer zwei.«

Sie schluckt. »Er hat sich vermehrt.«

»Und welcher war deiner?« erkundige ich mich, »der mit dem schmalkrempigen Hütchen, der kleine Rundliche, oder der Hagere mit der Leichenbittermiene?«

»Der Kleine«, sagt sie.

»Der Kleine«, sage ich, »so.« Doch bevor ich weiterfragen kann, warum sie geglaubt hat, daß einer wie der mich hätte beunruhigen können, läutet es bereits.

Wir benutzen als Glocke seit neuestem einen chinesischen Gong, sein tiefes Ding-dong-dang jedesmal eine Freude; nur in dieser Minute geht mir das fremdländische Geläut auf den Nerv. Auch meine Elisabeth steht da wie festgewurzelt und kaut auf der Unterlippe.

40

»Geh öffnen«, sage ich. »Die Herren möchten etwas von uns, und ich für mein Teil möchte wissen, was sie möchten.« Wir gehen beide zur Tür, Hand in Hand, gemeinsam ist besser. Der Kleine nimmt sein Hütchen vom Kopf und vollführt eine Art Kratzfuß; der Hagere läßt seine prächtigen Zähne blinken, »Herr und Frau Bodelschwingh, wenn ich nicht irre?«

Ich heiße in der Tat Bodelschwingh, Bodelschwingh wie der berühmte Pastor, obwohl keinerlei verwandtschaftliche Bindung besteht zwischen ihm und meiner Familie, und meine Elisabeth erwarb den Namen durch Eheschluß.

»Dürften wir?« sagt der Hagere.

Das Auge meiner Elisabeth glänzt wieder, aber es ist ein anderer Glanz als vorher, düster und bedrohlich, ihr Trotzalledem-Blick, wie ich ihn nenne.

Der Kleine streicht sich die Schuhsohlen ab auf der Türmatte, sorgfältig und lange: als ob ihm das Haus gehörte, fährt es mir, ich weiß nicht wieso, durch den Kopf. Und während er sein leichtes, staubfarbenes Mäntelchen ablegt, stellt er sich vor, »Prottwedel, Elmar, wenn Sie gestatten.« – »Angenehm«, sage ich.

»Schwiebus«, sagt der andere, und reicht mir ein Kärtchen, »Dr. jur. Schwiebus von Schwiebus, Schwiebus und Krings, Beratung in Liegenschaften.«

»Wir«, sagt meine Elisabeth, »bedürfen keiner Beratung.«

Inzwischen hat sich Herr Prottwedel mit einer Zielstrebigkeit, die man nur als nachtwandlerisch bezeichnen kann, durch die offene Schiebetür in unser Wohnzimmer begeben und steuert auf den Biedermeier-Ohrensessel zu, den wir vor kurzem erst unter großen Mühen, man finde bei uns mal einen Polstermeister und einen so stilechten, gold- und blümchengestreiften Stoff, haben restaurieren lassen, sinkt mit einem Ächzer auf den für einen Hintern wie seinen wie geschaffenen Sitz und sagt, »Dieses war meines Opas Lieblingssessel. Nur war er grün bezogen damals, der Sessel, grün mit lila Röschen. Mein Opa ist darin gestorben: Herzversagen.«

Meine Elisabeth erbleicht. Nicht wegen der Sterbeszene, sondern wegen der Möglichkeit, daß der Sessel tatsächlich von Herrn Prottwedels Opa stammen könnte; wir haben ihn nämlich nicht selber angeschafft, auf uns ist er gekommen von unserm Vorgänger, dem Genossen Watzlik. Als wir das Haus von ihm übernahmen, es stand mir zu als Abteilungsleiter, sagte Watzlik, den Sessel überlaß ich dir, Genosse Bodelschwingh, wir werden uns modern einrichten in der Hauptstadt.

»Vielleicht«, Herr Dr. Schwiebus hat einen sehr gepflegten Akzent, Lübecker Gegend wohl, »vielleicht«, sagt er zu Herrn Prottwedel, »sollten wir den Zweck unsres Besuches erklären.«

»Es wäre«, sagt meine Elisabeth, »an der Zeit.«

Herr Prottwedel verzieht sein Mündchen zu einer Art Knopfloch. »Sie werden, Frau Bodelschwingh, meine vormaligen Anwesenheiten vor Ihrem Grundstück bemerkt haben.«

»Zweimal«, nickt meine Elisabeth, »zweimal.«

»Ich habe Sie nicht erschreckt, hoffentlich«, sagt Herr Prottwedel. »Es geht mir nur um Erinnerungen. Eine glückliche Jugendzeit, die ich hier verbrachte, mit einem der liebenswürdigsten Väter, welcher notabene dieses Haus zusammen mit dem Grund, auf dem es steht, seinerzeit erwarb.«

»Herr Prottwedel«, sagt Dr. Schwiebus, »lebt Gott sei Dank in guten Umständen. Er ist Eigentümer einer bei uns im Westen nicht unbekannten Brauerei sowie weiterer Interessen, die ihm genügend abwerfen. Er befindet sich also in keinerlei Notlage, die es als geraten erscheinen lassen könnte, sich um die Wiederinbesitznahme ihm eigentlich zustehender Liegenschaften zu bemühen.«

42

»Wiederinbesitznahme!« Die leichte Röte, die meiner Elisabeth ins Gesicht steigt: ich kenne das, ein Warnsignal. »Wiederinbesitznahme«, sagt sie, »wie verstehe ich das?«

»Auch freut es mich«, sagt Herr Prottwedel, »feststellen zu können, daß Sie, Herr und Frau Bodelschwingh, den Besitz in gutem Zustand gehalten haben.«

»Wie denn auch anders«, nickt Dr. Schwiebus. »Nutzen die Bodelschwinghs, uns als zuverlässige, saubere Menschen beschrieben, den Besitz doch selber.«

Der rosafarbige Hauch auf dem Gesicht meiner Elisabeth ist deutlichem Rot gewichen. »Wir nutzen das Haus nicht nur«, sagt sie, »es gehört uns. Damit Sie's wissen, Herr Prottwedel, und auch Sie, Herr Dr. Schwiebus: Wir haben es gekauft und bezahlt dafür, samt dem Sessel. Da ist ein Kaufvertrag, ein gültiger, und alles ist im Grundbuch eingetragen und rechtens, Sie können sich selber überzeugen.«

»Herr Dr. Schwiebus hat sich bereits überzeugt«, sagt Herr Prottwedel, »im Grundbuch. Aber trotzdem wird man das Haus doch besuchen dürfen und sich darin umschauen?«

»Wir verstehen, Herr Prottwedel«, sagt meine Elisabeth, »Ihr Bedürfnis, Ihren Erinnerungen nachzugehen.« Und setzt, eine Art Nachgedanke, hinzu, »besonders wo es Sie nichts mehr kostet, nicht einmal, wie vor kurzem noch, die fünfundzwanzig Mark für den Grenzübertritt.«

»Jetzt«, sagt Herr Prottwedel, »würde ich mir doch gern das Obergeschoß besehen.«

Die Schritte, bald von da kommend, bald von dort, und widerhallend in meinem Gehirn: zum Verrücktwerden.

»Warum«, sage ich, »schmeiße ich die Kerle nicht hinaus?«

»Es ist nicht ihr Haus«, sagt meine Elisabeth, »daß sie darin herumstreunen können nach Belieben.«

»Sie benehmen sich«, sage ich, »wie Eroberer.«

»Und das Bad«, sagt meine Elisabeth, »ist nicht aufgeräumt.« Der Ausbruch, so lange schon angekündigt durch
ihre Rotverfärbung, ist da. »Und daß wir«, ruft sie aus, »uns
das selber auf den Hals gewünscht haben!«

»Zügle dich«, mahne ich, »sie sind nicht taub.«

Aber sie ist nicht zu halten. »Es ist unser Haus! In unserm
Haus schrei ich herum, soviel ich will!«

Dann Stille. Dann die Stimme des Herrn Prottwedel. »Da
wären wir wieder!«

»Und wie war der Rundgang?« fragt meine Elisabeth.

Herr Prottwedel schiebt sich hinter den Ohrensessel, als suche er Schutz dort vor ihrem Blick. »Die Anlage der Zimmer«,
sagt er, »ganz wie in meiner Erinnerung.«

»Erinnerung«, sagt Dr. Schwiebus, »ist das halbe Leben.« –
»Und die Einrichtung«, sagt Herr Prottwedel, »so gediegen!«

Nach einer nachdenklichen Pause sagt Dr. Schwiebus, er
verstünde nur unsre ablehnende Haltung nicht, um nicht zu
sagen unser Ressentiment: neben der Auffrischung seiner Erinnerungen habe Herr Prottwedel doch einzig die Absicht, die
Eigentumsfragen bei Haus und Grundstück – hier zieht er hinter dem Tüchlein in der äußeren Brusttasche seines Jacketts
einen Zettel hervor – Marschall-Konjew-frühere Hindenburgstraße 27 baldigst zu klären.

»Was gibt's da zu klären!« Meine Elisabeth stampft mit dem
Fuß auf. »Haus und Grundstück sind unser Besitz, und Besitz
steht unter staatlichem Schutz, immer und überall, Ost wie
West.«

Darum, sagt Dr. Schwiebus, gerade darum; oder läge es
nicht auch in unserm Interesse, eventuelle Auseinandersetzungen zu vermeiden, die sich ergeben könnten, nachdem die
beiden deutschen Staaten sich glücklich wiedervereint hätten, mit entsprechenden rechtlichen Folgen? Und entnimmt
seiner Aktenmappe, schwarzes Maroquin, eine Anzahl von

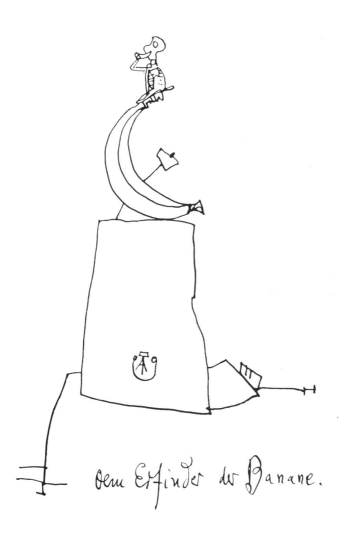

dem Erfinder der Banane.

Bogen, die er vor mir auf den Tisch breitet. Aus diesen Schriftstücken, doziert er dabei, gehe hervor, daß Herr Dietmar Prottwedel, der verstorbene Vater seines Freundes und Mandanten Elmar Prottwedel, Haus und Grundstück ehemalige Hindenburgstraße 27 im Jahre 1936 von einem Herrn Siegfried Rothmund, welcher Deutschland kurz darauf mit unbekanntem Ziel verließ, rechtmäßig erworben habe, und zwar, schicksalhafter Zufall, zu dem gleichen geringen Preis von 35 000 Mark, zu dem wir, das Ehepaar Bodelschwingh, den Besitz von unsrer Kommunalen Wohnungsverwaltung erhielten: und hier sei der Kaufvertrag.

»Nicht«, sagt Herr Prottwedel, »nicht daß wir auch nur im Traum daran dächten, Sie vor die Tür setzen zu wollen.«

Die Lippen meiner Elisabeth zittern. »Vor die Tür unsres eigenen Hauses!«

»Oder«, lächelt Herr Prottwedel, »Anforderungen anderer Art an Sie erhöben zur Zeit.«

»Sollen wir etwa«, sage ich, »für das, was wir längst schon bezahlt haben, noch einmal zahlen?«

»Von Geld«, schaltet Dr. Schwiebus sich ein, »war in keiner Weise die Rede.« Und doziert wieder, wie es Herrn Prottwedel und ihm viel mehr um Titel und Recht gehe, wobei unsere, der Familie Bodelschwingh, Ansprüche auf Haus und Grundstück jetzige Marschall-Konjew-Straße 27 gar nicht in Zweifel stünden. Nur habe eben auch Herr Prottwedel Ansprüche, und es frage sich, wessen die älteren seien und, was wichtiger noch angesichts der sich verändernden Rechtslage, auf welche Art Person oder Personen, von denen wir besagten Besitz erwarben, diesen ihrerseits erworben hätten, und ob die Art jenes Erwerbs nach dem wohl bald auch in unserm Teil Deutschlands wieder gültigem Recht gesetzlich und in Ordnung gewesen wäre.

»Mein Elternhaus wurde nämlich«, erklärt Herr Prottwedel,

»enteignet.« Und verdreht genüßlich die Augen, »Entschädigungslos.«

Dies verdammte Warten. Wir wußten, sie würden wiederkommen. Nur wann, wußten wir nicht, und oft ertappte ich mich, wie ich, heimgekehrt von meiner längst sinnlos gewordenen Arbeit in meinem längst sinnlos gewordenen Amt, im Zimmer saß und auf jedes Geräusch von draußen lauschte. Es hat uns aufgeweckt mitten in der Nacht, man spürt, wenn der andere wachliegt neben einem, ein zu kurzer Atemzug, eine plötzliche Bewegung, und man fängt an nachzudenken: das kann doch nicht wahr sein, denkt man, die ganze Zeit ging das Leben seinen Gang, und nun auf einmal stürzt zusammen, was für die Ewigkeit schien, und wenn nicht für die Ewigkeit, dann doch für beträchtliche Fristen; aber immerhin stand noch das Haus und gehörte uns, ein Dach war da, unter das man kriechen konnte.

»Nein«, sagt meine Elisabeth, »es wird nicht laufen, wie die sich das denken. Ein Staat oder zwei, Besitz ist Besitz, und besonders die drüben, wo kämen die hin, wenn sie zuließen, daß einer so einfach daherkommt und sagt, das war der Lieblingssessel von meinem Opa.«

Da hilft kein Schweigen; die Angst muß heraus, sonst wirst du verrückt. »Aber sie sind die Sieger«, sage ich. »Und wir selber haben sie ins Land geholt. Aufgerissen die Mauer und Deutschland, Deutschland! Gewiß, das vorher war auch kein Honigschlecken, Jahr um Jahr das ewige Ja und der ewige Gehorsam und als Lohn dafür was, eine Vergünstigung hier und da; aber das Haus wenigstens, das sie dich haben ließen, war deines und du hattest Ruhe in deinem Bett.«

»Du gibst dich geschlagen«, sagt sie, »schon vor dem ersten Schuß. Wer ist Herr Prottwedel? Ein mieser kleiner Geschäftsmann, wie sie herumlaufen bei denen zu Tausenden.

Und du? Wie viele Leute hast du geleitet in deiner Dienststelle? Wenn du so gar niemand wärst, sie hätten dich lange schon gefeuert. Und du meinst, die drüben, die Herren Minister und Staatssekretäre und Generaldirektoren, sie bräuchten nicht solche wie dich, die hier die Fäden kennen und wie sie geknüpft waren und die Beziehungen von Amt zu Amt? Wart ein Weilchen, und du wirst den Prottwedel und Schwiebus das Loch weisen können, das der Zimmermann gelassen hat im Haus für sie.«

Das ist meine Elisabeth, hellwach für jede sich bietende Chance. Und ich erkenne: so anders sind die Regeln gar nicht, nach denen die Dinge sich bewegten in dieser Republik und nach denen drüben die Oben und Unten einander begegnen, und ich fühle mich richtig gerührt und sage, »Du hast, Elisabeth, wieder einmal recht. Wir werden uns doch nicht ins Bockshorn jagen lassen von solchen wie denen.«

Dennoch erschraken wir beim neuerlichen Knirschen des Kieses und dem Ding-dong-dang kurz darauf.

»Es wird der Postbote sein«, sage ich, und denke, wie lächerlich, wenn er's tatsächlich wäre. In den Augen meiner Elisabeth ist wieder der Glanz, und sie nimmt mich bei der Hand, was sie, wenn sie glaubte, es wäre der Postbote, nie getan hätte, und so stützen wir einander, moralisch, auf dem Wege zur Haustür. Aber es ist weder der Postbote noch der Herr Prottwedel oder sein Freund Dr. Schwiebus; es ist eine Frau, die da in der Tür steht, dunkler Typ, mit ganz eigenartigem Gesichtsschnitt, und die, da wir überrascht zur Seite weichen, eintritt und, mit ebensolch nachtwandlerischer Sicherheit wie kürzlich erst der Herr Prottwedel, dem Ohrensessel zustrebt.

»Ich nehme an«, sage ich, »das war Ihres Opas Lieblingssessel.« Sie stutzt. »Woher wissen Sie?«

»Und Sie heißen Rothmund?«

»Eva Rothmund«, bestätigt sie, »aus Tel Aviv«, und läßt sich in den Sessel fallen, in dem sie allerdings schmaler wirkt als Herr Prottwedel.

»Und auch Sie suchen Ihre Erinnerungen«, sage ich, »jetzt, wo es nichts mehr kostet, nicht einmal die fünfundzwanzig Mark für den Grenzübertritt.«

»Ich habe keine Erinnerungen«, sagt sie. »Nicht an dies Haus, und nicht an Deutschland, außer einer indirekten: an diesen Sessel, von dem mir mein Großvater oftmals erzählt hat.«

»Und was wünschen Sie dann?« sage ich.

»Ich bin die Erbin.«

»Sind Sie das«, sage ich, und dann, da mir ein Gedanke kommt, ein bösartiger, »ja, das eröffnet ganz neue Perspektiven!«

»Wieso?« fragt sie. »Und welche?«

»Zusammen mit Ihnen, Frau Rothmund«, verkünde ich, »fordre ich Prottwedel und Schwiebus in die Schranken.«

Meine Elisabeth jedoch scheint davon wenig zu halten.

»Aber hat denn, Frau Rothmund«, fragt sie, »Ihr Großvater diesen Besitz nicht an einen Herrn Prottwedel verkauft?«

»Verkauft?« Frau Rothmund erhebt sich aus Ihres Großvaters einstigem Lieblingssessel und entnimmt ihrer Handtasche, billiges braunes Leder, eine Anzahl von Bogen, die sie auf den Tisch breitet. »Aus diesen Schriftstücken geht hervor«, sagt sie, »daß ich die rechtmäßige und alleinige Erbin meines Großvaters Siegfried Rothmund bin und daß dieser am 23. Februar 1936, bedroht seitens des SS-Sturmführers Dietmar Prottwedel, man werde ihn verhaften und in ein Konzentrationslager verbringen, besagtem SS-Sturmführer Prottwedel sein Haus und Grundstück Hindenburgstraße 27 überschrieb.«

Deutsche Theokratische Republik

»Was heißt hier Bedrohung«, sagt meine Elisabeth.

»Entscheidend für den Besitzstand einer Liegenschaft ist nicht, was bei der Verhandlung darüber geredet wurde, sondern ob Ihr Herr Großvater die Kaufsumme von 35 000 Mark dafür erhalten hat oder nicht.« Und ich sehe, was vorgeht in ihrem Kopf: ihr ist die Dame aus Israel, so diese denn wirklich das Urrecht hat an unserm Besitz, die größere Gefahr; mit Prottwedel und Schwiebus würde sich, besonders nach dem Auftauchen der Frau Rothmund, eine Einigung eher herstellen lassen; West oder Ost, man war da unter Deutschen.

»Entscheidend, sagten Sie«, sagt Frau Rothmund, »entscheidend für den Besitzstand sei der Erhalt der Kaufsumme?«

»Wir haben«, sagt meine Elisabeth, »den von Ihrem Großvater mit dem Herrn Dietmar Prottwedel abgeschlossenen Kaufvertrag selber gesehen.«

»Hier«, sagt Frau Rothmund und greift nach einem der Papiere, »ist ein Affidavit mit meines Großvaters eigenhändiger Unterschrift, geleistet am Tag vor seinem Ableben in Anwesenheit eines öffentlichen Notars, des Inhalts, daß der Verkauf des Hauses und Grundstücks Hindenburgstraße 27 mitsamt dem zugehörigen Kaufvertrag null und nichtig sind, da der Käufer, SS-Sturmführer Dietmar Prottwedel, die meinem Großvater vertraglich zugesicherten und sowieso nur einen geringen Teil des wahren Werts der genannten Liegenschaft darstellenden 35 000 Mark einbehalten und unterschlagen hat.«

Meine Elisabeth schnappt nach Luft. »Aber wo stehen *wir* dann?« sagt sie schließlich, und, nach einer langen Minute, »Sie müssen doch auch an uns denken, Frau Rothmund!»

Ich weiß nicht, ob das ganz das richtige war, der Frau Rothmund zu sagen, die doch extra aus Israel gekommen war; doch was soll man auch sagen in einer solchen Situation, jetzt wo sich alles bei uns ändert?

53

Der Zauberlehrling

»Goebbels«, sagt er nachdenklich, »du erinnerst dich doch?«

Dabei blickt er wie in weite Fernen, die Augen groß, dunkel, das Weiße darin durchzogen von feinen Äderchen, kein Wunder nach so vielen Jahren, wie weit liegt das auch schon zurück, 1945.

»Goebbels«, wiederholt er, »weißt du nicht mehr, was du damals gesagt hast?«

Irgend etwas über den Mann im Dunkel des Bunkers, vermute ich, muß es gewesen sein, und die Stimmung, die da unten geherrscht haben mag, und den Suizid, samt Familie. Und sage, »Du hast das bessere Gedächtnis, Michael, das habe ich nie bestritten.«

Er nippt an seinem Scotch. Er trinkt schon eine ganze Weile, praktisch seit er gekommen ist, aber man merkt es ihm nicht an. »Du hast gesagt«, sagt er, »du hättest dir manchmal überlegt, wie dem Mann zumute gewesen sein muß am Ende. Er war ja kein schlechter Psychologe, hast du gesagt, und er hatte Ideen. Und dann hast du mir erklärt, und hast gelächelt dabei, das Geschäft brauche eben, um zu funktionieren, eine Ausgangslage, die zumindest einige Chancen biete; wenn schon alles kaputt ist, hast du gesagt, und die Menschen spüren, wie die gewohnten Strukturen um sie herum zusammenbrechen, dann nutzten auch die schönsten Überredungskünste nichts mehr und die originellsten Gedanken wären für die Katz.«

Das Geschäft, über das ich ihn damals belehrte, jetzt fällt es mir wieder ein, war die Psychologische Kriegsführung, und ich betrachte meinen plötzlichen Gast, gestern abend war er noch in New York, wie er da sitzt, das schwere Glas in der Hand, und die Eisstückchen gegeneinander bewegt, und auf einmal wird mir auch klar, warum er die alte Geschichte um den Dr. Goebbels, den ich gehaßt habe, heute und hier aufs Tapet bringt: Du, mein Alter, will er mir damit sagen, befindest dich in einer ganz ähnlichen Situation wie der selige Propagandaminister.

»Michael«, sage ich, als müßte ich jede Silbe hinter mir herziehen, »Michael Heidenheim...«

»Hyde, bitte«, sagt er, »von Bryan, McKinley, Siskind & Hyde, Consultants.«

Jeder von uns hat das schon erlebt, glaube ich: wenn man mit Menschen, die man einst gut kannte, eine Zeitlang wieder zusammengesessen hat, ist es auf einmal, als schälten die Jahre wie tote Haut sich von den Gesichtern, und diese selber erscheinen, verschwommen zwar, aber deutlich erkennbar noch: eine Art Reflexbild in Spiegeln von gestern: das seine, das ich jetzt sehe, ist Haut und Knochen; so hatte es sich mir eingeritzt ins Gedächtnis, als er zu uns in die Redaktion kam damals, zerlumpt und verlaust, und mit dem Schrecken noch in den Augen, dem Schrecken des Lagers, und wenn er die Lippen breitzog, zeigten sich zwischen ihnen die schwarzen Löcher, wo sie ihm die Zähne ausgeschlagen hatten, die SS. Wir saßen zu jener Zeit in der Zentralredaktion der Blätter, die die U.S. Army für die lieben Deutschen machte, um sie auf andere als Nazi-Gedanken zu bringen, und irgendwie spürte ich, es steckte mehr in dem Jungen als beim ersten Blick sichtbar, und ich gab Anordnung, ihn aufzufüttern und auszu-

56

staffieren und ihm ein Bett zu verschaffen irgendwo und ihn auf die Gehaltsliste für deutsches Zivilpersonal zu setzen als Volontär, und er war mir dankbar wie ein zugelaufenes Hündchen, dem man ja auch gelegentlich einen Tritt gibt, und allmählich begann ich, fast so etwas wie väterliche Gefühle für ihn zu entwickeln, möglicherweise weil er mich eines Tages wissen ließ, ich ähnelte, im Ton der Stimme und in der Art, wie ich mich bewegte, seinem Vater; dann jedoch stellte sich heraus, daß er von seinem Vater schon getrennt worden war in einem Alter, als er noch kaum feste Erinnerungen an ihn gehabt haben konnte.

»Wenn du meinst...«, sage ich. Und konzediere ihm, »Doch, du magst recht haben. Ein paar Tage lang hab ich geglaubt, wir hätten gesiegt, ich und die Handvoll mir Gleichgesinnter.«

»Jedenfalls sahst du so aus dort auf der Tribüne: wie ein minderer Caesar nach seinem Siege.« Er trinkt wieder, einen gehörigen Schluck. »Seinem Sieg über irgendwelche unbedeutende Stämme.«

»Du schmeichelst mir«, sage ich. »Die Wandlung von Heidenheim in Hyde und dein Aufstieg aus der bundesdeutschen Medienlandschaft ins Chefbüro von Brian, McKinley, Siskind & Hyde in der Park Avenue, nach nützlichem Umweg über den Seitenflügel des Weißen Hauses, hat nichts von deiner naturgegebenen Bosheit abgeschliffen.«

»Du hast, scheint's, meinen Weg verfolgt«, sagt er.

»Wo werde ich denn nicht«, sage ich. »Ich habe dir deine schönen Kenntnisse doch beigebracht, von der Manipulation der Worte bis zu der der Menschen.«

»Ich bin nicht boshaft zu dir, du täuschst dich.« Er streicht sich über das krause, nun auch schon ergraute Haar an der Schläfe, unter der es zu zucken begonnen hat. »Ich habe Angst.«

»Um wen? Mich?«

»Auch.«

»Ich bin ein alter Mann«, sage ich. »Was soll mir noch passieren?«

»Man kann auch seelisch zugrunde gerichtet werden.« Seine Lippen verziehen sich. Die Zähne, die sie ihm ausgeschlagen haben, sind längst ersetzt, ein prachtvolles Gebiß. »Sie werden dich hernehmen und dir ihre Messer zwischen die Rippen stechen, nahe der Herzgegend.«

»Und bist du gekommen, Michael Heidenheim, mir das zu sagen?«

Er meidet die Antwort. »Auch ich«, sagt er, »habe deine Tätigkeit mit Interesse beobachtet – deine Essays gelesen, deine Reden mir exzerpieren lassen, deine Video Tapes gesehen: der alte Meister. Und wie du das aufgebaut hast über die Jahre, deine Autorität im Lande, gegen so viele Widerstände, und single-handedly, wie sagt man das im Deutschen, auf eigene Faust? – nein, das faßt es nicht – das Englische ist eine viel brauchbarere Sprache in vielem: *ein* Mann, gegen einen ganzen Apparat . . .«

»Es gab auch andere«, sage ich, und ärgere mich über ihn, wie es mich schon damals geärgert hat, wenn er mir um den Bart ging, sobald er etwas von mir wollte.

»Und nun sitzt du da«, sagt er und hebt das Glas und blickt mich an durch das Honiggelb der Flüssigkeit, als sähe er mein Gesicht zum ersten Male, »sitzt da wie dein Dr. Goebbels selig, nachdem er sein letztes Aufgebot noch in den Kampf geschickt hat, erinnerst du dich, wir haben das Photo vorgefunden in der Ecke eines Schreibtischfachs in der Redaktion, ihn zeigend in seinem Ledermantel, und die verschreckten Augen der Kindersoldaten unter ihren großen, zerknitterten Feldmützen, schrecklich, und kein Flugblatt, das noch etwas hätte bewirken können, und keine Ansprache

Das Hohe Hotaus

im Rundfunk, die noch einer gehört hätte, und die Zeitungen erscheinen auch längst nicht mehr, nur die Übermacht der Amerikaner steht gegenüber und millionenweis flattern ihre Passierscheine vom Himmel und werden aufgelesen von den müden Landsern, *Kommt herüber, wir garantieren euch Leben und Sicherheit, gute Behandlung, gutes Essen,* und die Wehrmacht entschwindet gen Westen, so wie deine DDR-Menschen heute, und du nichts dagegen machen kannst, nichts, nichts: Psychologische Kriegsführung, mein Alter, doch diese unter den herrlichsten Voraussetzungen!«

Trotzdem sieht er nicht glücklich aus, mein ehemaliger Musterschüler, jetzt bei der Firma Brian, McKinley, Siskind & Hyde, Consultants, und ich sage, »Das hab ich mir lange gedacht, daß das ein Job gewesen ist von einem aus unserer Branche, und der Text auf unsern alten Passierscheinen war nicht mal gar so anders als das, was heute abgeleiert wird, die großen Versprechungen, was sie alles erhalten würden an Schönem und Gutem, die Lieben, und ganz umsonst, wenn sie nur brav kämen mit erhobenen Händen, *Ei ssörrender.* Aber wer, frage ich, hat das Ding jetzt gedreht? Den plötzlichen Wandel im Gehirn der Leute von *Wir sind das Volk* zu *Wir sind ein Volk...* Du, das ist fast genial, diese totale Umkehr von Sinn und Bedeutung eines Schlachtrufs durch ein winziges Wort. Wenn er nicht so lange schon unter der Erde läge, hast du ihn übrigens besucht auf dem Friedhof in Ascona auf deiner letzten Reise, würde ich vermuten, der Gedanke stammte von Hans Habe.«

Er füllt sein Glas nach und hebt es mir zu, »Dem Andenken des teuren Toten!« Nur an der Stimme, die noch sonorer klingt als sonst, läßt sich erkennen, daß der Alkohol zu wirken beginnt.

»Oder das«, sage ich, »auf einem Riesenspruchband, schwarz-rot-gold, in Leipzig: *Kommt die D-Mark nicht hier, gehn wir hin zu ihr!* Das ist die beste Definition von Deutschland, einig Vaterland, die ich je gesehen habe.«

»Gut, nicht?« sagt er, mit einem Anflug von Stolz, so hört es sich an.

»Fast genial!« wiederhole ich, und mutmaße, »In Bonn war es keiner; ich kenn doch die Typen in den zuständigen Ämtern; du brauchst sie nur kurz zu betrachten, wenn sie herumwieseln dort, wichtig, wichtig, wichtig, und ihre Nasen hervorstecken hinter einem Ministerrücken und dem erstbesten Fernsehmenschen ihre Weisheiten vorerzählen, und du weißt Bescheid.

Und die Burschen in dem Hamburger Wochenblatt da – gelehrige Clowns, bar jeder Originalität. Dem Goebbels könnt keiner von denen das Wasser reichen, geschweige denn echten Profis wie dir oder mir.«

Er lacht, vom Bauche her, der Scotch schwappt gefährlich. Und er läßt erkennen, wie stolz er ist, daß ich ihn so direkt an die Spitze der Profis stelle. Und sagt, »Aber du bist der Größte.«

Das läßt mich nun doch aufhorchen. »Michael«, sage ich, »Michael Heidenheim«, und mein Blick fixiert sich auf seinen Adamsapfel, der damals, als wir uns kennenlernten, aussah wie ein Stück Hühnerknochen, ihm steckengeblieben im dürren Halse und ihn zu ersticken drohend, und jetzt da eingebettet liegt in solides Fett, »Michael, warst *du* das?«

Er grinst. Aber das Grinsen gefriert ihm, und die Hand, die das Glas hält, bebt ihm plötzlich, so als verspürte er große Angst.

»Trink«, sage ich ihm, »du mußt den Alkoholspiegel halten, sonst kippst du um.«

»Genial!« Für einen Moment ringt er nach Luft; dann geht es wieder. »Genial! hast du gesagt.«

»Fast genial«, korrigiere ich.

Er weiß, was ich jetzt denke von ihm, und in welchen Kategorien. Wasser sammelt sich ihm in den Augen, tatsächlich, gleich wird er anfangen zu flennen. »Du weißt ja nicht«, schnieft er, »was ich leide.«

»Du«, sage ich, »leidest. Wieviel haben sie gezahlt an Brian, McKinley, Siskind & Hyde für die Beratung?«

»Ich bin kein Judas!« Er richtet sich auf, so gut es geht. »Ich bin einfach gegen die Kommunisten. Sie haben ja auch dich kaputt gemacht. Oder hast du's nicht schwer genug gehabt, wie sie dir noch im Nacken saßen? Und jetzt sind sie kaputt, Gesindel, elendes, kaputt und erledigt.«

»Was jammerst du dann?« frage ich.

»Warst du nicht erfolgreich? Ein ganzes Volk, und was für eines, von den Füßen, auf denen sie gerade zu gehen lernten, auf den Kopf gestellt. Hast du sie dann gesehen? Und gehört? Wie haben dir die Texte gefallen, und die Töne? An wen hast du gedacht dabei? Deinen ermordeten Vater? Oder gar an dich selber, in der Zeit, da du zu uns gekrochen kamst, mehr tot als lebendig?«

Eben war das Glas noch halb gefüllt; jetzt hat er's geleert. »Hilf mir«, sagt er, mit schwerer Zunge. »Du mußt mir helfen. Du kannst es. Mach es rückgängig irgendwie, eine neue Linie, neue Texte, neue Methoden, alles neu, alles anders, ganz gleich, was es kostet, ich bekomme das durch, glaub mir, und du kannst es schaffen, wenn einer, dann du, du bist der Meister, ich hab's doch erlebt, damals, wir blocken es ab, sonst kommt eines zum andern, diese Grenze, jene Grenze, Jubel, Hurra, ein Reich, ein... Und dann ist kein Halten mehr, und es schwemmt uns alle fort, dich, mich...« Er richtet sich auf, mit Mühe, die Knie wollen ihm versagen, er klammert sich an mich, keucht, »Hilf mir doch!«

»Besen!« sage ich. »Besen, Besen, seid's gewesen!«

Er starrt. Die Augen, schwarz, dunkel, treten hervor. Dann

beginnt er zu verstehen. »Goethe!« sagt er. Und dann, »Das ist alles?«

»Aber es paßt doch auf die Situation«, sage ich. »Oder etwa nicht?«

Alte Bekanntschaft

Ich habe mir seit je die größte Mühe gegeben, nicht aufzu-
fallen, und habe mich stets einzufügen gesucht in die Reihen
der Durchschnittlichen, deren Interesse im Leben nur eines
ist: sich rechtzeitig anzupassen an das Gängige, Konflikte zu
meiden, besonders mit denen oben, und eine möglichst kosige
Nische zu finden.

Aber es hat nichts genützt. Vielleicht habe ich irgendwann
doch etwas geäußert, was den Behörden zu denken gab, so
daß sie seither ein Auge auf mich haben. Oder mein Miß-
geschick rührt daher, daß Regierungsämter und deren Be-
dienstete nach Mustern funktionieren, in die einer wie ich
nicht hineinpaßt; fast könnte man meinen, mein Körperge-
ruch sei anders als der behördliche; die Vertreter der Staats-
macht brauchen nur kurz Witterung zu nehmen, und schon
regt sich in ihnen Verdacht: sie spüren das fremde Etwas im
Raum, eine Gefahr, noch undefinierbar und gerade deshalb
um so gravierender.

Mein Freund Wohlrabe hält nichts von der Geruchstheo-
rie. Eher, sagt er, könnte es an meinem Gesichtsausdruck liegen. Besonders in meinem Blick säßen die Zweifel, die einen
Untertan bei der Obrigkeit unbeliebt machen; und in der Tat,
wenn ich mich beim Rasieren im Spiegel betrachte, oder beim
Knoten der Krawatte, die ich gelegentlich noch trage, muß ich

feststellen, daß Wohlrabe mit seiner Meinung sehr wohl recht haben könnte.

Er ist ja auch ein Kenner der Materie. Wohlrabe hat, für seine Bedürfnisse, eine ganze Physiognomielehre entwickelt, in die er mir, wenn er so gelaunt war, Einblick gewährte: neben den Augen, sagt er, seien es die Stirn, die Lippen, das Spiel der Muskeln um Kinnbacken und Schläfe, die charakterliche Anhaltspunkte lieferten; er läse diese Sorte von Merkmalen wie etwa ein Schiffskapitän die Linien auf seiner Seekarte, hier befänden sich Untiefen, dort sollte man glatte Fahrt machen können. Einem Manne, so denke ich, der seine Umgebung auf diese Weise beobachtet, dürfte es an Kurzweil nicht fehlen – beneidenswert.

Aber wenn Sie mich jetzt um eine genauere Angabe des Zeitpunkts bäten, zu dem ich Wohlrabe kennenlernte, müßte ich passen; vor drei, vier Jahren etwa, als die ersten Risse sich zeigten in dem vorher anscheinend so festen Gefüge von Staat und Partei, trat er ganz unvermittelt in mein Leben, sagte, er sei Journalist, freischaffend, und blieb, ohne sich irgendwie aufzudrängen und oft kaum bemerkt, präsent. Es gibt derart Menschen; es ist, als trügen sie, wenn auch nicht ständig, eine Tarnkappe, und mehr als einmal geschah es, daß ich im Glauben, er stünde hinter mir, mich nach ihm umwandte, ihn jedoch nicht vorfand. Aber selbst wenn er deutlich und dreidimensional anwesend war, schien er öfters wie abgekapselt; in Gesellschaft verhielt er sich, und dies bis zuletzt, bis unsere Wege sich trennten, eher schweigsam; wenn er aber sprach, sprach er klug und zum Wesentlichen, sogar bei kontroversen Fragen, obwohl er sich da nur selten festlegte.

Mit der Zeit wäre es auch einer weniger mißtrauischen Natur als mir aufgefallen, daß der Zufall uns beide häufiger zusammenführte, als ein normaler Zufall es getan hätte; ohne ersichtlichen Grund tauchte er, sich meist im Hintergrund haltend, bei Besprechungen auf, die von Themen handelten, welche ihn überhaupt nicht betreffen konnten, besuchte Zusammenkünfte von Kreisen, denen er in keiner Weise sich zugehörig fühlen durfte, und drängte sich in Parties ein, zu deren Besuch ich wenige Stunden vorher noch gar nicht entschlossen gewesen war. Ich hatte einen Schatten gewonnen, der mir auf beinah rührende Weise anhing, und nach anfänglichem Unbehagen gewöhnte ich mich nicht nur an ihn, sondern fühlte mich sogar unsicher, wenn er aus irgendeinem Grunde nicht erschien. Rechnet man hinzu, daß ich ein eher schutzbedürftiger Mensch bin und die Einsamkeit, in der ich seit dem Hinscheiden meiner Frau lebe, mich zusätzlich belastet, so wird meine Haltung noch verständlicher werden. Wenn ich nachts durch die Vorortstraßen, in denen aus dem Dunkel die Betrunkenen grölen, meiner Wohnung zustrebe, wage ich kaum, mich umzusehen, und um so willkommener ist mir dann die Nähe jemandes, der mir zur Not Beistand leisten kann, nicht im Wortstreit, da weiß ich mich durchaus zu behaupten, aber physisch, und Wohlrabe hatte, Schultern, Hüften, Gang bewiesen es, einen glänzend durchtrainierten Körper. Und wenn er gar, der offenbar einen Wagen besaß oder zumindest zur Verfügung hatte, aus einer Seitenstraße aufkreuzte, ein paar Schritte neben mir herfuhr, die Fensterscheibe herabkurbelte und, freundlich grüßend, sich erkundigte, ob er mich nicht nach Haus fahren dürfte, nahm ich das Anerbieten gerne an, obwohl es mich verpflichtete, ihn noch auf einen Drink oder eine Tasse Kaffee zu mir einzuladen.

In einer solchen Stunde, es ging auf Mitternacht, fragte ich ihn offen heraus, wie es denn käme, daß er seit geraumer Zeit sich in meinem Leben, er möge das Wort mir bitte nicht verübeln, eingenistet habe, und ob dahinter eine Absicht stecke, und wenn ja, welche und von welcher Seite; ich sei, setzte ich hinzu, doch nicht der Typ, der irgend jemandem gefährlich werden könnte und daher einen Aufpasser bräuchte; auch seien, wie er wohl wisse, meine persönlichen und gesellschaftlichen Verbindungen ein offenes Buch; und schon gar nicht besäße ich verborgene Reichtümer oder in meiner Schublade Entwürfe von Erfindungen, die irgendwelchen Gruppen oder Organisationen von Bedeutung sein könnten: kurz, woher sein Interesse an mir, warum verfolge er mich?

Er antwortet nicht, oder nicht sofort. Doch nach einigem Nachdenken fragt er mich, ob ich denn, wenn ich ehrlich mit mir wäre, ihm nicht konzedieren würde, daß ich behördliche Aufmerksamkeit verdiente: die Gefahren für Staat und Gemeinwesen lägen weniger im Tun einer Person – dieses sei leicht zu erkennen und zu bekämpfen – als in deren Gedanken. »Gedanken«, sagt er, »springen über von einem zum andern. Überprüfen Sie doch einmal, was da herumsprüht in Ihrem Kopfe und noch mehr in Ihrer Brust: würden Sie nicht auch, säßen Sie anstelle der für Ruhe und Ordnung Verantwortlichen, einen wie Sie im Auge behalten?«

»Sie sind also, Herr Wohlrabe«, sage ich, »auf mich angesetzt, sozusagen.«

»Ich könnte«, erwidert er, »für jedes unsrer Zusammentreffen durchaus stichhaltige Gründe nachliefern, die jeden in dieser Richtung laufenden Verdacht ausräumen würden; doch in der Häufung unserer Begegnungen, das läßt sich nicht leugnen, liegt das Mißliche, das geeignet ist, unser Verhältnis zu trüben.«

»Unser Verhältnis«, wiederhole ich. »Was denn empfinden Sie für mich, daß Sie es noch erhalten möchten, nachdem Sie mir soeben die Motive für Ihre, sagen wir, Anhänglichkeit eingestanden haben?«

»Soll denn einer«, Wohlrabes Gesicht verzog sich, als litte

er tatsächlich, »soll denn einer wie ich kein Innenleben haben dürfen? Keine Sympathien, keine Gefühle von Freundschaft?«

»Und womit«, frage ich, »habe ich Ihre Sympathien verdient? Was habe ich Besonderes für Sie getan? Oder läuft unser Denken so parallel? Oder haben Sie gar Neigungen, die ich bei meiner Veranlagung zu erwidern nicht imstande wäre?«

»Lassen Sie die Frivolitäten«, sagt er. »Fragen Sie sich lieber, ob einer, der auf dienstliche Anordnung hin einem Mitbürger ein gewisses Maß von Wachsamkeit widmet, auch unbedingt dessen Feind sein muß? Und selbst wenn unser beider Anschauungen mitunter differieren, schließt das jede andere Beziehung von Mensch zu Mensch aus?«

Er stützt sich, als seien ihm Kopf und Schultern auf einmal zu schwer, auf seine Ellbogen. Und lag nicht auch, dachte ich, ein geheimer Reiz in einem engeren Verhältnis zwischen Lauscher und Belauschtem? Dann lehnt er sich vor, »Ganz abgesehen davon, daß Sie sich selber eine Menge Unannehmlichkeiten ersparen und zugleich mir meine Aufgabe ganz ungeheuer erleichtern könnten, wenn wir ein wenig kooperierten. Eine Behörde ist wie eine Wildkatze im Käfig: harmlos, wenn regelmäßig gefüttert und nicht durch Lärm oder spezielle Gerüche gereizt.« Womit er auf einen Zettel deutet, den er plötzlich in der Hand hat, »Sehen wir einmal, was die wissen möchten« – wobei die Betonung des *die* keinerlei Werturteil enthält, der hinweisende Nominativ pluralis hätte sich ebensogut auf ein Paket Nudeln beziehen können.

Sollte man die Sache nicht doch eventuell probieren, dachte ich. Was ich ihn an Informationen wissen lassen würde, kontrollierte ja schließlich ich!

Er nahm mein Schweigen wohl als eine Art Einverständnis und stellte ein paar unverfängliche Fragen, jederzeit bereit, wieder zurückzuweichen, und nichts würde gewesen sein zwischen uns beiden. Ich erinnere mich nur noch ungefähr, was sie damals über mich zu erfahren wünschten: etwas über meinen Umgang mit Dozenten an der Ingenieurhochschule, glaube ich, und über meine Reisepläne im März und April des Jahres; Wohlrabe und ich beschlossen, ihnen ein knappes halbes Dutzend Namen zu liefern von Leuten, deren dienstliche Kontakte mit mir längst zutage lagen, und was die Reisen betraf, die komplette Liste plus einem nichtamtlichen Abstecher; die kleinen persönlichen Sünden freuen sie am meisten, erläuterte Wohlrabe; die häufeln sie auf für eventuelle künftige Verwendung.

Nun könnte jemand einwenden, mit dem Teufel sei nicht gut Kirschen essen; am Ende möchtest du selber als einer der Teufel dastehen, dir zum Abscheu: erst ein kleiner Verrat, ein winziges Denunziatiönchen, niemandem eigentlich schädlich; dann eines, das schon von Bedeutung, wenn auch von geringer; dann ein größeres, das diesen Genossen den verdienten Aufstieg kostet oder jene Genossin den Job; und so weiter und so fort, bis du endlich auch Geld dafür nimmst und teilhast an den Vorrechten und Genüssen der Kameraden von der unsichtbaren Front und ihnen verfällst mit Haut und Haar.

Etwas der Art sagte ich Wohlrabe auch, und fügte hinzu, dieses werde er von mir nicht erhalten, das schwöre ich ihm. Und wirklich bekam er von mir nur was man, unter Fachleuten, als Spielmaterial bezeichnet, und da er selber mitspielte in dem Spiel, fiel es mir nicht gar so schwer, mir die Finger relativ sauber zu halten; die größeren Schwierigkeiten dürfte er gehabt haben: mehr als einmal deutete er an, daß seine Freunde ihn um solidere Fakten bedrängten als die, die ich ihm vorsetzte, und daß er es nicht leicht hatte, sie hinzuhalten.

Aber warum begnügte er sich mit seinen begrenzten Er-

Argumente gewisser Kreise
sind schlagende Beweise.

meine
Damen & Herren.

gebnissen? Er hätte mich doch unter Druck setzen können: Hör zu, Bursche, hätte er nur zu sagen brauchen, du hast uns den kleinen Finger gereicht; jetzt gib uns gefälligst die Hand. Dann hätte ich zu entscheiden gehabt, ob weiterzumachen und zum Schufterle zu werden oder mich von ihm zu trennen und so den Zorn seiner Freunde auf mich zu ziehen, einen Zorn, dessen üble Folgen jeder kannte. Oder erklärte sich seine Genügsamkeit dadurch, daß unser gemeinsam erarbeitetes Spielmaterial doch genügend ernsthaften Stoff enthielt, um den Ansprüchen seiner Freunde zu genügen und gegen all meine Absichten Unheil anzurichten, für das ich dann verantwortlich wäre?

Gespräche, schicksalsbestimmende besonders, kommen meistens ganz unbemerkt zustande, oft weiß man hinterher nicht einmal, welcher der Partner den Anstoß dazu gab. Im Gedächtnis ist mir Wohlrabes Bemerkung geblieben, ziemlich am Anfang der bewußten Unterredung, wie die Zeiten sich doch änderten und ob ich nicht auch das Gefühl hätte, daß, was gestern noch unbeweglich erschien, sich heute zu rühren begänne, und ob auch ich es für möglich hielte, daß wir uns einem jener Momente näherten, da, laut Hegel, Quantität umschlug in eine neue Qualität.

Auf genau einen solchen Moment, das war ja der tiefere Grund für das Mißtrauen der Ordnungsmächte mir gegenüber und für Wohlrabes Allgegenwart in meiner Nähe, hatte ich längstens hingearbeitet, und die Bestätigung, just von ihm kommend, daß der Moment kurz bevorstand, erfüllte mich mit Genugtuung, mehr noch, mit innerem Jubel.

»Sie müssen doch, nehme ich an«, sagt er, »sich oft schon gewundert haben über meine, nennen wir es Toleranz. Ich bin ja auch, offen gesagt, nicht ausgeschickt worden, um Sie zu päppeln.«

»Sondern?«

»Zuerst«, sagt er, »dachte ich, ich käme am weitesten bei Ihnen auf die weiche Tour.«

»Und wie weit sind Sie gekommen?«

»Dann«, sagt er, »begannen Sie mir leid zu tun. Gesetzt den Fall, dachte ich, ich hätte Sie ausgenommen, wie wir es gewohnt sind zu tun, Ihre sämtlichen Innereien fein säuberlich auseinandergepickt und auf die übliche Weise verwertet: was wäre aus Ihnen geworden!«

»*Ich*«, sage ich, »begann Ihnen leid zu tun. Was sind Sie, ein Engelchen?«

»Sie haben's mit den Jenseitigen«, sagt er. »Irgendwann äußerten Sie bereits, mit mir zu verkehren hieße mit dem Teufel Kirschen zu essen. Schöner Teufel, angekränkelt innerlich und leid des Menschenpacks, das er aufspießen und rösten soll über einem Feuer, das nur noch qualmt.«

»Warum machen Sie dann nicht Schluß?« frage ich. »Jetzt. Gerade rechtzeitig noch vor dem Hegelschen Punkt.«

»Weil das nicht geht«, sagt er. »Einmal in dem Verein, immer in dem Verein. Seien Sie froh, daß ich Sie davor bewahrt habe.«

»Großen Dank«, sage ich. »Aber was jetzt?«

»Ich weiß nicht«, sagt er, »was kommen wird. Aber Sie können ja, falls Sie einmal gefragt werden, bestätigen, daß ich von gutem Charakter bin, mit Absichten und Motiven, die man wahrlich nicht als bösartig bezeichnen kann.«

»Ich werde«, sage ich, »in dem Sinne aussagen.« Und da ich an seiner Stirn und dem Ausdruck der Augen, und an dem Spiel der Muskeln um seine Kinnbacken und Schläfe, an all den Stellen also, an denen, wie er mir beibrachte, Wesen und Stimmung des Menschen ablesbar sind, erkenne, wie ihm zumute ist, ergänze ich, »Es dürfte aber, Herr Wohlrabe, kaum notwendig werden.«

Ich sah ihn an jenem denkwürdigen 4. November des Jahres 1959; er kam, in voller Sicht der auf den Dächern rundum montierten Videokameras der Polizei, auf den Alexanderplatz marschiert und trug, zusammen mit einem mir Unbekannten, ein Transparent, darauf mit großen, dilettantisch gezogenen schwarzen Lettern zu lesen stand, *Stasi in die Produktion!*

Auch er mußte mich gesehen haben, denn er grinste mir zu, als wollte er mir gratulieren; dann war er vorbeigezogen, und ich fand ihn an dem Tag nicht wieder. Dafür klingelte es etwa eine Woche danach an meiner Tür, und er stand da, eine Flasche in der Hand, und fragte, ob er hereinkommen dürfe; es bestünde kein Grund mehr zu irgendwelcher Geheimhaltung unsrer Beziehung, und sowieso sei alles zu Ende, worauf diese gegründet gewesen sei, Prost, Gesundheit!

Ich war doch irgendwie berührt: er war das Nächstbeste zu einem Freund gewesen, und ich fragte mich, ob, und wann, wir uns noch einmal begegnen würden. Und sage, »Eines Tages werden die Leute sich noch zurücksehnen nach einer Zeit, wo man wußte, wer zu fürchten war.«

»Es wird«, sagt er, »eine große Unsicherheit sein im Volke, und sie werden nach neuen Feinden suchen: Juden, Kommunisten, Fremden, allen, die irgendwie aus der Reihe reden.«

»Der gleichen Garnitur«, sage ich, »die euch schon als Freiwild diente.«

»Aber natürlich«, sagt er. »Sind wir nicht Fleisch vom Fleische dieses Volkes?«

»Touché«, sage ich. Und erkundige mich, »Was werden Sie nun tun? Sie, Major Friedrich Karl Wohlrabe. Persönlich, meine ich.«

»Wenn ich das wüßte«, sagt er, »würde ich es Ihnen nicht sagen. Aber ich weiß es nicht. Noch nicht.«

Man kann davon ausgehen, daß zwischenmenschliche Beziehungen stets von irgendwelchen mehr oder minder egoistischen Beweggründen motiviert sind; kennt man diese, so werden die Beziehungen gedeihen; andernfalls bleibt immer, bewußt oder unbewußt, ein Bündel beunruhigender Fragen.

Bei ihm wußte ich, was ihn trieb; unser Verhältnis war also klar gewesen und ohne störende Zwischengedanken; man konnte sich aussprechen mit ihm und relativ sicher sein, daß er nur das, worauf wir uns einigten, weiterberichten würde; um so mehr vermißte ich ihn nun.

Einzig die Tatsache, daß alles im Lande sich mit so rasantem Tempo entwickelte, verhinderte, daß ich mich der Trauer um ihn des längeren hingab; ich mußte erleben, wie rasch die Blütenträume, die ich mit mir herumgetragen, welkten, und mußte mich, wollte ich überhaupt ein paar Karten im Spiel behalten, kurzfristig umstellen: mit sichtlichem Erfolg; die Partei, der ich mich anschloß, delegierte mich alsbald zu Tagungen und Konferenzen auch außerhalb der Grenzen, und ich muß sagen, daß ich die Betriebsamkeit und das Hin und Her genoß, eine Zeitlang wenigstens, bis mir klar wurde, daß sich das Ganze nur in der Richtung, in der gesteuert wurde, nicht aber in seinen inneren Strukturen von dem Vorherigen unterschied; oft geschah es sogar, daß ich beobachten konnte, wie dieselben Leute, die ich von früher als gehorsame Diener der Macht kannte, in wieder derselben Funktion und derselben Manier die Knochen, die man ihnen zuwarf, apportierten.

In derlei Gedanken versunken, saß ich in der Bar des Hotels, das uns im Konferenzort zugewiesen, und spürte auf einmal wieder jenes Gefühl im Nacken, das mir einst angezeigt hatte, daß mein ständiger Begleiter nahebei war, ob dreidimensional oder im Schutz seiner Tarnkappe. Eine Weile ließ ich das Gefühl auf mich einwirken, ohne zu reagieren; ich war nicht mehr der, der ich gewesen, und es war eine andere Zeit,

Er denkt marktwirtschaftlich.

und ein anderes Land, und ich würde mich nicht narren lassen. Schließlich aber wandte ich mich doch um, mit einem Schwung nach rechts, den der drehbare Sitz des Barhockers mir erleichterte: Wohlrabe war, ganz wie erwartet, nirgends zu sehen.

Dann jedoch, aus dem Nichts links neben mir, die bekannte Stimme, »Wie wär's mit unserm alten Arrangement?«

Er hatte ein halb geleertes Glas Martini vor sich auf der blanken Theke; das Stückchen Zitronenschale darin verlieh der Szene die Realität, die ich ihr zuerst nicht zuzubilligen bereit war.

»Nun?« fragt er, mit allem, was ihn je auszeichnete, im Blick.

»Sie sind wieder im Dienst?« sage ich.

Er nickt.

»Bei wem?«

Er zögert. Dann sagt er, »Was ist der Unterschied«, und legt mir den Arm um die Schulter, väterlich fast: »Hier oder dort: solange die einen die Macht haben und die andern keine, bleibt die Rollenverteilung immer die gleiche.«

Rette sich wer kann

Was heißt, der Laden gehört mir nicht.

Natürlich gehört er mir nicht, aber wer soll sich denn sonst darum kümmern? Das Politbüro vielleicht, das es seit Herbst nicht mehr gibt und von dem nichts weiter geblieben ist als ein großer Gestank? Das Ministerium? Die Hauptverwaltung? Da weiß doch längst keiner mehr, auf welchem Stuhl er sitzt, und ob er überhaupt noch auf einem Stuhle sitzt oder schon draußen. Oder das Volk gar? Schließlich läuft der Laden unter dem Kürzel VEB, VEB Dreh-und Bohrmaschinen, und ich bin der ökonomische Direktor, und über mir steht, rangmäßig, nur noch der Genosse Seybold, und der läßt sich hier kaum mehr blicken.

VEB, Volkseigener Betrieb. Aber wer ist das Volk? In all den vierzig Jahren Republik, hat uns je einer erklärt, wer das Volk wirklich ist, bis das Volk dann anmarschiert kam auf der Straße und lauthals verkündete: *Wir* sind das Volk? Doch das ist auch nur eine Redensart, die so gut wie nichts bedeutet, wenn es um Reales geht, etwa um Besitzverhältnisse. Ist das Volk eine Person, eine juristische wenigstens? Ist es haftbar zu machen, wenn der Betrieb zusammenbricht? Was versteht das Volk vom Geschäft, von Saldo und Bilanzen und Kredit und Verlust? Nur zahlen muß es immer, das Volk, aber das ist überall so auf der Welt und nicht nur bei uns.

Was bleibt also? An wen sollen sie sich halten, die Herren von Wesendonck & Brendel, die ihren Sitz haben in Duisburg und Basel und Glasgow, wenn sie sich für mehr interessieren als ein bloßes Joint Venture in unserer demnächst verflossenen Deutschen Demokratischen Republik und statt dessen einen richtigen soliden Einstieg wünschen: an wen, wenn nicht an mich?

Das ist die neue Entwicklung, die keiner erwartete. Oder vielleicht doch. Und es war ausgerechnet der Genosse Seybold, der mir, Monate vor der berühmten Wende schon, damals in Willershagen, die Möglichkeit angedeutet hatte, Genosse Generaldirektor Siegmund Seybold, der meines Wissens bis dahin nie einen auch nur im geringsten ketzerischen Gedanken geäußert hatte. In Schloß Willershagen, das einst den Großherzögen gehörte, hielt das Ministerium alljährlich seine Lehrgänge für Wirtschaftliche Leiter ab, und in der Pause, im Park, wo nur die Schwäne auf dem Teich ihn hören konnten, sagt Seybold zu mir: »Was hältst du von Müller-Kraschutzki?«

Müller-Kraschutzki, Bruno, Dr. jur., Dr. rer. oec. war Staatssekretär, und ein Betonkopf, wenn es je einen gab.

»Wieso fragst du?« frage ich.

»Weil er«, sagt Seybold, »auch dieses Jahr wieder die alten Sprüche vom friedlichen Übergang vom Kapitalismus zum Sozialismus loszulassen für nötig hielt.«

»Und warum sollte er nicht?« gebe ich zu bedenken.

»Weil«, sagt der Genosse Seybold, »es auch umgekehrt kommen könnte.«

»Wie meinst du das?« frage ich, und es rieselt mir dabei kalt über den Rücken.

»Vom Sozialismus zum Kapitalismus«, präzisiert Seybold, »könnte es ja auch laufen, nicht?« Und wirft den Schwänen ein paar Brotbrocken zu – ein Mann mit Herz.

Das Rückgrat der deutschen Staaten:

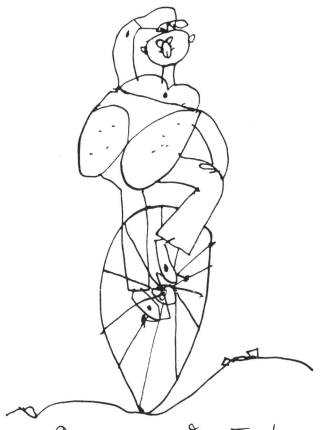

die Radfahrer – Demokraten.

Es war die reine Prophetie gewesen.

Im Nachhinein läßt sich natürlich leicht behaupten, daß alles damals schon erkennbar war. Trotzdem, meinen Respekt vor dem Genossen Seybold, der nicht nur vorauszusagen, sondern auch vorauszuhandeln verstand.

Da hockt er nun in meinem Büro, und die getreue Paula, meine Sekretärin, hat den Kaffee gebracht, und wir reden, Seybold und ich, über die neuen Zustände und welches die Perspektiven seien und ihr Wieso und Warum, und wie doch die ganze Wirtschaft vor die Hunde gegangen wäre in der Republik und kein Unternehmen mehr rentabel arbeite, auch mein Laden nicht, und wie lauter neue Löcher aufgerissen würden, nur um die alten zu stopfen, und je eher wir Anschluß fänden an eine Wirtschaft, in welcher die regulativen Kräfte des Marktes segensvoll wirkten, desto besser, und gar in der Politik, wer habe denn da noch das Sagen, und wer denn sei eigentlich legitimiert, legitimiert, auch so ein Wort, das Sagen zu haben, die alten Parteien vielleicht, oder die neuen Gruppen etwa und die Bürgerkomitees mit ihrem dauernden Palaver und ihren verschiedenen Tischen, runden und eckigen? Aber nicht für ihn, Siegmund Seybold, diese Hektik, in der sich so viele der führenden Genossen verlören, dieser allgemeine Trieb, Rette sich wer kann, samt öffentlicher Lossagung von allem, was einst galt; obwohl einer natürlich auch sehen müsse, wo er bleibe. Dann lehnt er sich zurück und sippt, genüßlich, ein Schlückchen aus seiner Tasse. »Zeit des aufrechten Ganges! ... der deutschen Einheit! ... der Öffnung zur Welt! ... Weißt du, was für eine Zeit dies ist? – die Zeit der Generaldirektoren.«

»Also verhandelst du schon«, sage ich, »mit Wesendonck & Brendel?«

»Wenn ich's nicht tue«, sagt er, »tut es Müller-Kraschutzki. Und dann sitzen wir beide, du und ich, in der Kälte.«

Später, nachdem er gegangen, dachte ich, wie lieb es von dem Genossen Seybold doch gewesen sei, mich so unter seine Fittiche zu nehmen. Aber er brauchte mich ja auch, denn über VEB Dreh- und Bohrmaschinen verfügte de facto ja nicht er, sondern ich. Und außerdem stand auch ich bereits im Gespräch mit Wesendonck & Brendel.

So eine Revolution, auch wenn sie nur Wende heißt, bringt ständig Neues. Keine drei Tage sind vergangen seit Seybolds Visite, da kommt die getreue Paula zu mir gehastet. »Von der Pforte«, sagt sie, »haben sie angerufen: ein großer Regierungswagen.«

»Und wer«, frage ich, »sitzt darin?«

»Das«, sagt Paula, »hat der Pförtner nicht erkennen können.«

Der Besucher tritt in mein Zimmer: Müller-Kraschutzki, in voller Größe. Die markigen Züge heute besonders gestrafft, winkt er mir huldvoll zu: »Bleib sitzen Genosse; wir beide bestehen doch wohl nicht auf Formalitäten.«

Wenn einer so anfängt, meine Erfahrung, dann will er etwas von dir, was dich teuer zu stehen kommen wird, oder, ist er einer der Mächtigen, so hat er möglicherweise auch Angst. Doch der Genosse Müller-Kraschutzki befindet sich in keiner Situation, in welcher er Angst haben müßte vor irgend jemandem; rechts und links von ihm rollten die Köpfe, aber seiner saß fest auf den Schultern, denn die Fakten, die geheimen, die darin gespeichert waren, schützten ihn und würden, falls keiner ihm in den Rücken fiel, ihn auch weiterhin schützen.

»Kaffee?« offeriert die getreue Paula.

Ein Blick auf Müller-Kraschutzki, ein kurzer; dann winke ich ab. Und dann sind wir ohne Zeugen, Müller-Kraschutzki und ich, es sei denn die Wanze, von der ich weiß, daß sie irgendwo eingebaut ist, funktioniert noch; aber das ist kaum mehr wahrscheinlich, und wer soll denn auch ihre Texte noch auswerten?

Müller-Kraschutzki mustert mich, lange und mit einem Anflug von menschlicher Wärme. »Du hast es gut«, seufzt er. »Ich wünschte, ich säße an deiner Stelle.«

»Ich«, sage ich, »hätte es gut? Ich habe nichts als Schwierigkeiten. Der Absatz stockt total, das Material kommt nicht, und keiner weiß, was mit dem Laden wird; unsere Werktätigen fürchten sich, werden sie morgen noch Arbeit und Lohn haben, und alle schauen sie auf mich; und was, bitte, soll ich ihnen sagen?«

»Du«, sagt Müller-Kraschutzki, »hast es gut, weil du etwas von Wert in der Hand hast, einen ganzen Betrieb nämlich, selbst wenn er heruntergewirtschaftet ist; es läßt sich, mit Know-how und Investitionen, noch immer einiges daraus machen. Aber was habe ich an verkäuflichen Werten? Einen Bürosessel, Typ Staatssekretär, und einen Schreibtisch mit doppeltem Korb für Ein- und Ausgänge und drei Telephonen darauf. Du verhandelst mit Wesendonck & Brendel?«

Also wußte er. Ich hätte die Sache zwar ableugnen können, aber das hätte unser Gespräch unnötig verlängert. »Es sind«, so sage ich dann, »nur Vorverhandlungen, genauer, Vorvorverhandlungen.«

Das Wort schien ihn zu belustigen. »Ich könnte«, sagt er, »das stoppen, deine Vorvorverhandlungen. Dafür langt meine Macht noch. Aber ich will das nicht. Ich will, daß du weiterverhandelst. Und da ich Verschiedenes einbringen kann an Kenntnissen und Verbindungen, besonders den Osten betreffend, wird eine deiner Bedingungen sein: Herr Staatssekretär Dr. jur., Dr. rer. oec. Bruno Müller-Kraschutzki wird Vizepräsident des um deinen und wohl auch noch andere hiesige Betriebe vergrößerten Hauses Wesendonck & Brendel.«

Ich kann nicht sagen, daß ich mich wohlfühlte bei seinem Vorschlag, so naheliegend er war. Müller-Kraschutzki bemerkte das auch; ein Mann in seiner Funktion muß, will er die täglichen Auseinandersetzungen bestehen, ein Gefühl auch für das Seelische seiner Kontrahenten entwickeln. »Nun?« fragt er.

»Zu meinem Leidwesen«, sage ich, »habe ich das Gleiche bereits dem Genossen Seybold versprechen müssen, der, wie er mir mitteilte, an verkäuflichen Werten noch weniger besitzt als du: statt dreien, nur zwei Telephone.«

»So«, sagt er, »hat er nur zwei?« Und dann, »Mach dir da keine Gedanken. Wer ist schon Seybold. Sie werden sich freuen bei Wesendonck & Brendel und es dir hoch anrechnen, wenn du mich ihnen zuführst. Kapiert?«

»Kapiert«, sage ich.

Dann stürzte der Genosse Müller-Kraschutzki doch.

Niemand hatte erwartet, daß solches ihm zustoßen könnte; alle Welt war überzeugt, daß er rundum und flächendeckend abgesichert war, besser noch als der Genosse Seybold; vielleicht würde Müller-Kraschutzki, so hatte es geheißen, nicht in seiner Position als Staatssekretär überdauern, die möglicherweise doch etwas zu exponiert war in diesen Zeiten – aber ein derart totaler Sturz! Manche behaupten sogar, das habe Müller-Kraschutzki wahrlich nicht verdient, und Seybold hätte sich zurückhaltender äußern sollen vor dem Untersuchungsausschuß; aber wer will da den ersten Stein werfen; weiß denn einer, wie er sich verhalten hätte an Seybolds Statt.

Sicher ist nur dies: von mir wußte Seybold nichts von Müller-Kraschutzkis Plänen und von der Rolle, die mir darin zugeteilt war; ich gedachte, wenn es denn nach all den Vorvor- und Vorverhandlungen dazu käme, den Herren von Wesendonck & Brendel beide Genossen zu empfehlen, Seybold wie

Mutter Bäumlein
Hausbesitzer

Müller-Kraschutzki; vielleicht akzeptierte die Firma dann sogar alle beide, und ich wäre damit aus dem Schneider.

So aber geschah es, daß der Genosse Seybold plötzlich vor den großen Untersuchungsausschuß zitiert wurde, als Zeuge in Sachen Müller-Kraschutzki. Dabei blieb unklar, wer das Verfahren gegen Müller-Kraschutzki eigentlich angezettelt hatte und wie es überhaupt dazu gekommen war; klar war nur, daß die Angelegenheit ganz überraschend und wie aus heiterem Himmel vom Ausschuß aufgegriffen worden war, und daß eine Frau Schmidthenner, die zu einer der radikalen Gruppen im Umfeld der Kirche gehörte, sich als einer der Hauptverfolger des mächtigen Staatssekretärs hervortat. Spitznasig und dünnlippig, wie mir mein Gewährsmann berichtete – mir selber war es nicht möglich, in den Sitzungssaal zu gelangen – feuerte sie Frage um Frage gegen Müller-Kraschutzki, Fragen, die sämtlich eine intime Kenntnis der Vorgänge in dessen Apparat verrieten; Müller-Kraschutzki habe zunächst recht ruhig und gefaßt gewirkt, abgeklärt, könnte man fast sagen; erst als der Genosse Seybold aufgerufen und von der Dame Schmidthenner in die Zange genommen wurde, habe er Nervosität gezeigt.

Dabei, so mein Gewährsmann, sei Seybold durchaus kein aussagewilliger Zeuge gewesen; die Schmidthenner, rot im Gesicht und mit allen Anzeichen moralischer Entrüstung, mußte ihm jede Antwort auf ihre immer verfänglicher werdenden Fragen einzeln abringen; aber am Ende habe Müller-Kraschutzki ziemlich entblößt dagestanden: Seybolds Zeugnis zufolge schuldig des Machtmißbrauchs wie so ziemlich aller anderen Vergehen, die sich einem Wirtschaftsfunktionär des alten Regimes vorwerfen ließen. Die Medien, eifrig bedacht, ihre Reformfreudigkeit zu zeigen, verlangten schon am Abend des denkwürdigen Tages die Verhaftung des Genossen Müller-Kraschutzki; als, am Morgen darauf, mehrere

Reporter vor seinem Haus auftauchten, fanden sie nur die Haushälterin vor; der Herr Staatssekretär, sagte sie, sei in der Nacht noch verreist; wohin, habe er ihr nicht mitgeteilt.

Noch so ein Wort von meinem Vater: Nicht die Menschen, hat er mir gesagt, machen die Zeiten; die Zeiten machen die Menschen. Wie also, bitte, soll ich urteilen über den Genossen Seybold? Er kommt und sagt, »Gehen wir essen; ich weiß da ein kleines Lokal, altmodisch noch, aber jetzt werden sie's bald aufputzen für die Westkundschaft, und dann wird man nicht mehr hingehen können. Wir haben uns eine stille Stunde verdient, du und ich.«

Sagt er. Und wie wir beim Nachtisch sitzen, sagt er, »Sie war groß in Form, das mußt du doch zugeben, die Schmidthenner.«

»Hast du sie gekannt?« frage ich.

»Muß man sie alle kennen?« sagt er. »Ein ehrliches Mädchen, arm und ehrlich, eine solche kannst du nicht korrumpieren, nicht für Geld und nicht für gute Worte. Aber sie möchte sich, so erzählt man in ihrer Gruppe, gern profilieren.«

»Profiliert«, sage ich, »hat sie sich. Und den Genossen Müller-Kraschutzki auch.«

»Dann laß uns«, sagt Seybold, »systematisch vorgehen: sozusagen Schritt um Schritt. Du wirst, höre ich, eine Belegschaftsversammlung machen in deinem Laden, mit allen, die dort arbeiten, für die Herren von Wesendonck & Brendel, wegen guter Public Relations, wie es heutzutage heißt, zwischen dem künftigen Management und unseren Werktätigen.«

»Eine Versammlung der Art«, sage ich, »wird stattfinden. Und Wesendonck & Brendel werden, hat man mich informiert, die Ausgestaltung übernehmen.«

»Es wird ein Ereignis sein«, sagt Seybold, »von geschichtlicher Dimension, für VEB Dreh- und Bohrmaschinen wie für

Wesendonck & Brendel. Und du wirst doch«, setzt er hinzu, »dich freuen, mich dort zu sehen?«

Ich dachte an Müller-Kraschutzki, dem ein ähnliches Ereignis durchaus vorgeschwebt haben mochte, nur mit ihm als Partner und künftigem Vizepräsidenten von Wesendonck & Brendel und als Sitznachbarn am festlich gedeckten Vorstandstisch bei der Veranstaltung in der großen Halle von VEB Dreh- und Bohrmaschinen, und ich fragte mich, wo er sich jetzt wohl aufhielte und was er wohl täte.

Ja, der Westen.

Ich habe mir immer geschmeichelt, ich wüßte, wie man mit unseren Werktätigen umgeht; war ich doch selber Arbeiter gewesen, vor langer Zeit allerdings. Aber verglichen mit den bei Wesendonck & Brendel für Moral und Motivierung der Betriebsangehörigen verantwortlichen Herren bin ich ein Waisenknabe.

Nun haben diese Herren allerdings die besseren Bedingungen. Wollte ich, obwohl Ökonomischer Direktor, zu irgendwelchen Feierlichkeiten oder Festtagen meinen Leuten auch nur ein Bier mit Bockwurst zukommen lassen, so mußte ich das praktisch durch Unterschlagung aus dem Prämienoder anderen festgelegten Fonds finanzieren; die Kontrollorgane, deren leitende Genossen sich selber aus der öffentlichen Kasse nicht zu knapp bedienten, rechneten, wenn es um die Arbeiter ging, jeden Groschen zweimal nach.

Bei Wesendonck & Brendel dagegen schöpften sie aus dem Vollen. Die Herren ließen zu unsrer Belegschaftsversammlung die feinsten Delikatessen liefern, aufs appetitlichste angerichtet, und mit den seltensten Südfrüchten, mit englischen Whiskys und französischen Brandys und sowjetischen Wodkas, dazu Bieren und Weinen und für die Magenkranken Alkoholfreies; wichtiger aber waren noch die eleganten

Broschüren, bunt illustriert, auf teurem Glanzpapier, die in persönlich gehaltenem Ton sich an die Ostproleten richteten: da erfuhren die lieben Kollegen und Kolleginnen von VEB Dreh- und Bohrmaschinen nun von dem Uropa Wesendonck, der die Firma begründet hatte in der Gründerzeit, stets mit dem Wohl seiner Arbeiter im Auge, und von den Brendels aus Basel und Glasgow, die zum genau richtigen Zeitpunkt das Kapital einbrachten, welches der Uropa brauchte zum Ausbau des Stammhauses und zur Herstellung der neuen Großmaschinen, für die Wesendonck & Brendel berühmt werden sollten, und wie, unter den Söhnen und Enkeln der Wesendoncks wie der Brendels, die Firma immer weiter aufblühte und sogar nach der Not am Ende des Krieges sich bald wieder herausmauserte, und wie hoch die Aktien von Wesendonck & Brendel heute gehandelt wurden an den führenden Börsen der Welt, und wie angenehm sich's in den verschiedenen Werken der Firma arbeitete, und welch besondere Sozialleistungen den Mitarbeitern zugute kamen, und was für Pläne das Management für die Zeit nach der deutschen Wirtschafts- und Währungsunion hege, wenn auch das ehemalige VEB Dreh- und Bohrmaschinen mit seinen vielen tüchtigen und fleißigen Werktätigen zu der großen Familie gestoßen sein werde.

Das war's, was auch Wesendonck junior, von dem es hieß, er sei seinem Uropa wie aus dem Gesicht geschnitten, vor der Belegschaftsversammlung in etwa erklärte, und unsere Werktätigen lauschten ihm mit größtem Interesse und zollten ihm Beifall. »Kein Wunder«, flüstert Seybold mir zu, »hast du jemals, oder ein anderer führender Genosse, so einfühlsam und zu Herzen gehend mit ihnen gesprochen?«

Dann kamen die Fragen, vereinzelt zuerst nur und verschüchtert von den Versammelten, und die Angst vor der Zukunft der unbekannten, stand im Raum: wer würde bleiben dürfen in seinem Job und wer gehen müssen, und wie würde die Arbeit sich gestalten und wie die Bezahlung, und was war mit der Versicherung und was mit dem Urlaub und der Zusatzrente, würde die Firma sich auch daran beteiligen, und dies noch und jenes und was dergleichen mehr, und die Herren von Wesendonck & Brendel zeigten die größte Geduld, auch wenn es ihnen schwerfiel, denn sie beherrschten die Sprache nicht, die unsre Werktätigen zu hören gewohnt waren von ihren Funktionären, und einmal, als der Junior gar selber ins Stottern geriet, meldete sich, zu meiner Überraschung, der Genosse Seybold zu Wort und rettete mit ein paar geschickten Sätzen, die den Leuten sofort eingingen, die Situation, und Wesendonck junior lächelte und entschuldigte sich, der Herr in der Leitung der Firma, der in solchen Fragen besser versiert sei als er, hätte längst anwesend sein sollen, doch habe die Maschine aus Moskau, auf der er anreiste, sich offenbar verspätet.

Hinterher saß man noch im kleinen Konferenzraum beisammen, bequem in den kürzlich erst angeschafften Klubsesseln, die Gäste aus dem Westen und ein paar von meinen leitenden Ingenieuren und ich, und auch der Genosse Seybold. Die Sache war ein Erfolg gewesen, und man war entspannt; nur Seybold, bemerke ich, zeigt Unruhe; er erwartet, scheint's, das Wort, das entscheidende, von Wesendonck junior, doch der redet nur Allgemeines, sicher würden sich, sagt er, auch Positionen auftun für Herren mit Erfahrung im Ostgeschäft; aber das ist auch alles, und kein Ton über die spezifische Zukunft des Genossen Seybold; vielleicht, so schießt es mir durch den Kopf, wartet der Junior auf den Ostfachmann in der Leitung der Firma, dessen Maschine sich verspätet hat.

Und da, wieder, meine getreue Paula. Sie kommt hereingehuscht, direkt hin zu mir; doch ich traue meinem Ohr nicht; das kann doch nicht wahr sein, was sie mir da zuflüstert; sie ist hysterisch geworden, sieht Gespenster. Dann sehe ich es auch, das Gespenst, und sehe, wie Wesendonck junior sich aus seinem Sessel erhebt. »Ah, Herr Doktor!« ruft er. »Schön, daß Sie's noch geschafft haben!« Und zu mir und dem Genossen Seybold, »Die Herren kennen einander ja wohl. Dr. Müller-Kraschutzki ist seit kurzem für Wesendonck & Brendel tätig, als Vizepräsident zuständig für unsre neuen Absatzgebiete.«

Seybold ist blaß geworden. Ich packe ihn am Ellbogen, um ihn zu stützen. Doch er faßt sich, zumindest so weit, um sagen zu können, »Herr Staatssekretär Müller-Kraschutzki und ich sind alte Freunde, und ich hoffe, wir werden es bleiben.«

Ausstellungseröffnung

Schmitt-Murnau ist ein Genie.

Sie kennen Schmitt-Murnau nicht?

Das ist kein Wunder, denn Schmitt-Murnau behält die Tatsache für sich. Um ein Genie zu sein und zugleich als Genie zu gelten, muß man die richtigen Verbindungen besitzen oder wenigstens wissen, wie man diese herstellt; man muß einen Instinkt dafür haben, in wessen Händen Macht liegt und wessen Bekanntschaft zu pflegen sich lohnt, und welcher Partei man anzugehören und auf welche Weise man dort mit wem zu sprechen hat.

Von dergleichen Taktiken hielt Schmitt-Murnau nichts; schlimmer noch, wo er sie praktiziert sah, wandte er sich gelangweilt ab: mochten andere sich abstrampeln; er zog es vor, sich seinen Zeichnungen zu widmen und seinen Graphiken, in denen er mit ein paar anscheinend krakeligen Strichen das Innere der Menschen, die er scharfen Auges beobachtete, so entblößte, daß dem Betrachter eine ganze Welt, Schmitt-Murnaus Welt, sich auftat, die am Ende wahrer erschien als die reale.

Aber das war nur eines von seinen Talenten. Wenn er sich elend fühlte, und die Umstände, unter denen zu leben wir in diesem Lande gezwungen waren, und die Frauen, von denen keine ihn wirklich verstand, gaben ihm genug Anlaß zu Depressionen, oder wenn ihn der Zorn packte über die Dummheit und Eitelkeit so vieler seiner Zeitgenossen, vertauschte er die Zeichen- mit der Schreibfeder – er gebrauchte tatsächlich eine altmodische Stahlfeder, in schwarze Tusche getaucht, und seine Manuskriptseiten sahen aus wie frühes 19. Jahrhundert – und schrieb Kurzdialoge höchst skurriler Art, die man als Übersetzung seiner Zeichnungen ins Literarische hätte auffassen können, wenn sie, auf vertrackte Weise, nicht noch vernichtender gewirkt hätten als jene.

Geld machen ließ sich mit solchen Künsten nicht viel. Die geringen Summen, die er benötigte, beschaffte er sich größtenteils durch die Nutzung seines untrüglichen Sinns für Form. Mit einem Schriftkatalog neben sich und einem leeren Bogen Papier vor sich entstanden unter seinen fähigen Händen Druckentwürfe von erregenden Proportionen. Die Ausstatter in den Verlagen und die Funktionäre der Künstlerverbände wußten sehr wohl um diese seine Fertigkeit und bedienten sich ihrer, wo sich das tun ließ, ohne das Gehege anderer, mit dem Segen der Parteimitgliedschaft versehener Zunftgenossen zu verletzen.

So auch diesmal wieder, bei der Vorbereitung der großen Jahresausstellung des Kunstvereins, des wohl repräsentativsten republikweiten Ereignisses auf dem Gebiet der bildenden Künste. Da saßen sie nun beieinander, wie Michael Treufreund, der Sekretär des Vereins, es mir später beschrieb: der große Püschel, als Präsident amtierend, neben Wilhelm Wuttke, seinem Vize, und ihm, Treufreund, um Art und Ausstattung des Katalogs zu debattieren, welcher, bei den Druckverhältnissen im Lande, fast ein Jahr vor dem Datum der Veranstaltung schon in Vorbereitung gehen mußte. Lassen wir, so fragte Treufreund, den Schmitt-Murnau unsern Katalog machen oder nicht?

Dieses hänge, meinte Wuttke, von der politischen Atmosphäre und anderen Umständen in der Woche der Eröffnung der Ausstellung ab, welche sich leider nicht voraussehen ließen; gehe man von der Möglichkeit aus, daß Partei und Regierung endlich durchgriffen gegen die ständig zunehmende Demoralisierung im Lande, sei es besser, man beauftragte einen politisch weniger fraglichen, wenn denn auch weniger begabten Graphiker; liefen jedoch die Aufweichungserscheinungen ungehindert weiter, so werde das ebenfalls Konsequenzen haben, personelle und andere, besonders auf künstlerischem Gebiet, und dann könne man sich einen von Schmitt-Murnau gestalteten Ausstellungskatalog durchaus leisten, ja, man liege dann sogar genau auf der richtigen Linie.

Treufreund, warum sollte ein Sekretär sich unnötigerweise festlegen, enthielt sich einer eigenen Meinung; so fiel die Last der Entscheidung auf die leicht gerundeten Schultern des großen Rainer Püschel, der nach längerem Schweigen doch dazu riet, den Auftrag dem Kollegen Schmitt-Murnau zu erteilen; notfalls könne man dessen Namen ja aus dem Impressum noch auslassen, bevor das Heft in Druck gehe: ein Versehen des Druckers; nicht nur Künstler, auch Handwerker konnten irren.

Nun, Sie wissen, was kurz nach dieser an sich unbedeutenden Besprechung Weltgeschichtliches geschah, unter aktiver Beteiligung so zahlreicher unsrer Künstler, Rainer Püschel einer der prominentesten unter ihnen. Püschels Züge, die als markant hätten gelten können, wäre die untere Hälfte seines Gesichts nicht etwas zu schwammig geraten, erschienen alle zwei oder drei Tage in den Print- wie den elektronischen Medien, und seine politischen Äußerungen, in denen er sich von den Größen des gestürzten Regimes zwar mit Zurückhaltung, aber doch eindeutig distanzierte – schon immer, erklärte er, hätte ein geschultes Auge von seinen Gemälden ablesen können, daß für ihn nur Menschlichkeit und Demokratie zählten – seine politischen Äußerungen also wurden weithin zitiert, Ost wie West.

Beim nächsten Treffen der leitenden Herren im Präsidium des Kunstvereins, als Genossen bezeichneten sie sich schon seit den Ereignissen des historischen Leipziger Oktober nicht mehr, kamen, wie denn anders, die Wandlungen zur Sprache, welche die besagten Ereignisse in den Strukturen und Aktivitäten des Vereins hervorgerufen hatten und noch hervorrufen würden, wenn möglich unterstützt durch eigene Initiativen. Von einem neuen Kongreß der bildenden Künstler war da die Rede, den man jedoch noch gründlicher als bisher vorbereiten müsse, und von eventueller Zusammenarbeit mit oder gar Anschluß an Organisationen mit gleicher oder ähnlicher Aufgabenstellung im Westen, vor allem aber von der großen Kunstausstellung, die man, schon aus Prestigegründen, nicht hatte absagen können und die daher, da ihr Eröffnungsdatum nahte, sofortige Beschlüsse des Präsidiums erforderlich machte.

Notwendigkeiten der Art antizipierend, so erzählte mir Treufreund, hatte er Schmitt-Murnau zu der Besprechung hinzugeladen, nicht als gleichberechtigten Teilnehmer etwa, vielmehr als Konsultanten ausschließlich bei den Tagesordnungspunkten *Ausstellung* und *Ausstellungskatalog;* also saß Schmitt-Murnau, geduldig wartend, in Treufreunds Vorzimmer im Büro des Vereins, neben sich eine Flasche von Treufreunds bestem Bärensiegel, und blätterte ohne sonderlichen Eifer in den Druckfahnen des Katalogs, die Treufreund durch Versprechungen, von denen er wußte, daß sie sich nicht einhalten ließen, dem Drucker speziell für diese Präsidiumstagung entlockt hatte. Schon wollte Schmitt-Murnau, sein sowieso nur spärliches Interesse ermüdet, die Fahnen

100

Jeder Volk, ob es greint oder grient,
hat die Regierung, die es
verdient.

weglegen, als er plötzlich aufmerkte; die letzten Seiten mit dem Register der ausstellenden Künstler taten es ihm an. Da standen sie ja sämtlich aufgelistet, einer nach dem andern, in alphabetischer Folge, mit Geburtsdatum, Geburtsort, akademischen Titeln etcetera, die Püschel und Wuttke und Haussmann und Rehmüller und Katzenstein und Willuweit und wie sie alle hießen, und, auf die Daten zur Person folgend, jeweils die Orden und Ehrenzeichen, systematisch nach Rang und Gewicht, die man ihnen verliehen: ihre Karl-Marx-Orden und Vaterländischen Verdienstorden in Gold, Silber und Bronze, ihre Nationalpreise in dito, ihre »Banner der Arbeit« und Kunstpreise und Preise für künstlerisches Volksschaffen und Johannes-R.-Becher-Preise, samt ihren Ehrentiteln, »Verdienter Künstler des Volkes« als mindestes und »Verdienter Aktivist« und Dr. h. c. und Dr. Dr. h. c., und ihren Ehrenmedaillen für ausgezeichnete bzw. hervorragende Leistungen, und all dies gehäuft, so als hätten Hühner es hinter den einzelnen Namen zusammengescharrt, oft zu mehreren Zeilen hintereinander, je nach der Wertschätzung, die der Preis- und Ordensträger in der zuständigen Abteilung des Zentralkomitees oder bei dem Sekretär für Kultur im Politbüro oder, auch das gab es, beim Generalsekretär selber genoß.

Schmitt-Murnau war daher, als er von Treufreund in den Sitzungsraum gebeten wurde, in heiterster Stimmung und voll lächelnder Verbindlichkeit gegenüber den Präsidialen des Vereins, einschließlich Püschel und Wuttke, und zeigte durch häufiges Kopfnicken und gegrummelte Laute der Billigung sein absolutes Verständnis für deren Probleme, die allgemeinen ebenso wie die mit dem Ausstellungskatalog, der ja, da alles sich so herrlich gewendet, nun auch nicht bleiben konnte wie vordem konzipiert. In weiser Voraussicht, ließ Püschel Schmitt-Murnau wissen, habe man bei der Auswahl der Ausstellungsstücke von vornherein eine gewisse

Vorsicht walten lassen; daher müßten jetzt, neben einer Anzahl von minder wichtigen, eher unansehnlichen Objekten, die keiner vermissen werde und die teilweise nicht einmal separat angeführt gewesen waren im Manuskript des Katalogs, nur relativ wenige Exponate wegen zu offensichtlichen sozialistischen Realismusses aus der geplanten Ausstellung wie von den Seiten des Katalogs entfernt werden: ein Haussmann mit dem Titel »Und golden fließt der Stahl«, ferner das Triptychon von Willuweit über die Schweinezucht-LPG in Groß-Kulla bei Greiz, und, da dieser inzwischen zurückgetreten, Violetta Katzensteins Porträt eines Staatsanwalts und, last not least, Rehmüllers Block in rosa Granit, welcher, obzwar von Rehmüller selber als zu dessen abstrakter Periode gehörig eingestuft, wie ein Leninkopf aussah, wenn man ihn, bei Nachmittagslicht, von schräg links unten betrachtete. Wilhelm Wuttkes Zyklus über den Bauernkrieg, den einige Präsidiumsmitglieder angesichts der neuerlichen Geschichtseinschätzung in Frage gestellt hatten, müsse allerdings bleiben; das Werk sei bereits zu bekannt, um es zurückzuziehen, ohne sich der Gefahr öffentlicher Lächerlichkeit auszusetzen; doch habe Wuttke den Titel verändert; statt »Die Enkel fechten's besser aus« heiße das Werk nun »Aus deutscher Vergangenheit«.

Schmitt-Murnau nahm Püschels Ausführungen mit aller Aufmerksamkeit, die ihm nach dem Genuß von Treufreunds Bärensiegel noch zur Verfügung stand, zur Kenntnis, und machte sich, um mögliche spätere Fehler zu vermeiden, genaue Notizen auf den Rand der Druckfahnen: mußten doch, so zog er in Betracht, nicht nur Teile des Katalogtexts, sondern auch die entsprechenden Illustrationen eliminiert werden, was einen erneuten Umbruch nötig machte. Dabei sei ihm, vertraute er mir später an, die Idee zu einer Zeichnung durch den Kopf gegangen, die er, sobald er nach Haus

zurückgekehrt, in Angriff zu nehmen plante: in winterli-
cher Landschaft das hintere Ende eines Schlittens, darauf
der große Püschel mit wehendem Schal um den Hals, wie er
Haussmann, Willuweit, die Katzenstein und Rehmüller den
hinter ihm herhechelnden Wölfen in elegantem Bogen zuwarf; mochte sein, daß dieses erheiternde Bild ihn davon
abhielt, sich Gedanken über eventuelle weitere Änderungen im Heft zu machen; außerdem bezahlte man ihn ja für
die Gestaltung des Katalogs und nicht für dessen Redaktion.

Auch der große Püschel war's zufrieden und bedeutete
Treufreund mit einer Handbewegung, Schmitt-Murnau aus
dem Raum zu geleiten; in der Tür wandte Schmitt-Murnau
sich noch einmal um und winkte dem Präsidenten fröhlich
zu, eine Geste, die dieser irgendwie unpassend fand, aber
nicht mehr die Gelegenheit hatte zu monieren.

Der Katalog war, das mußte auch ich zugestehen, als Schmitt-
Murnau mich sein Vorausexemplar sehen ließ, ein Pracht-
stück: die Farben stimmten, die Balance der Seiten, der
Wechsel zwischen Text, Bebilderung und Leerräumen; dazu
hatte Schmitt-Murnau eine Schrift benutzt, um die jeder
Kundige ihn nur beneiden konnte, eine Variante von Bodoni,
die er irgendwo in der Provinz in einer alten Druckerei aus-
gegraben hatte. Und, die Hauptsache, das Ding war fertig,
just für die Ausstellungseröffnung, vollständig ausgedruckt
und tadellos gebunden. »Nicht daß dieser Verein das verdient hätte«, so Schmitt-Murnau. »Sind doch sämtlich die
alten Mittelmäßigkeiten, die einander hochgepustet im Lauf
der Jahre; aber was soll's.«

Schmitt-Murnau hatte fest erwartet, daß sie vergessen würden, ihn zur Eröffnung einzuladen; aber am Tag davor rief er
mich an: die Einladung sei doch gekommen, und ob ich ihn
begleiten wolle. Da ich, als einer der minderen Feuilletonre-

dakteure, sowieso zum Besuch der Ausstellung verpflichtet
war, sagte ich zu, und wir betraten gemeinsam die geheilig-
ten Räume.

Zuerst schien es mir, als böte sich uns das vertraute Bild
und sonst nichts; noch standen die Offiziellen unter die
Gruppen gemeiner Besucher gemischt, die zu derartigen Gelegenheiten zusammenzuströmen pflegen: Angehörige und
Freunde der ausstellenden Künstler; Leute vom Fach und
solche, die vorgaben, es zu sein, wichtig darunter die Damen und Herren vom Kultusministerium; dazu Vertreter der
Presse, Ost wie West, und Personal der anderen Medien, die
Kameras in Position, die Scheinwerfer zum Teil schon angeschaltet. Nach einer Weile jedoch wurde die Unruhe spürbar,
die sich in den Ausstellungsräumen verbreitete, von den
vorderen allmählich den hinteren zu; die Neugierigen, die gegangen waren, einen fürwitzigen Blick auf die Bilder an den
Wänden und die mit Bedacht gestreuten Plastiken zu werfen, drifteten zurück in die Eingangshalle, und die Hungrigen
lösten sich von den weißgedeckten Tischen, auf denen die
Platten mit den lecker belegten Broten und die Weinflaschen
samt zugehörigen Gläsern standen, und kamen, um zu erfahren, was es denn gäbe, und zum ersten Mal hörte man:
der Katalog! Wo war der Ausstellungskatalog, von dem man,
da er von Schmitt-Murnau entworfen, soviel erwartete? Und
es ging nicht nur um das Ästhetische dabei; man hätte doch
gern auch gewußt, von wessen Hand etwa das mit Nr. 17 A
bezeichnete graugerahmte Farbengewirr stammte und ob es
in der Tat eine Sicht von den Ahrenshooper Dünen darstellte, wie die einen meinten, oder eine Abbildung tanzender
Neger in den Bayous von Louisiana, wie Dominik Rums-
feld behauptete, der bekannte Kunstkritiker, oder ob die
Plastik Nr. 763, die aussah wie eine verbeulte Kinderbade-
wanne mit rechtsseitig verdickten Rostflecken, in der Tat ein

. VER EINIGUNGS FEST . .

echter Beuys war, aus dem Nachlaß stammend und von der Witwe als Zeichen der inneren Verbundenheit des Meisters mit den Menschen der Deutschen Demokratischen Republik dem Kunstverein als Vermächtnis übergeben, oder das Werk eines seiner mehreren örtlichen Nachahmer, die nun, da die absolute künstlerische Freiheit absolut gefahrlos praktiziert werden konnte, einander an Kühnheit übertrafen.

Ja, wo waren die Kataloge geblieben? Was war geschehen? Auf dem länglichen Tisch gleich hinter dem Eingang, auf den derlei Gedrucktes gewöhnlich placiert wurde, dem Publikum zur Auswahl, befanden sich ein paar alte Poster und Häufchen von Postkarten, sonst nichts. Hatte der Drucker versäumt, die Kataloge zu liefern? Doch diese, Schmitt-Murnau hatte sie selber gesehen, hatten ja sauber gebündelt in der Auslieferung der Druckerei bereitgelegen. Hatte der Zensor sie beschlagnahmen lassen? Aber es gab ja gar keine Zensur mehr! In sämtlichen Räumen des Hauses, in dem die Ausstellung stattfand, neun an der Zahl, glaube ich, existierte nur ein einziges Exemplar, leicht geknickt und verschmuddelt, des Katalogs: in Schmitt-Murnaus Rocktasche.

Schmitt-Murnau zieht es heraus. Die Schultern gestrafft, hält er es zwischen Daumen und Zeige- und Mittelfinger seiner Rechten in die Höhe, einem Wimpel ähnlich, wie er in alten Zeiten an den Lanzen der Ulanen flatterte, und marschiert auf den großen Püschel zu, der sich unwillkürlich hinter Wuttkes und Treufreunds soliden Rücken und dem schmaleren der Violetta Katzenstein zu verkriechen sucht.

»Ah, der Kollege Püschel!« ruft Schmitt-Murnau mit einer Stimme, wie ich sie noch nie von ihm kommend gehört, halb Trompete, halb Knurren eines ungarischen Hirtenhundes, Sie kennen die Sorte, dunkle Zotteln, Vorder- und Hinterende des Tiers kaum zu unterscheiden, »wo, Kollege Püschel, sind die Kataloge?«

Inzwischen haben die Leute, Skandal witternd, sich gesammelt; Püschel kann sich nicht länger in Deckung halten; er rafft sich zusammen; die beste Verteidigung, erinnert er sich, besteht im Angriff; und so ruft er, viel zu schrill, »Das fragen Sie mich, Schmitt-Murnau?«

»Das«, sagt Schmitt-Murnau, »frage ich Sie, allerdings.«

»Ich habe sie einstampfen lassen«, antwortet Püschel, »schweren Herzens, und Sie, Schmitt-Murnau, werden für den Schaden, den Sie uns angerichtet, aufkommen.«

»Welchen Schaden?« Schmitt-Murnau schlägt sein Katalogexemplar auf, das eine und einzige noch vorhandene, und schiebt es Püschel vor die Nase. »Ist nicht alles, was und wie Sie's wollten, Kollege Püschel, entfernt worden? – Haussmanns Goldstahl und Willuweits Schweinezucht und der Staatsanwalt des Fräulein Katzenstein und Rehmüllers rosa Granit und was sonst noch Sie aussortierten an nunmehr Unbrauchbarem; nur Wuttkes Tableau blieb wie gewünscht, das riesige, weil Wuttke es umbenannte, den neuen Bedingungen entsprechend. Was für Schaden also?«

Püschel merkt, er hat sich von Schmitt-Murnau hineinreiten lassen in eine Situation, in der es kein Zurück mehr gibt; aber vor ihm liegt gleichfalls ein Abgrund, und alles wartet auf seinen nächsten Schritt.

»Bitte«, sagt Schmitt-Murnau, »wo also liegt mein angeblicher Fehler?«

»Sie wissen genau, was ich meine«, krächzt Püschel. »Das ganze Register, mit den...«

»Ah so!« Schmitt-Murnau spricht sehr ruhig. »Die Orden und Ehrenzeichen hinter den Namen, Ihrem und denen der andern Kollegen... Aber es hätte eines Wortes nur von Ihnen bedurft, und ich hätte auch das noch gestrichen. Nur eines will mir nicht in den Kopf: was gestern eine Ehre war, von Ihnen allen dankbar akzeptiert, soll heute ein Schandmal sein?«

110

»Es will ihm nicht in den Kopf!« Püschels Gesicht ist eine Studie in mehreren Schattierungen von Rot. »Vierzig Jahre lang sind wir belogen worden und betrogen; und es will ihm nicht in den Kopf!«

»Ich war niemals in Ihrer Partei, Kollege Püschel«, sagt Schmitt-Murnau, »und habe nie irgendwelche Orden und Ehrenzeichen erhalten oder Kunst- und Nationalpreise. Wie also soll mein armer Kopf derart Sinneswandel begreifen?«

Treufreund klatscht in die Hände. »Hiermit erkläre ich«, verkündet er feierlich, »die große Ausstellung des Kunstvereins für eröffnet. Wenn auch der Katalog uns fehlt, Wein und festliche Häppchen sind für unsre Gäste reichlich vorhanden.«

Schmitt-Murnau, wie gesagt, ist ein Genie. Aber ich befürchte, er wird auch in der neuen Zeit kaum reüssieren.

Filz

*Gedanken über das
neueste Deutschland*

*Und fünf Zeichnungen
von Horst Hussel*

FUR ArBeitslosigkeit
wir sind ein volk
FUR höhere Mieten
für höhere
wir auch
FUR MEHR Bureaucratie
Für höhere Steuern

FÜR INGE, MIT DANK
FÜR RAT UND TAT

Inhalt

Präzedenzfall

Am 27. März 1979 erstattet die Abteilung Zollfahndung der Zollverwaltung der Deutschen Demokratischen Republik Anzeige gegen Heym, Stefan, geb. am 10. 4. 1913 in Chemnitz. Heym, Stefan, heißt es, werde verdächtigt der Durchführung bzw. Veranlassung ungenehmigter Devisenwertumläufe (§ 17 Abs. 1 Devisengesetz), begangen durch Vornahme von Veröffentlichung auf Honorarbasis im Devisenausland. Erhärtet werde der Verdacht, laut Anzeige, durch die am 23. 3. 1979 am Postzollamt Berlin festgestellte Sendung vom Absender Verlagsgruppe Bertelsmann mit 10 Stück in Folie eingeschweißten Büchern mit dem Titel »Collin«, die an den Verdächtigen gerichtet war.

Am 17. April 1979 beantragt die Zollverwaltung gegen den Bürger Heym, Stefan, Konteneinsicht, und diensteifrig erläßt der Generalstaatsanwalt der Deutschen Demokratischen Republik am gleichen Tag noch »zur Sicherung zu erwartender Ansprüche« einen Arrestbefehl über das Konto 6752-69-650268 bei der Sparkasse der Stadt Berlin, und am 19. April 1979 übergibt, laut Protokoll über den Vollzug des Arrestbefehls, der Beschuldigte Heym, Stefan, sein Sparbüchel an den mit dem Vollzug des Befehls beauftragten Zollhauptkommissar.

Nach diesen Präliminarien nimmt das Spiel seinen vorge-
schriebenen Lauf. Der Beschuldigte wird, gleichfalls am 19.
April, zum Verhör zugeführt, und es wird ihm, laut Proto-
koll, gesagt, »Sie werden beschuldigt, ohne Genehmigung
Devisenwertumläufe veranlaßt bzw. durchgeführt zu haben.
Äußern Sie sich zusammenhängend dazu!«

Der so als Devisenschieber Beschuldigte erklärte darauf-
hin: »Ich möchte die Frage eines angeblichen Devisenverge-
hens getrennt behandelt sehen von der Nichtbefolgung der
Verordnung zur Wahrung der Urheberrechte und dem Wirken des sogenannten Büros für Urheberrechte. Das Büro für
Urheberrechte vereinigt zwei Funktionen, die Registrierung
von Devisen von Schriftstellern und die Genehmigung für
die Vergabe von Rechten an den Werken dieser Schriftsteller. Die letztere Funktion ist im Effekt eine Zensurtätigkeit,
sie ist die Übertragung der Zensur innerhalb der Grenzen der
DDR auf den Rest der Welt. Die Zensurbehörde der DDR,
die das Büro für Urheberrechte als ihr Werkzeug benutzt,
steht im Widerspruch zur Verfassung der DDR und zu allen
literarischen Grundsätzen, die in zivilisierten Ländern gelten.
Ich habe mich daher seit je geweigert und weigere mich auch
jetzt und werde mich weiter weigern, mich diesen Zensur-
maßnahmen zu fügen, und vergebe also meine literarischen
Rechte ohne Rücksicht auf besagtes Büro. Außerdem machten meine Erfahrungen mit der Zensurpraxis in der DDR es
mir klar, daß der Roman ›Collin‹ hier sowieso nicht genehmigt werden würde, so daß dieser Punkt zusätzlich zu meiner
bereits erwähnten prinzipiellen Ablehnung des Büros für Urheberrechte hinzukam. Da aber laut Regierungsverordnung
das Büro für Urheberrechte in meinem Fall zuständig ist, bin
ich, selbstverständlich ohne jede kriminelle Absicht, in eine
Situation geraten, wo ich, indem ich mich gegen die Zensur
zur Wehr setze, automatisch gegen das Devisengesetz versto-

ßen muß, und insofern habe ich den devisenrechtlichen Bestimmungen entgegengehandelt.«

Der letzte Satz wird von den vernehmenden Beamten als Geständnis betrachtet; die Gründe für seine Übeltat, die der Beschuldigte so ausführlich dargestellt hatte, interessieren die Zollfahndung weniger. Auch in einem zweiten Verhör, am 9. Mai 1979, gehen die Behördenvertreter auf diese Gründe nicht ein, sondern wollen wissen, wie der Beschuldigte das Manuskript ins Devisenausland verbracht hätte – er trug es selber über die Grenze –, und wieviel westliche Währung ihm die Veröffentlichung gebracht habe – schätzungsweise DM 25 600, gibt der Beschuldigte an, für vier Jahre Arbeit; aber der »Collin« sei ja gerade erst in die Läden gekommen.

Im Stadtbezirk Köpenick findet dann der vorläufig letzte Akt statt, vor der Direktorin des Gerichts, einer lieben, etwas verschüchterten Frau, die dem Beschuldigten mitteilt, das Gericht habe die Akten und den staatsanwaltlichen Antrag geprüft und befunden, die gegen ihn erhobenen Beschuldigungen bestünden zu Recht; er habe durch sein Handeln eindeutig die genannten Gesetze verletzt. Im übrigen sei er ja in seiner Vernehmung selber davon ausgegangen, daß er gegen die devisenrechtlichen Bestimmungen verstoßen habe.

Darauf übergibt sie ihm seinen Strafbefehl, lautend auf eine Geldstrafe von 9000 Mark und Einziehung der bereits beschlagnahmten Exemplare des »Collin«. Der Beschuldigte, sagt sie weiter, könne innerhalb einer Woche Einspruch erheben. Nach kurzer Beratung mit seinem Anwalt erklärt der Beschuldigte, daß er angesichts der politischen Motivierung des Urteils annehme, die nächsthöhere Instanz werde dieses nur bestätigen; er verzichte deshalb auf sein Recht auf Einspruch.

Nach einigen Wochen erhält er das arrestierte Sparbüchel zurück; die 9000 Mark sind bereits abgebucht.

Zeit verstreicht. Am 10. September 1990 schreibt der Generalstaatsanwalt der Deutschen Demokratischen Republik, »In der Strafsache gegen Stefan Heym, geb. am 10. 4. 1913 in Chemnitz, wegen Verstoßes gegen das Devisengesetz der DDR, beantrage ich Kassation des Strafbefehls des Stadtbezirksgerichts Berlin-Köpenick vom 22. 05. 1979 zugunsten des Verurteilten.

Die Entscheidung des Gerichts stellt eine schwerwiegende Verletzung des Gesetzes dar.

Das Verhalten des Verurteilten erfüllt zwar formal den angeführten Straftatbestand; unter Berücksichtigung der von Herrn Heym damals bereits angeführten Umstände und Auswirkungen waren und sind seine Handlungen jedoch nicht gesellschaftswidrig und daher gemäß § 3 StGB nicht strafbar. Herr Heym hat damals bereits unwiderlegt erklärt, daß er gegen die Anmeldepflicht des Devisengesetzes verstoßen habe, weil sie einer verfassungswidrigen Zensur seines schriftstellerischen Wirkens gleichkam. Das Büro für Urheberrechte war sowohl für die Vergabe von Rechten in das Ausland als auch für die Registrierung von Devisenforderungen zuständig und maßte sich an, Büchern von Herrn Heym die Genehmigung für ein Verlegen im Ausland zu versagen, weil sie Verhältnisse in der DDR real widerspiegelten.

Unter diesen Umständen stellte die strafrechtliche Bewertung seiner unterlassenen Anmeldung der Devisenforderungen als Straftat in der Tat lediglich den Versuch dar, Herrn Heym mundtot zu machen und ihn von weiterer gesellschaftskritischen Veröffentlichungen abzuhalten. Das Gericht hätte dem Antrag des Staatsanwalts auf Erlaß eines Strafbefehls daher nicht stattgeben und die Sache wegen fehlender gesetzlicher Voraussetzungen für eine Bestrafung zurückgeben müssen.

Ich beantrage,

1. den Strafbefehl des Stadtbezirksgerichts Berlin-Köpenick vom 22. 05. 1979 aufzuheben;

2. Herrn Stefan Heym gemäß § 322 Abs. 1 Ziff. 3 StPO i. d. F. vom 29. 06. 1990 freizusprechen.«

Am 19. September 1990 beschließt das Oberste Gericht der DDR auf Antrag des Generalstaatsanwalts der DDR vom 10. September in der Strafsache gegen Stefan Heym die Kassation des Strafbefehls des Stadtbezirksgerichts Berlin-Köpenick vom 22. Mai 1979 für zulässig zu erklären.

Aber entschieden wurde über den Kassationsantrag selber noch nicht, und am 3. Oktober, dem Tag der großen Vereinigung, beendet der Generalstaatsanwalt der DDR seine Tätigkeit und übergibt seine Akten an den Generalstaatsanwalt beim Kammergericht in West-Berlin, der die Sache wiederum auf dem Umweg über den 5. Strafsenat des Bundesgerichtshofs und das Landgericht Berlin an die Staatsanwaltschaft beim Kammergericht weiterreicht. Diese nun beantragt am 20. März 1991, das als Antrag auf Kassation anzusehende Begehren des Betroffenen Stefan Heym, geboren am 10. April 1913, als offensichtlich unbegründet zu verwerfen.

Die Überprüfung des summarischen Strafverfahrens, schreibt die Staatsanwaltschaft beim Kammergericht, habe »keine den Verurteilten beschwerenden schwerwiegenden Rechtsfehler im Hinblick auf das Zustandekommen des Schuldspruchs erbracht«. Und Anhaltspunkte dafür, daß es bei dem Schuldspruch »um eine reine unter Verletzung grundlegender Verfahrensvorschriften zustandegekommene Willkürentscheidung handeln könnte«, seien nicht ersichtlich.

Der Paragraph 270 der Strafprozeßordnung der DDR »erforderte vielmehr nur, daß neben den den hinreichenden Tatverdacht begründenden weiteren Beweismitteln ein den Tatvorwurf rechtfertigendes Geständnis vorlag«.

Und weiter: »Die DDR-Verfassung vom 6. April 1968 kannte in Artikel 27 nur ein Recht auf freie und öffentliche Meinungsäußerung sowie der Freiheit der Presse, des Rundfunks und des Fernsehens, nicht jedoch die Kunstfreiheit. Soweit Grundrechte in Artikel 27 DDR-Verfassung verbürgt waren, standen sie unter Gesetzesvorbehalt.« Die Entscheidung von Berlin-Köpenick beruhe daher nicht auf einer schwerwiegenden Verletzung des Gesetzes. Im Gegenteil: »Selbst wenn die erkannte Strafe als hart anzusehen wäre, wäre sie deshalb noch nicht ungerecht. Selbst der Betroffene dürfte die für ihn nachteilige Ermessensausübung im konkreten Fall für vertretbar gehalten haben, da er gegen den Strafbefehl keinen Einspruch einlegte.«

Aus dem Juristendeutsch übersetzt heißt das: die Köpenicker Richter und ihre Hintermänner haben keineswegs eine Willkürentscheidung getroffen, um dem Heym endlich das Maul zu stopfen, sondern sie haben sich strikt an die Verfassung der DDR gehalten, die keine Kunstfreiheit kennt und außerdem ihren Artikel 27, wo von Meinungs- und Pressefreiheit die Rede ist, ausdrücklich unter Gesetzesvorbehalt stellt. Und wenn der Kerl auch noch selber zugibt, er hätte gegen das Devisengesetz verstoßen, geschieht's ihm recht, wenn sie ihn dafür bestrafen.

Nur eines haben die Staatsanwälte bei dem Kammergericht zu Berlin nicht bedacht: Wenn das DDR-Gesetz recht und billig ist für einen Autor, um dessen Verurteilung aus dem Jahr 1979 aufrechtzuerhalten, dann muß es auch recht und billig sein für Staatsratsvorsitzende und Devisenbeschaffer und

Spionagechefs, und für Mauerschützen sowieso, die sämtlich genau nach diesem, vom West-Berliner Kammergericht noch jetzt als rechtsgültig betrachtetem DDR-Gesetz gehandelt haben. Was Freiheit! Was Moral! Was Demokratie! Gesetz ist Gesetz, und Devisengesetz erst recht.

Die Sache mit der Kassation des Urteils gegen den Devisenschieber Heym und ihrer Behandlung bei dem West-Berliner Kammergericht schafft nämlich einen Präzedenzfall: der Genosse Honecker kann jetzt ruhig nach Deutschland zurückkehren, es wird ihm nichts passieren, denn alles, was er getan hat, tat er seinem DDR-gesetzlichen Auftrag entsprechend, und Markus Wolf handelte gleichfalls nur nach DDR-Gesetz, von Schalck-Golodkowski gar nicht zu reden; und die Mauerschützen schossen auch nach gesetzlichem Befehl.

Wie schön, daß es die klugen Staatsanwälte bei dem Kammergericht zu West-Berlin gibt, die der DDR nachträglich bescheinigen möchten, daß sie ein Rechtsstaat war.

Und jetzt kommt der große Purzelbaum.

Es fand ja um etwa dieselbe Zeit wie das Verfahren in Berlin-Köpenick gegen Autor Heym ein ganz ähnlicher Prozeß beim Kreisgericht Fürstenwalde statt, und zwar gegen den Professor Robert Havemann; die Anklage lautete gleichfalls auf mehrfaches Devisenvergehen, begangen durch unerlaubte Veröffentlichung seiner Schriften im Devisenausland. Bemerkenswert ist, daß Havemann, ohne deshalb mit Heym Kontakt aufgenommen zu haben, zu seiner Verteidigung beinahe wörtlich das gleiche Argument wie dieser anführt. »Es entsteht«, sagte er, »der Eindruck, daß dieses Verfahren nicht wegen Verletzung der Devisenvorschriften angestrengt worden ist, sondern in Wirklichkeit dem Zweck dient, die Freiheit der Meinungsäußerung zu unterdrücken.«

Trotzdem wird Havemann am 20. Juni 1979 von den Fürstenwalder Richtern nach §17, Abs. 1, Devisengesetz, zu einer Geldstrafe von 10 000 Mark verurteilt und eine Anzahl von Gegenständen aus seinem Besitz werden eingezogen. Im Gegensatz zu Heym aber geht Havemann in Berufung; diese wird denn auch, wie zu erwarten, vom Bezirksgericht Frankfurt (Oder) am 18. Juli als »offensichtlich unbegründet« verworfen.

Havemann stirbt; sein Begräbnis wird zu einer ersten großen Demonstration gegen die Regierung der DDR, und nachdem diese gestürzt ist, fordert Frau Katja, seine Witwe, Kassation des Urteils von Fürstenwalde. Und wieder befürwortet der Generalstaatsanwalt der DDR die Kassation, und wieder gerät das Verfahren, nach dem 3. Oktober 1990, an ein Gericht der Bundesrepublik; nur befindet sich dieses, da Fürstenwalde ins Brandenburgische gehört, in Potsdam.

Dort aber sitzen im 2. Kassationssenat des Bezirksgerichts drei Richter, welche am 3. Juli 1991 einstimmig beschließen, in entsprechender Anwendung von §349 Absatz 4 StPO in Verbindung mit Anlage I zum Einigungsvertrag vom 31. 8. 1990, Kapitel III, Sachgebiet A, Abschnitt III, 14., Maßgabe h, dd, ff, gg, 311 ff. StPO/ DDR in der Fassung vom 29. 6. 1990, das Urteil der Strafkammer des Kreisgerichts Fürstenwalde vom 28. 11. 1979 aufzuheben, den Verurteilten freizusprechen, und die Kosten und notwendigen Auslagen der Verfahren sowie die Kosten des Kassationsverfahrens der Landeskasse aufzuerlegen. Die insgesamt ungesetzlichen Verfahren von Fürstenwalde und Frankfurt (Oder), so erklären die drei, wurden mit dem Ziel durchgeführt, den Betroffenen einzuschüchtern und davon abzuhalten, öffentlich Kritik an der damaligen DDR und der sie beherrschenden SED zu üben. Dem entspreche es, daß in der öffentlichen Hauptverhandlung die Einlassung des Angeklagten, es gehe in dem Verfahren nicht um Devisenvergehen, sondern darum, ihn mundtot zu machen, geflissentlich unterdrückt wurde, und es bedürfe keiner näheren Erläuterung, »daß mit dem Verfahren einschließlich des Urteils, das nur den Zweck verfolgte, den Betroffenen unter Druck zu setzen und ihn so an der Wahrnehmung seines Rechts auf freie Meinungsäußerung – Artikel 27 der Verfassung der DDR – zu hindern, gegen die Grundsätze der Gewährung der Gesetzlichkeit und der Achtung der Menschenrechte verstoßen wurde«.

Die Frage ist jetzt, wer wirklich recht hat; jene, die, wie die Staatsanwälte bei dem Kammergericht, nach dem alten Satz entscheiden wollen, daß doch nicht Unrecht sein kann, was gestern noch Recht war, oder die andern, die, wie die Richter von Potsdam, eher der Meinung sind, daß das Unrecht von gestern heute nicht zu einem Recht höchst zweifelhafter Art verbogen werden darf.

Diese Frage ist nicht nur akademischer Natur, noch betrifft sie ausschließlich die Erben des Professor Havemann oder den Autor Heym. In praxi scheiden sich hier die Wege der Rechtspflege im gesamten wiedervereinigten Deutschland und damit die Wege seiner Bürger, besonders der in der ehemaligen DDR: hie Rechtsstaat, hie Rückzug in die alten Verhaltensmuster.

Bei Drucklegung erhält der Autor die Nachricht, daß die 6. große Strafkammer des Landgerichts Berlin – Kassationsgericht – in ihrer Sitzung vom 17. Januar 1992 einstimmig beschlossen hat: »*Der Strafbefehl des Stadtbezirksgerichts Berlin-Köpenick – 710 S 220/79 (131-265-79-16) – vom 22. Mai 1979, rechtskräftig seit dem 30. Mai 1979, wird entsprechend §349 Abs. 4 StPO aufgehoben.*«
In der Begründung heißt es u. a.: *Das Kassationsgericht hat bereits erhebliche Zweifel, ob das gegen den Kassati-*

onsführer seinerzeit geführte Strafverfahren überhaupt in ordnungsgemäßer Anwendung der gesetzlichen Vorschriften erfolgte, oder ob nicht vielmehr mit einem nur nach außen hin justizförmig ausgestalteten Verfahren in Wirklichkeit sachfremde, politische Zwecke verfolgt werden sollten. Hinweise darauf lassen sich den Akten des Ministeriums für Staatssicherheit entnehmen, in denen sich zum Beispiel eine Aufforderung an die »Abteilung Postzollfahndung« aus dem Jahre 1971 befindet, nach der bis auf Widerruf gegen den Kassationsführer eine Postzollfahndung einzuleiten ist und alle anfallenden Sendungen inhaltlich zu dokumentieren sind. Ferner existiert aus dem gleichen Jahr eine sogenannte »Einschätzung des Operativ-Vorganges ›Diversant‹«, wonach die weiteren Maßnahmen darauf zu konzentrieren sind, »den Verbindungskreis des Heym zu zersetzen, seine politische Einflußnahme und Wirksamkeit einzuschränken«.

Auch die Behandlung des Strafverfahrens durch höchste Dienststellen bei der Staatsanwaltschaft und auf Direktionsebene der Gerichte läßt darauf schließen, daß das Strafverfahren – wie der Kassationsführer selbst einwendet – den Zweck hatte, einen Schriftsteller mundtot zu machen und eine Veröffentlichung seines Schaffens zu unterbinden.

Denkmuster

Wer des Nachts aufwacht und nicht wieder einschlafen kann, der kennt das: die Fragen, die einem dann durch den Kopf gehen, manchmal sehr abseitige Fragen, manchmal auch solche, die einen selber direkt und schmerzlich betreffen. In dieser Nacht, war es der Vollmond draußen, war es ein Traum gewesen, floh mich der Schlaf dann, und aus dem Gewirr der Gedanken kristallisierte dieser eine sich heraus: Wieso eigentlich war das alles auf einmal zusammengebrochen, dieses System, das aussah, als sei es so festgefügt, und in dem jeder jeden zu überwachen schien – zusammengebrochen ohne besondere Anwendung von Gewalt seitens irgendwelcher Angreifer, und ohne daß aus den Zwingburgen die Verteidiger herausgetrabt kamen in disziplinierten Kolonnen und die Verderber aufs Haupt schlugen – sondern einfach so?

War die berüchtigte Macht des Staates innerlich derart ausgehöhlt gewesen, daß sie fast ohne Anstoß von außen in sich kollabierte, und wer oder was hatte sie so ausgehöhlt, und warum war da keiner, der ihr zu Hilfe eilte in der Stunde ihrer Not, obwohl sie doch Tausende und Abertausende ernährt und begünstigt hatte mit klug dosierten Gaben?

Und warum standen sie am Schluß, die einst so Mächtigen, gleich Abc-Schützen, die ihre Lektion vergessen, hinter ihren Amtsschreibtischen, ihre sorgfältig gehäuften Papiere, die sie wie Schätze gehütet, plötzlich ohne Wert und gut höchstens noch, um andere zu denunzieren bei den neuen Herren?

Ich benutze bei meinen Überlegungen bewußt keine Akte der Geheimpolizei, um die Denkmuster aufzuzeigen, nach denen in den Köpfen der herrschenden Schicht und ihrer Lakaien alles ablief, von der Prämisse über die Folgerung bis zum scheinbar logischen Schluß, welcher dann behördliches Handeln erfordert. Polizeiakten, ob aus dem geheimen Apparat stammend oder von einer harmloseren Dienststelle, zeigen immer nur das Funktionieren einer bestimmten Art von Geist; mir jedoch scheinen, für unseren Zweck, die ganz gewöhnlichen Gedankengänge ganz gewöhnlicher Institutionen mehr auszusagen, weil sie den Alltag des Systems bloßlegen und uns erlauben, die wesentlichen Gründe seines Zusammenbruchs zu erkennen.

Einer der Vorteile eines Umsturzes ist, daß einem da Dokumente in die Hände fallen können, die sonst unter Siegel und Verschluß geblieben wären. Hier war es ein simples Verlagsgutachten, wie sie, verfaßt möglichst von Fachleuten, jeder DDR-Verlag der zuständigen Abteilung des Kulturministeriums vorlegen mußte, wenn er die Zuteilung von Papier zum Druck eines Titels beantragte – oder wenn ein Grund gesucht wurde zur Verdammung eines Buches. Das Verlagsgutachten war also auch eine Vorstufe der Zensur.

Dieses Gutachten behandelte eine lange Novelle von mir, betitelt »Die Schmähschrift«, die zum ersten Mal im Jahre 1970 als Buch gedruckt worden war, allerdings in der Schweiz, und die, so meinte ich, eine Veröffentlichung auch in der DDR verdiente. Es wird darin von einer Begebenheit im Leben des Schriftstellers Daniel DeFoe erzählt, der 1702, anonym, eine Schmähschrift erscheinen ließ, *The Shortest*

Way with the Dissenters, zu deutsch, »Das kürzeste Verfahren mit den Abweichlern«. Der Ich-Erzähler meiner Story ist eine fiktive Gestalt mit Namen Josiah Creech, persönlicher Referent, wie wir's heute nennen würden, des Earl of Nottingham, des Staatssekretärs der südlichen Abteilung der Regierung Ihrer Majestät der Königin Anna von England; Creech ist betraut mit der Feststellung und Verfolgung des anonymen Autors der Schmähschrift; das Manuskript seines Tagebuchs aus der Zeit erhielt ich, wie ich im Vorwort meines kleinen Bandes andeutete, während des Londoner Blitzes aus den zarten Händen einer Miss Agnes Creech; und da am nächsten Tag eine deutsche Bombe das Haus zerstörte, in welchem Fräulein Agnes gewohnt hatte, konnte ich ihr, so schrieb ich, das Manuskript ihres Urahnen Josiah nicht mehr retournieren.

Das Ganze war also eine sorgfältig kaschierte Fiktion, die aber auf geschichtlichen Fakten beruhte: Daniel DeFoe hatte eine solche Schmähschrift tatsächlich verfaßt und in ihr die Dogmen der herrschenden Kirche durch nur geringfügige Übertreibungen ad absurdum geführt; und mein Mr. Creech ermittelte ihn sehr bald als Autor der Broschüre und veranlaßte seine Verhaftung und ein Gerichtsverfahren gegen ihn: DeFoe wurde verurteilt, an drei Tagen hintereinander an drei verschiedenen Londoner Plätzen am Pranger zu stehen, eine lebensgefährliche Prozedur, falls nicht das Volk sich zugunsten des Delinquenten entschied.

Im Falle DeFoe geschah gerade dies. Die Bürger von London umkränzten den Pranger mit Blumen und ließen den Mann hochleben, der da mit dem Kopf im Querholz stand, unfähig sich zu rühren; und zu seinen Füßen wurde eine Neuauflage seiner amtlich verbotenen Broschüre mitsamt seinem neuesten Werk verkauft, der »Hymne an den Pranger«, in welcher der Autor aufzählte, wer von rechtswegen statt seiner

an den Pranger gehörte: »Die Börsenmakler und die Speku-
lanten, die kirchlichen Würdenträger, das Juristenpack, und
die Bullen der Regierung, drauf abgerichtet, Unschuld'ge zu
Tod zu hetzen!«

Die Bullen taten's dem Gutachter besonders an, wiesen sie
doch auf die Polizisten auch der DDR-Gegenwart hin, die,
zumindest im Unterbewußtsein des Gutachters, eine gewisse
Ähnlichkeit mit den Bütteln der Königin Anna zu haben
schienen. Ja, noch mehr: nachdem er zugestanden, daß es
ihm nicht gelungen sei, in einschlägigen Literaturgeschich-
ten herauszufinden, ob es tatsächlich ein Pamphlet DeFoes
mit dem Titel »Das kürzeste Verfahren mit den Abweichlern«
gebe, und daß selbst neuere englische Wörterbücher keinen
adäquaten Begriff für die ganz und gar moderne deutsche
Wortbildung ›Abweichler‹ verzeichneten, stellt er fest, »Autor S. H. identifiziert sich selbst mit der Figur des Dichters
DeFoe auf der geistigen Grundlage der ›absoluten Freiheit des
dichterischen Gedankens‹ und verteidigt diesen Standpunkt
gegen, wie er es gestaltet, engstirnige, orthodoxe (sprich: dog-
matische) Staats- und Kirchen- (sprich: Partei-)vertreter. Das
Buch ist also gleichnishaft und symbolisch zu verstehen, und
im Grunde gibt es kaum eine Zeile darin, die nicht voller bösartiger Anspielungen und Bezüge steckt. H.s ›Schmähschrift‹
ist eine Schmähschrift im wahrsten Sinne des Wortes – eine
Schmähschrift wider uns«!
  Nachdem der Gutachter dieses erkannt, sucht er nach Beweisen für seine These, daß es dem Autor S. H. weder um
den historischen Daniel DeFoe geht noch um die gesellschaftlichen Mißstände des frühkapitalistischen England. Das hi-
storische Gewand, so schreibt er, sei Verkappung und Mum-
menschanz zur Tarnung eines ganz andern Anliegens: einen
Angriff vorzutragen nämlich gegen unsere Partei und die Re-

gierung der DDR, insbesondere ihre Kulturpolitik im Zusammenhang mit dem 11. Plenum von 1965. Ganz deutlich werde die Sache, schließt er, schaut man sich die Hauptpersonen der kleinen Geschichte an.

»Es wird hier vom ›Staatsrat‹ und seinen Mitgliedern gesprochen. Lord Nottingham, der Dienstherr des Erzählers Creech, soll ganz offensichtlich die in der Karikatur verschlüsselte Person des Genossen Prof. Kurt Hager wiedergeben. Das reicht sogar bis ins Wortspiel hinein: ›Lang und hager‹, steht der Lord im persönlichen Dialog seinem Widerpart DeFoe gegenüber, und er ›kaut an seiner schmalen Unterlippe‹.

Der Mr. Robert Stephens, genannt Robin Mastschwein, zielt wohl auf die Person des Genossen Axen, und Lord Godolphin gar, der Lordschatzmeister, der die Verfolgung DeFoes aus ›Mitteln des Geheimdienstes‹ finanziert, soll offensichtlich die Person des Genossen Erich Honecker verkörpern. Und so redet DeFoe/Heym frank und frei von der Leber weg: ›Ich habe die Reden geistig beschränkter Dunkelmänner gehört, die eine bigotte Vergangenheit zurückersehnen, und plötzlich war mir, als vernähme ich das glorreiche Lachen meines verstorbenen Königs William (gemeint ist wohl Genosse Wilhelm Pieck!), dem zu dienen, und das Echo der Revolution, für die zu kämpfen ich die Ehre hatte, und ich erkannte, daß ich nichts weiter zu tun brauchte, als die Sache der regierungsamtlichen Dummköpfe bis ins letzte darzustellen, um sie in ihrer eigenen Lächerlichkeit zu ertränken.‹«

Gott segne den Mann und sein Gutachten. Besser hätte er nicht darstellen können, wie die polizeilichen Normen, denen zufolge ein jeder a priori verdächtig war, und die detektivische Akribie der Geheimdienste das Denken und die Gefühle sonst sicher ganz vernünftiger und dem Sozialismus ergebener Bürger pervertierten und die Resultate ihrer Überlegungen zu Absurditäten werden ließen. Aber er geht noch weiter in seinem Bedürfnis, dem Autor der »Schmähschrift« auf die Schliche zu kommen. S. H. bediene sich, schreibt er, sogar der Zahlensymbolik: »Die Quersumme der Jahreszahl 1703 – die hauptsächliche Zeit der Handlung des Buches – ergibt 11 (11. Plenum!). Und auch in den Wochentags- und Monatsdatierungen sucht er sich stets der Quersumme 11 anzunähern (3. 8. = 11; 10. 1. = 11; 7. 4. = 11, usw.).«

Man kann ihn direkt sehen, den braven Genossen Gutachter, wie er da sitzt und über den Daten in dem Buche grübelt, und hinter ihm den gespenstischen Schatten des Mannes mit der Zensurschere, den Exekutor seiner Gedanken. Dabei will er doch verhüten, daß der Verlag, der sein Gutachten angefordert, und das Kulturministerium das Gift, welches er mit geschärftem Instinkt in der Story vom Sieg des Autors De-Foe über die Regierung der Königin Anna erkennt, auf dem Umweg über die Drucklegung der Sache in die Hirne eines nichtsahnenden DDR-Publikums gerät, und in der Tat bleibt das Werkchen östlich der Elbe vier Jahre lang unveröffentlicht.

Man kann sich heute gut lustig machen über solche wie ihn. Außerdem hatte der Mann ja recht, es gibt deutliche Parallelen zwischen den Geschehnissen des Jahres 1703 in London und den eher farcenhaften Konflikten, in welche ein paar Schriftsteller um die Zeit der 11. Plenarsitzung des Zentralkomitees der SED im Jahre 1965 gerieten – darum ja hatte es mich gereizt, über DeFoe und die Folgen seiner Schmähschrift zu schreiben; ich hoffte, der Leser könnte bei der Lektüre der Sache ins Nachdenken geraten, und Denken, das glaubte ich zu wissen, fördert die politische Bewegung.

Alles andere in dem Gutachten aber war das Produkt der

Ängste seines Verfassers, der, wie jener Josiah Creech, be-
fürchtet haben mußte, daß das Volk sich mit dem kritischen
Autor, heiße er nun DeFoe oder Heym, solidarisieren könnte,
am Fuße der Prangers oder sonstwo. Und es waren diese Ängste, die ihn veranlaßten, nach Läusen zu suchen, die nur in seiner Einbildung existierten, und Zusammenhänge herzustel-
len, die es gar nicht gab.

Und so wie er haben sie alle denn gesucht, die Polizisten
selber und die, die Schutz und Sicherheit nur sahen in Polizei
und immer mehr Polizei, haben gesucht und gesammelt, zwischen den Zeilen der Bücher und in Briefen und Gesprächen,
auf der Straße, in der Kneipe, im Betrieb, in den Schulen und
auf den Ämtern und in den Toiletten der Bahnhöfe, und haben ihre Funde numeriert und registriert und zusammenge-
klebt und ausgewertet und immer wieder bebrütet, und haben doch nicht gewußt, was vor sich ging im Lande, obwohl
doch alles so einfach war – sie hätten nur ein Ohr haben müssen für die Lächerlichkeit ihrer Formeln und Dogmen und für
das wahre Echo der glorreichen Revolution, in deren Namen
sie zu handeln vorgaben, und hätten die Freiheit des Wortes,
und ein paar andere Freiheiten, für welche der Schriftsteller
DeFoe am Pranger zu stehen bereit gewesen war, gewähren
sollen, statt das Wort immer wieder zu unterdrücken mit ihren Polizeistempeln und ihrer Polizeigewalt. Sie waren durch-
organisiert und durchbürokratisiert wie kaum irgendwo, und
kaum etwas entging ihrem mißtrauischen Blick, aber sie such-
ten den Feind am falschen Ort und nicht dort, wo er wirklich
war: in der eigenen Brust und im eigenen Gehirn.

Aber war das, so mögen wir fragen, ein besonderes Verhalten der herrschenden Schicht und ihres Apparats nur in
der ehemaligen DDR? Liegt es nicht vielmehr im Wesen aller
Gruppierungen der Art? Und verbreitet das Virus sich nicht,
jetzt und in dieser Minute und morgen und übermorgen, just

unter den treuesten Dienern und den devotesten Anhängern der Mächtigen allüberall? Man lese doch nur was da steht in den Spalten der vornehmsten Blätter des größeren, des vereinten Deutschland, und höre, was da geredet wird vor den Mikrophonen der lautesten Sender.

Der Gutachter zitiert in seinem Schriftstück den Earl of Nottingham: »Eine Armee von Verbrechern, Mr. Creech, stellt keine Bedrohung der bestehenden staatlichen Ordnung dar. Aber ein aufsässiger Schriftsteller gehört nach Newgate hinter Schloß und Riegel, und ich rate Ihnen, Mr. Creech, ihn so rasch als möglich dort zu haben.«

Die DDR, mit ihren Polizeiköpfen und ihrem Polizeidenken, ist zugrunde gegangen, verdientermaßen.

Schnallt euch fest, Boys, es geht wieder los.

Der Scribent als
moralische Instanz.

Mich hat ja keiner gefragt

Mich hat ja keiner gefragt.

Keiner. Obwohl ich im vorigen Herbst zum Bundesbürger avancierte mit allen Rechten, die mir dadurch erwachsen, darunter das Recht, mitreden zu dürfen auch über die Geographie des Landes und ein Wörtchen beizusteuern – und sei's auch ein Ja oder Nein nur! – zu so gewichtigen Fragen wie jener, ob denn das Volk, das wieder vereinte, von Berlin aus zu regieren sei oder von Bonn.

Hätte jedoch mich einer gefragt, ich hätte geantwortet: *Bonn.*

Und hätte das gesagt als Berliner, der ich seit langen Jahren nun bin. Gerade als Berliner – und nicht nur aus der großzügigen Lässigkeit heraus, die vielen Berlinern eigen, nach dem Muster etwa: ach laßt den armen Kerlen am Rhein doch ihr Spaßvergnügen! Nein, aus purem von Vernunft und Erfahrung diktiertem Egoismus.

Wir lebten ja schon, erinnern wir uns, zumindest wir Ossis, in einer Hauptstadt zusammen mit einer Regierung. Wer sieht nicht noch vor seinem geistigen Auge die großen blauen Schilder entlang der Autobahn, *Berlin, Hauptstadt der DDR,* die uns erinnern sollten, daß wir nicht in ein Fischerdorf an der Spree kamen, wenn wir das Holperpflaster spürten unter unseren Reifen bei der Einfahrt in die Kapitale. Ah, welcher Hauptstadtduft, welches Hauptstadtflair, besonders in der Normannenstraße im Stadtbezirk Lichtenberg!

Aber unsre neue Regierung, so höre ich Stimmen, das ist doch was ganz anderes. Das sind, bittesehr, aufgeklärte und demokratisch denkende Herrschaften, tolerant, klug und mit anerkannt großem Herzen auch für den kleinen Mann. Und die Mitglieder dieser Regierung sind, von der Spitze bis zum hinteren Ende, gewählt, wirklich und wahrhaftig gewählt!

Zugegeben. Und dennoch scheint mir, im Licht der Weltgeschichte, als ähnelten die Regierungen, seit es Regierungen gibt, einander doch sehr – wenn nicht im Background ihres Personals, so doch in Wesen und Gehabe.

Und was ist denn, gebe ich zu überlegen, so schön an einer Regierung, auch der besten, daß man sie unbedingt in der Nähe haben muß?

Die Herren und Damen, die sich hochgerangelt haben im Parlament und in der Exekutive und nun auf den Stühlen der Macht sitzen und ihre Gesichter – ach täten sie's weniger häufig! – in die Fernsehkameras hängen? Oder das Ritual der Empfänge und die Karossen und die Eskorten, die zu den alltäglichen Staus noch die offiziellen hinzufügen? Oder die Scharen von Schranzen, die um die Großen herumwieseln und wiederum andere, kleinere Schranzen um sich herumwieseln lassen? Oder die Ministerien und Ämter, die ewig sich vermehrenden, untergebracht in protzigen Burgen, die nützlicheren Bauten den Platz streitig machen und die Quadratmeterpreise ins Astronomische treiben?

Gewiß, das Gefolge, das eine Regierung mit sich herumschleppt, konsumiert allerlei Güter, auf unsere Kosten übrigens; und reichlich dotiert von ihren Oberen fördern die beamteten Massen den hauptstädtischen Handel und Wandel;

aber es ist doch fraglich, ob der dadurch entstehende wirtschaftliche Nutzen die Belastung der Bürger aufwiegt, die eine jede Bürokratie für die Bürger der Stadt bedeutet, über welche sie herfällt.

Ja, wenn die Regierenden uns wenigstens, mit funkelnder Krone, blitzendem Schwert und dramatischer Rede eine Schau böten, die unsre Seele erbaute, oder Charaktere zeigten, um die zu bangen sich lohnte! Aber die meisten von ihnen strahlen nichts aus als Langeweile, und die Weisheiten, die sie von sich geben, sind Gemeinplätze, noch dazu schlecht vorgetragen. Und wäre es nicht für den gelegentlichen Skandal, mit dem sie uns aufwarten, sie wären schon vor ihrem ruhmlosen Abtritt vergessen.

Ich weiß, vielerorts wird man mich nicht lieben für derlei Ansichten. Und ich höre den warnenden Ruf schon von Freundesseite: Philister über dir! – und sehe sämtliche Bodenbesitzer und Grundstücksmakler, Wessis wie Ossis, sich auf mich stürzen, um mich mit ihren zur Unterschrift neuer, noch profitablerer Mietsverträge bereits gezückten Kugelschreibern zu erdolchen.

Sei's drum! Ich sage trotzdem: Wir haben schon so viele Regierungen gehabt in Berlin, brauchen wir diese da auch noch?

Wir hatten den Kaiser, den mit dem vergüldeten Helm über dem gezwirbelten Schnurrbart; der ging dann nach Doorn in Holland, und übte sich im Holzhacken. Dann hatten wir den dicken Ebert, der in die Inflation schlidderte, und den Feldmarschall Hindenburg, der den ganzen bankrotten Laden an Hitler übergab, und Hitler zog in die Wilhelmstraße und starb in dem Bunker dort, als die Sowjets auf dem Reichstag ihre Fahne hißten, die rote. Und dann hatten wir den Genossen Ulbricht und den Genossen Honecker, und Honecker verkriecht sich jetzt mit seiner Margot in irgendwelchen fernen Winkeln – ja, ich glaube wirklich, sagen zu können, daß Berlin eine Unglücksstadt ist für deutsche Regierungen, sie enden alle böse hier, und wenn ich ein deutscher Regierungschef wäre, heute, ich zöge lieber, als daß ich nach Berlin käme, in den Kyffhäuser wie der Kaiser Barbarossa selig und ließe meinen Bart durch den steinernen Tisch hindurchwachsen dort – oder ich bliebe wenigstens in Bonn.

Aber mich fragt ja keiner.

Und nun kommen sie schon, obwohl sie eigentlich gar nicht kommen möchten, denn sie hatten sich ja so schön eingerichtet in ihren stillen Bonner Ämtern und Datschen entlang des Rheins. Sie kommen und lassen sich extra zahlen, hoch über Tarif, für die Unbequemlichkeit und den entbehrungsreichen Umzug und all die anderen Opfer, die das Leben in einer Halb-Kolonie so fordert, und suchen sich unter dem in der Noch-nicht-Hauptstadt Verfügbarem das heraus, wofür sie den Ausdruck »Filetstück« gefunden haben, und zeigen uns, wie man regiert.

Nicht, daß wir's nicht brauchen könnten, einmal regiert zu werden, wie sich's gehört, oder gar uns selber zu regieren; was wir an Regierung hatten bisher, war ja auch, daß Gott's erbarm. Aber vielleicht sollte der Haupttroß der neuen Regierung doch noch ein Weilchen bleiben, wo er zur Zeit sich befindet, denn wenn sie erst alle hier in Berlin sind, Minister und Staatsräte und Abgeordnete und Hardthöhe und BND und was alles noch, und sie sich so, statt in der Abgeschiedenheit ihrer Bonner Bungalows, in der Nähe der Volksmassen offenbaren, das möchte doch sehr entblößend wirken. Familiarity, sagen die Engländer, breeds contempt; nähere Bekanntschaft erzeugt Verachtung.

142

Zurück nach Bonn!

Welch grausame Losung, an die Regierung gerichtet, für die Bürger Bonns! Waren denn mehr als vierzig Jahre Regierung am Ort nicht genug für die arme Stadt? Und ich entschuldige mich ausdrücklich bei ihren Bewohnern dafür, daß ich Bonn noch mehr Bonner Regierung auf den Hals gewünscht hätte, hätte man mich gefragt.

Denn ich sympathisiere zutiefst mit ihnen und freue mich für sie, daß sie nun einer geruhsamen Zeit entgegensehen können. Ich kannte Bonn ja, bevor es Bonn war. Ich kam nach Bonn, kurz nach Kriegsende, in amerikanischer Uniform, und fand es versponnen wie eh und mit einem gewissen stillen Charme, und mein Captain sagte, »Das soll sie nun sein, die künftige westdeutsche Hauptstadt«. Und ich fragte, hinter der Schnapsidee einen amerikanischen General vermutend, »Welcher Idiot hat sich denn das wieder ausgedacht?«. Und der Captain sagte, »Ein gewisser Adenauer. Wohnt in der Nähe von Bonn und möchte keine zu lange Anfahrt zu seinem Büro«.

Und ich suchte mir vorzustellen, wie das wohl aussehen würde, dieses Bonn, bei dem man an Beethoven dachte, als Hauptstadt. Aber auch die lebhafteste Phantasie wird übertroffen von der Realität, der Realität dieses liebenswürdigen, anheimelnden, sauber gefegten Städtchens, in dem selbst die Hunde sich genieren, ihre Kringel vor staatlichen Gebäuden zu hinterlassen, und aller Art Beutelschneider einträchtig mit den Politikern frühstücken.

Und nun suche ich mir ein Bild zu machen von Bonn als Ex-Hauptstadt, mit Büschen wilder Rosen um den Kanzler-Bungalow, durch deren Dornen keiner mehr durchdringt, und der lange Eugen von Efeu überwuchert bis zum obersten Geschoß, und der neue Bundestag eine Investruine, mit all den Baggern und Kränen gestoppt mitten beim Baggern und Liften, und der Koch in der Saarländischen Vertretung, den Arm erstarrt, mit dem er dem Küchenjungen eben noch die Ohrfeige geben wollte, und sämtlich warten sie auf den Pater Basilius Streithofen, der aus dem Kloster Walberberg angeritten kommen soll, um die Bonner Dornröschen wachzuküssen und ihnen die Beichte abzunehmen für ihre Sünden und ihnen, in strengstem Vertrauen natürlich, mitzuteilen, wie man dies Deutschland denn so richtig zu regieren habe.

Ein Märchen? Mag sein; ein Märchen für kluge Kinder.

Doch wir in Berlin sitzen nun fest mit Berlin. Mich hat ja keiner gefragt.

144

Denkmalspflege

Große Ereignisse zeugen große Veränderungen: Stein verschwindet und Bronze; ein verwaister Sockel bleibt oder gar nur ein leerer Fleck.

In meinem Dorf stand einst am Ufer des Langen Sees, der eigentlich nichts ist als ein versprengtes Stück Spree, das Denkmal des Deutschen Sports. Es stammte noch aus der Kaiserzeit und war, architektonisch gesehen, eine Art Mini-Ausgabe des Leipziger Völkerschlachtdenkmals; das besondere waren die Steine, aus denen es zusammengefügt war; ein jeder von diesen war von einem der damaligen Sportvereine gestiftet worden, die dafür ihren Namen auf ihren Stein eingravieren lassen durften: Kaiserlicher Yachtklub Kiel, oder Kgl. Sächsischer Kleinwildjägerverband zu Dresden, oder Kgl. Bayrischer Alpenjodlerverein.

Das Denkmal, ein beliebtes Seezeichen für die vorbeisegelnden Binnenschiffer, mißfiel aber, vom Politischen her, der damals aus SED und entsprechenden Blockparteien zusammengesetzten Stadtverwaltung. Statt aber Aufkleber mit den Namen von DDR-Sportvereinen herstellen zu lassen, etwa Dynamo Dresden oder Union Schilda, und mit deren Hilfe die ungeliebten historischen Vereinsnamen zu kaschieren, befahlen die Genossen, das ganze Ding von der Köpenicker Erde zu vertilgen.

Ich hätte mir gerne einen der Steine für mein Vorgärtchen geholt, aber meine Hände waren zu schwach für ein solches Vorhaben, und meine Nachbarn ließen sich in jener Zeit lieber nicht mit mir blicken.

Auch der Stalin an der Stalinallee mußte verschwinden, nachdem der Genosse Chruschtschow die Betriebsgeheimnisse der Regierung seines Vorgängers ausgeplaudert hatte. Und nun, dank der freundlichen Mithilfe Gorbatschows bei dem Zusammenschluß der beiden deutschen Staaten, ist der Lenin dran am Leninplatz, und nicht nur der, die Liste ist lang. Was das alles kosten wird! Und was stellt man hinterher hin? Eine leere Stelle erinnert doch in noch peinlicherem Maße als das Denkmal selber an die gefallene Größe aus vergangenen Zeiten!

Ich frage: Reißt man denn eine Straße ab, nur weil sie nach einer nicht mehr erwünschten Figur einer nicht mehr erwünschten Geschichte benannt ist? Lieber hängt man doch einfach ein neues Straßenschild an die Ecke.

Daher mein Vorschlag: Die Stadtbehörde lasse nur den Kopf des Lenin-Denkmals abnehmen und ihn durch einen anderen, weniger anstößigen ersetzen, gleich mit Gewinde am Hals, damit er bei Sturm auch festsitze. Als Ersatzkopf für den Lenin läßt sich etwa ein Bismarck-Kopf denken; auch der Kanzler Bismarck hatte markante Züge und war, als Gründer des Reichs, eine Art Vorgänger unsres Dr. Kohl. Oder auch ein Kopf von Wilhelm Busch, dem beliebten Erfinder von Max und Moritz; ein Künstlerkopf wird eher von Dauer sein als der eines Politikers, und die Leninallee könnte dann Max-und-Moritz-Allee heißen, was in jedem Fall phantasievoller wäre als der Name, den unsre heutigen Stadtväter und -mütter sich dafür ausgedacht haben. Und die vor der Nikolaikirche so hübsch gruppierten Engels (stehend) und Marx (sitzend) könnten mit den Köpfen von Goethe und Schiller sehr rasch in ein viel weniger kontroverses Dioskurenpaar verwandelt werden.

Und so in allen neuen Bundesländern durch Wandel der Köpfe ein Wandel der Zeiten. Aber die abgenommenen Köpfe bitte hübsch aufheben – für eventuelle spätere Wenden.

Wie jedoch, wenn das ganze Denkmal aus nichts besteht als einem Kopf? Was machen wir mit dem riesigen Marx-Kopf in Karl-Chemnitz-Stadt, der uns, von seiner Hauswand her, quer über die Straße mit vorwurfsvollem Blicke verfolgt?

Sogar dafür gäbe es eine Lösung. Statt dem steinernen Ungeheuer mit Hammer und Meißel zu Leibe zu rücken, setze man ihm einen Helm auf aus Gips oder Plaste, mit zwei Hörnern dran, und schon wird aus dem Trierer Juden Marx der Cherusker Armin, der Germanenheld, der die Römer schlug im Teutoburger Wald und so sein Teil zur Entstehung der glücklich vereinten neuen, größeren Bundesrepublik Deutschland beitrug.

Und auch dieser Helm ließe sich, sollte sich's so ergeben, wieder abnehmen.

Erinnerungen

Da war ich nun bei Tucholsky. Er liegt in Mariefred, übers Wasser von Schloß Gripsholm, das er so geliebt hat; aber der dicke Stamm der alten Eiche auf dem kleinen Friedhof, unter der zu ruhen er sich wünschte, versperrt ihm die Aussicht auf die drei roten Türme im Mittagsdunst. Auf dem schweren flachen Stein mit den Trageringen steht zu lesen, alles Vergängliche sei nur ein Gleichnis – und die Jahreszahlen: 1890–1935. Wie jung er doch war, als er am Leben verzweifelte! Die Schweden, berichtete mir mein Begleiter, hätten ein schlechtes Gewissen heute gegenüber Tucholsky; er mußte um sein Asyl fürchten, das sie ihm nur unter Bedingungen gewähren wollten, die zu erfüllen ihm unmöglich schien.

Und während ich da stand und über den Mann unter der Eiche nachdachte, der der Welt noch so viel hätte geben können, Heiteres, und Trauriges und Bitteres wohl auch, zündeten die Skinheads in Hoyerswerda den Asylanten das Dach überm Kopfe an und brüllten die alten Losungen, die der Tote auf dem Friedhof zu Mariefred auch schon gehört hatte, in dem Deutschland vor 1933.

Und dann habe ich mir die Filme angesehen, welche die unbestechliche Kamera aufgezeichnet von den Gesichtern dieser sächsischen Rambos, während der Aktion und danach, und ich dachte, wo hab ich die nur schon erlebt, und dann fiel es mir ein: nur damals hatten die Kerle braune Mützen getragen und braune, schlecht sitzende Hemden, und die Molotow-Cocktails waren noch nicht erfunden; das Brändelegen war mühsamer.

Und da war das liebreizende junge Mädchen, das blonde Haar eng anliegend am schöngeformten Schädel, und der Teint so makellos weiß – aber der Blick der blauen Augen, direkt gerichtet ins Objektiv, hart, hart, hart, und das Lächeln grauenerregend, als einer sie fragte, was nun, wenn die Kinder im Zimmer dort verbrannt wären? Der Schäferhund, wo war der Schäferhund, der zu ihr gehörte, und die Peitsche, die lederne Peitsche der KZ-Kommandeuse?

Und das Schlimmste: die Gesichter der anderen, der Zuschauer, der braven, sonst so untertänigen Bürger, der Frauen vor allem, dicklich schon die meisten mit den Falten, welche der tägliche Frust in die Haut kerbt, doch nun freudig erregt dreinblickend, denn hier wurde aufgeräumt, endlich, und gesäubert, Deutschland den Deutschen, nach vierzig Jahren, wo einem verwehrt war zu sagen, was man dachte.

Wie ich sie kannte, alle, aus der Zeit der Kristallnacht – aber auch später, als sie durch die Ruinen schlurften und den Siegern erklärten, nein, sie trügen keinerlei Schuld.

Und die Regierung? Ich meine die heute, die in Dresden wie die in Bonn.

Die Regierung kniff. Die Regierung überließ das Schlachtfeld den Angreifern und verlud die Menschen, die da verstört in den feuergeschwärzten Räumen des Asylantenheims hockten, in Busse und schickte sie hinaus in die Nacht, Bestimmung unbekannt, und einer der Busfahrer hielt dann an, mitten im Nirgends, und befahl seinen Passagieren, »Raus!«, und da standen sie nun, ein neudeutsches Gruppenschicksal.

Gut, das war in Hoyerswerda, im finstersten Osten.

Aber wo ist Hoyerswerda nicht?... Die Spur der Gewalttätigkeit, der faschistischen, zieht sich kreuz und quer übers Land, West wie Ost, nur im Osten zeigt sie sich stärker, weil hier der soziale Zündstoff sich sammelt.

Und es soll mir doch keiner einzureden versuchen, daß diese Überfälle so spontan kommen, aus der reinen Seele unsrer patriotischen Jugend. So unfähig kann doch sogar die frisch zusammengepappte Einheitspolizei nicht sein, daß sie nicht feststellen könnte, wie da die Fäden laufen und wer daran zieht.

Meinen Respekt vor den Politikern, die niedliche, saubergeschrubbte dunkle Asylantenbabys auf den Arm nehmen, als wären's die eigenen – doch würde meine Achtung vor den Herren noch steigen, wenn sie auch Order gäben, dem Spuk ein Ende zu setzen. Order – wem? Einer Beamtenschaft, die insgeheim glaubt, geschieht diesen Ausländern ganz recht, wenn sie mal eine Abreibung kriegen, was wollen sie hier überhaupt, schmarotzen herum bei uns und machen krumme Geschäfte, und wir füttern sie noch durch und geben ihnen freies Quartier; und die Ost-Ordnungshüter sagen sich außerdem, bei dem Bruchteil, den ich kriege vom Gehalt der Kollegen drüben, und weiß ich, ob ich morgen den Job überhaupt noch habe, da soll ich mir heute den Schädel einschlagen lassen von den Glatzen, nein danke.

Und dann die Politiker selber – die sind doch auch beeindruckt von den Massen derer, die den Schlägern wohlgefällig zunicken, oder? Was Wunder, wenn sie da nicht folgerten, das sind doch, bittesehr, meine Wähler, soll ich mir die vielleicht auch noch verprellen dieser elenden Neger wegen und der Fidschis und Zigeuner, und wegen der Juden, der russischen, die die jeweilige Regierung in Moskau uns schickt?

Das höre ich gern, die DDR wäre an allem schuld.

Die DDR hätte die armen Kinder unterdrückt, vierzig Jahre lang, und nun, da sie, diese Kinder, wir sind ein Volk, sich befreit hätten von dem Druck, ließen sie eben, schon bei Freud sei derlei nachzulesen, ihren Aggressionen freien Lauf; da müsse man doch Verständnis haben, und sich an einen mehr oder weniger runden Tisch mit den Kindern setzen und gemeinsam mit ihnen über ihre seelischen Probleme reden. Die Theorie ist mir lange schon bekannt, und wenn ich mich recht erinnere, war es Tucholsky selber, der dazu dichtete, *Küßt die Faschisten, wo ihr sie trefft.*

Die DDR hat Kinder unterdrückt, jawohl, aber ganz andere Kinder – Kinder, die Kerzen trugen und auf dem Ärmel einen Aufnäher mit dem Prophetentext Schwerter zu Pflugscharen, und die sich Gedanken darüber machten, wie man den Sozialismus mit Demokratie und den lieben Gott mit den Bedürfnissen der Arbeiterklasse in eins bringen könnte. Und als die ersten Skinheads in der DDR auftauchten, in den achtziger Jahren, haben Mielkes Leute sie sogar gelegentlich benutzt, um denen mit den demokratischen Flausen im Kopf eins über die Rübe zu geben; und als jemand dem Genossen Honecker von den neuartigen Schlägern berichtete und ihn darauf hinwies, welch ein Gezücht da in den Schulen seiner Gattin aufwuchs, ließ er in den Betrieben nachfragen und erfuhr, daß die Skins dort bekannt dafür seien, daß sie fleißig an ihrer Maschine werkelten und sich sauber hielten, und dieser Bescheid beruhigte ihn ungemein.

Nein, das kroch nicht nur aus DDR-Schoße. In beiden deutschen Staaten blieben die faschistischen Muster erhalten, sich fortpflanzend von Vätern zu Söhnen, weil keiner, weder Ost und noch West, sich wirklich die Mühe gemacht hatte, über das eigene Verhalten in der Vergangenheit nachzudenken und mit dem seelischen Unrat aufzuräumen, der sich da an-gehäuft hatte. Und was die östlichen Schläger und deren Anhang betrifft, so wurden deren psychische Deformationen weniger durch die DDR-übliche stupide Schulmeisterei erzeugt als durch die innere Unsicherheit der Menschen, besonders der jungen, welche ein Nebenprodukt ist der neuen Marktwirtschaft. Die Kehrseite der großen Freiheit, die dem einen gestattet, Millionen zu scheffeln, während der andere seiner Arbeit beraubt wird und damit seines Lebensinhalts, ist die große Hilflosigkeit, die zur Aggression führt.

Und wer, einmal ins Aus gestoßen und von Selbstzweifeln geplagt, an den gleichen Symptomen leidende Gleichgesinnte findet und gleich ihnen an der gleichen Ecke stehen und in der gleichen Kneipe saufen und gar noch den gleichen Feind, einen schwächeren natürlich, zusammenstechen darf, der wird, gestärkt und gestützt von seinesgleichen, sich plötzlich riesenhaft vorkommen und die deutsche Einheit erst so richtig genießen. Heil Hitler.

Das ist die eine Seite. Die andere, das sind die Asylanten.

Asylant, zu englisch Refugee, einer, der ein Refugium sucht, eine Fluchtstätte vor politischer Verfolgung und vor Gefahr an Leib und Leben. Tucholsky war einer, und auch ich, nur hatte ich mehr Glück als er und durfte, nach langem Hin und Her und großen Ängsten, in Amerika bleiben. Ich weiß also, wie einem zumute ist, der Schutz und Sicherheit sucht, und jener Artikel im Grundgesetz, der die deutsche Regierung verpflichtet, Asyl zu gewähren den Verfolgten, entsprang einer edlen Emotion.

Aber sind sie nun sämtlich politisch Verfolgte, die da in das reiche Deutschland hineinwollen? Oder ist nicht auch der gewöhnliche Hunger ein Verfolger, vor dem man zu fliehen sucht?

Und wer trifft da die Entscheidung, welcher Bürokrat, und

wie lange dauert es, bis er sie trifft, und was, wenn der Antragsteller nicht echt ist und sich nur hineinschmuggeln möchte in unser Wirtschaftsparadies zum Hütchenspielen oder zum Drogenverkauf? Oder, wenn's eine Frau ist, zur Prostitution? Und wohin mit den Leuten, wenn endlich feststeht, daß sie kein Anrecht haben auf den Segen des Artikels 16, Grundgesetz? Welches Land nimmt sie uns ab? Nicht mal ihr eigenes.

Da könnte einer schon auf den Gedanken kommen, die Skinheads hätten recht, wenn sie tabula rasa machen möchten: weg mit ihnen allen, die uns da kommen mit ihrer fremdartigen Haut und ihren watschelnden Weibern und ihrer ganzen lärmenden Brut.

Und doch haben sie unrecht, die Skins und die, die ähnlich denken wie sie. Denn auch der Terror gegen die Ausländer nützt nichts, in Hoyerswerda oder irgendwo. Es sind ihrer nämlich zu viele schon, die begehrlich blicken nach den Ländern, in denen die Läden noch voll sind mit Eßbarem, und mit Elektronik. Habt ihr die Schiffe gesehen aus Albanien, an deren Bordwand die Menschen wie Trauben hingen, bevor sie hinabsprangen auf den Quai, den italienischen? Was wäre, wenn die Schiffe statt in Bani in Bremerhaven angelegt hätten? Was wäre, wenn die in Calcutta, wo sie zu Hunderttausenden im Staub der Straße liegen und um eine Handvoll Reis betteln, sich aufmachten nach Hoyerswerda oder, näherliegend, die Russen herkämen, sollte dort drüben noch mehr schiefgehen als schon schiefgegangen ist? Müssen wir dann alle zu Skinheads werden, oder neue Mauern bauen an unseren Grenzen – und wie hoch müßten die sein, um dem Ansturm standzuhalten?

Denn Hoyerswerda ist ein Weltproblem.

Nur die Skinheads, die das aufgezeigt haben, wissen es nicht; und ob es die in Bonn wissen, ist zu bezweifeln, sonst würden sie, statt sich zu erhitzen über Paragraphen, dem Übel an die Wurzel zu gehen versuchen, im Verein mit anderen Regierungen, und würden, als erstes, ein Fax schicken an den Papst Woytila mit der dringenden Bitte, er möge doch endlich aufhören, bei jedem befruchteten Ei darauf zu bestehen, daß es auch aufwachse zu einem Wesen, für das keine volle Schüssel mehr da ist.

Damals, als ich die Gesichter zum ersten Mal sah, die ich jetzt wiedergesehen, wußte ich nur, daß sie Unheil bedeuteten – aber welcher Art und wie groß das Unheil sein und welche Opfer es fordern würde, konnte ich nicht einmal ahnen.

Heute wissen wir mehr, viele von uns haben miterlebt, in was für Zeiten wir hineingerieten. Laßt die Gesichter von Hoyerswerda uns eine Mahnung sein darum, und tun wir alles, um zu verhindern, daß neues, noch schlimmeres Unheil über uns kommt.

Treuhand aufs Herz

Treuhand aufs Herz – wer weiß eigentlich mit Sicherheit, was für ein Laden das ist, der da, versehen mit einer Macht, wie sie nur das Politbüro hatte, über das Wohl und Wehe von Hunderttausenden, nein, Millionen Menschen in der ehemaligen DDR entscheidet und Schicksal spielt mit ihnen?

Wer, und was, ist diese Treuhandanstalt, die da gleichsam über Nacht auftauchte und, ohne daß irgendeiner auch nur die leiseste Frage nach ihrer Berechtigung stellte, über das gesamte Volksvermögen auf dem Gebiet, das später »Die neuen Länder« genannt wurde, verfügt? Wie ist dieses Machtmonopol zustande gekommen? Wer hat es legitimiert? Und warum müssen wir, die wir selber uns, einst in den Oktobertagen, zum Volk erklärten, vor dieser Institution hocken wie das Kaninchen vor der Schlange und uns, früher oder später, von ihr schlucken lassen?

Der Ur-Skandal war, daß in dem sogenannten real existierenden Sozialismus die Produktionsmittel, die nach den Maßgaben der Erfinder der eigentlichen Idee, der Genossen Marx, Engels und Lassalle, dem Volke gehören und von diesem zum Nutzen aller Menschen gebraucht und verwaltet werden sollten, einer ebenso selbsternannten Körperschaft unterstanden wie es die Treuhandanstalt heute ist, nämlich dem bereits er-

wähnten Politbüro der allein alleswissenden, allein allesbe-
herrschenden Partei.

Kaum aber war dieses Politbüro gestürzt, und kaum war
die Chance da, daß das Volk sich seines Eigentums endlich
bemächtigen und bedienen konnte, wurde die Chance vertan:
zwar gab es Betriebe, in denen Versuche in dieser Richtung
unternommen wurden, vergebliche leider, aber im großen
Ganzen waren die Menschen, und man kann sie auf Grund
ihrer Geschichte verstehen, mehr an den neuen Konsum-
möglichkeiten interessiert als an den neuen Möglichkeiten
einer Produktion, deren Ergebnisse nicht mehr der Firma
Honecker, Mittag & Schalck, sondern ihnen selber gehören
würden.

Es gab jedoch in jenen Wendetagen ein paar Leute bei den
neuen Gruppierungen an den runden Tischen, denen der an
sich lobenswerte Gedanke kam, man müsse sich doch vielleicht um die nun herrenlos herumliegenden Werte kümmern,
um all den Grund und Boden, all die Gebäude und Maschinen, und was derlei noch vorhanden und nicht bereits zugrunde gewirtschaftet war. In jenen Kreisen besann sich einer, oder vielleicht waren es auch mehrere, des frühbürgerli-
chen Begriffs der Treuhand – ein Treuhänder verwaltet nach
bestem Treu und Glauben etwa das Erbe von minderjährigen
Waisen – und so sollte auch eine Treuhandgesellschaft her für
das kollektive Erbe des plötzlich verwaisten DDR-Volkes, damit dieses nicht etwa auf den Gedanken käme, selber etwas
damit anzufangen.

Nun hatten die meisten jungen Leute in diesen Gruppen –
noch heute bestehen ein paar Gruppen der Art und ihre nicht
sehr zahlreichen Vertreter im Bonner Bundestag dürfen dort
gelegentlich fünf Minuten lang reden – diese Leute also hatten
sich in den Tagen vor und während der DDR-Wende auf ihre

158

basisdemokratische Manier durchaus klug und tapfer verhalten, im Gegensatz zu all jenen, die das Maul erst recht aufrissen, nachdem das nicht mehr mit irgendeiner Gefahr verbunden war. Aber es mangelte ihnen an einer gründlicheren politischen Erfahrung und vor allem offenbar an Kenntnis der Tatsache, daß die Macht über die Produktionsmittel die Macht im Staate bedeutet, und daß ein Unternehmen, heiße es Treuhand oder sonstwie, dem man eine solche Macht aushändigt, sie kaum je wieder hergeben wird.

Auf der Spurensuche nach den Ursprüngen der Treuhand findet man tatsächlich im Gesetzblatt der DDR vom 8. März 1990 unter dem Titel »Beschluß zur Gründung der Anstalt zur treuhänderischen Verwaltung des Volkseigentums (Treuhandanstalt)« unter Punkt 1 schon die Feststellung: *Zur Wahrung des Volkseigentums* wird mit Wirkung vom 1. März 1990 die Anstalt zur treuhänderischen Verwaltung des Volkseigentums gegründet.

Aber dann kam der kleine dürre Herr de Maiziere, gesponsert von dem großen dicken Herrn Kohl, an die Regierung, und da las sich's plötzlich anders. Im Gesetzblatt vom 22. Juni 1990 wird die Sache nun »Gesetz zur Privatisierung und Reorganisation des volkseigenen Vermögens (Treuhandgesetz) vom 17. Juni 1990« genannt.

Also nicht mehr *Wahrung des Volkseigentums,* sondern dessen *Privatisierung und Reorganisation,* soll heißen Ausverkauf und Vernichtung. Vom Volk, dem das Ganze ja eigentlich gehörte, ist in diesem neuen Gesetz überhaupt nicht mehr die Rede, nur von den verschiedenen Bürokratien und ihren Zuständigkeiten im Rahmen der Anstalt. Das Volk kann sich sein Eigentum in den Rauchfang schreiben.

In der Zeit, erinnere ich mich, erhielt ich einen Anruf von Arbeitern der Narwa-Werke in Berlin, man stellt dort elektrische Birnen her und ähnliches. Ihre Gewerkschaft, sagten sie, sei nicht mehr existent, ditto Gott sei Dank auch ihre Parteiorganisation; ob ich ihnen vielleicht einen Rat geben könnte, wie sie mit ihrem Eigentum, den Narwa-Werken, verfahren sollten.

Ich ging hin. Da saßen mehrere hundert Männer und Frauen in ihrer Arbeitskleidung und machten sich Sorgen um ihren Betrieb, der allerdings in keinem besonders guten Zustand zu sein schien – aber jedenfalls produzierten sie noch und berichteten, Osram, ihre alte Firma drüben, sei an einer Zusammenarbeit mit ihnen interessiert.

Ein anderer sagte, man würde Osrams Hilfe zweifellos brauchen, und würde dafür auch zahlen müssen; möglicherweise könnte man ein Joint Venture mit Osram machen, aber achtet darauf, Kollegen, daß ihr 51 Prozent der Narwa-Anteile für euch behaltet.

An die Treuhand dachte noch keiner; Volkseigentum war Arbeitereigentum, und Narwa war ihres. Die Treuhand wird wissen, wem sie den Narwa-Betrieb dann zugeschustert hat, und wie viele von den Kollegen, die sich damals um ihren Betrieb bemühten, noch darin arbeiten.

Wer erinnert sich des Dr. Peter Moreth, des ersten Chefs der Treuhandanstalt, den der Genosse Modrow noch einsetzte, oder des Herrn Rainer Maria Gohlke, einstigen Direktors der Bundesbahn, der diesem im Amt folgte. Beide begriffen irgendwie nicht ganz, was von ihnen gewollt wurde seitens der Herren, die in Bonn das wirkliche Sagen hatten, und so mußten sie abtreten, sang- und klanglos.

Dann kam Karsten Rohwedder. Rohwedder begriff nur zu gut, worum es ging, und handelte danach, und wo man auch hinblickt in der ehemaligen DDR erkennt man die Resultate seines Wirkens.

Ich möchte nicht, ich wiederhole *nicht,* mißverstanden werden: ich bin gegen jedweden individuellen Terror und gegen die bübischen Anschläge, die von derart Terroristen vollführt werden, also auch gegen das Attentat auf Rohwedder. Mord ist kein Argument, er ist eine Bluttat, und an die Stelle des Ermordeten tritt ein anderer und setzt dessen Werk, sei es gut oder böse, fort.

In diesem Fall war der Nachfolger eine Frau, Birgit Breuel. Sie ist eine kluge Frau, heißt es, und ein Organisationstalent, aber kühl, kühl bis ins Herz. Und Frau Birgit Breuel setzt nun fort, wo Rohwedder abbrechen mußte, und alles, was noch einigermaßen brauchbar gewesen aus den Beständen der alten DDR, denken wir nur an die Interflug, wird abgewickelt und vernichtet, und alle Werte, die man noch nützen könnte, Grund und Boden etwa und Gebäude, werden ihren eigentlichen Besitzern, dem Volk, unterm Hintern wegeskamotiert und zu Billigpreisen verscherbelt, an wen eigentlich, bitteschön, und, wie ich gerade in der Zeitung lese, wurden jetzt sogar eine Million Flaschen Weißbier, in Sechserpackungen für den Export, aus der auch von der Treuhand geschlossenen Weißenseer Brauerei, auf den Müll gekippt, weil die Treuhand die Lagerhalle, in der das Bier lag, einem Interessenten eilig zugeschoben hatte.

Wir sind das Volk! – Da hätten sie uns doch wenigstens jedem eine Flasche Bier geben können, mit den Komplimenten der Treuhand.

Die Sache hat natürlich ihren sozialen Sinn.

Hat sich mal einer überlegt, warum immer die Ostbewohner, seien sie Arbeiter, Ingenieure, Verwaltungsleute, Ärzte oder was auch, ihre Jobs verlieren? Warum nicht auch mal ein westlicher Deutscher? Sind die im Osten wirklich fauler und dümmer als die Brüder und Schwestern drüben? Ich habe immer gefunden, daß ein östlicher Handwerker, wenn mal ein Ersatzteil fehlte, sich besser zu helfen wußte als der Westkollege; das Improvisieren hat er ja jahrelang geübt.

Wo ist die Gleichberechtigung? Haben sich zwei Teile eines Volkes in Freiheit vereinigt, oder hat der eine, der reichere, sich den anderen, ärmeren, untertan gemacht und verfährt nun mit ihm nach Gutdünken, nach dem Gutdünken der Treuhand?

Oder ist es gar so, daß der ganze Osten des Landes als Produktionsstätte gar nicht gebraucht wird, weil die westdeutsche Industrie die fünf neuerworbenen Länder ohne weiteres mitversorgen kann, bei erheblich erhöhter Rendite, versteht sich?

Nun sollen Beschäftigungsunternehmen eingerichtet werden für die Abertausende von Arbeitslosen, die es jetzt bei uns gibt, und die Treuhand soll sich mit zehn Prozent an dem Projekt beteiligen. Ja, es ist besser, daß die Menschen irgend etwas tun, auch wenn es nicht produktiv ist, und dafür bezahlt werden, als wenn sie herumsitzen und für ein Almosen die Daumen drehen. Ich würde die milde Gabe akzeptieren, wie auch alle andern milden Gaben seitens der Regierung und ihrer Treuhand – aber ich würde auch, wie die Arbeiter das früher getan haben, an die Herren die Frage stellen: *Gut, das ist der Groschen, aber wo ist die Mark?*

Vielleicht könnte man sich auch dafür interessieren, wer die Damen und Herren sind, die nicht nur in der Berliner Zentrale der Treuhand sitzen, sondern auch in ihren Provinzfilialen und darüber bestimmen, wer morgen noch früh zur Arbeit gehen darf und wer aus dem nützlichen Leben ausscheiden soll.

Wenn das alles nur Westler sind, eingeflogen in den Osten, um hier tabula rasa zu machen, so ist das schlimm genug, denn sie kennen die Menschen hier nicht und richten schon deshalb eine Menge Unheil an, selbst in bester Absicht. Aber man hört, daß da auch eine ganze Anzahl von Leuten sitzen, die zu jenen gehörten, die in der guten alten Honeckerzeit bereits alles zugrunde wirtschafteten und die nun, von neuen Schreibtischen aus und versehen mit dem neuen Amtssiegel, diese Art von Tätigkeit fortsetzen.

Wirklich, man hat das Gefühl: eine Treuhand wäscht die andere.

Gott helfe uns, amen.

Kleines Gespräch mit Herrn Dr. K.

Höflich und in aller Ruhe – wenn ich ihm begegnete, mehr oder weniger zufällig, würde ich ihm sagen: Meinen Sie nicht auch, Herr Dr. K., es wäre an der Zeit, daß Sie zurücktreten? Jetzt, jawohl, da Sie es noch tun können, ohne dazu gezwungen worden zu sein durch Aufruhr oder Skandal, und da das Schiff noch schwimmt, auf dem Sie und ich und wir alle uns befinden, und da um Ihr Haupt noch ein Schimmer zu spüren ist der Glorie des großen Vereinigers, als den Sie sich so gerne sehen.

Ich weiß, ich weiß, und jeder weiß es, der Ihr Gesicht studiert hat und den Blick Ihrer Augen, welcher so offen und treuherzig erscheint und in Wahrheit alles verbirgt, was in Ihnen vorgehen mag: Sie glauben, auch dieses überstehen zu können, oder aussitzen, wie man es wohl in Ihren Kreisen nennt. Und mit gewisser Berechtigung – stand das Glück nicht immer auf Ihrer Seite? Und haben Sie nicht immer dieses untrügliche Gefühl für den rechten Moment gehabt, da es zuzugreifen und zuzuschlagen galt? Und warum, werden Sie denken, sollte Ihr Glück Sie jetzt verlassen, Ihr Instinkt versagen, der Ihnen seit je so nützlich gewesen?

Und doch, davon bin ich überzeugt, rühren sich bereits in Ihrem Herzen die Zweifel.

In Ihrem Ostvolk, das Ihnen in einer Stunde kindlichen Zutrauens einst zurief, »Helmut, nimm uns bei der Hand, und führ uns ins Wirtschaftswunderland!« sagen sie jetzt, »So haben wir uns das nicht vorgestellt«. Haben *Sie* es sich so vorgestellt, Herr Dr. K.?

Haben Sie sich überhaupt etwas vorgestellt? Haben Sie eine Konzeption gehabt, wie das wohl funktionieren würde, zwei solch ungleiche Teile eines Landes, reich der eine, arm der andere, und bewohnt von Menschen mit solch ungleicher Vergangenheit und von solch ungleichem Wesen, auf einmal zusammengewürfelt, zusammengewirbelt – oder haben Sie einfach gedacht, als Sie da umjubelt standen in Dresden: das reißen wir uns unter den Nagel, die wollen's ja so haben, und die paar Bimsen, die es eventuell kostet, die schaffen wir mit links.

Und nun sind da, bei Ihrem Ostvolk die Ängste, und bei dem Westvolk der Ärger, und alles nur, weil Sie weder genug Kenntnis noch genug Phantasie hatten, um zu erahnen, daß man sich auch verschlucken könnte bei der Riesenschluckaktion, und daher dem Ostvolk wie dem Westvolk das Blaue vom Himmel herunter versprachen.

Ja, Ihre Versprechungen.

Muß ich sie aufzählen? Jeder kennt sie, jeder erinnert sich, die für das Ostvolk wie die für das Westvolk berechneten. Ich habe sie damals gehört, die schönen runden Sätze, keiner wird, keiner soll, wie sie im Brustton der Überzeugung aus Ihrem Munde kamen, Herr Dr. K., und habe mir im Stillen gedacht, sein Wort in Gottes rechten Gehörgang.

Aber Gott war, wie zu erwarten, taub auf dem Ohr, und nun sitzen wir da, das Ostvolk mit seiner Arbeitslosigkeit und seinen zerbrochenen Hoffnungen und das Westvolk mit seiner neuen, unerwarteten Bürde, und allesamt fassungs-

Mütterchen Treuhand

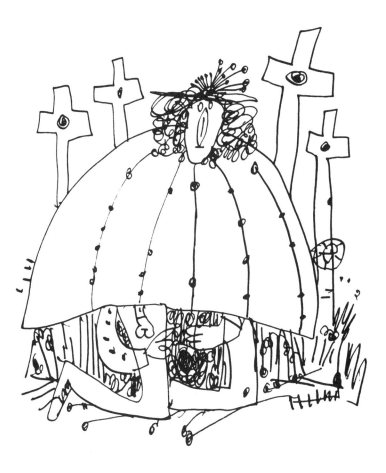

los angesichts dieser Zustände. Und von Ihnen, Herr Dr. K., was vernehmen wir? Es könne ja sein, dieses mit leicht gequetschter Stimme, Sie hätten die Schwierigkeiten ein wenig unterschätzt; und darauf gleich wieder volltönend und ermunternd: aber wenn nicht diesen Sommer, dann im nächsten oder schlimmstenfalls übernächsten werde die Talsohle erreicht sein, und danach ginge es aber los, steil nach oben; an Geld werde es nicht fehlen; das deutsche Volk müsse sich nur auf seine Tugenden besinnen.

Aber Regierungen, das wissen Sie selbst, können sich derart falsche Einschätzungen nicht leisten; und ich glaube auch nicht, daß Sie etwas falsch eingeschätzt haben; Ihr nahezu perfektes Timing und Ihr Geschick bei der gewaltlosen Übernahme der DDR beweisen Ihre Fähigkeiten auf dem Gebiet der Machtspiele. Nein, Sie haben schon um die Probleme gewußt, die auf Sie und auf uns zukommen würden bei diesem Anschluß; nur haben Sie Ihr Wissen von sich geschoben und verschwiegen, vor dem Ostvolk wie dem Westvolk, und vielleicht sogar vor sich selber.

Wenn Sie wenigstens hören könnten, Herr Dr. K.!

Ich meine auf die Schattierungen in der Stimme der alten Rentnerin, die in der DDR schon jetzt nur knapp über der Hungergrenze gelebt hat und nun nicht weiß, sogar das Briefporto hat sich verfünffacht, wie sie noch leben soll; auf die gequälten Worte der jungen Mutter, die, allein und ohne Mann, ihre zwei Kinder zu nähren, zu kleiden, und zu erziehen hat, von der Miete ganz abgesehen; auf das kurze, verzweifelte Lachen, ja, so etwas gibt es, des Arbeiters, der das Tor seines Betriebs hinter sich ins Schloß fallen hört, zum letzten Mal und für immer.

Das klingt ganz anders, gewiß, als bei Ihrem Wahlbesuch der Jubelchor fahnenschwingender Jugendlicher, die Fahnen waren eigentlich für ein Sportereignis, ich weiß schon nicht mehr welches, gekauft und von Ihren Helfern zweckentfremdet worden. Aber das sind die Töne, die wirklich zählen, weil sie sich in Aktion umsetzen könnten – und vergessen Sie doch nicht, Herr Dr. K., Sie haben es nach der Wende auch mit jenem Teil des deutschen Volkes zu tun, das schon einmal, und so lange ist das gar nicht her, eine Regierung gestürzt hat.

Aber selbst wenn Ihr Ohr auf diese Töne nicht eingestimmt ist, so lesen Sie doch, Politiker, der Sie sind, die Statistiken Ihrer Wirtschaftsgremien und die Berichte Ihrer Meinungsforschungsinstitute, und sehen die farbigen Linien, welche die Stimmung in den Schichten und Gruppierungen der Bevölkerung und deren Ursachen auch dem Taubsten zum Bewußtsein bringen. Brauchen Sie wirklich noch eine Feuerschrift an der Wand, um Ihnen das Mene Tekel deutlich zu machen?

Und wie, Herr Dr. K., schlagen Sie vor, dem zu begegnen? Haben Sie, wenn es Ihnen am Anfang der ganzen Sache schon jeder Konzeption ermangelte, jetzt wenigstens eine?

Ich kann verstehen, wenn Ihre Partei Hemmungen hat, Ihnen meinen Ratschlag nahezulegen; Ihre Leute wissen, eine Persönlichkeit mit Eigenschaften wie den Ihren findet man nicht so leicht wieder, und sie fürchten um die eigne politische Haut; dabei müßte ihnen doch klar sein, daß ihre Haut eine bessere Chance hat, heil zu bleiben, wenn Sie, Herr Dr. K., sich aus dem öffentlichen Leben verabschiedeten – in allen Ehren, selbstverständlich, und Ihre Position jemandem überließen, der besser und feinfühliger als Sie auf die großen Nöte der Menschen im Lande zu reagieren imstande ist, und der die Courage hat, außer den erzkonservativen Gedanken von der freien Marktwirtschaft und den absoluten Vorrechten des Privateigentums und den sattsam bekannten Volkstugenden auch ein paar neue Ideen zu entwickeln.

Ich will keine Namen nennen, die da in Frage kämen, denn ich möchte die Betreffenden nicht in Verlegenheit bringen; wir alle wissen, daß Sie mit möglichen Thronfolgern eine höchst unsanfte Art haben.

Und nun bin ich gespannt, wie es mit Ihnen wird, Herr Dr. K. Und ich bin nicht der einzige.

Präsident Lear

Sonst zahlt man, um eine gute Shakespeare-Aufführung zu sehen; diesmal bekamen wir's umsonst; einschließlich Schlachtenlärm und Helden und Narren, und Spannung bis zum Ende. Wenn, heißt das, wir schon am Ende des Stückes sind.

In König Lear, Akt I, 3. Szene sagt einer der Ritter zum König, »Mylord, ich weiß nicht, was vorgeht, aber nach meiner Ansicht begegnet man Eurer Hoheit nicht mehr mit der ehrerbietigen Aufmerksamkeit, wie man pflegte; es zeigt sich ein großes Abnehmen der Höflichkeit sowohl bei der Dienerschaft als auch beim Herzog und Eurer Tochter selbst«. Darauf der König, »Du erinnerst mich nur an meine eigne Wahrnehmung. Ich bemerkte seit kurzem eine sehr kalte Vernachlässigung, doch schob ich's mehr auf meine argwöhnische Gemütsart als auf einen wirklichen Vorsatz und absichtliche Unfreundlichkeit. Ich will genauer darauf achtgeben.«

Da ist es jedoch schon zu spät: Lear hat sein Reich verteilt an seine Töchter Goneril und Regan, die ihm Treu und Liebe heuchelten; die dritte und jüngste, Cordelia, die sich weigerte, ihm nach dem Munde zu reden, ließ er leer ausgehen und verbannte sie; so nimmt die Tragödie ihren Lauf, und sein Narr wird ihm sagen, »Der ist toll, der auf die Zahmheit eines Wolfs baut, auf die Gesundheit eines Pferdes, eines Knaben Liebe, oder einer Hure Schwur«.

Wir alle haben, sei's im Fernsehen, sei's in der Zeitung, die Galerie von Gesichtern gesehen, die den Mitgliedern jenes Notstandskomitees eigen, welches drei Tage lang in Moskau regierte. Oh, dieser Janajew, diese Pugo und Jasow! Kein Regisseur, der einen Gangster-Film drehte, würde es wagen, ausschließlich Schauspieler mit derart Physiognomien als Darsteller seiner Mafiosi auszuwählen aus Furcht, man könnte ihm vorwerfen, er übertreibe; und der bärtige Herr, der in der Pressekonferenz am Abend der Rückkehr Gorbatschows diesen fragte, wie es denn käme, daß er gerade solche Leute in Positionen höchster Macht gehievt habe, brachte den Präsidenten in ziemliche Verlegenheit: es sei ihnen doch, sagte der Bärtige, auf die Stirn geschrieben gewesen, was für Schurken sie waren.

Er habe, erwiderte Gorbatschow schließlich, sich in dem einen oder anderen geirrt; doch erklärt das nicht, warum er sich irrte. Nun gut, er mag in den zweiundsiebzig Stunden seiner Isolierung auf der Krim an Dringlicheres gedacht haben als an eine Analyse seiner Torheiten.

Aber die Gründe liegen auf der Hand; es sind die gleichen, die zu der sonderbar schwankenden Politik Gorbatschows führten, zwei Schritt vorwärts und dann wieder zurück, heute Reform und morgen die Scheu davor.

Alle Geschichte, das lehrte den jungen Gorbatschow schon sein Instrukteur auf der Parteischule, ist die Geschichte von Klassenkämpfen. Und welche Klasse, so wird er sich wohl in schlafloser Nacht auf der Krim gefragt haben, war es denn nun, die sich da in diesem August 1991 in einer Art unedler Verzweiflung in den Kampf stürzte gegen ihn? – Doch wohl seine eigene: die Nomenklatura, die Natschalniki in der Wirtschaft und die Höheren unter den Militärs und jene Beamten und Funktionäre, deren er selbst so lange einer gewesen.

174

Aber bildeten diese denn, wird er sich weiter gefragt haben, eine Klasse? Das Merkmal einer Klasse, so hatte der Instrukteur erklärt, war ihr sozialer Besitzstand; die Kapitalisten besaßen die Produktionsmittel, die Arbeiter ihre Hände. Ein Nomenklatur-Kader dagegen, das hatte nun wieder die eigne Erfahrung ihn, Gorbatschow, gelehrt, besaß außer dem Hintern, mit dem der Genosse seinen Bürosessel ausfüllte, nichts; seines Postens enthoben, war er wieder nur der arme Schlucker, als der er einst angefangen hatte.

Der Sessel also war das Merkmal dieser Klasse, ihr Besitzstand, und obwohl das Ding nicht mehr kostete als ein paar Rubel, war es wertvoller, viel wertvoller als Aktienbesitz oder Banknoten, Land oder Bauten und Maschinen, und man kämpfte darum mit Zähnen und Klauen. Denn der Sessel war Macht. Im Besitz dieses Möbels verfügt man über alles, was das Leben reich und komfortabel machte, über Datschen und Limousinen, französische Moden, englisches Leder, japanische Elektronik, und, als Wichtigstes, über die Menschen.

Klar, daß diese Macht ohne eigenen Grundstock, dieser Besitz ohne Besitztum, sich nur halten ließ, wenn die Klasse zusammenhielt.

Als sie ihn damals erwählten aus ihrer Mitte, den Jüngsten unter ihnen, denn die Älteren starben ihnen zu rasch weg, da ahnten sie nicht, weder im Politbüro noch in anderen höheren Stellen der Nomenklatura, daß er den Zaum so bald zwischen die Zähne nehmen und ihnen davongaloppieren möchte. Hoah! riefen sie und Halt!, und drohten ihm, und redeten dunkel von Verrat. Er aber hatte gut hingehört in der Parteischule, als der Instrukteur, die großen Geister des Marxismus zitierend, verkündete, daß eine Klasse abtreten müsse, die sich als Hemmnis bei der Entwicklung der Produktivkräfte erwies.

Und genau das war die Nomenklatura geworden im Lauf der Jahr, eine Klasse, die, wie die Priester, nach immer gleichem Ritus redete und in immer gleichem Schritt sich bewegte, unschöpferisch, eine Last den Menschen. Und da er dieses erkannte und sah, daß es so, wie es bisher war, nicht weitergehen konnte, bei Strafe des allgemeinen Untergangs, er aber nicht stark genug war, seiner Klasse den verdienten Tritt zu geben, es wohl auch nicht getan hätte, hätte er diese Kraft besessen, erfand er die Perestroika, den Umbau, die große Veränderung, und hoffte, die Kerle würden sich selber auch verändern im Verlauf des Prozesses, wenn er, Gorbatschow, ihnen nur mit genügend Geduld zuredete und ein wenig Druck machte mit Glasnost, und würden einsehen, daß alles, was er tat, in ihrem Interesse geschah, im Interesse ihres Staates und seiner und ihrer Partei.

Und deswegen, im Vertrauen auf diese Einsicht, hatte er Janajew und die anderen, die ihm dann das Ultimatum stellen würden, das seinem Selbstmord gleichgekommen wäre, seinem politischen, und die Wachen ihm vor die Tür setzten, damit er ihnen nicht entkäme, zu seinen vertrauten Weggenossen ernannt, sie und er stammten aus dem gleichen Stalle und hatten den gleichen, vertrauten Stallgeruch an sich: so rochen Verräter nicht, hatte er sich gedacht in seinem alten Funktionärshirn.

Goneril und Regan sind Aristokratenweiber, wie denn auch Lear ein Aristokrat, dessen größter Schmerz es ist, daß ihm die Töchter sein Gefolge beschneiden, von hundert Rittern auf fünfzig auf fünfundzwanzig, und dann auf null; nur der Narr verbleibt ihm und der als einer aus dem Volk verkleidete Kent. Im Gegensatz zu ihrem Vater wissen Goneril und Regan jedoch, was Macht ist und zeigen ihm, was einem passiert, der, im Glauben an das Gute im Menschen, de facto seine Klasse verrät, indem er deren Macht leichtfertig verschenkt.

176

So auch die Genossen vom Notstandskomitee. Ihnen saß der Schreck noch in den Knochen von damals, als er ihnen auf den Leib rückte mit seiner Glasnost; der Schreck und die tiefe, instinktive Feindschaft gegen den trotz aller Ähnlichkeiten Andersartigen, und die Furcht vor ihm; hätten sie ihn nicht immer noch gefürchtet, sie hätten ihn wohl unsanfter behandelt, als sie ihn besuchen kamen in der Krim; irgend einer von ihnen hätte die Pistole gezogen und gesagt, »Wir geben dir dreißig Sekunden, Michail Sergejewitsch, deinen Rücktritt zu unterschreiben«, und das wär's dann gewesen.

Aber es fand sich kein Stalin unter ihnen und kein Dserschinski, sie waren allesamt zweitrangige Leute, mit schlechtem Gewissen.

Gegen Schluß des Stücks, seine besten Absichten in ihr Gegenteil verkehrt, wird der König von Wahnsinn befallen. Die Szene ist nicht ein Ort in der Krim, sondern England.

LEAR: Sie schmeicheln mir wie Hunde. – Ja und Nein zu sagen zu allem, was ich sagte! – Ja und Nein zugleich, das war keine gute Theologie. Als der Regen einst kam, mich zu durchnässen, und der Wind mich schauern machte, und der Donner auf mein Geheiß nicht schweigen wollte, da fand ich sie, da spürte ich sie aus. Nichts da, es ist kein Verlaß auf sie...

Unter uns – den Platz gewechselt und die Hand gedreht: wer ist Richter, wer Dieb? Sahst du wohl eines Pächters Hund einen Bettler anbellen? – Und der Wicht lief vor dem Köter: da konntest du das große Bild des Ansehns erblicken; dem Hund im Amt gehorcht man.

Wie, kein Entsatz? Gefangen? Bin ich doch
Der wahre Narr des Glücks. Verpflegt mich wohl,
Ich geb' Euch Lösegeld. Schafft mir 'nen Wundarzt,
Ich bin ins Hirn gehaun.

Zweimal, so scheint es, war er dicht an der Grenze, die Lear bereits überschritten hatte. Da ließ sich, live im Fernsehen, das jedem Arzt vertraute Irrlichtern erkennen in seinen Augen: das erste Mal, als er berichtete, wie die, die zu seinem Schutz mit ihm gereist waren, zu seinen Gefangenenwärtern wurden, und das zweite Mal, als er von sozialer Gerechtigkeit sprach und vom Sozialismus, und was diese trotz alledem für ihn bedeuteten, und als er zu ahnen begann, daß diese seine Botschaft, obwohl wahr und richtig, keinen seiner Zuhörer mehr überzeugte.

Wie allein und erniedrigt muß er sich gefühlt haben, als Jelzin, der Retter, in seiner Gegenwart und während er noch am Rednerpult stand, den Ukas unterzeichnete, der die Partei verbot, deren Generalsekretär er in dem Moment noch war und für die er gerade gesprochen hatte. Und wußte dabei doch, daß diese Partei drei Tage feige geschwiegen hatte, während die Regan und Goneril, sein eigen Fleisch und Blut, ihn des letzten Rests seiner Macht beraubten, und daß ihm, wollte er leben, nur blieb, auf ganz andere zu hoffen, von denen er nie viel gehalten hatte und die ihn mit großer Wahrscheinlichkeit eines Tages ebenso entmündigen würden, wie seine eignen Leute es gerade zu tun unternahmen; und wußte jetzt auch, wenn er's nicht vorher schon gewußt hatte, daß diese seine Partei, welch Heldentaten sie in der Vergangenheit auch vollbracht haben mochte, nicht die Partei war, die den Sozialismus, an den er immer noch glaubte, je durchführen konnte oder durchzuführen auch nur beabsichtigte.

Einst hatte er gesagt, »Wer zu spät kommt, den bestraft das Leben«. Das bezog sich auf einen anderen, aber möglich ist doch, daß er dabei auch sich selber im Sinn hatte. Jedenfalls ist er, was immer ihm noch geschehen mag, eine tragische Figur, und daher von Interesse für die Dichter.

Und was ist mit dem Volk, in Shakespeares Stück verkörpert durch den weisen Narren? Mit dem Volk, mit dem die Verschwörer nicht glaubten rechnen zu müssen, und das sich, bedenkt man es recht, ganz unmarxistisch verhielt, indem es nämlich das Fressen keineswegs der Moral vorzog, sondern sich für die Freiheit in die Bresche schlug wie 1917 einst und später gegen Hitler?

Dieses Volk, so darf man annehmen, wird uns noch einiges Unerwartete zu sagen haben, darunter manches, was nicht besonders süß und angenehm klingen wird in unserm Ohr und in den Ohren derer, die dem Volk jetzt soviel Beifall zollen.

Eine andere Welt

Plötzlich wird einem bewußt, wie sehr sich alles verändert hat. Die vertrauten Muster, deren Linie man zu folgen gewohnt war, wenn man sich klar zu werden versuchte über die Vorgänge des eignen Lebens wie im Leben der anderen sind außer Ordnung geraten und außer Gleichgewicht; sie haben sich auf höchst sonderbare Weise verschoben; sie hängen schief, sozusagen; wo einst links und rechts deutlich erkennbar gewesen, scheint nur noch eine Seite vorhanden, und auch diese lappt über den Rand des Geschehens, schlaff und ohne Façon, ähnlich einer der Uhren des Salvador Dali.

Offenbar fehlt etwas, was vor kurzem noch den Dingen Halt gab und begehbare Wege vorzeichnete.

Es fehlt der Feind.

Es fehlt der Widersacher, der ewige Gegenspieler, der die Alternative vertrat zu allem, was uns hoch und heilig, und den man hassen konnte im Konkreten wie im Grundsätzlichen, und dessen Komplotte man überall witterte, und gegen den es sich zu rüsten galt, moralisch, ökonomisch, atomar.

Wirklich, was tun wir, die wir seit kurzem sämtlich angesiedelt sind im Reich des Guten, wenn sich kein Reich des Bösen mehr findet? Wer ist noch da, den wir mit Nutzen verfolgen, beschimpfen, prügeln könnten?

Wem das Haus über dem Kopf anzünden? Gegen wen unsre Top-Agenten entsenden? Auf wen oder was unsre Raketen richten, unsre atomkopfbestückten?

Wer hat das nicht schon beobachtet, auf der Straße oder im Park: die zähnefletschende Dogge, die den kläffenden Mops zu zerfleischen droht, bis der sich plötzlich auf den Rücken legt, alle viere nach oben, und dem Großen den wehrlosen Bauch darbietet, den fetten, rosigen? Welch Sieg für den Großen! Total! Absolut! Aber bald schon wendet der Triumphator sich ab, enttäuscht und angewidert: da gibt's nichts mehr zu bekämpfen, das Leben ist freudlos auf einmal, ja, scheint all seinen Sinn verloren zu haben.

Im übrigen ist auch der Mops nicht glücklicher, obzwar er glücklich überlebte. Was ist denn seins nun für ein Leben: in ewiger Abhängigkeit den Großen umschwänzeln zu müssen und nie, nie wieder sich mopsig machen zu dürfen?

Man sieht es am Mienenspiel des unglückseligen Gorbatschow, wenn er auf dem Kanapee sitzt neben Bush beim Phototermin oder Arm in Arm mit dem dicken Kohl am Ufer eines Bächleins entlanghüpft im Kaukasusgebirge. Und wie die Sieger gönnerhaft grinsend sich mühen, das Triumphgeheul zu unterdrücken, das ihnen vom Bauch her aufsteigen will durch Schlund und Kehle!

Und die stolzen Sowjetgeneräle, die einst die Wehrmacht schlugen, wie sie da stehen, Doppelkinne markig unter den Riesentellermützen, und von den Perrons der ostdeutschen Bahnhöfe her zuschauen, wie ihre Riesenraketen hinweggekarrt werden zu dem Müllhaufen der Geschichte, und alles nur, weil die verdammten Kapitalisten mehr und bessere Güter zu produzieren wußten als die großmächtigen Bürokraten in den Staaten des real existierenden Sozialismus. Das Weltreich zerfallen, die hehren Statuen gestürzt in den Staub!

Und nicht einmal einen anständigen Putsch zustandebringen zu können dagegen!

Und hier im neu geeinigten Vaterlande, wie sich die Bilder doch gleichen – nur sind sie hier kleinformatiger und deutscher: es wird mehr noch gekrochen als anderswo von den Verlierern und größere Fladen Speichel werden geleckt, und wem's glückt, ein Plätzchen zu finden am wärmenden Busen der Sieger, der ist alsbald westlicher noch als die Wessis.

Ist ja auch schwierig, so aus dem Stand heraus, ohne Plan, ohne Konzeption, ohne Philosophie, ganze oder auch halbe Völker umzupolen vom real existierenden Sozialismus auf den real existierenden Kapitalismus. Umgekehrt ja, da gab's Modelle die Fülle, jede größere Parteihochschule hatte eins vorrätig. Aber für das, was dann wirklich auf uns zukam – nicht einmal eine provisorische Skizze.

Wie soll das in Wirklichkeit gehen, so ganz ohne Gegner? Was für ein Rennen, in dem nur ein Einziger läuft, was für ein Wettbewerb, den ich nur mit mir selber betreibe?

Aber man übersehe doch nicht, so wird amtlicherseits eingewandt, die Macht der Privatkonkurrenz, welche neben der Sehnsucht nach gesteigerter Rendite die Triebkraft ist der freien Wirtschaft – Schmidt & Co. gegen Schulze Kg gegen Müller GmbH –, und die alles befruchtet und wachsenden Segen schafft Jahr um Jahr für ihre Teilhaber.

Doch ist Schmidt kontra Schulze kontra Müller nur Kleinkram verglichen mit der großen, der geschichtsbildenden Konkurrenz gesellschaftlicher Systeme, dem Gegensatz von Klassenpositionen, dem Hickhack der Ideologien, hie Marx, hie Erhard, welch alle nun geschwunden. Es war die Präsenz der jeweiligen Anti-Welt, die, Ost wie West, die Oben zwang, die Unten zu päppeln – im real existierenden Kapitalismus durch Krankengeld, Altersrenten, Arbeitslosenunterstützung, Mietsubventionen, Urlaubsbonus, Weihnachtsgeschenke, und und –, und die so, Schritt um Schritt, Veränderungen schuf, welche aus der freien, brutalen Marktwirtschaft eine halbwegs soziale machten und aus dem Zerrbild von Sozialismus, mit dem wir gesegnet waren, die Gorbatschowiade oder Jelzins Tohuwabohu. Natürlich lag solcher Entwicklung die reine Erpressung zugrunde: denn ständig bohrte, solange das Andere, die Alternative, vorhanden, in den Hirnen der Oben die dumpfe, kaum je in Worte gekleidete Drohung der Unten: Wir können auch anders!

Im Falle des real existierenden Sozialismus machten die Unten die Drohung wahr: sie zerbrachen die Mauer, und prompt fiel das ganze Gebilde zusammen.

Doch fiel damit auch das System der Alternativen, welches, beginnend mit dem Oktober Siebzehn, das Auf und Ab der Historie dieses Jahrhunderts bestimmte. Und die Unten werden es zu spüren bekommen, daß der Hebel zerbrochen ist, vermittels dessen sie Druck auszuüben vermochten, bei guter Gelegenheit, auf die Oben.

Zerbrochen der Sozialismus, oder das, was man so nannte: eine Puppe, mit der die Kinder zu grob gespielt, seine Inhalte weniger wert noch als das Sägemehl, das dem armen Ding aus der zerfledderten Brust rinnt. Zerbrochen der Sozialismus, selbst in China und Kuba, wo man nach dessen Riten noch betet, und heimatlos die Linken in der westlichen Diaspora, die bis vor kurzem noch Fünkchen von Hoffnung hegten, es könnte vielleicht noch ein Licht kommen aus dem Lande, welches einst Lenin geprägt.

Aber, und das ist notierenswert, geblieben sind Oben und Unten, auch unter den neuen Bedingungen; und in den nunmehr sozial und politisch zu gedeihlicher Einheit zusammengequirlten Bereichen erscheint der Graben tiefer denn

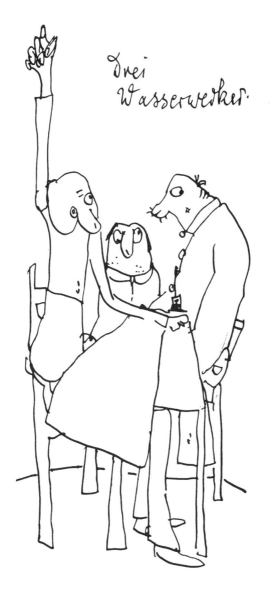

drei
Wasserwerker.

je, der seit Urzeiten gegähnt zwischen den Mächtigen und den Machtlosen. Und dies wird neue Probleme erzeugen, neue Konflikte und Widersprüche, nur daß jetzt die Alternative fehlt, die einst real existierte, so schäbig sie auch gewesen sein mochte.

Und wie umgehen mit den neuen Problemen unter den neuen Umständen? Woher die neuen Ideen nehmen, die man da bräuchte? Die deutsche Linke – und nicht nur die deutsche – ist ein einziger Wirrwarr, seit sie aus der luftigen Höhe ihrer runden Tische herunterpurzelte auf den Boden der Realität. Ach, wir Armen! Marx hat sich, so hallt es von überallher, als Versager erwiesen, Lenin gar nicht zu erwähnen; wer, oder was, ist uns geblieben zum geistigen Trost? Freud? Aristoteles? Der Apostel Paul? Oder, als letzter Helfer in Not, unser Dr. Kohl, der ewig sprudelnde Urquell hausbackener Weisheiten?

Dabei kocht es und brodelt es sichtbarlich an allen Ecken und Enden des Globus. Statt der großen Feindschaft zwischen den Reichen des Guten und des Bösen, welche, im Gleichgewicht ihres Schreckens, wenigstens eine gewisse Stabilität boten, brechen hundert kleinere, doch ebenso dumme und haßerfüllte Feindschaften aus, Blut fließt auf den Kontinenten, die umspült sind von verseuchten Meeren; Erde und Luft vergiften sich zusehends, ganze Völkerschaften, von Armut getrieben und Krieg, wandeln sich zu Asylsuchenden und machen sich auf zu den wenigen Inseln des Wohlstands – eines relativen nur, – und jeder Gebirgsstamm entdeckt sich als Nation und fordert, unter heftigen Drohgebärden, einen eigenen Luftraum und eigene Zollhäuseln und, nach der Anerkennung durch Bonn, Kredite.

Und statt des Klassenfeinds – wie kann es den Klassenfeind noch geben, wenn, wie es heißt, keine Klassen mehr da sind! – richten wir unsern Haß gegen alles, was sich nicht fügen will in unsern blöden, beschränkten Horizont, gegen Ausländer und Juden besonders; da werden wir doch sehen, wer hier das Sagen hat auf der S-Bahn, und in der Regierung!

Eine andere Welt als die uns gewohnte, und keine behagliche. Wäre es nicht an der Zeit, zu ergründen, was *diese* Welt nun im innersten zusammenhält, wenn überhaupt, und wie man sie gestalten könnte, sofern sie sich noch gestalten läßt?

Eine ganz besondere Wissenschaft

Die Medizin ist eine ganz besondere Wissenschaft.

In der Medizin geht es immer, direkt oder indirekt, um Tod und Leben. Ich muß dem Arzt, in dessen Hand ich mich begebe, vertrauen können, und zwar nicht nur in seinem Wissen, seinem diagnostischen Geschick, seiner Fähigkeit mit dem Skalpell: er darf mich nicht verraten, er darf mich nicht im Stich lassen, er muß meine Not über seine eignen Nöte und Bedürfnisse stellen. Der Arzt, kurz gesagt, muß eine Art Engel sein, oder das Nächstbeste zu einem Engel. Zwei oder drei solche Ärzte habe ich kennengelernt in meiner Zeit, und wenn ich heute noch am Leben bin, verdanke ich ihnen das.

Natürlich gibt es andere Ärzte auch. Schließlich ist auch der Arzt nur ein Mensch, und in der Regel steht auf der Wertskala des Menschen am höchsten das eigene Ich. Woraus sich der Rest der Sache ergibt: der Arzt als Opportunist, als Werkzeug der Mächtigen, gierend nach Geld und Gut, und, auch das hat es gegeben, als Mörder. Auf der Rampe des Konzentrationslagers stand immer ein Arzt.

Ende der sechziger Jahre beschäftigt sich ein junger Assistenzarzt an der Universitätsklinik in Halle mit dem Eigenbau einer Dialyse-Maschine. Solche Maschinen, im Westen werden sie schon industriell hergestellt, braucht man, wenn die Nieren versagen; dann wird dem Nierenkranken das Blut abgezapft, durch die reinigende Maschine getrieben und zurück in den Körper gepumpt; dies muß periodisch geschehen, zwei- oder dreimal die Woche; es ist aufwendig und teuer, aber der Patient, der sonst hätte sterben müssen, bleibt so wenigstens am Leben. Besser wäre es natürlich, man könnte ihm eine neue Niere einsetzen anstelle der alten, nicht mehr funktionsfähigen, und wirklich beginnen in jener Zeit die Urologen, im Bund mit den Chirurgen, gesunde Nieren, meist gespendet von Blutsverwandten, in den Leib des Kranken zu transplantieren. Und auch diese Operation erfordert, bis das Transplantat seine Arbeit aufnimmt, die Dialyse-Maschine.

Der junge Arzt, Peter Althaus sein Name, bastelt tatsächlich, mit Hilfe seines Vaters, der Ingenieur ist, und unterstützt von ein paar Technikern aus einem Merseburger Werk, eine ganz brauchbare Maschine der Art zusammen, die man auch in Halle einsetzt, bis etwas Professionelleres zur Verfügung stehen wird.

Dann nimmt sich die Regierung der DDR des Problems an. Sie hat keine Devisen, oder benutzt die, die sie hat, für andere als medizinische Zwecke; aber sie gibt Auftrag, eine Dialysemaschine Made in GDR zu entwickeln, und ein Werk in Aue baut das Modell »Aue«, gepriesen als wahre DDR-Errungenschaft, da gänzlich ohne westliches Know-how und westliche Lizenzen hergestellt, und die prominenten Ärzte, die daran mitgewirkt haben, erhalten den Nationalpreis, und das Werk in Aue eine Prämie, und sogar die Bruderländer werden damit beliefert – nur einen Fehler hat das neue Spitzenprodukt: es funktioniert nicht.

Der junge Dr. Althaus, dem man die Maschine aus Aue auch hingestellt und der sie bei einer schweren Operation verwendet hat, tobt: das Ding ist tödlich; der Patient überlebte nur, weil Althaus' altes Eigenprodukt noch in der Ecke stand und angeschaltet werden konnte. Aber wenn ein DDR-Bürger über Wohltaten der Regierung schimpft, erhält er Besuch. Der Besuch stellt sich vor: Hartloff, Udo, vom Ministerium für Staatssicherheit; bitte, Herr Doktor, erzählen Sie doch mal.

Dr. Althaus erzählt. Wer denn, denkt er, wenn nicht die Genossen von der Staatssicherheit, könnte die Urheber dieser verbrecherischen Fahrlässigkeit ausfindig machen und gegen sie vorgehen. Hartloff, Udo, hört aufmerksam zu; er wird da einen Bericht schreiben müssen, sagt er, und Dr. Althaus ist ihm dafür dankbar. Und in der Tat verschwindet »Aue« nach einiger Zeit aus den Krankenhäusern; eine neue Dialyse-Maschine wird in der DDR gebaut, diesmal nach einem amerikanischen Verfahren und mit amerikanischer Lizenz; bis diese zur Verfügung steht, benutzt man in Halle noch das Althaussche Bastelwerk.

Hartloff, Udo, aber besucht ihn auch weiterhin, vorzugsweise zu Hause, und mit Gattin. Ein Verhältnis, das Dr. Althaus und dessen Frau für Freundschaft halten, entwickelt sich, man macht sogar gemeinsame Ausflüge, und zum Zeichen, wie ehrlich Hartloff, Udo, es meint, vertraut er dem Dr. Althaus an, daß er eigentlich gar nicht Hartloff heiße, sondern Kirmse, und stellt ihm bei seiner Versetzung nach Berlin, als Direktor für internationale Beziehungen der Akademie der Wissenschaften, seinen Nachfolger im Amte vor, einen gewissen Träger, mit dem Dr. Althaus aber nur ein einziges Mal spricht, nämlich als der ihn bittet, seine, Trägers Frau wegen ihrer chronischen Bauchspeicheldrüsenentzündung zu behandeln.

Soweit, Dr. Althaus zufolge, seine Kontakte mit dem Ministerium des Genossen Mielke, dessen Stellvertreter, den General Beater, er in den kommenden Jahren operieren wird, viermal hintereinander.

Ende Juli 1991 erhält Dr. Althaus – inzwischen ist er Professor geworden und Leiter der Urologischen Klinik an der Charité und gilt als einer der vertrauenswürdigsten Operateure auf diesem Gebiet – von einer Frau Schnoor, die beim Senator für Wissenschaft und Forschung in Berlin arbeitet, einen Brief, darin seine fristlose Kündigung. Er ist nicht der einzige Empfänger eines solchen Schreibens; mehreren Kollegen an der Charité, von gleichem Range wie er, ergeht es ähnlich. In dem Brief an Althaus heißt es, seine Weiterbeschäftigung sei unzumutbar; Begründung: »Nach den vom Sonderbeauftragten der Bundesregierung für die personenbezogenen Unterlagen des ehemaligen Staatssicherheitsdienstes (Gauck-Behörde) überprüften Unterlagen waren Sie... für das ehemalige Ministerium für Staatssicherheit/Amt für Nationale Sicherheit vom 30. 06. 1973 bis 11. 12. 1986 in der Funktion eines inoffiziellen Mitarbeiters für Sicherheit/zur Sicherung der Konspiration Hauptabteilung/Abteilung XV (Staatsapparat, Kultur, Opposition, Gesundheitswesen) der Bezirksverwaltung Halle, Hauptverwaltung A (Aufklärung) tätig. Ihnen zugeordnete Führungsoffiziere waren Kirmse und Träger. Am 7. 10. 77 erhielten Sie die Medaille für treue Dienste der NVA. Im Jahre 1988 waren Sie weiterhin unter dem Decknamen Junghans erfaßt.«

Nun ist der eigentliche Dienstherr des Professors Althaus der Rektor der Humboldt-Universität. Nur dieser kann ihn entlassen, und nicht der Senator für Wissenschaft und Forschung, selbst wenn der sich als juristisches Feigenblatt eine Kommission vor den Nabel hängt, bestehend aus drei Vertretern der Senatsverwaltung und dreien der Universität, unter letzteren auch der Professor Mau, der Dekan der Medizinischen Fakultät. Aber abgesehen von dieser Frage der Zuständigkeit drängt sich dem Leser des Briefes der Frau Schnoor noch eine ganz andere auf: Was ist das für eine Demokratie, was für ein Rechtsstaat, in dem ein Mann von einer Verwaltungsinstanz für schuldig erklärt und bestraft werden kann, ohne daß ein Beweis seiner Schuld vorgelegt, ohne daß er selber auch nur gehört worden wäre von einem der hohen Herren der Kommission, – *audiatur et altera pars,* verlangten die alten Römer schon – nur auf Grund der Äußerung einer Behörde, deren Anspruch auf Zuständigkeit einzig auf einem Haufen noch nicht einmal durchgeordneter alter Akten beruht?

Entsprechend entsetzt und empört ist der Professor Althaus. Weder, sagt er, war er zu irgendeiner Zeit ein Mitarbeiter, offiziell oder inoffiziell, der Hauptabteilung XV oder irgendeiner Abteilung des Ministeriums für Staatssicherheit, noch waren Kirmse und Träger seine Führungsoffiziere, noch kannte er den Namen Junghans, geschweige denn, daß er ihn als Decknamen getragen hätte, noch erhielt er jemals, oder erblickte auch nur, eine Medaille für treue Dienste der Nationalen Volksarmee.

Dieses teilt er am 30. Juli dem Professor Erhardt, dem Senator für Wissenschaft und Forschung in Berlin, mit, zusammen mit einer langen Aufzählung seiner Mühen und Verdienste um die Heilung seiner Patienten und die Entwicklung der Urologie und besonders der Kunst der Nierentransplantation an der Charité, ein Thema, das für den Senator von minderem Interesse ist.

Dann wendet er sich um Hilfe an seinen alten Freund, eben jenen Professor Mau, Dekan der Fakultät; der teilt ihm nur mit, da ließe sich leider nichts tun, und wenn ihm seine Entlassung nicht schmecke, könne er ja beim Arbeitsgericht klagen; ihm, Mau, als Mitglied der Kommission des Senators, habe man jedoch mitgeteilt, daß eine Verpflichtungserklärung zur Mitarbeit bei der Stasi mit der Unterschrift »P. Althaus« durchaus vorhanden sei.

Ich, sagt Althaus, habe nie so etwas unterschrieben.

Auf meinem Tisch habe ich eine Photokopie der bei der Gauck-Behörde aufbewahrten, von Hand »30. 6. 73« datierten und mit »P. Althaus« gezeichneten angeblichen Verpflichtungserklärung des Professors Althaus zur Mitarbeit bei der Stasi; daneben liegen, zum Vergleich, zwei Arbeitsverträge des Mannes mit seinen Unterschriften aus etwa der gleichen Zeit und ein graphologisches Gutachten, welches nahelegt, daß die Unterschrift aus dem Hause Gauck gefälscht sein könnte.

Ich bin kein Graphologe, aber auch mir scheint, daß das Autogramm auf dieser Verpflichtungserklärung mit seinen sorgfältig aneinandergereihten steifen Buchstaben sich von den beiden »Althaus« auf den Arbeitsverträgen unterscheidet wie die Nachahmung von Papas Unterschrift, die der Junior, die Zungenspitze im Mundwinkel, mühevoll herstellt, von dem echten Signum seines Erzeugers. Dennoch konzediere ich die Möglichkeit, daß der Professor Althaus geirrt haben könnte, als er jegliche Mitarbeit bei der Staatssicherheit ableugnete: daß er die Sache total aus seinem Bewußtsein verdrängt hat. Das menschliche Hirn ist ein sehr merkwürdiges Organ, und was 1973 geschah, liegt eine lange Zeit zurück, und inzwischen hat der Mann am Operationstisch buchstäblich tausendmal mit dem Tode gerungen.

Und wir reden hier auch nicht nur von dem Professor Althaus. Er wird vor Gericht gehen, und dort wird, wann immer es endlich zum Prozeß kommt, der Sonderbevollmächtigte der Bundesregierung wohl endlich vorzeigen müssen, was er an Beweisen gegen Althaus hat. Wir reden von den Zuständen in diesem Lande, wo ein Mensch seine Existenz, seinen Ruf, seinen inneren Frieden verlieren kann, zeitweilig oder für immer, und nur auf Grund der Angaben einer Behörde. Wir reden von der Art der Vergangenheitsbewältigung, die hierzulande betrieben wird, jener Vergangenheitsbewältigung, welche man in Westdeutschland nach 1945 durchzuführen versäumte und die man nun, am Objekt DDR, mit aller Strenge nachholen möchte. Wir reden von der großen Abwicklung, welche die Institutionen der DDR, gleich ob sie unnütz waren oder nützlich, zu Schatten ihrer selbst macht; wir reden von Posten und Pöstchen, von Einfluß, von Lehrstühlen, und von Geld, viel Geld. Und wir reden von Recht und Gesetz, und von Machthunger und Machtspielen, und von der Gefahr, daß die Methoden der Stasi, die gleichfalls Menschen nach Willkür abstrafte und ins Aus stieß, auf dem Umweg über ihre hinterlassenen Aktensammlungen fröhliche Urständ feiern.

Ich habe die Herren – und Damen – von der Stasi vor meinem Hause gehabt, vierundzwanzig Stunden am Tag, und in meinem Hause; Herr Gauck verwaltet elf Bände Akten über meine Person; ich stehe also wohl außer Verdacht, ich könnte diese Gestalten verteidigen wollen. Aber ich will, daß man scheidet zwischen Schuldigen und Unschuldigen, und ich bin gegen Pauschalurteile, besonders von Leuten, die selber eine Durchleuchtung nicht bestehen würden.

Also ließ ich mich überzeugen, in der Kommission des letzten Innenministers der DDR, des Herrn Diestel, mitzuarbeiten, die sich mit der künftigen Verwendung der Stasi-Archive befaßte. Unsere Hauptsorge war, zu verhindern, daß die darin enthaltenen personenbezogenen Akten einer Lynchjustiz zunutze sein könnten; man weiß ja, welche Motive den berühmten Richter Lynch im wilden Westen Amerikas bewegten, wenn er seine Opfer zum Hängen am Strick verurteilte, bis sie tot wären. Die Diestel-Kommission, in der auch der Pfarrer Gauck aus Rostock mehrmals gastierte, war zu schwach, um ihr Ziel gegenüber den Ansprüchen gewisser Bundesämter durchzusetzen, und die Vertretung der DDR bei den Einigungsverhandlungen mit der Bundesrepublik war zu willfährig und eilfertig, nicht nur in diesem Punkt.

Eine Folge des Verhaltens der DDR-Herren damals ist unter anderem, daß der Osten Deutschlands heute beherrscht wird von zwei Behörden, welch beide, zusammen und für sich allein, mehr Macht haben, als sie das Politbüro je hatte, und welch beide, gottgleich, über die Schicksale der Bürger entscheiden: der Treuhandanstalt, und dem Amt des Sonderbeauftragten der Bundesregierung für die Unterlagen des ehemaligen Staatssicherheitsdienstes, mit seinen Akten, die auf Regalen von insgesamt etwa zweihundert Kilometern Länge gespeichert sind – Sachakten und, zum geringeren Teil, personenbezogenen.

Die ersteren werden völlig geheimgehalten, denn in ihnen steht einiges über die Interna von vierzig Jahren deutsch-deutscher Beziehungen; aus den anderen wirft die Gauck-Behörde bei besonderen Gelegenheiten, wie etwa im Falle Althaus, Informationen aus, welche sie selber exzerpiert und welche der Rest der Menschheit auf Treu und Glauben zu akzeptieren hat – und welche genutzt werden, um ausgesuchte Leute abzuurteilen und zu verstoßen, ohne daß die so Gestraften je Einblick erhielten in die angeblichen Beweise ihrer Schuld oder sich auch nur verteidigen könnten.

Da ging es sogar bei der Inquisition milder zu: wenn einer die Folter lebend überstand, wurde ihm vergeben. Und bei dem berüchtigten Senator McCarthy wurde man wenigstens angehört.

Dabei sollte doch selbst ein Pfarrer aus Rostock nicht so tumb sein, um anzunehmen, daß seine Stasi-Akten die Wahrheit und nichts als die Wahrheit enthielten, nur weil sie von einer deutschen Behörde stammen. Wer je Recherchen betrieben hat, der weiß, wie unsicher die Quellen, wie oft die Berichte persönlich gefärbt sind, aus was für Gründen auch immer. Und selbst im Hause Gauck müßte man doch erkannt haben, wes Geistes Kind die Lauscher und Gucker waren, die uns da auf den Hals geschickt wurden von der Stasi – und die werden nun nachträglich zu Gewährsleuten für die Tugend, oder Untugend, bisher nicht bescholtener Bürger. Die geistige Elite, die da in der Eckkneipe saß oder bei einer Party mit auf dem Kanapee, wieviel bekamen die Kerle denn überhaupt mit von dem, was gesagt wurde, und wer sagte ihnen denn etwas! Aber bezahlt wurden sie nach Länge und Inhalt ihrer Berichte, und die Führungsoffiziere nach Anzahl und Rang der von ihnen Geführten. Was wurde da nicht erlogen und gefälscht und zurechtgeschneidert nach Wunsch und Bedarf! Man lese doch einmal auf ihren Wahrheitsgehalt hin die Protokolle der Prozesse, die auf der Grundlage von Nachforschungen und Angaben der Untergebenen des Genossen Mielke geführt wurden! Bei Gaucks aber gelten die Texte in den Stasi-Akten, als kämen sie geradewegs aus der Bibel, und er selber hat uns versichert, er habe bisher nur ein einziges Mal erlebt, daß da etwas nicht stimmte. Selig sind, man weiß schon wer, denn ihrer ist das Himmelreich.

Vielleicht, so meine ich, sollte der Bundesminister des Inneren sich überlegen, ob man nicht auch bei der Benutzung von Mielkes Erbe, das schon genug Unheil gestiftet, nach den Grundsätzen eines Rechtsstaats vorgehen sollte. Auch die, deren Namen in diesen Akten auftauchen, gleich in welchem Zusammenhang, verdienen Gerechtigkeit: nicht mehr, nicht weniger.

Denn, wie die Medizin, ist auch die Politik eine ganz besondere Wissenschaft, bei der des Menschen Wohlergehen und nicht selten sogar sein Leben auf dem Spiele stehen.

Schuld und Sühne

So, nun ist es soweit. Die Herrn und Damen, die hinter – und vor – den Bonner Kulissen agieren und die zu zartbesaitet sind, ihrer Polizei Order zu geben, mit den glatzköpfigen Neo-Nazis aufzuräumen, sie genieren sich durchaus nicht, den betagten Bürgern in die Magengrube zu treten, die, als sie noch jung waren, die Courage hatten, gegen die Original-Nazis zu kämpfen.

Die DDR gab ihnen, mehr als ein paar tausend davon sind's nicht mehr, für ihre Haltung damals und für die Leiden, welche sie darum auf sich genommen hatten, eine Sonderrente, etwa 1700 Mark monatlich: höher als sonst die DDR-Renten waren, aber für Westverhältnisse bescheiden genug. Auch die wenigen überlebenden deutschen Juden, die in der DDR geblieben waren, erhielten das; andere Entschädigungen, wie sie den Juden in Westdeutschland zuteil wurden, bekamen sie nicht.

Und jetzt, so verlautet es aus dem Ministerium des Herrn Blüm, eines bekannten Verfechters humanitärer Prinzipien, sollen diese Sonderrenten ab Januar 1992 auf 750 Mark herabgesetzt werden; die Abgeordneten im Bundestag, die sich selber gerade wieder eine Erhöhung ihrer Bezüge genehmigt haben, müssen den Vorschlag aus dem Hause Blüm nur noch absegnen.

Hinter der Maßnahme, welche Blüms Staatssekretär Gero höchst temperamentvoll verficht, steckt natürlich auch der Gedanke, daß unter den Empfängern der Rente für Kämpfer gegen den Faschismus, wie sie offiziell hieß, auch alte Kommunisten waren; und die müssen jetzt für ihre Schuld sühnen. Aber erstens befanden sich unter denen, die sich Hitler widersetzten, nicht nur Kommunisten, sondern ebensoviele Sozialdemokraten, Katholiken, Protestanten und was noch; und zweitens nahmen auch die Kommunisten damals, so wie die anderen, Haft, Folter, Konzentrationslager oder Exil auf sich; und drittens habe ich nie erlebt, daß alten Nazis von Herrn Blüm ihre Ehrenbezüge gekürzt worden wären oder daß derart Pläne überhaupt bestünden.

Aber das alles paßt in das neue Bild, welches die Bonner Regierung von dem vereinten Deutschland zeichnet: mit den Neureichen und den Neuarmen, und dem neuen Rassismus, und den neuen Ungerechtigkeiten.

Und das, sagen die, die dereinst auf dem Alexanderplatz zu Berlin für eine neue demokratische Ordnung demonstrierten, haben wir nicht gewollt.

Candide

Candide, die Zentralfigur des gleichnamigen Romans von Voltaire, ist ein sanftmütiger junger Mann, der auf dem Rittergut des Freiherrn Thunder ten Tronckh in einem aus des Autors Phantasie stammenden Westfalen aufwächst, wo es archaisch-freundlich hergeht, bis die bulgarischen und avarischen Heere dort aufeinanderstoßen. Candide ist völlig argloser Natur und erwartet, daß andere Menschen, gleich ihm, auch nur die besten Absichten haben, und sein Hauslehrer, der berühmte Dr. Pangloss, bestärkt ihn noch in seiner Haltung, indem er ihm beibringt, daß die Welt die beste aller möglichen Welten sei und daß für alles, was geschieht, stets ausreichende Gründe vorhanden sind. Als Candide und die Tochter des Hauses, die dicke Kunigunde, einander hinter dem Vorhang küssen, werden sie von dem Freiherrn erwischt, und Candide wird mit wuchtigen Tritten in den Hintern in diese beste aller Welten hinausbefördert, wo er nach und nach erfährt, daß seine Erwartungen eines sind, die Realität aber etwas anderes. In der realen Welt wird gelogen und betrogen, geraubt und gemordet, vergewaltigt und gefoltert, und über all dem thronen Kirche und Staat; und würde Candide nicht, bei allem frommen Bedauern, einen gesunden Egoismus entwickeln und gelegentlich auch rascher mit dem Degen zustechen als die, die ihm nach dem Leben trachten, Voltaires Roman wäre wohl kürzer ausgefallen, als er ist, und erheblich weniger amüsant.

Ich kann mir nicht helfen, aber bei meinen Begegnungen mit Bürgern der Ex-DDR werde ich, ihre Berichte und Klagen mir anhörend, an den Candide erinnert. Da ist die gleiche Bereitschaft, das Gute zu sehen in seinem Mitmenschen und dessen Wort ungeprüft zu akzeptieren, und die Erwartung, daß auch jener die besten Absichten habe, fair und gerecht mit einem zu verfahren, und darauf die gleiche Überraschung angesichts der bösen Wirklichkeit, das gleiche Erstaunen wie das des Candide.

Nun war die verblichene DDR mit dem westfälischen Paradies des Ritters Thunder ten Tronckh höchstens insofern zu vergleichen, als auch dort die Kenntnis der Zustände außerhalb der Mauern des Schlosses sehr begrenzt war und der Chefideologe, der Dr. Pangloss, Zweifel an seinen Thesen nur ungern sah; aber eigentlich genügten solche Beschränkungen schon, um eine Unzahl von Menschen zu erzeugen, die, über Nacht konfrontiert mit dem real existierenden Kapitalismus, einen erheblichen Schock zu erleiden vorbestimmt waren. Nicht daß die Großmoguls der Agitation in der DDR den Kapitalismus idealisiert hätten; eher im Gegenteil. Aber da die Herren immerzu und auf die plumpeste Weise logen, glaubte man ihnen auch nicht, wenn sie, was selten genug, die Wahrheit über etwas sagten, über gewisse Eigenheiten der freien Marktwirtschaft zum Beispiel; und die Gestalt, in der sich diese Wirtschaft darstellte in den Köpfen der Leute, ergab sich daher aus dem Fernsehen (West), den mitunter doch recht geschönten Berichten von Freunden und Verwandten, und aus dem Reichtum an Westgütern im Intershop.

Man war also, östlicherseits, unvorbereitet auf das, was man nach vierzig Jahren real existierenden Sozialismusses erlebte und erhielt.

Oder doch nicht so ganz. Es hatte ja, neben der offiziellen Ökonomie, eine Schattenwirtschaft gegeben, die nach ganz anderen Gesetzen verlief als jene. Geld, es sei denn, es war westliches, spielte darin keine Rolle; vielmehr wurde getauscht, Messingschrauben gegen Lederjacken, Badezimmerfliesen gegen Autoreparaturen, und auf diese Art wurde der Händlergeist des Ostmenschen geschärft und sein Instinkt für Wert und Unwert einer Sache aufs beste entwickelt. Aber stets war, bei Wahrung des eigenen Nutzens, die Grundlage solch schwarzer Geschäfte eine gewisse Redlichkeit der Beteiligten; Betrüger, ob groß oder klein, wurden bald herausgefunden und aus dem illegalen Kreislauf ausgeschieden.

Jetzt aber, nach der Vereinigung, bekam man es mit Profis zu tun. Diese zeigten sich zuerst in der Maske von Biedermännern; war man nicht, zu beiden Seiten der Grenze, ein- und desselben Blutes, ein Volk von Brüdern und Schwestern, die einander doch nicht übers Ohr hauen würden? Laßt uns euch helfen: wir wissen, wie man umgeht mit Banken und Behörden, und wir kennen die Shortcuts und die Regeln.

Der erste große Reibach kam mit dem Geldumtausch. Die harmlosen Ostler, gewöhnt an den schwarzen Kurs von 5 oder gar 10 Mark Ost gegen eine Mark West, erhielten nun, und amtlich gar, 2 zu 1 – wie reich, freuten sie sich, waren sie auf einmal geworden, und was konnte man sich nun nicht alles leisten, Reisen und schicke Kleider, Westautos (aus zweiter Hand, meistens), Elektronik aller Art; und über all dem vergaß man, daß man sein Geld ursprünglich ja 1 zu 1 verdient hatte, Arbeitskraft gegen entsprechenden Lohn.

Und nachdem man auf diese Weise die Hälfte seiner Ersparnisse verloren hatte, kam es Schlag auf Schlag: die Löhne und

Renten waren nicht etwa dieselben wie die der Brüder und Schwestern im Westen, sondern erheblich niedriger, Steuern und Abgaben aber gleich hoch wie deren; die Treuhand verhökerte zu Schleuderpreisen, was eigentlich Eigentum der Arbeiter und Bauern war, während Mieten und andere Kosten stiegen; oft genug war auch der Job plötzlich unsicher; und wer glaubte, er könne das System überlisten, indem er zum billigsten Anbieter ging, erfuhr bald genug, daß der billigste nicht immer der billigste war, sondern nur der schlaueste.

Es brauchte seine Zeit, bis die Candides des real existierenden Sozialismus mitbekamen, daß die freie Marktwirtschaft tatsächlich weniger auf einem fairen Spiel von Angebot und Nachfrage beruhte als auf den Bräuchen des orientalischen Basars, wo die Preise nach oben offen sind wie die berühmte Richter-Skala, nach der man die Stärke der Erdbeben bemißt, und daß die Verdienstspanne bei einer Ware weniger von deren Herstellungskosten abhängt als von der Unverschämtheit, mit der ein Händler die Lage seines Ladens, und seine Verbindungen zu den Ministeriellen der jeweiligen Regierung, und die Naivität des Kunden, ins Spiel bringt.

Was nicht heißt, daß der oben erwähnte Sozialismus etwas Besseres oder Humaneres gewesen wäre; auch dort wurden die Menschen betrogen, sogar von Staats wegen; aber immer erwies sich, das zeigte der rasche Zusammenbruch des östlichen Großreichs, das System der privaten Schieber und Halsabschneider, Profitmacher und Grundstückshaie als das effizientere; es förderte Ehrgeiz und Initiative und dadurch den allgemeinen Fortschritt; und für den Einzelnen stellten sich Glück und Erfolg, oder auch Pleite und Untergang, nur als eine Frage des individuellen Geschicks dar und einer möglichst nahtlosen Anpassung an die herrschende Räuberethik – wobei die Westverwandtschaft, gestehen wir's zu, einen Vorsprung von Jahren und Jahrzehnten besaß.

204

Die Westbrüder und -schwestern hatten die Geschäftstricks nämlich peu à peu gelernt, und sie gerieten nicht in helle Aufregung bei jedem Reklameschrieb, den ihnen der Postbote in den Kasten schob, bei jeder Kaffeefahrt, die ihnen angeboten, bei jedem Lotteriegewinn, der ihnen als todsicher angepriesen wurde. Sie, die Westverwandten, waren es gewohnt, kühl zu vergleichen, Versicherungspolicen, Kreditangebote, Billigreisen, und nicht jedes Versprechen, komme es von Marktschreiern oder von Politikern, für bare Münze zu nehmen.

Nicht so die Ostler. Das Kleingedruckte, auf das es ankommt, war ihnen lästig und fremd, und da war keiner, der sie bei der Hand nahm und sie führte und ihnen klarmachte, was wo auszufüllen war und wofür und auf wie lange sie sich verpfändeten und was die Folgen sein würden ihrer Unterschrift; dabei sehnten sie sich nach genau diesem väterlichen Rat; und alle möglichen Luftexistenzen, dieses witternd, boten sich ihnen an als selbstlose Anwälte und ehrliche Makler und machten sich dann davon, in der Tasche das Ersparte der Witwen und Waisen.

Und wie im einzelnen, so insgesamt. Manipuliert jahrzehntelang und an kurzer Leine gehalten, hatten die einstigen DDR-Bürger sich losgerissen von ihrer Regierung mit stiller, doch unwiderstehlicher Gewalt, hoffend, endlich Herr zu werden im eigenen Haus und frei entscheiden zu können über das eigene Schicksal, und erkannten nicht, daß sie schon wieder in die Hände von Manipulatoren geraten waren, Leuten allerdings, welche mit sanfterem Druck operierten und mit geschickteren Losungen, als die Machthaber von früher benutzt hatten.

Als sie dann merkten, daß sie abermals in der Schlinge saßen, ihre Freiheit beschränkt, ihr Tatendurst gelenkt in der Obrigkeit genehme Bahnen, empfanden sie es dennoch als angenehm, daß der Strick am Halse nicht mehr so schmerzhaft rieb wie in den alten Zeiten; selbst wenn man die Arbeit verlor, langte das Unterstützungsgeld noch zur täglichen Videokassette und zum Bier an der Ecke; die neue Regierung in ihrer Weisheit sorgte dafür, daß, wenn einer fiel, der erste Aufprall nicht zu hart wäre. Nur die Zukunft...

Aber warum sich darüber unnötig Sorge machen? Irgend etwas würde sich immer finden, Vorruhestand oder ABM oder Sozialfürsorge oder ein Schulungskurs mit anschließendem Praktikum, für welch alles die Brüder und Schwestern im Westen würden zahlen müssen. Nur die ganz Alten und die, die nirgends eine Nische für sich organisieren konnten, die Untüchtigen und Unbrauchbaren also, die gingen vor die Hunde: die Notärzte in ihren Heulewagen wissen ein Lied zu singen von der Suizidrate.

Doch waren die Schwachen nicht immer am Wege gefallen? Außerdem konnte man sich nicht um alles kümmern; jeder war, in dieser neuen, real existierenden Ordnung, sich selber der Nächste.

Ah, Dr. Pangloss! Voltaire hatte ihn aufhängen und danach wieder auferstehen lassen, und man kann ihm, in dieser besten aller Welten, jederzeit und in jeder Regierungsabteilung als Pressesprecher begegnen, die Wogen glättend und die Kritiker besänftigend und, wo nötig, mit der Rute drohend.

Candide aber endet, nachdem er den halben Globus umzirkelt und seine Kunigunde, obwohl diese gealtert und geschrumpelt, geehelicht hat, als eine Art Schrebergärtner in der Umgebung von Konstantinopel; sein Schlüsselerlebnis war die Begegnung mit einem freundlichen alten Mann, der unter seinem Pomeranzenbaum frische Luft schöpfte und auf die Nachricht, der Kalif habe zwei seiner Wesire und den Mufti erdrosseln und mehrere ihrer Freunde pfählen lassen, ihm sagte, er kenne den Namen weder des Muftis noch der Wesire, vermute jedoch, daß im allgemeinen die Leute, die sich mit öffentlichen Angelegenheiten befaßten, elendiglich umkämen, wie sie es übrigens auch verdienten.

So schließt denn Voltaires Roman, der bis dahin durchaus realistisch, als Märchen; bei uns, wie wir wissen, blühen und gedeihen die Muftis und die Wesire und werden immer fetter.

Seelenschmerzen

Man wird mir sagen, daß es in dieser Zeit Wichtigeres gibt als die Seelenschmerzen der Literaten.

Auch ich bin dieser Meinung. Aber da ich hier in einem Literaturhaus spreche und zur Eröffnung von Literaturtagen, erlaube ich mir ein paar Worte zu dem Thema, in der Hoffnung, daß meine Ausführungen auch Zusammenhänge außerhalb der esoterischen Kategorien beleuchten könnten, in denen unsereins sich gemeinhin bewegt.

In den etwas mehr als zwei Jahren seit jenem denkwürdigen Meeting auf dem Alexanderplatz, wo ein paar Autoren und Schauspielerinnen plötzlich in eine Herzensverbindung gerieten mit den Massen, hat sich im Osten unseres vereinten Vaterlandes mehreres verändert in bezug auf Rolle und Reputation der Schriftsteller, und nicht zum besseren; im Westen war die alte Sterilität, gegründet auf kommerzielle Zwänge, sowieso geblieben, unberührt von dem Gezeitenwechsel.

Man mag darum streiten, ob das, was da in der DDR in den Tagen der Wende vom Oktober zum November 1989 geschah, eine Revolution gewesen ist oder nicht; früher jedenfalls hätte kein Historiker und kein Soziologe sich gescheut, Ereignisse, die zur kompletten Umstülpung eines ökonomischen Systems führten, als Revolution zu bezeichnen.

Und tatsächlich folgte auf jenen Morgen am Alexanderplatz ein Umsturz im östlichen Drittel Deutschlands, wie man ihn sich fröhlicher nicht vorstellen könnte: Bücher und Stücke, bis dato unterdrückt, kamen plötzlich heraus, eine Presse, die nichts gewesen war als ein langweiliges Sammelsurium von Kopfblättern der Agitationsabteilung des Zentralkomitees, trieb über Nacht tausend bunte Blüten, und Fernsehen und Funk, von ihren Fesseln befreit, entwickelten innerhalb von Wochen und mit fast dem gleichen Personal wie vorher eine Qualität, welche die der Öffentlich-Rechtlichen im Westen um ein beträchtliches übertraf und die, bei Nachrichten- wie Unterhaltungssendungen, durch entsprechend höhere Einschaltquoten belohnt wurde.

Demokratie in den Medien! Eine Demokratie, geschaffen von Menschen mit neuen Konzeptionen, die es danach verlangte, Neues auszusagen! Leichtigkeit und Freude, und ein Schuß Ironie, und der Beginn einer Auseinandersetzung mit dem Gestern! Und ein Bedürfnis, den Leuten im Publikum das Gefühl zu geben, daß auch sie frei seien zu sagen, was sie empfanden, und abzuschütteln, was sie bedrückte!

Aber so hatten sie nicht gewettet, die Herren der D-Mark, die wahren Sieger der europäischen Geschichte. Eine DDR-Demokratie, eine echte, mit allem, was sich daraus ergäbe, sozial und kulturell, und sogar mit Dichtern, die sich da engagierten! – das nicht, nein; das könnte die eignen Schäfchen, die frommen, fügsamen, am Ende selber noch infizieren.

Und so das Marionettentheater mit den zwei Ost-Kasperles an den Schnüren, dem einen, der nebenher die Viola spielte, dem andern, der völlig amusisch; und der Verkauf von Land und Leuten und Hoffnung und Zukunft um ein Linsengericht, ein nicht gar gekochtes noch dazu; und dann los und schnellstens eingesackt, was noch vorhanden an Gütern, und abgewickelt, was noch funktionstüchtig war an Einrichtungen und Institutionen.

Die Amerikaner hatten das rüde Spiel vorexerziert in Grenada, aber das war nicht das eigene Land gewesen, bevölkert von Brüdern und Schwestern, sondern ein kleiner karibischer Flecken, und sie hatten wenigstens noch landen müssen mit ihren Schiffen und ein paar Schüsse gewechselt; hier aber, sehnsüchtig nach Freiheit und Farbe und Düften und Grenzenlosigkeit, hatte eine ganze Bevölkerung sich freiwillig der Gewalt der neuen Herren ausgeliefert.

Ein anderes war, daß das, was man aufgab, von fraglichem Wert gewesen, und die Strukturen brüchig, und die Bürokraten, denen man endlich den Tritt gab, von miserablem Charakter und die personifizierte Unfähigkeit.

Nur wen, oder was, erhielt man im Austausch? – Die Treuhand. Die Gauck-Behörde. Und jenes Mischgewebe aus neuem und altem Filz, das sich alsbald über das Land breitete wie der Ölteppich des Saddam Hussein über die Strände Arabiens.

Mit den Künstlern, besonders den Literaten, war das vordem so gewesen: im Westen zählten sie, wo sie Unterhaltungs-, eventuell noch Bildungswert besaßen; ihre Produkte mußten »sich rechnen«, wie es jetzt so schön heißt, gleich jeder anderen Ware auf dem Markt – eine Marktfrage also.

Doch eine moralische Instanz? Neben dem einen Böll – wie wenige westlich der Mauer, der ehemaligen, durften von sich behaupten, sie wären eine Instanz irgendwelcher Art gewesen, geschweige denn, eine moralische?

Östlich dagegen wurden die Kollegen von Amts wegen zu solch einer Instanz ernannt, ob sie es wollten oder nicht; und die meisten wollten. Talent war da weniger wesentlich; im Gegenteil, je talentloser, desto moralischer. Doch wenn einer gar fähig war, halbwegs richtig konstruierte Sätze im Zusammenhang zu schreiben, vielleicht noch mit einem Witzchen drin, damit es auch geistreich klinge – der war King.

Der Grund für die Inflation an mit hohen Würden ausgestatteten Großpriestern der Kunst und Literatur des real existierenden Sozialismus lag in dessen feudalistischem Wesen. Hatten nicht auch die Fürsten von einst, mangels eigenen Geistes, ihre Hofphilosophen, Hofschreiber, Hofnarren gehabt? Wie bedurfte solcher Schranzen dann erst jene Ansammlung halbgebildeter Kleinbürger, die im Auf und Ab der Geschichte, der sowjetischen wie der deutschen, ins Politbüro gespült worden waren! Ängstlich besorgt um ihre kostbare führende Rolle, mußten sie ihren Ruf und ihr Renommee tagtäglich bestätigt haben von moralischen Autoritäten, auch wenn diese großenteils selbstgestrickt.

Das Wort aber ist eine höllische Versuchung: das Wort, mit dem man nicht nur verhüllen und verschönen kann, sondern auch aussprechen was ist.

Und so geschah es, daß aus der Schar jener Künstler und Schriftsteller, die ausgewählt und gesammelt und speziell geschult und bezahlt und mit zugehörigen Ämtern ausgestattet worden waren zum Zweck der Verbreitung im Volke des höheren Ruhms und der glorreichen Gedanken der führenden Genossen an der Spitze der führenden Klasse, der eine oder andere der Versuchung dennoch erlag und ausbrach aus der Phalanx der Gehorsamen und, eine Andeutung hier und ein Farbtupfer da und eine Nuance dort, der Wahrheit Bahn brach und auf einmal wirklich zu einer Art moralischer Instanz wurde im Lande.

Gewöhnlich legte die Behörde den Rebellen nahe, das Land zu verlassen, und denen, die dem amtlichen Drängen folgten, tat sich die Mauer prompt auf, und das war's dann: lauter kleine persönliche Tragödien, denn obwohl die Armen nicht weiter als von Deutschland nach Deutschland gingen, war der Boden, auf dem sie gewachsen, ihnen entzogen, und die Ziele, auf die sie vordem geschossen, nicht mehr erkennbar; und sobald das lärmige Willkommen, das die westlichen Medien ihnen boten, verklungen, saßen sie da, fremd in der Fremde und innerlich ausgehöhlt.

Und das Schlimmste: als dann die Revolution doch kam in der DDR, unter Mitwirkung derer, die sich nicht hatten vertreiben lassen, fand sie ohne die Exulanten statt; und als diese dann zurückkamen, auf Gastrollen die meisten nur, hörten die Leute wohl ihre Verse an und ihre Ratschläge, höflich applaudierend, aber es war ein Nicht-Ereignis.

Diejenigen aber, die im Lande geblieben waren und weiter versucht hatten, wo immer die Gelegenheit sich bot, die Wahrheit zu sagen, zu schreiben, zu singen, zu filmen, und die so Teil geworden jenes geheimen Bündnisses mit dem Volke, das auf dem Alexanderplatz zu Berlin sich aller Welt offenbarte, sie sahen sich bald schon diskreditiert und désavouiert und denunziert von den feinsten der Feinen im literarischen Establishment des neugeeinten Deutschland und von den gelernten Meinungsbildnern. Sie seien, hieß es, viel zu feige gewesen und leisetreterisch; schlimmer noch, durch ihr Verbleiben im Osten hätten sie dem Unrechtsregime eine Aura verliehen von Toleranz und Kulturfreundlichkeit; und überhaupt taugten sie nichts, auch und besonders als Künstler; man habe sie nur hochgejubelt aus politischen Gründen seinerzeit und die Weiber zu Heiligen Jungfrauen stilisiert, fast, und die Kerle zu veritablen Genies; aber jetzt, da die DDR im Orkus, könne man sich's ja endlich leisten, die ganze Bagage auf das Niveau zurückzustufen, auf welches sie gehöre.

Das ist so unklug nicht gedacht: wenn man die paar Leute vom Sockel holte, die dem Volk noch etwas gelten, so blieben die Unten gänzlich ohne Vertrauenspersonen, die auf ihre Fragen eingehen, ihre Nöte ausdrücken, ihre Beschwerden abfassen könnten. Und daß sich's mit Hilflosen leichter umgehen läßt als mit aufsässigen Bürgern, die ihre Stichworte von kritischen Literaten erhalten, das wird jede Dienststelle eines jeden Ministeriums freudig bestätigen.

Darum also die systematischen Verbalinjurien der Schicki-Micki-Feuilletons wie der Tittenjournaille gegen gerade die Künstler und Schriftsteller, die einst schon den Schmährufen aus dem Politbüro standhielten und den Boykottmaßnahmen der Kulturbosse erfolgreich Widerstand leisteten. Man muß diese Nachwende-Kampagne in einer Linie sehen mit den plumpen Bonner Bemühungen, die noch funktionsfähigen Institutionen der Ex-DDR, als da sind Universitäten, Akademien, Schulen und Forschungsstätten, Museen und Kliniken, Funk und Fernsehen, Betriebe, Klubs, Kindergärten, abzuwickeln oder zumindest zu beschneiden – alles überhaupt, was den Ost-Menschen Anlaß und Gelegenheit geben könnte, über die Werte, die sie schufen, nachzudenken und über ihren eigenen Wert.

Das ist ein uraltes Verfahren. Schon in grauester Antike beseitigten die Sieger bei den Besiegten zuerst die Sänger und die Schreibkundigen, denn deren Wort barg Gefahr. So radikal geht man heut nicht mehr vor, zumindest in Mitteleuropa: man mordet nicht mehr die Person, nur ihren Ruf.

Im Namen von Freiheit und Demokratie, der gleichen Freiheit, der gleichen Demokratie, von der die Menschen überall so lange geträumt.

Das ist der Pfenning,

aber wo ist die Mark.

Vergangenheitsbewältigung

Als ich, damals in amerikanischer Uniform, am Ende des Zweiten Weltkriegs nach Deutschland kam, hieß das Ding noch nicht Vergangenheitsbewältigung; aber allenthalben traf ich auf Leute, die, sobald ich sie ernsthaft befragte, was sie denn in den letzten Jahren so getan hätten, mit aller Kraft zu bewältigen begannen. Nein, erklärten sie in der Mehrheit, Nazis seien sie natürlich nie gewesen, vielmehr hätten sie mit den Juden, wo sie nur konnten, deutlich sympathisiert; einige wenige aber fanden, daß ein Geständnis, ja, sie seien in der Partei gewesen, man habe doch gar nicht anders gekonnt und sie hätten auch nie jemandem ein Härchen gekrümmt, ihnen jetzt die Gelegenheit zu lauthals demonstrierter Reue bot; sie wußten, daß der reuige Sünder mehr galt als jener, der einfach die Fakten aufzählte; aber da ich kein Feldkaplan war, sondern ein ganz gewöhnlicher GI mit Sergeantenstreifen am Ärmel, rührten mich ihre Geständnisse nicht so sehr, wie sie gehofft hatten.

Später merkten sie dann, daß die Amerikaner sie noch gegen die Russen brauchen würden, und die Notwendigkeit für jede wie immer geartete Vergangenheitsbewältigung fiel weg und man widmete sich erfolgreich dem Wiederaufbau West; es gibt Leute, die meinen, vielleicht hätte man sich anno dazumal doch nicht so rasch von der Beschäftigung mit seiner

Vergangenheit abkehren sollen, und die das Versäumte von damals, bei guter Gelegenheit nun, in dem sogenannten Beitrittsgebiet nachholen lassen möchten.

Da kam einer zu mir; er müsse, sagte er, unbedingt mit mir reden; es sei ganz außerordentlich wichtig.

Und was war das Wichtige? Er sei, sagte er, von der Staatssicherheit auf mich angesetzt gewesen, und nannte die Punkte, die er habe für die Polizei in Erfahrung bringen sollen; und dann blickte er mich treuherzig an, als wolle er sagen, »Nu?«.

Und plötzlich wußte ich, der Mann wollte tatsächlich Absolution. Er war ein kleiner Handlanger gewesen, nicht mehr; und nun wünschte er, von mir zu hören, was für ein bedeutender Sünder er wäre und wie es mein Herz erfreute, daß er so gründlich in sich gegangen sei, und nun möge er hingehen und nicht mehr sündigen, besonders nicht für den Bundesnachrichtendienst, für den er, nach eigener Angabe, nebenher auch gearbeitet hatte.

Scharen von Menschen im Osten des wiedervereinigten Vaterlandes sind plötzlich Opfer eines Beichtsyndroms geworden; kein Wunder, angesichts des Einflusses, den so zahlreiche Gottesmänner seit der Wende in den Neuen Bundesländern gewonnen haben. Dem einen Teil der Bevölkerung wird unentwegt zugeredet, er möge nur vortreten zur medienwirksamen Beichte, dann würde allen wohler werden, politisch und überhaupt; und der andere lechzt danach, daß ihm was Sensationelles vorgebeichtet wird; es ist eine neue Variante eines alten Gesellschaftsspiels, mit Pfarrer Gauck, dem Herrn der Stasiakten, als Schiedsrichter.

Ich erinnere mich einer Versammlung, der ich kürzlich beiwohnte: da stand eine blasse Dame mittleren Alters auf und erklärte mit zitternden Händen, wir alle müßten nun aber, und öffentlich, uns mit unsrer Vergangenheit auseinandersetzen, sonst könnten wir unmöglich weiter in unserm Club bleiben; und tatsächlich hatte auch schon eines der Mitglieder gestanden, bei der Stasi mitgetan zu haben, und war demonstrativ ausgetreten, was alle höchst edel fanden, obwohl die meisten von uns längst wußten, welche Verbindungen der Kerl gehabt hatte.

Überhaupt haben die Bürger der DDR ja alle viel mehr gewußt, als die Prominenz, die sich bei der Premiere in der Lesestube der Gauckbehörde hat filmen lassen, zugeben mochte. Man kann nicht Jahre in diesem Lande gelebt haben, ohne erkennen zu lernen, wer bei der Firma mittat und wer nicht. Die Zeichen waren, in den meisten Fällen, auffällig genug, und die Knaben und Mädchen, die es so geschickt spielten, daß man keinen Verdacht schöpfte, waren selten. Man wußte, wer in der Telephonleitung hing und wo die Richtmikrophone standen und welche Autos einem hinterherfuhren, und man benahm sich entsprechend und fand Wege und Mittel, seine Post trotz allem an ihre Adressaten zu befördern; und wenn eine Ehegattin jetzt überrascht feststellt, daß ihr eigener Gatte sie bespitzelt hat, dann kann ich nur fragen, was muß das für eine Ehe gewesen sein, in der man so was nicht merkte.

Trotzdem könnte es einen schon reizen, zu erfahren, was die Berichterstatter über einen berichteten und zu welchen Themen die Behörde ihre Erkundigungen einzog. Und diejenigen gar, die unter behördlicher Willkür zu leiden hatten – und das sind nicht wenige –, haben ein Recht, Wiedergutmachung zu fordern. Ich frage mich nur, in welcher Währung? Auge um Auge? Zahn um Zahn? Oder in D-Mark? Bunte Scheine für erlittene Qualen und verlorene Jahre? Und wieviel Scheine für welche Schikanen? Und welcher Richter könnte da eine Tabelle aufstellen, die wahrhaft gerecht wäre? Und welches

Gesetz soll da gelten? Das weltliche? Aus welcher Welt bitte, und welchem ihrer Bereiche? Oder das göttliche – und welcher Bischof könnte, in diesem grausamen Zusammenhang, Gottes Gesetz gerecht interpretieren?

Und warum erst jetzt die nachgeholte Gerechtigkeit, und warum nur hier in der Ex-DDR? Warum nicht schon nach 1945, und in ganz Deutschland? Und warum nicht in anderen Ländern auch? Wo geschah denn kein Unrecht seitens Regierung und Polizei, wo geschieht es nicht heut noch? Wo herrscht denn nicht die Gewalt, die Gewalt des Knüppels wie die des Geldbeutels? Wo möchte man nicht dazwischentreten und rufen, Haltet inne! ... Wo?

Und wer hat eigentlich, im Jahre des Herrn 1992, zu Hohepriestern just jene Marktschreier ernannt, die vor den Kameras sich so wohlgefällig spreizen und dem Publikum mit so unnachahmlicher Selbstsicherheit erklären, wer als ein Schächer zu gelten habe und daher zu kreuzigen sei? ... Wer?

So viele Aspekte der Vergangenheitsbewältigung, so viele Probleme.

Vielleicht wäre es besser gewesen, es hätten mehr Leute die Courage gehabt, die Vergangenheit zu bewältigen, als sie noch Gegenwart war; oder man beschäftigte sich jetzt wenigstens etwas intensiver mit der jetzigen Gegenwart, damit nicht in abermals zwanzig oder dreißig Jahren von neuem Vergangenheitsbewältigung betrieben werden muß. Sich dieser Tage vor aller Augen an die Brust zu schlagen und zu jammern, »Weh ist mir!«, dient nur jenen zur Befriedigung, die einen Genuß daraus ziehen, wenn einer seine schöne Seele zur Schau stellt, oder jenen, deren Beruf es ist, schöne Seelen zu retten.

Es gehe, hielte ich für ratsam, ein jeder mit sich selber ins Gericht, und habe den Mut, aus seinem Urteil dann die Konsequenzen zu ziehen; es weiß doch eh jedermann, wo und wann er sich feige verhalten hat oder wie ein elender Schurke, und die Zeit ist gekommen für eine Abrechnung ganz neuer Art, eine Abrechnung des Gewissens. Und im übrigen kennt man doch die Burschen, die, obwohl sie ihr gerüttelt Maß Schuld tragen an dem, was uns alle belastet, schon wieder oben schwimmen wie das Fettauge auf der Suppe, und es gibt keine Polizei, die in einem Lande, in dem das Volk vor kurzem erst eine ganze Regierung gewaltlos gestürzt hat, verhindern könnte, daß solchen Leuten das Handwerk gelegt wird.

Nichts gegen die Beschäftigung mit der Vergangenheit – nur zu! Öffnen wir ihre Akten! Analysieren wir sie, mit all ihren Fehlern und Missetaten, und denken wir darüber nach, und lernen wir etwas daraus, für die Gegenwart und für die Zukunft.

Aber nicht als Ganztagsjob und Tag um Tag. Manchmal habe ich den Verdacht, es wird jetzt soviel von Vergangenheitsbewältigung geredet, damit die Leute sich von der Gegenwart abkehren, in der doch, alle wissen es, genug geschieht, auf das man ein Augenmerk haben müßte, wenn man nicht will, daß uns das Fell schon wieder über die Ohren gezogen wird.

btb

Stefan Heym bei btb:

Aus Freude am Lesen